"Mike Doogan's first full-length mystery, *Lost Angel*, kept me up till the wee hours. There is no doubt Doogan can write. This new tale, with its fascinating cast of contrasting characters, simply tells us he can write pretty much whatever he wants to, and do it with style and a convincing voice. Welcome to the mystery community, Mike. More, please." —Sue Henry, author of *The Refuge*

"Mike Doogan has taken on a theme as big as Alaska itself—lost Faith, both literally and figuratively—and has done it in this brilliant debut with humor, sincerity, and a love for his characters and his state. *Lost Angel* pulses with realism and a brilliant sense of place. Doogan may have created a new subgenre here: post-modern Alaska noir." —C. J. Box, author of *In Plain Sight*

"Doogan really knows the grit and the reality of living in Alaska, and with his first mystery novel, *Lost Angel*, he gives us an involving and hard-edged tale of life on the northern frontier." —*San Jose Mercury News*

"Gripping . . . The portrayal of a religious community that holds both secrets and dangers is fascinating. A top-notch start to a projected mystery series."
—*Booklist* (starred review)

"[An] auspicious debut . . . *Lost Angel* has all the earmarks of a successful series." —*Richmond Times Dispatch*

"Alaska's wide-open beauty gives novelist Mike Doogan a portal to a solid story about people living on the fringe in his promising debut . . . Doogan excels at plot and scenery . . . Nik is a character worth rooting for."
—*Fort Lauderdale Sun-Sentinel*

"Former *Anchorage Daily News* columnist Mike Doogan has created a complex character . . . The protagonist initially comes across as a Real Tough Customer but thankfully is much more than that . . . Inside he's riddled with doubts, sorrows, and fears about the future. In other words, he's a real human being."
—*Anchorage Daily News*

"[A] righteously appealing hero and terrific local color."
—*Kirkus Reviews*

"Engaging, lucid prose."
—*Publishers Weekly*

"Sign me up for the Mike Doogan fan club. This guy can really write. *Lost Angel* is a terrific debut novel."
—James Swain, author of *Deadman's Bluff*

"Alaska emerges as a tough, gritty place where danger lurks even in the most unassuming situations. Here's hoping that first time novelist and *Anchorage Daily News* columnist Mike Doogan will write many more mysteries with Nik Kane, one of the truly engaging new detectives on the scene."
—*Library Journal*

continued

Lost Angel

Mike Doogan

BERKLEY PRIME CRIME, NEW YORK

THE BERKLEY PUBLISHING GROUP
Published by the Penguin Group
Penguin Group (USA) Inc.
375 Hudson Street, New York, New York 10014, USA
Penguin Group (Canada), 90 Eglinton Avenue East, Suite 700, Toronto, Ontario M4P 2Y3, Canada
(a division of Pearson Penguin Canada Inc.)
Penguin Books Ltd., 80 Strand, London WC2R 0RL, England
Penguin Group Ireland, 25 St. Stephen's Green, Dublin 2, Ireland (a division of Penguin Books Ltd.)
Penguin Group (Australia), 250 Camberwell Road, Camberwell, Victoria 3124, Australia
(a division of Pearson Australia Group Pty. Ltd.)
Penguin Books India Pvt. Ltd., 11 Community Centre, Panchsheel Park, New Delhi—110 017, India
Penguin Group (NZ), 67 Apollo Drive, Rosedale, North Shore 0745, Auckland, New Zealand
(a division of Pearson New Zealand Ltd.)
Penguin Books (South Africa) (Pty.) Ltd., 24 Sturdee Avenue, Rosebank, Johannesburg 2196,
South Africa

Penguin Books Ltd., Registered Offices: 80 Strand, London WC2R 0RL, England

This is a work of fiction. Names, characters, places, and incidents either are the product of the author's imagination or are used fictitiously, and any resemblance to actual persons, living or dead, business establishments, events, or locales is entirely coincidental. The publisher does not have any control over and does not assume any responsibility for author or third-party websites or their content.

LOST ANGEL

A Berkley Prime Crime Book / published by arrangement with the author

PRINTING HISTORY
G. P. Putnam's Sons hardcover edition / August 2006
Berkley Prime Crime mass-market edition / August 2007

Copyright © 2006 by Mike Doogan.
Excerpt of *Capitol Offense* copyright © 2007 by Mike Doogan.
Cover photo of Plane © Chip Porter/Getty Images; Truck © Rich LaSalle/Getty Images; Mountain ©
Alan Kearney/Getty Images.
Cover design by Richard Hasselberger.

ISBN: 978-0-425-21666-8

BERKLEY® PRIME CRIME
Berkley Prime Crime Books are published by The Berkley Publishing Group,
a division of Penguin Group (USA) Inc.,
375 Hudson Street, New York, New York 10014.
The name BERKLEY PRIME CRIME and the BERKLEY PRIME CRIME design
are trademarks belonging to Penguin Group (USA) Inc.

PRINTED IN THE UNITED STATES OF AMERICA

10 9 8 7 6 5 4 3 2 1

For Kathy,
the woman who, thank God,
lets me live with her

ACKNOWLEDGMENTS

This book would not exist without the efforts of Pat Dougherty, Howard Weaver, and Gretchen Legler, who helped me learn the craft of writing; Dana Stabenow, who strong-armed me into writing mystery fiction; Kim Rich and Sue Henry, who helped me find the way to publication; my agent, Marcy Posner, whose suggestions made this a better book; Tom Colgan, my editor, who shepherded this book, and me, through the process with patience and humor; and, of course, my wife, Kathy, my reader and editor of first, and last, resort.

1

And the Lord God planted a garden, eastward in Eden. . . .

GENESIS 2:8

THE SINGLE-ENGINE BUSH PLANE STAGGERED ACROSS the sky, rocking and rolling on the air currents that rose from the jumbled land below. Nik Kane clenched his teeth and cinched his seat belt even tighter.

"Saint Joseph protect us," he muttered. Then he smiled. Some things we learn as children never leave us, he thought.

The pilot, who looked barely old enough to shave, gave him a pitying shake of the head.

"Don't worry, Pops," the pilot shouted. "These river valleys are always a roller coaster."

Kane could barely hear him over the engine's clatter. They had been flying north and east from Anchorage for almost two hours, and the trip included all the things Kane hated about flying in Alaska.

The cabin heater blew gas fumes into the cockpit, which made Kane regret the bacon and eggs he'd had for breakfast, but didn't raise the subarctic temperature. Kane was wearing high-tech boots, insulated coveralls, and a

wool cap, and he was still cold. He had a fat Air Force–
surplus fifty-below parka behind his seat, but there was no
way he could put it on in the tiny cabin. Unless he shoved
the pilot out of the airplane first.

The airplane banged its way through another set of air
pockets, lurched sideways, then dropped like it was falling
off a table, straightening out again with a jolt that set off a
cacophony of shrieks and rattles. Kane's forefinger stroked
the scar that ran from the corner of his left eye to his chin.
I'm accumulating quite a collection of nervous habits, he
thought.

"That's some scar," the pilot said. "How'd you get it?"

Kane gave the pilot a look that made the younger man
shrink back in his seat.

"Cut myself shaving," he said.

"Hey, I didn't mean nothing," the pilot said.

"Just fly the plane," Kane said.

He used the edge of a gloved hand to scrape at the frost
on the small window in the passenger door. The washed-
out winter landscape below was white, with streaks and
patches of brown or gray.

Looking at so much empty space made Kane feel light-
headed. I got used to small spaces inside, he thought.

To the right, he could see a flat, snowy, meandering,
bluff-lined track that he took to be the Copper River. A little farther along, a smaller river angled away to the left.

"That the Jordan?" he asked, pointing.

"Yeah," the pilot said sullenly.

The pilot slouched in his seat, one hand on the yoke,
like a kid cruising a low-rider down a boulevard. He had
sharp features dotted with acne scars and long, curly blond
hair that needed washing. He was wearing a leather jacket
over a Slayer T-shirt, jeans, and cowboy boots. He seemed
not to notice the cold.

The plane gave a series of sharp shudders. Kane cursed
and gripped the sides of his seat with both hands.

"Easy, Pops," the pilot called. "You'll give yourself a
heart attack."

Here's a guy who doesn't stay down for long, Kane

thought. I could strangle the little snot, but who'd fly the plane?

The bouncing continued for another ten minutes, then Kane began to see clumps of lights: a small patch on one side of the Jordan River, a small patch on the other, and farther along and higher up, a blaze of bright, industrial lighting.

That would be the Pitchfork mine, Kane thought.

Even though it was not quite noon, the winter day was dark enough to make the lights stand out sharply. Kane knew that the Glenn Highway ran through one of the groups of lights, but he couldn't make it out in the dim light.

"Almost there," the pilot said, sitting up and putting the small plane into a steep bank.

Three sharp gusts of wind tried to stand the airplane on its head, but the pilot got it around, around again, and lined up with an unlighted runway that had been carved out of the snow. He floated the little plane down and bounced it to a stop next to a Chevy Suburban that was idling at the side of the strip.

"Rejoice, you're in Rejoice," the pilot said, killing the engine.

Kane unclamped his hands from the seat, pushed open the door, and climbed unsteadily down onto the ice and snow. It seemed warmer at ground level, so he left the parka where it was.

A man got out of the Suburban. He was taller than Kane and bundled up.

"Mr. Kane?" he asked, putting out a gloved hand. "I'm Elder Thomas Wright." His voice was soft and gentle after the engine's racket.

"Pleased to meet you," Kane said, shaking the gloved hand with one of his own. Their breath formed small clouds that hung in the air between them.

Wright's eyes fastened on Kane's scar, then slid away. Kane was used to that. Most people were afraid to say anything. But they all looked.

"We should all get in out of the cold," Wright said. He

climbed into the driver's seat. Kane got in next to him. The heater whistled and blew hot, dry air over him. The pilot sat behind. Wright turned the Suburban around and headed for some lights about a mile away.

"You're probably wondering why we asked you here, Mr. Kane," Wright said.

"I am, Elder Wright," Kane said. "But the fellow in the back is my charter pilot, not my partner. If you want to keep our business private, you might want to wait until we're alone."

"I will wait," Wright said. He looked in the rearview mirror. "No offense meant to you, sir."

"No problemo," the pilot said. "But it's lunchtime, so I was hoping to find something to eat. And I don't want to let my bird sit there in the cold too long."

"We'll stop at our cafeteria," Wright said. "I'll arrange lunch for you. When you are finished, I'll have some of our brethren take you back to the airstrip with a canvas cover and a propane heater to keep your aircraft from freezing up."

"Sweet," the pilot said. To Kane, he said, "We can't take much more than an hour, or we won't have enough light to get back to Anchorage."

The road had been cut through a forest of scraggly black spruce and thin, ghostly white birch. Nothing grew tall or stout. It's like God ran out of gas here, Kane thought.

Nature is not hospitable in interior Alaska. The climate is rigorous: sixty below zero in the winter and ninety above in the summer. Not many living things can adapt to that. But the real problem is not enough water. The coastal mountains block moisture. Much of the interior is little more than high desert. Damn cold at times, but desert nonetheless.

A hodgepodge of buildings stood in clearings cut along the road: new wooden structures, ATCO construction trailers, mobile homes, even a few log cabins. Overhead electrical wires ran to most of them.

The buildings stood on a bench of land that began at the river and swept away to the north, rising gently to meet the foothills of the Alaska Range.

"This is quite a layout," Kane said.

"We've been here nearly forty years now," Wright said. "Possessions accumulate."

Wright pulled the Suburban nose-in to a big white wooden building. A long row of assorted vehicles was already parked there. The men got out of the Suburban, and Wright plugged in its engine heater. Then they walked to the building and through the staggered doors of an Arctic entryway.

They were in a well-lit hallway. In a big room to the right, about fifty people stood in a line with trays in their hands.

"Lunch is being served," Wright said.

Conversation stilled as Wright, Kane, and the pilot walked along the line to where four young men dressed for the outdoors were standing. Wright explained what he wanted, and he and Kane left the pilot with them.

"Our business is in the office building," Wright said. "We'll just walk through here and out the other end. "

The two men walked along the hallway. Opposite the cafeteria was another big room.

"That's our community hall," Wright said. "We hold gatherings and other community events there. We have some rooms off of it for smaller meetings."

Every person they passed ran an eye over Kane.

"I take it you don't get many visitors, Elder Wright," he said.

"I'm Elder Thomas Wright," the man said, putting a slight emphasis on his first name. "There is also an Elder Moses Wright. He is my father, and the founder of Rejoice."

The two men went out another set of staggered doors into the cold. They crossed an open space and went into a smaller building that looked to be four ATCO trailers clipped together. Inside was a warren of offices. Wright led Kane to a big one at the far end. Eleven men sat at a large, round table that was set for a meal. All were in shirtsleeves and wore ties. Most had close-cropped hair.

"This is the Council of Elders," Thomas Wright said,

and made the introductions. "Elders" didn't seem to be a term related to age. Theirs ranged from mid-thirties to what looked like early seventies. Each greeted Kane with the word "Welcome," a handshake, and eyes that quickly left his face to stare over his shoulder.

Elder Moses Wright, a short, fiery-eyed old ruffian with white hair that spilled over his collar, was the only exception. No welcome from him, only a defiant stare and a handshake intended to crush knuckles. Kane held the handshake and squeezed back until the old man seemed ready to call it quits. When he got his hand back, the elder rubbed it and gave Kane a considering look, like a logger trying to figure out just where to drop a big tree.

"I'm sure you'd like a chance to wash your hands and get out of those coveralls," Thomas Wright said. "I'll show you to the restroom."

When Kane got back, Thomas Wright was in shirt-sleeves and a tie, too. Unwrapped, he was a tall, thick, slope-shouldered man in his mid-thirties with an oval face and sorrowful eyes.

The scene looked like pictures Kane had seen of men's groups in the 1950s, Masons or Knights of Columbus. Only Kane, wearing wool pants and a polypropylene pullover, looked like someone from the twenty-first century.

"I guess I'm a little underdressed for the occasion," he said as he took the empty place at the table, "but I chose warmth over formality."

That got a chuckle from a couple of the elders.

Without a signal that Kane noticed, teenage girls brought food and withdrew. Lunch looked like stew of some sort. Kane picked up his spoon and dipped it into his bowl before he noticed that everyone else was waiting.

"It is customary for us to thank God for our food before eating," Thomas Wright said.

Kane set his spoon down and found himself holding hands with the men on either side of him. Moses Wright said grace in a booming voice, not a short prayer but a five-minute discourse on how God's bounty fell on even the most sinful. He seemed to be looking at Kane throughout the prayer. Kane stared back. With his wild white hair and beard, and piercing eyes, Moses Wright seemed to have stepped straight from the pages of the Old Testament.

The stew was wild game and delicious.

"Elder Pinchon's boy got the moose last fall," Thomas Wright explained. "He's our best hunter and a fine shot. We grow the potatoes and carrots ourselves. The bread is homemade, and the butter was churned from the milk from our own herd."

"Rejoice is very self-sufficient," Moses Wright growled, "and very prideful, too, it seems. 'Woe to the crown of pride,' it is written in Isaiah, and we all would do well to remember that."

Thomas Wright turned his attention to eating. Other elders hurried to fill the silence.

During the meal, they told Kane that Rejoice had about 230 residents, with another thirty or so away at the moment. The community—nobody used the word "commune"—had been founded in 1967 by Moses Wright, his wife, and a couple dozen others. Over the years, some people had died or drifted away, but more had joined. Children were born, and when they became adults, most stayed.

"You were born here?" Kane asked Thomas Wright.

"I was," Wright said. There was a tone in his voice Kane couldn't quite place. Not pride. More like resignation.

"Does everyone who comes here stay?" Kane asked.

The Wrights passed a look.

"This life is not for everyone," Moses Wright said. "Those of us who live here must sacrifice in the service of God."

The girls returned to clear away the bowls, then served dessert: blueberry pie à la mode.

"Let me guess," Kane said. "Blueberries from your own bushes. Homemade ice cream."

All the elders smiled. Except Moses Wright.

"Do you mock us, Mr. Kane?" he thundered.

"Why, no, Elder Moses Wright," Kane said. "You have much to be proud of."

"This is not our doing, but God's," the old man said, intoning:

"For the Lord thy God bringeth thee in to a good land, a land of brooks of water, of fountains and depths that spring out of valleys and hills;

"A land of wheat and barley and vines, and fig trees, and pomegranates; a land of oil olive, and honey;

"A land wherein thou shalt eat bread without scarceness, thou shalt not lack any thing in it."

"That's not exactly the description I'd give of this place," Kane said, "but the rest of it seems to fit: 'A land whose stones are iron, and out of whose hills thou mayest dig brass.' "

Silence greeted Kane's words.

"Are you a religious man, then, Mr. Kane?" asked the elder called Pinchon. He was, like Thomas Wright, in his thirties, but the resemblance ended there. Pinchon was one of the few men Kane had ever met who could fairly be called beautiful. He had fine, even features, dark hair and eyes, and eyelashes a supermodel would kill for. He had been introduced as the community's bookkeeper.

"I've had a lot of time to read in the past few years," Kane said.

" 'The devil can cite Scripture for his purpose,' " Moses Wright said.

"Shakespeare, too, I expect," Kane said, straining to keep his voice light.

The old man scowled. The other elders fought with varying degrees of success not to smile. The girls came in and cleared away the rest of the plates.

"Now, I suppose we had better get to the business that brings you here," Thomas Wright said briskly. His tone made it clear that a meeting had begun and he was in charge of it. "Perhaps, Mr. Kane, you wouldn't mind telling us a little of your qualifications."

Kane looked around the table.

"My name is Nik Kane," he said. "Except for some time in college and the Army, I've lived in Alaska my whole life. I am fifty-five and have been married for twenty-four years. We have three children, the last of them still in college. I put in twenty-five years on the Anchorage police force, fifteen of them as a detective. I'm here with the recommendation of the chief there, Tom Jeffords."

Moses Wright opened his mouth as if to say something, but closed it with the something unsaid.

"Why did you leave the force?" a thin, gray-haired elder asked.

"Surely you know that," Kane said, looking around the table, meeting the eyes of each man in turn. "The story was in all the newspapers."

A silence descended, broken by Moses Wright.

"Is this really the sort of man we want to invite into our community?" he asked. "A drunkard and a murderer?"

His son opened his mouth to speak, but Kane raised a hand to stop him. "Actually, the charge was manslaughter," Kane said, "and in the end I was exonerated. I haven't had a drink in more than eight years."

"Still . . ." the old man began.

"I'm not finished," Kane said quietly. "I'm here as a favor to a friend, not to solicit either your employment or your approval. If my presence here offends you, just say the word and I'll go back to Anchorage."

"Your presence here offends not only me, but God," the old man barked.

"Father!" Thomas Wright said.

Kane got to his feet.

"Thank you for a delicious lunch," he said to Thomas Wright. "I guess I'll be getting back now."

"Please, Mr. Kane," the younger man said, putting a hand on Kane's arm, "don't leave."

Something in the man's voice made Kane sink down into his chair again.

"As for you, father," Thomas Kane said, "we have discussed this and discussed it. You know the majority of the council does not feel as you do. Stop being obstructionist."

The old man bared his teeth at his son, then opened his mouth to speak.

"If all of your experience is in the city," a balding, pop-eyed fellow said quickly, "do you think you can work out here?

"Detecting is detecting," Kane said. "And I know my way around the woods."

Silence descended. It was clear the group had at least one more question, but no one wanted to ask it. Finally, a young man said, "There's sort of a rough element out here. You may run into them in your work."

Kane smiled and ran a hand over his close-cropped hair.

"I have a lot of experience with the rough element," he said, "both as a police officer and more recently. I'll be okay."

"How many men have you killed?" Moses Wright asked.

"Do you want me to count the war?" Kane asked.

"Is that where you got the scar?" the old man said with a vicious grin. "The war? Or is it perhaps punishment for more recent sins?"

"That's enough, Father," Thomas Wright said. "Mr. Kane didn't come here to be put on trial."

"The Lord said, 'Thou shalt not kill,'" Moses Wright growled.

Kane looked at the old man for a long moment.

"Your Lord sets a high standard," he said. "Are you so holy that you always meet it?"

That brought silence. Thomas Wright looked around the table and got nods from everyone but his father.

"Now, perhaps, Mr. Kane, you'd like to hear what it is we'd like you to do," he said.

"That's why I'm here," Kane said.

Wright cleared his throat and began.

"As my father said, not everyone is cut out for this life," he said. "This is a community in every sense of the word. We live together and worship together and laugh together and weep together. We raise our children together. We own everything you see together.

"That togetherness is too much for some people. So is the religion that binds us. So is the lack of amenities: no movies, no television, no coffee stands. No coffee, for that matter."

"We allow no stimulants," the old man said.

"Coffee is expensive," his son said, "and we can't grow it ourselves. At any rate, we lose a few people every year. We have our own school, but there comes a time when many of our children go off to college or the military."

"You send people to the military?" Kane asked.

"We are not pacifists, Mr. Kane," the old man said.

"Nor are we trying to cut ourselves off completely from the larger world," said his son. "At least not all of us are. And because we cannot raise or make everything we need, we have to have money. So we own some businesses, both along the highway in Devil's Toe and in Anchorage and Fairbanks. Mostly tourism related. Our own people run those businesses.

"As you can see, a significant portion of our young-adult and adult population is exposed to the larger world. A few succumb to its charms."

"We wouldn't lose any if we kept them at home and prayed harder," the old man said.

His son ignored him.

"I'm telling you this so that you understand that we don't panic when someone leaves. We don't like to lose anyone. The community is diminished by their departure. But we understand that humans have different needs and the free will to seek to fulfill them."

"Get to the point," the old man barked.

"Having said all that," his son said, "we would like to hire you to find a member of our community."

"*They* would like to hire you," the old man said.

"Elder Moses Wright," his son said mildly, "we have discussed this and thought about it and prayed about it. This is what we agreed to do."

None of the other elders said anything, but Kane understood that they were sitting at the table, when they no doubt had plenty to do elsewhere, to demonstrate that the community agreed with Thomas Wright and not his father.

"Who would you like found?" he asked.

"My daughter," Thomas Wright said. "Faith."

"By your leave, Elder Thomas Wright," Pinchon said, "the others and I have affairs to attend to. I will assert that this is the man to do the job, and in the absence of any new disagreement"—he shot a glance at Moses Wright—"we will leave it to you to explain the task to him and negotiate his payment."

With that, the other men put on their outdoor clothing and departed, leaving Kane and the two Wrights.

"This is unwise," the old man said. "Rejoice has always handled its own problems."

"Father," the younger man said, "you can be a help or a hindrance. Either way, we are decided to do this."

Now that the other men were gone, the differences between the two remaining were even clearer. And there was something about the younger man that Kane couldn't quite put his finger on. Something about the way he talked or sat or held his head seemed familiar.

"I have counseled against bringing in an outsider," the old man said, "particularly this outsider. I will continue to speak against it."

"In that case, Mr. Kane," Thomas Wright said, "perhaps we should continue our discussion elsewhere. So that my father may return to his prayer and meditation."

The two men put on their outdoor gear and retraced their route to the Suburban.

"There's something I wanted to show you anyway," Wright said. He started the Suburban, pulled away from the building, and aimed for the foothills. As he drove, he talked.

"Faith is almost eighteen. She has been gone four days now, since Friday," he said. "We don't know where she has gone or with whom. Some think she has chosen the world over Rejoice. Others are afraid harm has come to her."

"What do you think?" Kane asked.

"I don't know what to think. Since she became a teenager, Faith has become a difficult person to fathom. She does what is expected of her and seems committed to our beliefs. But last year she insisted on attending the regional high school. She said it was because they offered programs she was interested in, but I can't help thinking she wanted time away from Rejoice.

"The truth is, I'm afraid I don't know my daughter very well."

"Might her mother be able to shed some light?" Kane asked.

Wright was silent for a moment.

"Her mother was called to God four years ago," he said.

"I'm sorry," Kane said. "How about friends?"

"I don't think Faith confided in anyone. I of course asked the young people if they knew anything about her—I'm not certain what to call it. Departure? Disappearance?—but got no information from them. I wasn't really sure what I should have been listening for, anyway.

"I'm not much of a detective, I'm afraid. And the local trooper says Faith is just another runaway. He couldn't be less interested. So we sent for you."

The two men drove the rest of the distance in silence. Wright pulled up next to a big greenhouse in an even bigger clearing and shut off the engine.

"I'm not sure how much good I can do you," Kane said as he followed Wright into the greenhouse. "Faith is nearly an adult. She's been gone long enough for the trail to be cold. There seem to be no clues. I don't know the area or the people. And my past . . ."

He had more to say, but the sight that greeted him in the greenhouse took his voice away. The two men stood in a vast flower garden, an explosion of color and fragrance and moisture. The flowers were sprawled in beds, and in pots that overflowed the crude tables on which they sat. After the monotony of the winter landscape, the flowers made Kane want to sing and, at the same time, stunned him into silence. He wasn't sure how much time went by before Wright spoke again.

"My father doesn't approve of this place," he said. "Most of our greenhouses are for vegetables, and a few fruits that we try to coax into growing. He thinks this place impractical and, somehow, ungodly. But man does not live by bread alone, or even by the word of the Lord. The people here need beauty in their lives, and some evidence during the long winter that nature is not all hostility and bleakness. This place provides these things. I love it here. So did Faith."

He paused and turned to face Kane. He had tears in his eyes.

"I don't want to force Faith to come back, Mr. Kane," he said. "I just want to stand here with her one more time."

Thus sayeth the Lord: Execute ye judgment and righteousness, and deliver the spoiled out of the hand of the oppressor.

JEREMIAH 22:3

"SO WHAT COULD I DO?" KANE SAID, SITTING UP STRAIGHT in the hard wooden chair that faced Tom Jeffords's desk. Jeffords didn't want anyone but himself to be comfortable in his office. "I told him I'd try to find the girl."

Jeffords sat behind the cherry wood desk in a padded leather chair that, with the addition of just a few jewels, would have been a throne. He was flanked by the red, white, and blue of the U.S. flag, the blue and gold of the Alaska flag, and the white-field-with-blue-anchor of Anchorage's city flag.

The wall between the flags was covered with certificates and plaques, each and every one of them awarded to Thomas Jeffords. Stretching out from the flags to the far walls were clusters of photographs of Jeffords with various dignitaries: Pope John Paul II, Ronald Reagan, Bill Clinton, two George Bushes, John Denver, B. B. King, Martha Stewart, Ted Nugent (the Motor City Madman), several prosperous-looking Asians. If you were wealthy or famous and visited Anchorage, it was hard to avoid having your picture taken with Tom Jeffords.

Jeffords drummed on his blotter with a letter opener.

"I'm glad to hear that," he said. "They need the help, and you need a new start."

It must be nice to sit on a throne and issue decrees, Kane thought.

"Look," he said, "I just spent four hours bouncing around the sky in a bush plane with a kid barely old enough to drive, and another with a bunch of Bible thumpers, all as a favor to you. So if you're looking for me to start gushing gratitude, don't."

"Angels," Jeffords said, trying to balance the letter opener on its point.

"What?" Kane asked.

"Angels," Jeffords said. He moved his hands slowly away from the opener. It started to fall. He grabbed it again. "Their neighbors call them Angels. It's not meant as a compliment."

"Why do you know so much about Rejoice?" Kane asked.

Jeffords was silent. He moved his hands again. The opener tilted to the side. He let it fall.

"Let's just say I have an investment in the area," he said.

Kane could believe that. Jeffords's title was chief of police, but he really ran Anchorage. Doing so had made him a rich man. Not from bribes and corruption. Jeffords was too smart for that. But for more than a dozen years he'd been on the inside of every good business deal in the city and many outside it. He could have any sort of investment in the area around Rejoice.

Kane didn't bother to ask what the investment was. He knew from experience that Jeffords would tell him what he wanted him to know and nothing more.

"What are they doing out there, anyway? The Angels?" Kane said.

Jeffords spun the letter opener and watched it wheel around until it stopped, business end pointed at Kane.

"I'm sure they could give you a better account than I," Jeffords said.

He gave the letter opener another spin.

"Seems like a hard place for a religious community," Kane said. "There's got to be more welcoming locations."

Once again the opener pointed at Kane.

"What's the point of having faith," Jeffords said, his words tinged with what might have been sarcasm, "if you don't test it?"

He spun the letter opener once more and both men watched it revolve until it stopped, pointing at Kane.

"Are you a religious man now, Nik?" Jeffords asked. "Do you believe in God?"

"What difference does that make?" Kane said, hearing the irritation in his voice. "Jesus, Tom, you've known me for more than thirty years. What are you asking me a question like that for?"

"Rejoice's preacher is said to be an eloquent and convincing man," the chief said. "It wouldn't pay to be too credulous. On the other hand, the Angels have created a religious culture out there. It would help to be able to speak their language."

"I'll get by," Kane said, wondering what Jeffords really meant by the question. Was the chief developing religious scruples as he aged? Or was he afraid that during his years in prison Kane, like so many other cons, had found Jesus?

He looked across the desk at the big, silver-haired man in the tailored police uniform and shrugged.

"This is probably a snipe hunt, anyway," he said. "By now the girl could be in Vancouver or Seattle or anywhere. Even here."

"I'm having my people keep an eye out for her," Jeffords said. "I've made inquiries of my friends in the state and the Lower 48. Even our Canadian cousins. Nothing so far."

"What is this girl to you?" Kane asked.

Jeffords's answer was a thin smile.

"She's a missing teenage girl from a respectable family," he said. "What else does she have to be?"

Classic Jeffords, Kane thought. An answer that doesn't answer anything.

"What are your plans?" the chief asked.

"I came back to collect a few things," Kane said. "I'll load up and drive out there tomorrow sometime."

"Good," Jeffords said. "Is there anything else I can do for you?"

"You can give me my job back," Kane said.

"You know perfectly well that can't happen," Jeffords said, holding up a hand to keep Kane from replying. "I know, I know. You've been cleared of the charges against you. But you still violated department policies. I'm taking a big political risk helping you out at all." Then his voice softened. "You're a good investigator, Nik, maybe the best I've ever worked with, but you'll never work here again."

"So the fact I was falsely convicted doesn't make any difference?" Kane asked. "Is that fair?"

Jeffords shook his head.

"Don't be childish, Nik," he said. "As my father used to tell me, fair is a place where men in overalls throw cow chips for distance."

"Your father was quite a card, wasn't he?" Kane said. "What if I sue?"

"Jesus, Nik," Jeffords said, his voice tired, "give it up. Start over. You made a mistake. You paid for it. Move on."

Kane bit down on an obscenity and swallowed it. He didn't really want to fight with Jeffords. Even if the chief had left him dangling in the breeze back then, he owed him a lot. Jeffords had quietly made sure he'd gotten a good defense lawyer. He'd quietly helped out Laurie, Kane's wife—soon-to-be ex-wife now—while Kane was in prison. He was quietly trying to help him now.

He owed Jeffords for all that, even though he knew the chief had done it for his own reasons. For much of Kane's time with the police department, Jeffords had been his boss. But he didn't consider the chief a friend. Tom Jeffords was all about Tom Jeffords.

"What are you doing in your dress blues, anyway?" Kane asked to fill the silence.

The chief looked at Kane, then at the big gold mariner's clock on his desk.

"You remember how this job is," he said. "It's always

twenty-four/seven. My budget is up before the Assembly tonight, then I've got to make an appearance at a fund-raising dinner with Gwendolyn."

"Political?" Kane asked.

"Not this time," Jeffords said. "Charity."

That was all the small talk Kane had in him, so he just sat there, waiting to hear what else was on Jeffords's agenda.

"Have you put in your papers for your pension?" the chief asked.

"No," Kane said.

"Why not?" Jeffords said. "You've got, what, twenty-five years in on the force?"

As if he hasn't been looking at my file, Kane thought.

"That's right," he said.

"Twenty-five years," Jeffords said, "and the expunging of your criminal record restored your pension rights. You're fifty-five. You're entitled to the money now. Why not claim it?"

Because if I draw my pension I can't come back on the force, Kane thought. But he didn't say it. Jeffords knew why he was stalling, and part of the reason he wanted Kane to make the application was to foreclose the question of re-hiring him once and for all.

"I just haven't had the time," Kane said.

The chief pushed a button on his desk. In a moment his longtime secretary, a canny, competent woman named Emily Lee, walked into the room. Her hair was gray now, and lines had appeared at the corners of her eyes and mouth, but she retained much of the beauty that had had cop after cop pawing the floor. When they were all younger, Kane had been sure that Jeffords had been fooling around with her. Then the chief had divorced his first wife to marry money, and their relationship now seemed strictly professional.

Emily Lee nodded to Kane.

"Hello, Emily," Kane said. "Is he still working you too hard?"

Emily Lee offered Kane a smile, and his heart jumped.

"Yes, he is," she said. "He's such a stern taskmaster."

She turned to the chief and briefed him on his schedule for the following day. When she was done, the chief said, "Nik here needs help with his pension paperwork, Emily. Why don't you get his information from personnel and fill it out for him? Then all he'll have to do is sign it."

The woman smiled, nodded, and left the room. The chief rose and got into a long overcoat. Kane stuffed his feet into the cold-weather boots, picked up his parka, and followed Jeffords out.

"What do you know about the rough element out there in Devil's Toe?" Kane asked as they walked down a long hallway.

"Every place has one," Jeffords said.

I wonder if they still call those Jeffordisms, Kane thought, those answers that don't answer anything.

Getting out of the building wasn't easy. Jeffords was stopped in the hall by three people who needed to consult, so Kane got to listen to conversations about materials procurement, delays in the delivery of new patrol cars, and the lack of minority applicants. He knew two of the people who stopped the chief, but they both ignored him. A lot of the department didn't know just what to think about Kane, and having him walking the halls was probably an embarrassment for them.

"Maybe you should keep me around as an object lesson," he said to Jeffords when the last of the conversations ended. "You know, 'There but for the grace of God . . .'"

"Nik . . ." Jeffords said.

"You know," Kane said, interrupting the chief, "if you'd stood behind me when all that happened, I might not have been sent to prison."

"I've explained that to you," Jeffords said. "There were political considerations."

"Yeah," Kane said, "there are always political considerations."

"And you were drunk," Jeffords said.

Kane could hear the edge in the chief's voice, so he

didn't respond. Besides, Jeffords was right. He'd been drunk.

"Do you need more money?" Jeffords said. Kane took the question to be an olive branch, and he was careful to reply calmly.

"No, thanks," he said. "I still have plenty from what you loaned me."

The two men continued in silence. Jeffords also stuck his nose into the watch commander's office and the dispatchers' bullpen. The watch commander was a guy named Rudy Jones, who got to his feet when he saw Kane and gave him a big hello and a handshake. Apparently there was a part of the force that saw him as a hero, Kane thought, or at least a guy who'd gotten more than was coming to him.

The watch commander didn't have much for the chief; Kane knew from experience that what Jones really wanted was for Jeffords to go home and leave him in charge. Two of the dispatchers were frosted at being forced to come in on mandatory overtime and let the chief know it. He laughed about it on the way through the lobby.

"The department would stop running without those women," he said, "and they're the first to tell you so."

The air outside was warmer and moister than it had been in Rejoice, but that wasn't saying much.

"Feels like snow," Kane said as he and Jeffords descended the steps of police headquarters. The building was well lit, the big towers of lights fighting the winter darkness to a standstill. The headquarters was new, built five years earlier with bond money approved by voters grateful to live in such a safe, smooth-running city.

The new building had everything. It was built on rollers and reinforced to withstand even the biggest earthquake. A civilian couldn't park a car within blast range or get past the armed, bulletproof glass–encased receptionist in the lobby with anything short of an RPG. One wing of the building housed an array of up-to-the-minute communications equipment. Temblor, terrorist attack, or Third World War, Jeffords was ready.

His driver had the chief's bulletproof car waiting in front of the building. Kane nodded to him and followed Jeffords into the backseat of the black Lincoln Town Car. A red-faced man in the blue-on-blue uniform of the Alaska State Troopers was waiting for them, sitting in the jump seat.

"This is Major Denton," Jeffords said to Kane as the car pulled away. "He's here unofficially to tell you a few things about the area into which you are venturing. Stanley, this is Nik Kane."

Kane didn't recognize Denton, and if the trooper knew who Kane was, he did a good job of hiding it. Kane wasn't really surprised to see him. The two departments cooperated pretty well, in part because Jeffords had gotten his start wearing a Smokey Bear hat.

"Whenever you're ready, Major," he said to the trooper.

"There are two communities in the area in question," Denton said. "I'm told you have visited Rejoice. Just across the river, on the highway, is the town of Devil's Toe.

"It's not much more than a wide spot in the road. Devil's Toe started out as a mining town, and when the mining played out, it shrank to little more than a roadhouse and grocery store catering to the Natives scattered around the area.

"It's still that today, although there's a component of the population composed primarily of riffraff who came up to get federal homesteads back in the sixties and seventies. Some of them proved up. Some didn't. The ones who stayed are dominated by a fellow who calls himself John Wesley Harding."

"John Wesley Hardin?" Kane said. "The Texas outlaw?"

"Harding, with a *g*," the trooper said. "This guy isn't from Texas, he's from back east somewhere. Real name's Francis Hogan."

"Probably got the name off the Dylan album," Jeffords said. "It's spelled with a *g* there."

Kane and the trooper looked at him.

"What?" Jeffords said. "I can't like Bob Dylan?"

The two men shrugged, and the trooper continued.

"Nobody around there seems to know him as Francis

Hogan," Denton said. "Everybody calls him Big John. He has a son, Little John, who is in his thirties, and another son, a teenager, whose name is, believe it or not, John Starship. His mother was a teenage runaway who called herself Brenda Starship."

"Big John was, what, in his fifties when the last boy was born?" Kane said. "He liked them young then?"

"Still does, as far as we know," Denton said.

Kane could feel himself relaxing. A police briefing was a familiar situation, and getting one reminded him of better times.

"The mother still around?" he asked.

"Long gone," Denton said. "She moved to Anchorage, did some hooking, then married a GI and left the state."

Kane looked out the window. The car was traveling through a part of town so generic everyone just called it midtown. What had once been perfectly good muskeg had been scalped, filled, and leveled, much of it while Kane had been in prison. In place of the trees and willow bushes, malls and big-box stores had erupted. In the block they were passing Kane counted seven fast-food outlets. Of course, it was a long block. The roadsides were decorated with a thin film of snow colored brown by the sand put on the roads to improve traction. The short trees planted here and there in the name of landscaping were leafless sticks. Hell must be a place much like this, Kane thought.

"What else?" he asked.

"There are also some solid citizens in the area: business owners, teachers, other state employees, even a few legitimate homesteaders," Denton said. "But Devil's Toe has more than its share of less-than-solid citizens."

"Got it," Kane said. "Lots of bad guys. Probably bad girls, too. Go on, please."

"For years, no one paid much attention to the area," the trooper said. "The Native people kept to themselves. The residents of Rejoice were quiet and hardworking, and the citizens of Devil's Toe were no better or worse than in a lot of road towns."

"What changed that?" Kane asked.

"Two years ago, the Pitchfork mine opened," Denton said. "And some of the entrepreneurs of Devil's Toe began to offer, shall we call it, entertainment for the mine workers."

"I don't suppose we're talking about movies?" Kane said. "Community theater?"

"Women," the trooper said. "Gambling. Drugs."

The car pulled up in front of Kane's apartment house.

"Why haven't you people closed the bad places down?" Kane asked.

Denton and Jeffords looked at one another.

"Don't be soft, Nik," Jeffords said. "You know that wherever you have a bunch of men working you're going to have vice. Nobody wants these guys driving back and forth to Anchorage or Fairbanks for their booze and nooky. Too dangerous."

"Too likely they won't come back, you mean," Kane said. "So letting the vice go on is just a service for the company. Keeping the workforce happy and productive." The silence in the car was broken only by the rumbling of the engine and the whine of the heater fan.

"Just what are you doing about the bad people in Devil's Toe?" Kane asked.

"Not much we can do unless we catch them red-handed," Denton said. "The protections of the legal system extend to criminals even out in the tules."

"But you have your best men on it?" Kane asked.

"We have one trooper for several hundred square miles," Denton said. "Budget constraints. Our man out there is named Jeremy Slade. He's just out of training."

"That's the best you could do?" Kane said. "A kid just out the of the academy?"

"These things are arranged by seniority," the trooper said. "None of the senior officers wants to live in Devil's Toe."

"Or to try to enhance his career by looking the other way, I'll bet," Kane said.

"Nik," Jeffords said, a warning tone in his voice.

Kane sighed.

"The people out in Rejoice say your man hasn't been much help with Faith Wright's disappearance," he said.

"His report says he's checked around without finding anything," Denton said. "His opinion is that the girl, who is nearly eighteen anyway, just ran off."

Well, Kane thought, if he'd done a better job, they wouldn't need me.

"Okay, you've got a situation out there that could explode at any time," he said. "So what do you want me to do about it?"

"What makes you think we want you to do anything about it?" Jeffords asked.

Kane looked at him.

"The mine is a centerpiece of the governor's economic development policy," Denton said. "He wouldn't like to see anything embarrassing happen there."

"Neither would the mine owners, who have their own concerns," Jeffords said. "They have a substantial investment in equipment. They have a significant amount of gold being stored and shipped. Every two weeks, they have a large sum of money on hand for payroll."

"Cash?" Kane asked.

"Checks would hardly have much value out there," Jeffords said. "The company offers the workers the option of direct deposit, but surprisingly few of them use it."

Kane's lips twisted in a sardonic smile.

"Wouldn't want the money where the IRS or child-support enforcement could find it," he said.

No one said anything for a moment.

"So that's it?" Kane said at last.

"That's it," the trooper said. "What everyone would like is for peace to descend on Devil's Toe, and particularly the Pitchfork mine. We don't mind them feeding booze to the workers, or even running a cathouse, but we want to be certain nothing worse is in the works."

He reached into his shirt pocket, produced a business card, and handed it to Kane.

"My private number is written on the back," he said, "in case you run into anything you need help with."

Kane put the card in his pocket and got out of the car.

"Oh, Nik," Jeffords called after him, "when you get out there, be sure to see the head of mine security first thing. You know him. Charlie Simms."

Kane closed the door and watched the car drive off.

Yeah, I know Charlie Simms, Kane thought. He's the guy who helped put me in prison.

3

The Lord hath chastened me sore: but he hath not given me over unto death.

PSALM 118:19

THE APARTMENT BUILDING KANE LIVED IN WAS ONE OF many thrown up quickly during the pipeline boom of the 1970s, then left to age ungracefully. It was three floors of plywood and two-by-fours, painted a nondescript gray on the outside and baby-shit brown on the inside. A large Yupik family with an ever-shifting cast of characters lived on one side of Kane; a good-looking young couple who had vigorous, noisy sex at every opportunity on the other. The people above him seemed to have a home business training elephants. Kane's ears told him what his neighbors argued about and what they watched on television; his nose informed him of what they ate and what they smoked.

Not all that much different from prison, privacy wise, he thought as he checked his mailbox and found, as usual, nothing but junk sent to "current occupant." He threw it away, climbed the stairs to the second floor, and let himself into his apartment. He locked the door behind him and felt the tension leave his shoulders and neck for the first time that day.

Kane had been out of prison for a little more than two

months. The proportions of the outside world were still all wrong. Everything was too big and too open, too bright and too loud, and there were too many people wandering around loose, driving, talking, laughing, looking him right in the eye in a way that, inside, would have brought on at least an exchange of threats. The world simply contained too much for someone accustomed to a small cell, cramped vistas, and the constant vigilance that kept him out of trouble.

Even his apartment, small by most standards, seemed too big to Kane. It really wasn't much: living room with kitchen attached, bedroom in the back with a bathroom off that. It had come furnished, and none of the pieces—the moldy couch, the rickety table with mismatched chairs, the double bed without headboard or foot board, the paper-thin wooden chest of drawers—was without its scratches, mars, or sags.

But every surface was spotless: the hairy brown carpets freshly shampooed and vacuumed, the kitchen linoleum swept and mopped, the bed made with a tautness that would have made even Kane's old drill instructor smile. The Wal-Mart dishes were clean and stowed away, the pot and pan shined. The little TV-VCR combo that sat on a metal stand gleamed. The apartment was as neat and barren as a monk's cell.

One exception, propped up on top of the chest of drawers, was a framed photo of Kane, Laurie, and the kids in camp during a raft trip on the Talchulitna River years before. He remembered everything about that picture: the sun on his back as he positioned the camera and set the timer, the fresh salmon they'd eaten for dinner after it was taken, how he and Laurie had made love so quietly in their tent that night, arriving together at the place very good sex takes you if you are lucky.

Another was an old picture his mother had given him that hung above the bed, a garish, bloody rendering of the Sacred Heart of Jesus that had scared the hell out of him as a kid.

How could anybody live with their heart outside them like that? he'd asked.

It's a miracle, his mother had said. Don't question God's miracles.

If you'd asked Kane why he'd hung that picture, he couldn't have answered. Even though his relationship with God, if there was a God, was much more complicated than his mother's, the picture looked like it belonged there.

Kane pulled off his outdoor gear and stowed it in the closet by the door, walked to the bedroom, navigated around the books piled there, and dressed for the gym. He put a change of clothes into his gym bag, put on a coat, and left the apartment, his nose noting that the Yupik family, the Sundowns, would be having fish for dinner. He started his pickup, got out to scrape the ice off its windows, disconnected the head-bolt heater from an electrical plug mounted on a short four-by-four cemented into the ground, got back in, and drove to the gym. As usual, the pickup's cab was just starting to warm up when he got to where he was going.

He pumped some iron, did an hour on the treadmill, then had a steam and a shower. After he toweled off, Kane looked at himself in a full-length mirror. A shade over six feet, 190, the same weight he'd played football at in high school. At the time of the shooting, he'd weighed thirty pounds more, but worry and exercise had pared that away. Self-discipline and prison cooking had kept it off.

Kane leaned closer to the mirror to examine his face. Except for the scar, unremarkable, he thought: black hair flecked with gray, still cut close, prison-style; brown eyes; an ordinary nose, ridged in a couple of places it had been broken, over somewhat thin lips; a jaw that was neither square nor pointed. The beginnings of jowls hung from the sides of that jaw, and when he bared his teeth the thin ropes of muscle in his neck jumped out.

Not getting any younger, he thought.

Back in the apartment, Kane stood in the kitchen assembling the ingredients for veal scaloppine. He'd never been a cook. Laurie had done all of that during their more than twenty years of marriage. Before that, institutions and restaurants had. Before that, his mother. But as he'd told the Rejoice Council of Elders, he'd had plenty of time to read in prison, and one of the things he'd found himself reading was cookbooks. He had one open now, an old copy of *The Joy of Cooking* he'd bought at a secondhand bookstore. Like most of the recipes, this one served three or four, and he was still trying to figure out how to cut them down to serve one.

As he sliced mushrooms and diced tomatoes, browned and baked, he thought about Jeffords's question. Was he a religious man? It was the same question the elder, Pinchon, had asked. Kane couldn't remember the last time anyone had asked him such a question, let alone two people on the same day. The cons and guards didn't discuss theology much, and neither had the cops he'd worked with.

Was he a religious man? He didn't think of himself as one. He had read the Bible in prison, true, but he'd read anything he could get his hands on to keep himself from thinking about where he was, how he'd gotten there, and how much longer he had. He couldn't remember the last time he'd been to Mass. The Catholic Church seemed like a big bureaucracy to him, the Army with bishops instead of colonels. And all that stuff about God, the devil, and evil? He'd seen enough in his time to believe in evil, but it seemed to him that everyone created his or her own. Jesus, the things people did to each other.

Kane put the scaloppine and steamed vegetables on separate plates; there was still far too much meat for one person. As he sat down, he heard the bed in the apartment next door begin its rhythmic squeaking. Here we go, he thought. He sat eating and reading other veal recipes as the pace of the squeaking increased, followed by the woman moaning, then the man joining in, the headboard banging against the wall, the noise level increasing until it sounded like the couple was going to come right through the wall, bed and all. Then, suddenly, silence.

That must be one stout bed, Kane thought, turning the page.

After he'd put the extra scaloppine in the refrigerator and cleaned up the dinner dishes, Kane took a cell phone from his pocket and punched in a number. When a man answered, he ran his finger down his scar and said, "I'd like to speak with Laurie, please. This is Nik Kane."

The man's hemming and hawing was quickly replaced by her voice.

"What do you want, Nik?" she asked in the tone of a mother dealing with a misbehaving child.

"I need to pick up a few things at the house," he said.

"Does it have to be tonight?" she said.

"It does," he said. "I'm heading out in the morning."

"Why did you leave this until now?" she demanded.

"I didn't leave it until anytime," he said. "I didn't think that coming by the house I still own to pick up some of my possessions would be a problem."

"Well, it is," she said.

"Well, I don't care," he said. "I'm coming over anyway. If that means you and your boyfriend have to put your clothes back on, tough."

"Oh, fuck you, Nik," she said, and slammed the receiver down.

That went well, he thought, stowing his cell phone away.

He put on a coat, went out, got into his pickup, and drove to his soon-to-be ex-house.

Kane told himself he'd have understood if Laurie had given up on him while he was in prison. But she hadn't. She wrote to him regularly and visited him once a week, tracking him as trouble drove him from one prison to another. The drive to where he'd ended up, at the prison in Kenai, was more than three hundred miles round trip, but she made it anyway, week in and week out, and never a word of complaint. He watched her hair grow longer and her body thinner, listened to her talk about the kids and her return to nursing, and wondered if he could make it without her. The cons' conventional wisdom was that having ties to the outside made you weak, but Kane figured that was just their way of making it okay not to have anyone outside. He had been—still was—immensely grateful to Laurie, and as he pulled into the driveway he was stricken with remorse for fighting with her.

Laurie was waiting for him, alone, her arms folded across her chest.

"We've got to talk," she said.

He followed her into their kitchen—her kitchen now—and sat at the table. Kane folded his hands in front of him and waited.

"Nik," she said, "we're getting divorced. I told you that before. You have to accept it. We can be friends or we can be enemies, depending on how we handle this. But we're not going to be husband and wife anymore. I've seen a lawyer. You'll be getting the papers soon."

Kane looked down at his hands. The knuckles were white. He forced himself to relax his grip, took a deep breath, and said, "I want to start by apologizing for how I just treated you. I had no right to do that. But I just can't get used to this. I thought about you for seven years, about coming back and being a couple again, and now that's all over? Why?"

Laurie sat up a little straighter, as if she were trying to put more space, even just a couple of inches more, between them.

"We talked about that, Nik," she said. "You're not the same man you were before you went in. I'm not the same woman. We don't have the kids to raise anymore. We've just grown apart. People do, even under normal circumstances."

Kane felt like he'd been punched in the stomach. He was having trouble breathing. He sat up straighter, took a couple of deep breaths, and said, "That's it? We've grown apart, so that's the end of more than twenty years of marriage? Couldn't we give it some time, maybe grow back together again?"

Laurie shook her head.

"That's not the way it feels to me," she said. "It feels

like this is over. Putting in more time would just make breaking up horrible and bitter."

Kane thought about that. Hiding somewhere in her explanation was something else, a real reason or reasons. He'd had this feeling before, questioning suspects, and he'd always been right. Was it that she felt like she didn't have that much more time, more time to find somebody else? Laurie was forty-three, and while she was still a good-looking woman, she had some gray hair and lines around her eyes and mouth. For a moment, Kane could see her as he first saw her at nineteen, a twinkle in her eye, her body turning her candy striper outfit into an incitement to riot. Laurie was right, the woman she was now was different. But did that have to mean the end of everything?

"Are you sure that's all there is to it?" he asked. He couldn't quite keep a tone of accusation out of his voice and he saw her stiffen.

"Another man, you mean," she said, her voice harsh. Laurie got to her feet and walked over to lean against the kitchen counter. "I told you before, there is no other man. I waited for you. I'm not saying I was a nun for seven years, but I passed up plenty of chances to hook up, as the kids say. I practically moved right out of my parents' house to yours. Why would I want to get involved again right away? I needed the time to figure out who I am."

Kane didn't understand that at all. *Who I am?* Who ever knows who they are? There's the person you want to be, the person other people want you to be, the person you have to be, and probably a lot of others. You do the best you can with all those people every day, and that's who you are.

"A man answered the phone," he reminded her.

"Antonio is just a friend," she said, exasperation in her voice. "I mean, he might be something more, but he hasn't been. He's just been there for me during a lot of hard times while you were away, and he's here for me now. But we're not sleeping together."

She blew air out of her mouth and paced, her movements jerky with anger.

"Listen to me," she said, "explaining myself to you. I don't owe you any explanations. You're the one who fucked up and brought us here."

"I know," Kane said. "I want to make it up to you."

"Make it up to me?" Laurie said, stopping in her tracks. She sounded really angry now. "How are you going to make it up to me? You going to give me the seven years back? You going to be here to help me finish raising the kids and see them off? You going to fix it so I don't spend the past seven years on my feet for ten hours a day, working my butt off, then coming home and working here, having to be cheerful every minute?" Kane watched as she regained control, saw the soft smile and the shake of her head. "You can't make it up, Nik. What's done is done. It's time to move on."

That's what Jeffords said, too, Kane thought. Time to move on. That's fine for people who have a place to move on to. But where am I going? I have a hard time just leaving my apartment.

"I wish there was something I could say that would change your mind," he said, a plea in his voice. He took a deep breath, then said more firmly, "Can you at least tell me what it is that convinced you we aren't right for each other anymore?"

He really was baffled about that. After seven years away, they'd spent three weeks together and she'd sent him away. He'd thought things were going okay, considering. He had been getting a slow start back into the world, it was true, and she'd seemed a little tense around him, prickly really. And there was the sex, which she didn't seem to really be participating in the way she once had. He was probably hard to get along with as well. You don't go from years of having walls and bars everywhere you looked to living in twenty-first-century America without needing some time to adjust. But he loved her, and he thought she loved him, and that would be enough to carry them over this rough spot.

"What good would it do you to know?" she asked.

"I don't know," he said. "It's just that you stuck with me for all that time and then, all of a sudden, it's over. I'm confused, I guess."

Laurie walked over and sat at the table again. She reached out and put a hand over Kane's folded ones.

"It wasn't anything big," she said. "It was a lot of little things. But the thing that did it was the way you dress."

"The way I dress?" Kane said.

"You wear the same clothes all the time," she said. "Blue shirt and jeans. You even had me buy another blue shirt, so you'd have one to wear while the other was being washed. Look at you. That's what you're wearing now. It's like you're still in prison and this is your uniform." She took her hand off his and laid it on the side of his face. He could feel its warmth, and calluses, too. "You're not the man I married, Nik, or the one I expected to get back from prison. Since you left, my world has gotten bigger, but yours has gotten so much smaller. You've got a lot of issues, Nik, a lot of things to resolve. And I just can't wait around until you work it all out, if you ever do."

Kane opened his mouth and closed it again. There wasn't anything to say to that. He'd been proud of the way he'd gotten through his sentence. Not proud of some of the things he'd done inside, but proud of not being broken by the experience. He'd thought it hadn't even marked him much, but Laurie saw it differently. He didn't understand the decision it had led to, but he had to accept it, like so many things that had come his way since that night.

I guess I'll have to do better living in the world, he thought, and for the first time he felt committed to going to Rejoice and finding the girl. At least it would force him to get out of the apartment.

He looked at Laurie's face. This is probably as close to her as I'll ever be again, he thought.

"Okay," he said, "if that's what you want. I'm not happy about it, I may never be, but you've got a right to your life."

He reached up and gently took her hand and laid it on the table. Then he got to his feet.

"I really do need to pick up a few things," he said. "I'm going out of town for a while. It's work. I'll get the rest of my stuff later, if that's all right. I'll be sure to call ahead.

And I'll sign the papers when I get back. Any way you want to settle things is fine."

He went into the garage and got a sleeping bag and some camping gear and his big thermos. He loaded all that into the pickup. He stood looking at his locked gun case for a long time but made no move to open it. A judge had said he was no longer a felon, so he could use firearms, but he didn't know if he'd ever handle one again.

He was taking out the last load, tire chains and his tool box, when he heard Laurie call, "Nikky."

He went back into the house. She was standing at the top of the stairs. God, she's beautiful, he thought.

"What is it?" he asked.

"Nothing," she said. "I guess I just wanted to see you one more time."

They stood looking at each other for several moments.

"Good-bye," Kane said. He wouldn't see her again if it could be avoided. He needed a clean break. He turned and walked away without another word.

Back at his apartment, he packed some clothes and shaving gear in a duffel bag and got ready for bed. He found he couldn't sleep. Somewhere somebody was watching a reality show on television, and it sounded like a domestic dispute was heating up down the hall. He lay in his bed thinking about Laurie and his life with her, saddened and amazed that it was over. Thinking about it made him want to take a drink. More than one. Instead, he turned on his bedside lamp and picked up Donald Frame's translation of Montaigne's essays.

"Those who make a practice of comparing human actions are never so perplexed as when they try to see them as a whole and in the same light," he read, "for they commonly contradict each other so strangely that it seems impossible that they have come from the same shop."

4

*And they journeyed from Oboth, and pitched at Ijeabarim, in the
wilderness which is before Moab, toward the sunrising.*

NUMBERS 21:11

KANE WAS AWAKENED EARLY THE NEXT MORNING BY THE
sound of squeaking springs next door. He got out of bed
and padded to the living room window. He couldn't see
two feet through the falling snow. He showered, dressed,
and drank a couple of cups of coffee.

As he waited for the caffeine to wake him up, he
thought about how strange it still was not to be on somebody else's schedule. He missed that in a way, missed the
predictability of it and not having to make decisions. That
must have been one of the changes Laurie saw, he thought.
Before I went in I was decisive, at home and especially at
work. Sometimes too decisive for her, I suppose. Now I
miss having someone tell me what to do with every
minute. What am I? A child? One of those cons who can't
make it outside? No wonder she wants to be rid of me.

He heated and ate the previous night's scaloppine,
washed the dishes and coffeepot, and loaded snacks and
bottled water into a day pack, along with as many books as
he could fit. He took one last look around the apartment,
put on a coat, picked up the duffel and day pack, and left,

locking the door behind him. He walked down a flight and knocked on the building manager's door. The guy, a recent arrival from someplace in Asia, looked like he hadn't been out of bed long. It took a while, but Kane finally got the idea across that he wanted the manager to hold his mail if he got any. The manager seemed happy that it wasn't a complaint of some sort, and closed the door nodding and smiling.

Downtown, Kane was lucky to find a parking spot in front of the Catholic cathedral. He let himself in a side door. The long wooden pews were empty, the only life in the big room coming from the flames of candles that danced in front of the statues of Jesus and his mother.

Kane had made his first communion in this church, wearing a hand-me-down white shirt and black dress shoes with holes in the soles. There were eight kids in his family—he was second-to-last—and never enough money for all the necessities, let alone luxuries. They'd been so poor that when his father drifted off in a cloud of failure and alcohol fumes the family's standard of living didn't drop much. He continued to attend the church through his youth and into his teenage years for reasons that were more practical than spiritual; without the parish's charity, the Kane family's situation would have been even more dire. His brothers and sisters approached the matter much the same way, but their mother had enough religious fervor for all of them.

When he went off to the military, Kane quit attending any church, and stayed away even after returning to Anchorage and joining the police force. But he'd been coming to the church again since he'd gotten out. He didn't know why, but the visits made him feel better somehow. He knelt in front of a rack of prayer candles, slipped a dollar bill into the slot beneath them, and lit a candle. His mind groped for a prayer to say for his parents and came up with the response from the rosary:

"Holy Mary, mother of God," he whispered, "pray for us sinners, now and at the hour of our death. Amen."

He said the same for each of the people he had killed. They ran through his mind like pictures fanned by a finger:

small brown men during the war, then a pair of hopped-up killers coming out of a convenience store, where they'd murdered the clerk and a pair of customers. The next picture, the one that had put him in prison, was blurred, a dark shape holding what looked like a gun. He skipped over it quickly. Then the man he'd killed in prison. A lot of bodies, when you added them all up, he thought.

Kane wasn't sure that the prayers would do any good for his soul, since he didn't really feel sorry for most of the killings. But maybe praying would help the souls of the dead somehow.

Kane got up from the bank of candles, walked back a few pews, and knelt. The church was dim and cool and quiet, soothing. He waited, as he had since he was a boy, for God to say something to him.

He would settle for any word from above, but he really wanted God to answer a list of questions for him. The list had grown long over the years; it was so long that Kane had forgotten many of the questions. He remembered the first one: Why had God allowed Shamrock, his dog, to be run over by a truck? He remembered the most recent: Why was Laurie leaving him? Now he had a new one: Where is Faith Wright?

He'd never heard so much as a whisper from God in answer. He didn't really expect one. He wasn't sure there was a God. Even if there was, he couldn't believe that God, whoever or whatever he, she, or it was, was directly involved in individual human lives. But somehow the awed boy in him continued to kneel in hope.

He tried to empty his mind but, as usual, failed. The blurry memories of the shooting kept creeping in. His pulse ran faster and faster and he clasped his hands harder and harder. But it was no use. He relaxed and let it all come back.

He was driving home from an after-work party. They'd been at the Blue Fox, celebrating his promotion to lieutenant. He was feeling no pain, humming to himself, but he had his home car completely under control. He was thinking about how to avoid an argument with Laurie about coming home late and, as she would put it, "stinko," when the *"Officer needs assistance"* call came over the radio. No cop could ignore that.

He was right on top of it, just two blocks away, so he was first on the scene. The neighborhood wasn't a good one. The scene was poorly lit by a single streetlight and lights from the surrounding houses. The unit was slewed in the road, the driver's door open, a shape sprawled half in, half out. Two figures were standing above it. One of them, the one closest, seemed to be doing some sort of dance.

His tires slipped when he braked, then grabbed as the studs dug in. He came out of the unit and drew his gun, keeping the door between himself and the two figures.

"Police officer!" he shouted. "Step away from the vehicle and put your hands on top of your head."

The second figure tried to say something, but Kane ignored him.

"I said step away, now!" he shouted.

The closest figure turned toward him and started to raise its arm. Everything seemed to be happening in slow motion now.

"Oh, Jesus, don't do that!" the second figure called.

But the arm kept coming up, and Kane could see something in the hand, something that looked like a gun.

"Drop that!" he called. "Drop it now or I'll shoot!"

The arm kept coming up. Kane centered his weapon on the figure's chest and fired three times. The bullets threw the figure back against the door. Then Enfield Jessup, described later in the newspapers as "a twelve-year-old mentally challenged African-American youth who was big for his age," fell on his face, dead.

"Oh, Christ, you shot Enfield!" the other figure screamed. "Why'd you wanta do that?"

"Get your hands up!" Kane shouted. The figure raised its hands. Kane moved out from behind the door, slipped on the ice, and went down, hitting his head. He must have been knocked out for a moment, he decided later, because the next thing he knew he was getting to his feet. He put a hand to the back of his head and it came away sticky with blood.

He could hear the sirens of other police vehicles approaching, but otherwise the only sound was his own labored breathing. A few faces peeked from behind curtains to see what had caused the gunshots. Even in the bad light, Kane could see both bodies lying as before. But of the other figure, there wasn't a trace.

Kane walked to the bodies. The officer was still breathing, but Enfield Jessup was not. There was no gun in his hand or anywhere else in sight. As a police car came sliding to a halt behind him, he sank to his knees thinking, What have I done? Where's the gun? What have I done?

Kane shook himself all over, got to his feet, and left the church. The snow was still coming down. The city was trying to go about its business, but the roads were littered with vehicles stuck in the snow. Beater cars, mostly, but he also saw an abandoned UPS van and a city bus that had gotten high-centered.

I hope this isn't God's way of telling me to stay put, he thought.

Traveling through an Alaska winter could be an adventure, and Kane was prepared. He wore long underwear, jeans, a blue work shirt, a pile vest, and old hiking boots over two pairs of polypropylene socks, one thick and one thin. He had a set of tire chains in the back of the pickup along with a shovel and a tow rope. An old parachute bag held camping gear, and his duffel of clothes sat on a foam pad and sleeping bag, his Kevlar vest lying beside it.

The cab contained cold-weather gear, hot coffee, snacks, and CDs. A set of United States Geological Survey maps of the area around Rejoice lay on the passenger's seat, along with Montaigne's essays and a copy of the Bible. He popped a Dylan CD into the player, and Bob started grating out "Love Sick."

About 350 road miles separate Anchorage from Rejoice. The highway follows the Matanuska Valley, climbs through a pass between the Talkeetna and Chugach mountain ranges, parallels the Copper River, then swings north and east along the Jordan to join the Alaska Highway.

Even in the snowstorm, there was a fair amount of traffic on the road between Anchorage and the Valley. The town of Palmer, about forty miles northeast of Anchorage, had started as the center of a social and economic experiment during the Great Depression, when families from the Midwest were relocated to establish agriculture in Alaska. But the coming of the container ship, the jet airplane, and the chain store made milk and vegetables from the West Coast cheaper than milk and vegetables from the Valley. Most of the people who lived in and around Palmer worked in Anchorage now, commuting because they liked the rural lifestyle and cheaper housing.

From Palmer on, only an occasional laboring semi marred the open road. On the long climb through the mountains, Kane watched the trees grow smaller and sparser, the houses fewer and farther between. He thought about why people came to Alaska and why they stayed. The Alaska they came to now was more like the rest of America than the one he'd been born in: more developed, more strident, and more polarized. But it retained its allure for people, at least certain kinds of people. Still the land of new beginnings and last chances, he thought.

On a good day, the drive from Anchorage to Rejoice takes five or six hours. It wasn't a good day. The snow slowed Kane to a crawl, and he had to stop well below the top of the pass to put on the tire chains, a wet, unpleasant job, then stop on the other side to take them off. There was, as usual, much less snow on the interior side of the mountains, but the air was much colder.

Kane looked at the trees he passed and the streams he drove over, wondering what it would be like to throw a pack on his back again and head off into the wild. He'd always loved the outdoors. When he was a boy, his father had taken him fishing and hunting. Then his father abandoned the family. But Nik was soon old enough to fish and hike in the summers with his friends and, later, hunt as well. He strapped on snowshoes as soon as he could, and skis not long after. The outdoors had been an escape from the troubles at home, and during the summers anyway, the source of fish, meat, and berries, much welcomed by his mother.

He'd done everything he could to show his own children the joys of the outdoors, with mixed success. Only his oldest daughter seemed to have caught his enthusiasm. His other daughter was an indoor girl all the way. And his youngest, his son? Kane had missed too much of his growing up to know.

His own attitude toward the outdoors seemed to have changed in prison. After so much time in confined spaces, the land that passed by the windows of his pickup looked too big and empty. I hope I get over this, he thought. I'd hate to lose the outdoors, too.

Kane was stiff, tired, and hungry when he pulled into the parking lot of the Devil's Toe Lodge a little after six p.m.

The lodge was a long, low log structure. Most of the logs were dark with age, but some were lighter, showing that someone had added on to the place. A door opened into a bar and café.

Inside the bar, a big, bearded drunk dressed in work clothes was yelling at a small, white-haired Native man wearing jeans, a flannel shirt, a ski jacket, and one of the nicest pairs of knee-high beaded moose-hide moccasins Kane had seen in years. A half dozen men in work clothes sat at a couple of tables, watching.

"We don't want none of you goddamn salmon-crunchers in here," the drunk was yelling. "Now get the hell out."

The old man stood with his head bowed, leaning slightly toward the man like his words were a stiff wind. The drunk towered over him. Kane's first instinct was to ignore the situation. It wasn't his problem. But that was prison talking. I've got to get out of prison sometime, he thought. He walked over and stepped between them, facing the drunk.

"Calm down," he said quietly, "or you'll break something."

The bartender looked at the two of them and scurried from the room.

Up close, the drunk looked to be Kane's age or a little older. He had small, bloodshot eyes and a beak of a nose etched with the red lines of a heavy drinker. His shirtsleeves were rolled up, and he had an ornate tattoo on his left forearm of a demon doing unspeakable things to a woman. The finger he shook at Kane had dirt embedded under its nail.

"Who the fuck are you?" the drunk screamed. "You keep out of this or you'll wish you had."

His breath smelled like the inside of a bourbon barrel.

He was taller than Kane and, with his ample gut, probably fifty pounds heavier. Kane wasn't worried. Every Anchorage cop had plenty of experience with big drunks.

"I'm just a guy came in here to have a quiet meal," Kane said reasonably, "which I can't do if you're carrying on like this."

"Fuck you," the drunk said, and wound up to throw a big right hand. Kane shifted his feet and kicked the drunk's brace leg out from under him. The drunk toppled over, banging his head on a table as he went down.

"Jumpin' jimminy," the old man said, "we're having fun now."

Kane looked around the room. All the men were standing. He turned to face them, arms at his sides and what felt like a big grin on his face. One of the men raised his hands and clapped them together. Slowly, the others joined him, until the café was filled with applause.

"Hit the rotten cocksucker again," one of them called. "We don't like him anyway."

The drunk put his hand to his head. It came away bloody.

"Son of a bitch," he said, and tried to get to his feet. Kane let him get to a knee before reaching over and shoving him onto his back.

"Stay there," he barked. "You get up again and you're just going to get hurt."

The drunk mumbled something but stayed put.

The bartender returned. He had a dark-haired young guy with him. The guy looked worn out to Kane, but he was carrying a metal baseball bat.

"What happened here?" he demanded.

"Relax, Little John," a voice called from one of the tables. "Henry just fell down."

"Yeah, twice," another voice called. General laughter followed.

"That what happened?" the guy with the bat asked Kane.

"More or less," he said, "leaving out the fact I helped him fall. You really should stop serving guys like him before their true personalities come out."

The guy gave Kane a tired grin and lowered the bat.

"Henry is a bastard," the man said, "but his money spends just as good as the next man's. As long as these boys don't break the place up, they're welcome."

He turned to the Native man.

"But you're another story, aren't you, Abraham?" he said. "You know what Dora will say when she finds out you were here again, don't you."

The Native man smiled and lowered his head.

"Maybe you should head on home," the man said, "before you get yourself—and me—in trouble."

"I can't leave," the old man said. "I'm going to meet my son here."

Kane looked toward the thin, wood-panel partition that separated the bar from the café.

"Let's go get a bowl of soup, uncle," Kane said. "If your son shows up, he can find us there."

The old man stopped and looked at the men at the tables. He looked at the man with the bat. He looked at Kane.

"Okie dokie," he said. "I like soup."

Kane took the old man's arm and led him toward the café.

A couple of the men helped the drunk to his feet. When he was upright, he shook them off and rushed toward Kane and the old man.

"Look out," one of them called. Kane pivoted, saw the drunk coming and stepped aside, nudging the old man out of the way. When the drunk reached him, Kane planted his feet, grabbed one of his arms, and heaved. The drunk went flailing past, and crashed into a table, tumbling over it. He lay there for a moment and got to his feet again.

"You know," Kane said conversationally, "being big isn't all there is to it."

The man rushed him again. Kane admired his gumption, but was getting tired of playing matador to his bull. He stepped aside again and as the big man floundered past Kane screwed his feet into the floor and put everything he had into a kidney punch. The man dropped like he'd been shot and lay there moaning, clutching his side.

A couple of the other men came over to help the big man into a chair.

"That was some punch," one of them said to Kane. "Henry here will be pissing blood for a week. Can't say he didn't deserve it, though." He laid a hand on the old man's arm. "We don't all share his views on race relations."

"This ain't over," the big drunk said through gritted teeth.

The other men in the bar laughed.

"Shit, Henry," one of them said, "you start up with that guy again and we'll be chipping in to buy flowers for your funeral."

Kane led the old man to a table in the café. A dark-haired young woman in tight jeans, a low-cut blouse, and sneakers brought them menus.

"What would you like to eat, uncle?" he asked.

"Just soup," the old man said.

He ordered chicken soup for the old man and a cheese-burger for himself. The café was about half full, single men or men in small groups mostly, but one family with a couple of kids. They gave off a buzz of conversation. Above it, Kane could hear noise from the bar next door: voices, laughter. A jukebox, or maybe a television set, started up.

Kane let the silence stretch out between him and the old man. He knew he'd have to do something with him, but for the moment he just sat and let the road miles and the tension from his encounter with the big drunk slip away.

While he sat, he examined his surroundings. The walls of the café were covered with photographs of Devil's Toe and its citizens, dating back quite a ways; the picture near-

est their table showed a half dozen men trying to push a
1930s Ford pickup out of the mud.

The waitress brought their food, bending low so that
Kane could get a good look at her lacy bra and what it held.

"If you see anything you're interested in," she said,
"just ask."

The old man picked up his spoon and began slurping.

"I like soup," he said. "These store teeth I got make it
tough to chew."

Kane had known a lot of Natives. He'd grown up with
them, gone to school with them, played sports with them
and against them. On the force he'd dealt with Natives of all
types: corporate leaders and street drunks, wife beaters and
crime victims, and fellow cops and neighbors. He'd known
a lot of Natives in prison—Native men ended up in prison
all out of proportion to their numbers—including the ones
who had helped him finally find peace of a sort. He'd done
some reading on their culture and found much to admire. It
gave them enough to keep going when disease and discrim-
ination and booze would have broken most other people.

For a moment, Kane was assailed by an urge to ask the
old man what it had been like to have his culture overrun
and nearly swept away. But he recognized the self-
indulgence and futility in that urge and kept quiet.

The two of them ate, the old man taking his time the
way old people do. Kane's cheeseburger was only a cut
above hunger. Just as he was finishing, a young woman
stormed in through the opening from the bar. She walked
directly to where the two men were sitting.

"Where the hell have you been?" she said to the old
man. "I've been looking all over for you."

She turned to Kane.

"Who the hell are you? And what are you doing with
my grandfather?"

She looked to be in her mid-twenties, with long, straight
black hair, high cheekbones, and copper-colored skin.

"Buying him soup," Kane said, "and looking after him.
Like somebody else should be."

The girl's shoulders slumped.

"He does this sometimes, he just takes off," she said. "When I get home from work, he's gone."

The old man stopped slurping soup.

"I'm here to meet my son," the old man said. "I promised."

He went back to eating.

Kane reached over and pulled out a chair.

"You could sit until he's finished eating," he said. "Would you like anything?"

The girl shook her head and sat.

"I'm Dora Jordan," the girl said. "This is my grandfather, Abraham."

"Nik Kane," he told her. "I'm here to do a job for the people over in Rejoice."

"The Angels?" the girl said. "What could you do for the Angels? They do everything for themselves."

The old man lifted the bowl and drank the rest of the soup. He set the bowl back down and smacked his lips.

"I seen an angel once," he said. "Back up behind where they're mining now. I used to have a trap line back up there. Too old now, and there's no animals on account of the noise."

The old man was quiet for several seconds.

"But I was up there checking my traps, me and my son, when I seen the angel. It was snowing pretty good, and out of the snow came this angel all dressed in white and carrying this beautiful woman. She had long yellow hair with red streaks in it. He didn't make a sound goin' past me."

The old man was quiet again. Just when Kane thought he'd finished, he said, "When I was done checking traps I went back to where I seen the angel. But there was no tracks. I guess because he was an angel. Or maybe the snow covered them up. I'll ask my son when I see him."

Kane cocked his head at the girl.

"His son, my uncle, went off to the Vietnam War," she said. "He never came back. I show grandfather the letter saying he's missing in action, but he doesn't understand."

Kane smiled.

"Or maybe, uncle, you just prefer living in a world where your son is coming back," he said. "A world with angels in it."

The old man smiled but said nothing. The girl helped him get up. She offered Kane some money, but he waved it away.

"My treat," he said.

The pair started out of the room.

"Oh, Dora," Kane called, "if those moccasins he's wearing are your work, they're beautiful."

The girl stopped and turned to face Kane.

"We're very good with our hands," she said sharply. She turned, put her hand on the old man's arm, and led him, shuffling, out of the dining room.

"Touchy, ain't they," the waitress said, bending low again to hand Kane the check.

"Yeah, but I expect you'd be touchy, too, if you were going through what she was going through," Kane said.

"Like my life's a day at the beach," the waitress said, turning to leave.

"Hey, wait," Kane said, "who do I talk to to get a room?"

"In the office," the waitress said, gesturing vaguely toward the bar.

Some of the men, the big drunk among them, had left. The ones who remained didn't say anything to Kane as he passed through. The bartender didn't even look up from his cell phone conversation.

A door on the far side of the bar led to a narrow hallway. The first door was open, and light poured from it. Kane went in. It was a small room divided by a counter. Behind the counter stood the young fellow from the bar. The baseball bat was nowhere in sight.

"Help you?" he asked, looking up. "Oh, it's you. Fighting with those men from the mine might not be too healthy."

"I'll try not to make a habit of it," Kane said. "Right now, I need a room for the night, someplace far from the bar and the noise. And a plug-in for the truck."

"We got warm storage around back," the man said. "Cost you twenty. Fifty for the room, eighty if you want your own bathroom."

"I'll take the bathroom," Kane said. He dug money out of his wallet and laid it in front of the man.

"Want a receipt?" he asked. Kane nodded and the man wrote one up.

"How about some company?" he asked.

"Company?" Kane asked.

"You know," the man said. "Female companionship. Tracy there, the waitress, would join you after her shift for a hundred. Or I got some numbers I could call."

His heart wasn't in his sales pitch. The idea of a warm body in bed with him sounded good to Kane, but he didn't want to have to deal with the hooker attitude he knew he'd get, and having to sleep with one eye open to keep his wallet from disappearing. Besides, if the Angels heard about it, there was no telling what would happen.

"Not tonight, thanks," he said.

"Suit yourself," the man said, handing Kane a key.

Kane drove his truck into the long, low garage at the back. He dug out his duffel, locked everything up, and, following the man's directions, carried the duffel to his room. When he got there, he closed and locked the door. Then he took a pair of wedges out of his duffel and shoved them under the door.

The room wasn't much bigger than a prison cell. He used the bathroom, brushed his teeth, and stripped off his clothes. He set his travel alarm for eight a.m., turned out the lights, and closed his eyes. He didn't even have time to think about how much he wanted a drink before falling asleep. He dreamed he saw an angel gliding over the snow, dressed all in black.

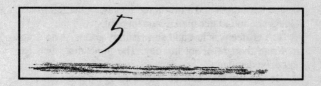

And the gold of that land is good; there is bdellium and the onyx stone.

GENESIS 2:12

THE ALARM CLOCK'S BEEPING PULLED KANE OUT OF HIS dream. He lay for a moment getting his courage up, then threw off the blankets, rolled out of bed, and hopped around for a minute on the frigid floor. He scraped a clear patch in the frost covering the room's small window and looked out. Too dark to see anything. He took a fast shower—you could never tell how long the hot water would last in a place like this—and dried himself on a towel as big and soft as a sheet of sandpaper. He repacked his duffel and walked along silent hallways to the café.

Tracy the waitress was standing behind the counter of the restaurant. She was wearing the same clothes. Kane wondered if she'd found some other customer ready to part with $100.

"This is some shift they've got you on," Kane said.

"Work's work," she replied. "Menu?"

"Just coffee," Kane said. "What's the weather like?"

"Cold," Tracy said, pouring coffee into a thick, chipped mug. "Thirty or thirty-five."

She didn't bother to say "below zero." She didn't have to.

Tracy put the coffee down in front of him, bending low from force of habit. Up close, she had lines of weariness beside her mouth and a bright red hickey on her left breast. Guess she found her man, Kane thought.

The coffee was hot and surprisingly good. As he drank it, Kane thought about his day. The mine first, then Rejoice, he decided.

He got another cup of coffee to go, put his coat on, picked up his duffel, and walked out to the warm storage shed. His breath escaped in white puffs. The cold deadened the skin of his face and froze the hairs in his nose. The only noises were the hum of the electrical line and the squeaking of his boots on the snow. Not a bird flew or a creature stirred.

Kane pulled the door open and went into the shed. He threw his duffel into the back of the pickup, backed out of the shed, got out, and closed the door, then drove off toward the bright lights that marked the Pitchfork mine.

He cruised along the highway for a few miles, the only thing moving. The community of Devil's Toe, not much more than a dozen buildings spread out along both sides of the road, was shut tight.

As he drove, he tried to ready himself for seeing Charlie Simms again. Simms had led the investigation of the shooting, and the last time Kane had talked to him was in an interrogation room at the station.

It was almost a week after the shooting. Kane was still feeling slow and fuzzy headed, disoriented from something, maybe hitting his head, maybe being the guy doing the listening rather than the talking.

"We can't find a gun, Nik," Simms said that day. "I'm telling you this because you're family. The other kid at the scene came into the station the next day. Lionel Simmons. Aka 'Train.' Seventeen. A pretty long juvie rap sheet. He said him and the retard, Jessup, were watching TV when they heard the shots. Jessup ran out to see what was what. Lionel followed, he says, to keep Jessup out of trouble. They were looking at the scene when you pulled up and started barking orders. He said he figured Jessup got confused, but it looked to him like the retard was starting to

*raise his hands when you shot him. Then you fell and hit
your head on the ice. He went over to check on Jessup. No
pulse. You groaned and he ran away."*

"Why'd he run?" Kane asked.

"Said he was afraid you'd shoot him, too," Simms said.

"That's it? His word against mine?" Kane asked.

Simms was silent for a moment.

"We went over it with him hard, again and again, but he
stuck to his story," Simms said. "We tested the clothes he
was wearing. No gunshot residue. We got a warrant and
searched his house and didn't find anything. None of the
neighbors said anything about seeing a gun, including one
old bag who said she watched the whole thing and saw you
shoot the kid for no reason, even though she can't see three
feet."

"What about the cop who was shot?" Kane asked.

"O'Leary?" Simms said. "Says he doesn't know anything. Says he went to answer a domestic dispute call and
didn't even get all the way out of the unit before he was
shot. Never saw anything. The bullets were from a nine-
millimeter. Half the men in Anchorage own a nine. And a
quarter of the women. All in all, nothing."

"So now what?" Kane asked.

Simms shook his head.

"We keep looking," Simms said. "Most of the force is trying to find out who ambushed O'Leary. You know how it is
when a cop is shot. But some of us are working your case."

*The word "case" got through to Kane. If the shooting
was a case, somebody could be charged.*

"What happens if you don't find anything?" he asked.

"That's up to the DA," Simms said.

"The DA?" Kane said. "To do what?"

"To decide whether to charge you," Simms said.

"Charge me?" Kane said. "Charge me for what? The
kid had a gun."

*Kane saw in Simms's eyes the look that cops gave sus-
pects.*

"You sure about that, Nik?" Simms said, his voice full
of doubt. "You blew a 1.6. You were pretty drunk."

Kane's thoughts took him right past a side road that seemed wide enough to accommodate heavy equipment. He stopped and backed down the highway, turned, and drove up the road. He followed it for a few more miles, twisting and turning and climbing steadily, until he reached a gate in a tall Cyclone fence topped with barbed wire.

"Pitchfork Gold Mine," a sign on the gate read, with "Alcan Mining Consortium" written below it. Then, in the biggest letters of all, "No Trespassing."

The place was lit up like a Hollywood premiere. From where he sat, Kane could see a big building that must have been the mill house, but not much else. There was a small guardhouse next to the gate, but its window was tinted and he couldn't tell if anyone was in there. He leaned on his horn.

The window flew open and a shotgun was thrust out. Behind it, Kane could make out a pale face dominated by a droopy mustache. He rolled down his window.

"You got business here?" a man's voice asked. Kane heard sleep in the voice and, beneath it, hundreds of hard whiskey nights.

"Shouldn't be sleeping on the job, Lester," Kane said. "Somebody might sneak up and steal your shack."

A smile appeared beneath the mustache. It was several teeth short of a full set.

"Anybody who tried would get a bellyful of double-ought," the man said. "Howdy, Nik. I heard you was out."

"Two months, eight days," Kane said. "I'm here to see Charlie Simms."

The man in the guardhouse gave Kane a look, then started shaking his head.

"I don't know about that, Nik," he said. "I'm sorry for what happened to you, but it weren't Charlie's fault."

Lester's seriousness made Kane smile. Much of life is a mystery to Lester, Kane thought, but not so baffling that he can't jump to the wrong conclusion.

"I'm not here to get even," Kane said. "Jeffords sent me."

"I'll check," the man said, and slid the window shut

again. After a few minutes, he came out, wearing a big beige parka and bulbous-toed white bunny boots. He threw a bolt and swung the gates wide.

"Just past the mill house on the left," he told Kane.

Simms's office was in a one-story prefab, next to the office belonging to the mine manager. A secretary dressed in a sweater and ski pants showed him in, asked him if he wanted coffee, and left him alone. Even though there were fifty yards between the trailer and the mill house, Kane could feel the steady shaking of the mills breaking rock.

Pictures of old mining operations dotted the walls: men in dark, bulky clothes standing next to long sluice boxes, men aiming water from high-pressure nozzles at seams of gravel, men jockeying bulldozers through creeks.

"The chief told me you'd be stopping by, Nik," a voice said. "You're looking pretty good."

Kane turned to face Charlie Simms. He was a big, balding fellow with a weightlifter's body and a drinker's complexion. Like Kane, he'd followed Jeffords through the ranks of the Anchorage Police Department. After Kane had gone to prison, Simms had finally made lieutenant and stalled behind a desk. He'd retired and gone to work for a private security outfit that, according to rumor, belonged to Jeffords.

Kane had worked with Simms from time to time, and had come to the conclusion he was dedicated but plodding. He was also a big-time skirt chaser, but then a lot of cops were. They'd socialized some, too, often sitting across from each other at poker games Jeffords put together. He'd called it team building, but Kane knew the chief had organized the games as a way of assessing his subordinates.

Simms had been at the Blue Fox that night, celebrating even though he'd been a sergeant in the running for the promotion, too. When Kane was on his way out, Simms had weaved over to shake his hand, then navigated his way back to a booth and put the hand up the skirt of a cop groupie.

"You okay, Nik?" Simms asked, drawing him back to the present. "You look a little peaked."

Kane gave Simms a twisted smile.

"Sorry, Charlie," he said. "Memories."

"Yeah, I had some, too, when the chief told me you were coming," Simms said. "Sorry about what happened."

"Wasn't your fault," Kane said. "You just did your job."

Simms closed the door, waved him to a chair, and went through the motions of hospitality. When those were out of the way, he said, "I'm surprised to see you, Nik."

"Why's that, Charlie?" Kane said. "I thought you said Jeffords told you I was coming."

Simms sat quietly for what seemed like a long time. I suppose he's thinking, Kane thought.

"I guess it's because the chief is involved," Simms said. "I know you never thought he did right by you."

"How do you know that?" Kane said.

Simms gave him a grin.

"Your wife told my wife, Nik," he said. "You know how that is."

Kane thought about telling Simms that he and Laurie were split up, but decided against it. Marriage trouble wasn't something men talked about. And he didn't really want to explain his attitude about Jeffords, either. On balance, he figured, the chief had helped him more than he'd not helped him. On a more practical level, Jeffords could still do him a lot of good or a lot of harm. And he found an odd kind of comfort in taking a case Jeffords gave him. It was an echo of his life before the fall.

Besides, he thought, how much reason do I need when my only alternative is sitting in a ratty apartment thinking about all the ways I've fucked up?

What he told Simms was, "That's all water under the bridge, Charlie. I'm trying to make a new start."

That seemed to satisfy Simms.

"I'm glad to see you, Nik," he said. "I'm glad you're doing okay. I'm glad that little bastard finally told the truth and that you're out with a clean record. And I can use the help. There's something bad coming. I can feel it."

"I'm not really here for you, Charlie," Kane said. "The

people over in Rejoice asked me to find a young woman for them."

"I know, Nik," Simms said. "I'd just really appreciate it if you keep your eyes open while you're going around. We produced three hundred fifty thousand ounces of gold last year, and that's a mighty big temptation. That, and the payroll. We bring in about a quarter-million in cash every two weeks, more when the mine's running full blast."

Kane whistled.

"I can see why that might be attractive to certain parties," he said, "but you've been operating for, what, eighteen months? Two years? Why so concerned now?"

"You ever done any remote site work?" Simms said.

Kane shook his head.

"Well, here's how it is," Simms said. "Most of the workers here, maybe eighty percent, are pretty solid citizens. Married, sending their money home, doing their jobs and happy to have them. Hell, some of them even moved their families out to Devil's Toe so they can go home to mama when their shift's over.

"The twenty percent, though, are a different proposition. They're just blue-collar bums, moving from job to job whenever somebody needs a truck driver or a mechanic. They've been drawing a good paycheck long enough to forget what it's like to be out of work. And they're getting tired of the job. Can't blame them, really. It's tough work, especially in winter. Plus they just don't like being in one spot too long. They get twitchy.

"So they're acting up more. Drinking, fighting. It's only a matter of time before one of them maims somebody or decides if he can just get away with the payroll he'll never have to work again."

"You're worried about your own employees robbing you?" Kane asked.

"I don't think any of them would try anything," Simms said, "except for those people over in Devil's Toe. That's just a bad lot over there, and when they get tired of taking the mine's money one paycheck at a time, they'll try something. That Big John, he looks like a fellow who would do anything, and he's smart enough to plan something that could work. Give him the right inside man, and there could be real trouble."

Real trouble could cost Simms his job, Kane thought, so he might be overreacting to the situation. But probably not. Simms wasn't the best man the department had ever produced, but he was usually steady. So if he was this antsy something was probably up. And, judging by his gate guard, he didn't have first-rate help.

"That was Lester Logan out at the gate, wasn't it?" he asked.

"Yeah," Simms said, "but what can I do? The good cops want to keep being cops." He noticed Kane's look and said, "No offense, Nik."

"None taken," Kane said. "So, to sum up, you're nervous but not about anything specific, and I'm here on other business. So why am I talking to you?"

Simms stood and walked to the door.

"For one thing, you're here to meet the mine manager," he said. "Why don't you follow me?"

They walked down a short hallway and entered a conference room. A fellow in his mid-forties, with dark, curly hair and wearing a suit and tie, stood at one end of the table. Clumped together along one of its sides were a half dozen or so Asian men in dark suits, white shirts, and dark ties. Some were grayer than others. Several wore glasses. But on the whole they seemed much more alike than different to Kane.

"Ah, Simms, you're just in time," the curly-haired man said. "I was just about to fill our visitors in on the Pitchfork mine. Why don't you and your guest sit down?"

"Well, ah, Mr. Richardson," Simms said, "Kane here isn't really a guest in that sense."

"Nonsense," the curly-haired man said. "The more the merrier. I can always use a bigger audience. Sit. Sit."

With a shrug, Simms sat. Kane followed suit. For the next half-hour, the mine manager explained in great detail, aided by a PowerPoint presentation, the workings of the

Pitchfork mine. One of the younger Asian men murmured a translation as he talked.

"Not many people know," Richardson began, flashing a photograph of five men, each holding a gold pan full of nuggets, "that most of Alaska's mines are not hard-rock but placer operations. Placer means they use water. There used to be placer mines here, but the Pitchfork is what's called a hard-rock mine, an open-pit mine. Essentially we dig a big pit in the ground and mine the ore out that way."

He flashed a photo of the mine taken from the air, a big gouge in the ground with the mine buildings down in the left corner. Then he was off on what was obviously a well-traveled trail:

"Most modern gold mines are mom-and-pop operations that use low-power explosives, bulldozers, and water." Photo. "But the big mines, like the Pitchfork, are much more sophisticated." Photo. "Explosives are used to loosen up the dirt and rock." Photo. "Huge loaders that can lift more than twenty cubic yards of rock and earth load it into one-hundred-fifty-ton dump trucks." Photo. "The trucks haul it to the crusher, where the dirt is separated and the ore crushed small enough to send along." Photo. "From there it goes by conveyor belt to the sag mill." Photo. "Which breaks it into smaller pieces." Photo. "Then to the ball mills that make it smaller still." Photo. "The ore in the mills wears out the ball bearings, so it costs us about fifteen thousand dollars a month to replace them." Photo. "The ore is dumped into a big pond, where a whirlpool spins the ore to separate it by size." Photo. "The ore goes through a series of processes." Photo. Photo. Photo. Chart. "To draw out the gold and purify it." Photo. "The final result is a gold bar worth between two hundred thousand and four hundred thousand dollars, depending on the price of gold."

From there, Richardson expounded on the overall economics of mining, stressing the profits when the price of gold was high, the difficulties of keeping equipment operating in such a harsh climate, and the logistics of feeding and housing about 150 workers at peak production. It was all very professional and, as nearly as Kane could tell, had absolutely no value to him.

Richardson gave a big smile when he'd finished.

"Do you have any questions?" he asked.

The youngest-looking of the men launched into a detailed series of questions about the mine's finances. Richardson spoke in response, but none of his words added up to an answer. When this completely uninformative exchange was finished, Richardson said, "Now, let's see the mine firsthand."

Kane and Simms exchanged looks and began to fade out.

"No, no," Richardson said, "you two, too. In fact, Charlie, if you wouldn't mind, you can drive one of the vehicles."

The two of them went back to Simms's office to get their coats.

"What the hell is this all about?" Kane asked.

"How should I know?" Simms said. "Maybe he just wants some white men with him. But what's it hurt? You're not in a big hurry."

The Asian men all came filing out of the building in identical cocoa-colored parkas and white hard hats. Half of them climbed into the new Ford Explorer that Simms drove, the other half into an identical vehicle driven by the manager. Then the group proceeded to visit for themselves everything they'd seen on the PowerPoint.

The visitors seemed to enjoy the tour. There was a lot of whispering, and a couple were taking notes. Kane reckoned they'd have the place mapped down to the last square foot before they left.

Richardson took their picture standing in the bucket of a front-end loader, another dwarfed by one of the dump trucks, still another next to the stockpile near the mill house. The visitors insisted that Simms and Kane pose in every photo with them. Kane could feel the cold working on his legs. I should have worn the padded overalls, he thought.

Fortunately, the tour turned indoors. The whole group put on big ear protectors, like the ones worn by the people who service jet airplanes, and went into the mill house.

The thrumming of the sag and ball mills rose through Kane's boots and shook him to the top of his head.

The mill house was warmer than the outdoors, and a lot noisier. As the group walked around, the mine manager made gestures, and the visitors gestured back. Kane had no idea what they might have been trying to convey. When the party stepped out of the mill house again, it was a great relief.

"I think my liver is somewhere up around my eyeballs," Kane said to Simms.

From there, they walked through a big building harboring the gold-removal processes. At the end, the Asian men, Simms, and Kane had their picture taken, clustered around a shiny gold bar.

"That's all the time we have for the tour," the mine manager said. "Now, if you'll just follow me back to the office, we've got a few mementos to give you, and then I've been told you have to get back to your airplane for the flight back to Anchorage."

Simms nudged Kane.

"We can go finish our talk," he said.

Back at the office the two men sat on opposite sides of the desk.

"Who were those guys?" Kane asked.

"I'm not sure," Simms said, grimacing. "Maybe potential investors. An operation like this one burns through money like a sailor on shore leave."

Kane remembered the grimace from the poker table. It was a tell; whenever Simms was bluffing, he'd grimaced like that.

"Okay," Kane said. "Now I've met the manager. Now what?"

"Now nothing," Simms said. "All I want is for you to keep your eyes and ears open and let me know if you hear anything I might be interested in. I can't add you to the payroll, but the company would be sure to give you a consulting fee if you turn up anything."

"You could start by paying me for all the time I wasted here today," Kane said. Then he sighed. "Never mind,

Charlie. Jeffords asked me to check in, so I'll see what I can do for you. Give me your telephone numbers."

Simms handed him a card, and Kane tucked it into his wallet.

"Now, you can tell me what you know about a girl named Faith Wright," Kane said.

Simms grimaced as he shook his head.

"Never heard of her," Simms said. "Why do you think I'd know anything?"

"Pretty young girl," Kane said. "A crew of young men with money, and you the security chief. I figured you might know something."

Simms shook his head again.

"I don't get off the mine property much," he said, "but I'll ask around."

"Now, Charlie, you'd tell me if you knew something, wouldn't you?" Kane asked, trying to keep his voice light.

The door to Simms's office popped open, and the mine manager stuck his head in.

"Ah, good, you're still here," he said to Kane. "Our guests have a little ceremony for us. The Asians are very big on ceremony, you know."

The three men walked out to the front of the office, where the group was waiting. With a bow, the youngest of them handed Richardson, Simms, and Kane large manila envelopes.

"Just small tokens," he said, "for your hospitality."

Kane started to undo the clasp on his envelope, but the man put his hand over Kane's.

"Please," he said, "it is considered bad luck to open a gift in the presence of the giver."

There was a flurry of mutual bows and handshakes, and the tour group left.

"Thanks for taking the tour," the mine manager said to Kane. "Charlie here tells me that you might be in a position to give us some help on the security front. We'd be grateful for anything you can do." He finished like someone who'd come to the end of his memorized material, shook Kane's hand, and walked quickly back toward his office.

Simms walked Kane to the door.

"Remember, Nik, pass along anything you hear," he said. "And I'll do the same."

Kane walked to his pickup, thinking about Simms's reaction to his questions. He tossed his envelope on the front seat, unplugged the head-bolt heater, drove back to the gate, and waited for Lester to open it.

"We going to be seeing you around, Nik?" the gate man asked.

"Damned if I know," Kane said, and rolled out onto the road.

Even though it was almost eleven a.m., the sun was just a rumor on the eastern horizon. Several of the businesses strung out along the highway were still closed. Kane wasn't surprised. Some probably closed for the winter. And the others? Well, the mine was one of the few places for hundreds of miles that kept to a set schedule. In his years in Alaska Kane had heard the phenomenon called things like "bush time" and "village time" and "Native time." It just meant that when you got out of town, people did things whenever they damn well pleased.

Kane slowed when he passed the state trooper station, but the small building was dark and there was no vehicle next to it. So he drove on. There was still hardly any traffic on the highway. When he got a few miles past Devil's Toe, he began looking for a turnoff to the left. He took a couple that quickly petered out into driveways. Finally, he struck the right one. It ran through the black spruce for about a mile, slid down a long bank to the river, crossed it on the ice, and climbed back out. Nothing moved anywhere along the way.

Once he had mounted the far bank, Kane pulled the truck to a stop, shut it off, and climbed out. Except for the ticking of the cooling engine, all he could hear was silence. From where he stood, Kane could see nothing but nature, which seemed to go on forever. The openness of the vista made him a little weak in the knees. He turned slowly in a circle. In the low light, everything he could see— mountains, trees, snow cover—was white, black, or gray. Some people saw God's majesty in this big, brutal country. If so, Kane thought, it wasn't a God he wanted to meet.

"Remember, son," his father had told him the first time the two of them had gone camping, "all of this"—he swept his arm around to encompass the trees, the mountains, the stream by which they'd pitched their tent—"all of this doesn't care about you at all. If you do something stupid, this will kill you if it can."

He felt the cold creeping into his bones. I hope this girl I've come to find isn't out here somewhere, he thought. I hope she hasn't done something stupid and been killed by the land. That would be bad for me, and very bad for her.

He climbed back into the pickup, started it, and drove on. The road brought him out on the side of the runway. Kane drove across it, then took the road he'd traveled a couple of days before. He pulled in to the community building, shut off his lights, and killed the engine. He was about to get out when he noticed the manila envelope the Asians had given him.

He opened the envelope and spilled its contents onto the seat. It held three bundles of used $100 bills and a pre-paid cell phone with an Anchorage number programmed into it. The phone showed a text message, so Kane punched it up.

"call when U R dun," the message said.

Kane dialed the Anchorage number. After a couple of rings, it answered. But in place of a voice or a recording, there was only silence. Kane was silent on his end, too. Finally, someone or something on the other end broke the connection. Kane shut the cell phone off and zipped it into an inside pocket of his coat.

The envelope also contained three eight-by-ten photographs: two of men, the third of a young, pretty woman with long, straight, blond hair.

Kane fanned one of the bundles of bills. Probably $5,000 a bundle, he thought. Then he sat thinking for a long time before the cold drove him out of the pickup and into the building.

The heart knoweth his own bitterness.

PROVERBS 14:10

KANE FOUND THOMAS WRIGHT IN THE OFFICE TRAILER, sitting behind a desk, talking on a cell phone. He took the seat Wright waved him to and waited.

"Sorry about that," Wright said when his conversation was over. "Business."

"That's okay," Kane said. "I'm surprised cell phones work out here."

"There's a string of towers along the highway system, if you can call the handful of highways we've got here a system," Wright said. "They actually make more sense than regular phones. No wires to maintain."

"I suppose that's right," Kane said. "Anyway, I'm here to get to work, Elder Thomas Wright."

"Please," the other man said, "call me Tom." He grinned. "Just don't call my father Mo."

"I won't be doing that anytime soon," Kane said.

"So, tell me about 'Nik,' " Wright said. "Is it short for Nicholas?"

This was a question Kane hated answering, but he couldn't see a polite way out of it.

"No, it's short for Nikiski," Kane said. "The place down on the Kenai Peninsula? When my father first came to Alaska, as a soldier in World War II, he saw the area and vowed he'd come back after the war and homestead there. But then he met my mom, and they got married and started having kids. They needed money and schools and medical care, so a homestead wouldn't work. Anchorage was as far as they got. My father went to work doing whatever he could. By the time I came along, he knew he'd never achieve his dream, so he named me to remind him of it. Fortunately, even he never called me anything but Nik."

"Nikiski Kane," Wright said. "Your father sounds like something of a romantic."

"I suppose he was," Kane said. "And then there's the fact he was dead drunk the day I was born. But that's another story."

The two men sat silently for a moment.

"Fathers aren't always what we'd wish them to be," Wright said.

"Too true," Kane said. "Anyway, have you told the other members of the community what I'm up to?"

"Yes," Wright said, "at last night's gathering. If you are here, I'd like to introduce you formally at tonight's gathering. But the members of the community already know to expect you to ask questions, and I asked them to answer as openly as possible."

"You don't expect members of your community to withhold information, do you?" Kane asked.

Wright gave him a wistful smile.

"Religion is important to most members of this community," he said, "but it is a community of human beings. Not saints."

"Or Angels?" Kane asked.

Wright's smile faded.

"I know others call us that," he said, "but it's not a name we picked for ourselves. 'Pride, and arrogancy . . . do I hate.'"

Kane cocked an eyebrow.

"Proverbs," Wright said, "slightly edited."

"It's possible that your neighbors aren't being compli-
mentary," Kane said. "There must be friction between a
community like this and, say, the people around Devil's
Toe who are engaged in more worldly pursuits."

"There is," Wright agreed. "But is that of concern to
you?"

"Until I find out more, everything is of concern to me,"
Kane said. "You don't suppose this friction might be connected to Faith's disappearance, do you?"

Wright was silent for a moment.

"You mean, someone took out their animosity toward
us on Faith? If that were the case, wouldn't whoever did it
want us to know?"

Kane looked at Wright, who looked back with an unruf-
fled expression. I wouldn't want to play cards with this guy,
Kane thought. He's smart, and he has a good poker face.

"They might," Kane said. "They might not. One thing I
learned in law enforcement is that people don't follow pat-
terns. Each one makes his own. Or her own.

"Anyway, I should get started." He took out a notebook
and a pen. "Let's start with a physical description. Height,
weight, eye color. All that."

Wright nodded.

"Faith is five-foot-six, about one hundred twenty
pounds. Shoulder-length blond hair, blue eyes."

"Any scars, distinguishing marks?"

"She has a small scar at the corner of her left eye, where
a dog cut her with a claw when she was a baby."

"That it? What was she wearing the last time you saw
her?"

Wright shook his head.

"I'm sorry, I just don't notice those things. Perhaps one
of her friends can tell you."

"A girl, you mean?" Kane asked. "Or is Faith the sort of
girl the boys notice?"

Wright squirmed in his chair.

"I don't think these are the sort of questions you can expect a father to answer. But Faith wasn't seeing anyone

here in Rejoice, and I don't believe she was attending any of the social events at the high school."

Kane had daughters of his own, so he understood Wright's reluctance to discuss anything bordering on sex. Every father wanted his daughter to remain the little girl who thought kissing was icky. And when she decided it wasn't, he didn't want to hear about it. It must have been tough for Wright, he thought, to have a daughter go through her teen years with no woman in the house.

"Okay," Kane said. "When did you see Faith last?"

Wright's story was straightforward. It had been the previous Friday. They'd attended the morning gathering together and eaten breakfast in the cafeteria. Faith had her nose buried in her history book most of the time; she said she had a test that day. She'd seemed normal.

"What's normal?" Kane asked.

"Friendly, but reserved," Wright said. "A little formal."

"A little formal? Even with her father?"

"Yes, even with her father. Maybe especially with her father. Her mother did most of the child-rearing and kept our family together. When she died, Faith and I grew apart."

Kane understood this, too. Even not counting the time he'd been in prison, Laurie had raised their kids almost on her own. Kane was out chasing bad guys and, truth be told, hanging out with other cops, who were the only people he'd ever felt entirely comfortable with. He'd brought home a paycheck and doled out punishment when called upon, but otherwise the fact that the Kane children were functioning adults had been Laurie's doing. If she'd died when the kids were young, God alone knew what would have happened.

"Faith said she had a couple of after-school activities, as she seemed to every day," Wright said, "but would be back before dinner. Then she got into her car and left."

"She had her own car?" Kane asked.

"None of us has his own car, but some of us have use of one. When Faith chose to attend the regional high school, the elders decided to grant her use of an old Jeep."

"Where's the Jeep now?"

"It's plugged in outside the cafeteria building. It was sitting in the parking lot of the high school, and we decided to bring it back before it froze up completely."

"Did anybody search it?"

"I looked around in it but didn't find anything."

"How about Faith's room?"

"I didn't find anything there, either." Wright gave Kane an embarrassed smile. "I probably didn't do the best job of searching anything. It seemed like an invasion of Faith's privacy to me."

"It is," Kane said, "but invading people's privacy is a big part of this job. I'll probably do a lot of it here. That might make some problems for you."

"We'll deal with those as they come along," Wright said. "What will you do first?"

"Search Faith's car and room," Kane said. "But before that I'll need the names of the people who knew Faith best and where to find them. Including your father."

"Faith and my father weren't really close, at least not in the past few years," Wright said, picking up a pen and writing.

"Why not?" Kane asked.

"I'm not sure," Wright said, handing him the piece of paper. "I think he thought Faith wasn't truly religious enough. And when she left Rejoice to go to high school, well . . ."

"Was that unusual?"

"As far as I know, Faith is the first child from Rejoice to do so."

Wright handed Kane the keys to both the Jeep and the log cabin he shared with Faith.

"You lock things up here?" Kane asked.

" 'Lead us not into temptation,' " Wright said.

Kane got to his feet.

"I'll be around here all day," he said. "Maybe more than one day. So if you've got a spare bed, that would be good. And somebody might tell whoever runs the cafeteria to feed me, too."

He turned to go.

"One more thing," he said, taking the pictures out of the manila envelope. "Do you know these people?"

Wright looked at the picture on top, which showed a man in his late twenties with long, unwashed black hair and an earring. The photo did not seem to have been posed; the man was captured in profile, apparently talking with someone off camera.

"I think this is the fellow they call Big John, although the picture has to have been taken thirty years ago," Wright said, holding it up. "At least that's what he calls himself. If he has a real name, I've never heard it. He owns the Devil's Toe Roadhouse and some other local, um, businesses. He doesn't run them anymore, though, or so people say. That work's done now by his son, who answers to Little John. There is another son, too, younger, named Johnny Starship. Named for his mother, they say. It's an improbable name, isn't it? Starship? Anyway, I don't think she ever married his father."

He stopped and shook his head.

"Listen to me, gossiping. 'Let every man be swift to hear, slow to speak.' "

"That's from the New Testament, isn't it?" Kane asked.

"Some of us read the New Testament, too," Wright said with a smile.

He set that picture down and looked at the second one, a man with shoulder-length brown hair and a bushy brown beard. Like the first one, this looked unposed; the man had been captured glaring at someone to his right. Wright was silent for a moment.

"This is an old picture of my father, one I've never seen before. It was probably taken not long after Rejoice was founded."

He gave Kane a questioning look, then picked up the third photograph. The blood seemed to drain from his face.

"Where did you get this?" he asked Kane.

"Someone had the pictures delivered to me. I'm not sure why."

"That seems strange."

"It does, doesn't it. Do you know her?"

"I do, although I've never seen this particular picture. It's my mother, Margaret Anderson Wright."

He looked at the photograph some more. This one had the appearance of being posed. The woman was looking at the camera, joy in her eyes, her lips slightly parted and smiling.

"I just don't understand why someone would give you her picture," he said. "She's been gone for so long."

"Neither do I," Kane said. "What can you tell me about her?"

Thomas Wright was silent for a long time.

"I'm not certain this is a subject I want to discuss," he said at last.

"Tom," Kane said, "if you expect me to work for you, you're going to have to answer my questions. No matter how odd they might seem. Or invasive. Detection isn't the straightforward, scientific process they make it seem on TV. It's a lot of fits and starts and detours and dead ends. So you'll have to humor me."

Thomas Wright sat silently for a while longer. Then he sighed and shrugged.

"It's not something we talk about much. And I was so young when it happened, I have no firsthand knowledge. All I know is that she left not long after my birth and was never heard from again. She just wasn't cut out for the pioneer life, I guess."

"Surely you know something. Take this picture. Was this taken before you were born or after? She looks pretty young here."

"I wouldn't know when the photograph was taken. My impression is that my mother was quite a bit younger than my father. As were most of those who came here to found Rejoice."

"That's it? Aren't you curious?"

"Of course I'm curious, but my father won't discuss it in any detail. I have asked others from time to time, but they were very circumspect. Today, with deaths and departures, I don't think there is anyone left in Rejoice who would remember her."

Wright sighed.

"I know very little. And I'm not sure that's a bad thing. After all, the woman left her infant son and has never made a single attempt to get in touch since. Whoever she was, whoever she is, she has no interest in me. Why should I be interested in her?"

"So you haven't tried to find her?"

"Really, Mr. Kane, do you have any idea what it's like to try to keep something as complex as this community going, let alone moving forward? Even if I wanted to indulge my curiosity, I don't have the time or the energy to do so. Or the resources, for that matter."

"I suppose there's no reason for you to try to find out something you don't care to know," Kane said. "Still, two pretty young blondes seem to have vanished from Rejoice thirty-five years apart. That's interesting."

"My mother didn't vanish, she ran away."

"How do you know that?"

"Everyone said so, and I've been listening to my father complain about it my whole life. In fact, you should ask him about it. He knows the details. Just stand back when you do."

"I'll do that," Kane said, gathering up the photos and returning them to the envelope. "Thanks for your time. I guess I'll get to work."

He left Thomas Wright staring off into the distance.

The things parents do to children, Kane thought. But then, I'm not exactly perfect on that score myself, am I.

7

Whose adorning let it not be that outward adorning of plaiting the hair, and of wearing of gold, or of putting on of apparel.

1 PETER 3:3

KANE TOOK HIS TIME GOING THROUGH THE JEEP, IG-noring the cold. A thickening stream of people headed for lunch passed him, but no one stopped to ask him what he was up to. This lack of curiosity surprised Kane, until he remembered that in small towns people spent a lot of time not poking their noses into their neighbor's business. That's how Anchorage had worked when he was a boy, before it grew beyond all recognition. Restraint was one of the things that made small towns work.

He didn't find so much as a gum wrapper. That was odd. Kane had been through the cars of dozens of young women, and every one of them had been a mess. Either Faith was very neat, or she didn't want to leave evidence of anything lying around. Or somebody else didn't.

The driver's seat was where it should have been for a driver of Faith's height, and when Kane inserted the key the engine fired right up. He examined the Jeep's seats with a flashlight, nose to the upholstery, and didn't find any-thing. If something bloody had happened to Faith, it hadn't happened in this car.

He walked back into the building and into the cafeteria. The tables were nearly full, and several women and girls stood behind the long counter, ready to serve. Women seemed like amazing creatures to Kane after his years in prison. Seeing them made him nervous in some way, and talking to them even more nervous. Well, he'd have to get over that. He walked up to one of them, a willowy, dark-haired woman in her thirties with intelligent eyes. She was dressed simply, in a way that neither accentuated her feminine attributes nor hid them. Of course, Kane thought, hiding that shape would take some doing.

"Excuse me," he said, "I'm doing some work here, and I was hoping to eat lunch."

"You must be the detective, then," the woman said. Her voice washed over Kane like a warm breeze. "Help yourself."

Kane got a tray and loaded it with chicken and vegetables while the woman watched him.

"Excuse me again," he said when he reached her. "Where will I find a hot drink?"

"I'm afraid we don't drink coffee here," the woman said, "but I can offer you a cup of tea."

"Why one and not the other?" Kane asked.

"Tea is in the Bible," she said.

"Then I'll take a cup," he said.

The woman came right back with a cup of hot water and a selection of tea bags.

"I'm afraid I don't know enough to make an intelligent choice," Kane said.

"Try the Earl Grey," the woman said, "most people like that."

She turned to go back to her work.

"Excuse me one more time," Kane said, "but do you know Faith Wright?"

The woman turned and looked at Kane. She had a smile on her face. Kane felt happy to have put it there.

"This is a small community," she said. "Of course I know Faith."

"Then, if you can spare the time, perhaps you could talk with me while I eat my lunch," Kane said.

She came out from behind the counter, and they took seats at the nearest table.

"You know," Kane said, dropping his tea bag into the water, "I'm certain Elder Moses Wright told me that the community doesn't allow stimulants."

"Elder Moses Wright doesn't run the cafeteria," the woman said matter-of-factly.

"And you do?" Kane asked.

"Yes, I do," the woman said with a smile.

Enough of those, Kane thought, and I might get light-headed.

"Then I'm sure the operation is in good hands," he said, smiling himself.

"Did you ask me over here just to flirt?" the woman asked. "With a woman whose name and marital circumstances you don't even know?"

"I'm sorry," Kane said quickly. "I didn't mean to flirt."

"It's okay," the woman said, placing her hand on Kane's. "Even we Angels recognize that the difference between men and women is a gift of God."

Kane slowly slid his hand away, then picked up his fork and began to eat.

"It's just that I've sort of forgotten how to behave around women," he said at last.

"I'm not surprised," the woman said. "We were told you'd been in prison. You killed somebody, didn't you?"

The woman's matter-of-fact attitude toward his history surprised Kane. It must have shown in his face.

"Don't worry," the woman said. She picked up Kane's spoon, lifted the tea bag from the water, set it in the spoon's bowl, wrapped the string around it and squeezed. Dark drops fell into the water. She unwrapped the tea bag, set it down on the table, and used the spoon to stir Kane's tea. "We were also told that you served many years in prison for a crime but were finally cleared by the authorities."

Kane was sure he was goggling at her by now. She laughed.

"We're used to talking about sins here, our own and other people's," she said. "We have many members who came here to get away from what they'd done elsewhere, to start over. So if you'd like to talk about it . . ."

To Kane's surprise, he found he wanted to tell her all about the shooting and the years in prison. But he shook his head.

"I don't think we have time for that right now," he said. "Perhaps you could tell me what you know about Faith Wright?"

The woman looked at him for a long time. As Kane looked back, he could feel something fluttering around in his stomach.

"Okay," the woman said, "some other time, then." She cleared her throat. "I've been here nine years now, so Faith was seven or eight when I arrived. She was bright, well-mannered, and seemed to be genuinely happy. She was a good student, and as far as I know didn't cause her parents a moment's worry.

"But then her mother, Martha, got sick. You could tell Faith was worried about her. The illness, cancer, moved along, and four years ago Martha died.

"About that time, Faith changed. She was still pleasant and well-mannered, but you couldn't call her happy. She seemed to go inside herself, somehow. Most people thought she was grieving her mother's death, but the change was permanent."

"So you don't think it was grief?" Kane asked.

"I don't know what to think," the woman said. "I have no training in psychology, but Faith's trouble seems to be something besides grief. Or in addition to it."

"Is she a popular girl?"

The woman seemed to think about that question.

"As I said, she is polite and quiet, she attends gatherings and behaves well, so I guess you could say she is popular among the adults. But she doesn't seem to be very close to the girls of her age."

"How about the boys?"

"Faith is a beautiful girl. She could be very popular with the boys if she wants to be. Several of them tried to get close to her, but she gave them no encouragement and they wandered off. Looking for a better reception else-where, no doubt."

"You don't seem to have a very high opinion of men," Kane said.

The woman smiled.

"I'm realistic about men," she said. "They want what they want." Her smile got bigger. "But, then again, so do women."

Kane found himself looking into the woman's eyes. He felt warm and unfocused, as if she had given him some sort of very pleasant drug. He drank some tea. Its bitterness brought him back to himself.

"Were you surprised when Faith decided to attend school outside Rejoice?" Kane asked.

Again, the woman seemed to think.

"No, I guess not," she said. "Faith is very much her own person, in a way that few people in Rejoice are. Oh, I mean, we're all individuals, but in mostly acceptable ways. Rejoice is a place with few rules but strong customs, and going against the customs is something most won't do. But doing so doesn't seem to bother Faith."

"How does she get along with her family?"

"With her father, you mean? They seem to get along all right, but on a superficial level. And sometimes, when he wasn't looking, she would give him a look that might have been anger. But if she thought someone was watching, she covered it up quickly."

"You seem to be very observant," Kane said.

The woman inclined her head and said, "When I came here I saw that there weren't really any written rules," she said, "so I watched others to learn. It suited my personality, anyway. I like watching people. I think they're fascinating. For instance, I think it would be fun to watch you do your investigation."

"Probably not," Kane said. "Most investigating is pretty tedious, asking the same questions over and over again. How did Faith get along with her grandfather?"

"All you want is the facts, eh?" the woman said. Again, she paused to think.

"You know, I don't believe I see her much with her grandfather," she said. "Oh, they are at meals and gatherings and so on, but they don't seem to interact very often. Can't say I blame Faith much. If he were my grandfather, I wouldn't spend any more time around him than I had to, either."

"You don't like Elder Moses Wright?" Kane asked.

"Let's just say that his view of the world is much more patriarchal than mine," the woman said, getting to her feet. "I'm afraid I have to get back to work. And you need to finish your lunch before it gets stone cold."

"Wait," Kane said. "You never told me your name and marital status."

"You're a detective," she said. "You find out."

The woman gave him a big smile and walked back behind the counter and into what Kane assumed was the kitchen. Watching her walk made Kane want to jump on the table and howl. Instead, he picked up his fork and finished his lunch, then took out a notebook and wrote some notes on his interview with Thomas Wright. When he read them over, Kane realized just how little the man had told him.

The Montaigne passage came to Kane's mind. Wright had a contradictory character, all right. It must take some grit to run Rejoice, but when it came to his family he was diffident to the point of timidity. Unless he was hiding something behind his reserve.

Kane added some notes about his interview with the woman, then stretched his cup of tea out as long as he could in the hope that she'd reappear. She didn't, so he carried his empty cup to the counter and went back to work.

Tom and Faith Wright lived in a log cabin about a quarter-mile from the cafeteria building. Kane decided to walk despite the cold. The sun was making its brief appearance over the mountaintops, painting the snow an almost painful white. As he thought about Faith and Rejoice, images of the woman in the cafeteria kept intruding. Stop acting like a damn teenager, he thought.

Kane kicked the snow off his boots and let himself into the cabin with the key he'd been given. The living room was small and tidy and missing something. A television set, Kane decided. Satellite TV had reached even the most remote settlements in rural Alaska. Few made the choice to forgo television.

The room contained a big, potbellied stove, a sofa that had seen better days, and a couple of chairs that looked hand-made. Tacked to the walls were big, bright primitive paintings of tropical scenes, signed "Faith" in a childish scrawl.

Kane went through the room thoroughly, and found nothing but dust bunnies. The kitchen contained basic cooking and eating utensils, some canned and dried food and nothing more. Probably just emergency rations, Kane thought. Who'd cook with the cafeteria so close? He walked back into the living room.

To Kane's right was a short hallway that ended in a bathroom. Bedrooms were to the left and right. He went into the one on the right and switched on the light.

The bed was covered with a wool blanket and made exactly the way they'd taught him to make one in boot camp. It was only when he opened the door to the small closet that Kane was sure he was in the girl's room. A single dress hung there, a blue summer dress with white flowers. The rest of the clothes looked as if they'd been chosen for warmth.

The small chest of drawers contained utilitarian underwear, socks, a scant assortment of T-shirts, and a couple of pairs of jeans. A bottle of hand lotion and a tube of lip balm stood on top. Nothing under the mattress or under the bed. No hiding places were possible in the log walls. The floor had no obvious hollow spots. Without a hammer and a wrecking bar, he wasn't going to find anything else.

Kane ticked off all the things that weren't there: cosmetics, jewelry, CD player, computer, magazines, posters. The room suited a nun better than a teenage girl. Like the Jeep, it told him absolutely nothing.

"Just what is it you're hiding behind all of this austerity, Faith Wright?" Kane asked the empty room.

Whatever it was, he didn't find it in the bathroom, either. It yielded shampoo, soap, and tampons. In frustration, he decided to toss Tom Wright's room, too. It was as bad as his daughter's. The only personal items were a pair of photographs in a plain wooden frame on his nightstand. One showed a young, pretty, blond woman holding a baby. Next to her stood a younger Thomas Wright. The other showed a different family in an almost identical pose: a very young, very pretty blond, a baby, and a dark-haired version of Moses Wright.

Moses is definitely next on my list, Kane thought.

He walked back into the living room and stood there, trying to imagine where a teenage girl would hide things she didn't want found. He looked into the stove, which was full of cold ashes, and into a medium-size wooden trunk, which held a collection of women's clothes that Kane figured had belonged to Wright's wife.

I don't suppose you can afford to throw anything away out here, he thought. Even difficult memories.

He was halfway out the door when he realized there was something else he hadn't found in Faith's room. A Bible. There was no copy of the Good Book in her father's room, either. Or anywhere else in the house.

"That's strange," he said aloud.

In fact, the whole situation was strange. And the more he looked, the stranger it got.

I hope this isn't one of those investigations where I end up more confused than when I started, he thought, and looking like a dope in the bargain.

On his walk back to the main building, he thought about the tidy, empty cabin and how little it had told him. Or how much. It reminded him of his apartment, and his prison cell. None was a home, just a place where people slept and marked time. Maybe Faith got tired of marking time, he thought. Maybe I will, too.

Only by pride cometh contention.

PROVERBS 13:10

MOSES WRIGHT SAT IN AN OFFICE OFF THE BIG ROOM where the community gatherings were held. The door was open. He was seated at a desk, a large volume bound in red leather open in front of him. His lips moved as he read. Kane sat across the desk from him. The old man ignored him.

Kane used the time to examine Moses Wright more carefully. The old man was short but, even well past his prime, had powerful shoulders and arms. His head, with its eruption of shaggy white hair and thick white beard, seemed too big for his body. Only the big shoulders kept it from looking freakish.

With his Old Testament appearance he would have been a good televangelist, Kane thought. People with big heads do well on television.

Something about him rubs me the wrong way, Kane thought. I'd better watch that. You can't let your personal prejudices warp the investigation.

The old man was, like all of the residents of Rejoice, dressed simply. He wore no jewelry, not even a watch. Just like the cons, Kane thought. Is Rejoice just another sort of prison? Did Faith break out?

Minutes passed. Wright's breathing was loud and steady as he read, pausing every now and then to make a note on a pad that lay next to the book.

Enough's enough, Kane thought, and dropped his hand on the desktop with a noise like a firecracker going off. The old man's head snapped up.

"Good morning, Elder Moses Wright," Kane said sweetly. "I have a few questions to ask you."

The old man glared at him.

"This book contains all the answers any man needs," he growled, holding the big volume up so Kane could see the words "Holy Bible" stamped on the front.

"Fine," Kane said with a smile, "just point me to the passage that tells me where your granddaughter is."

"Does blasphemy amuse you, Mr. Kane?" Wright asked.

The old man's hostility scratched against Kane's nerves like fingernails dragged across a blackboard, but he kept his temper in check.

"No," Kane said, "but I'm not here to inquire into religious matters. I'm here to find a young woman. What can you tell me that might help?"

The old man showed big, yellow teeth in a smile so unctuous that he must have wanted Kane to know it was phony.

"What makes you think I want to help you?" he asked. "I was against hiring you, but the other elders ignored me."

"Why wouldn't you want to help?" Kane asked. "Is your ego so much more important than the fate of your own flesh and blood?"

Wright's mouth twisted into a bitter grin.

"You really shouldn't talk about things you don't understand," he said.

"What's that supposed to mean?" Kane asked.

The old man was silent for a moment.

"One of the things it means is that I must weigh the souls of Rejoice in every decision," he said. "In your case, the question was whether it was better to have an outsider poking around here, particularly a murderer and convict, upsetting the residents, setting tongues to wagging, and exposing us all to the secular philosophy of the world, in the hope of finding one lost or more likely runaway girl, or to make our own quiet inquiries that would, no doubt, have discovered her whereabouts and left the community untroubled."

"You are confident that you would have solved the mystery?" Kane said. "How?"

"We have many friends outside Rejoice, and many more contacts. We have many competent men and women here. How hard could it be to find one girl?"

"Presumably you tried all that before calling me in and didn't learn anything."

"We didn't give it long enough. Besides, what is the fate of one body when compared to the danger to hundreds of souls?"

"So it doesn't matter that she's your granddaughter?"

The old man gave him another bitter grin.

"Faith is very important to me," he said. "You'll never know how important. But if the girl wants to live in the world, then it is better that she does. Better for her and better for Rejoice."

Kane sat trying to make sense of what the old man was telling him. Better to let a girl disappear than let one outsider spend time in Rejoice? Better for whom? How?

"Surely you don't think I can destroy the faith of those in Rejoice?" Kane said. "Doesn't the Bible say, 'For what if some did not believe? Shall their unbelief make the faith of God without effect?' "

"You are a most peculiar unbeliever, Mr. Kane," Wright said, "to quote the Bible so glibly. But we must be wary of unbelievers amongst us. For the Bible also says, 'Take heed, brethren, lest there be in any of you an evil heart of unbelief.' We should have much less to do with the outside world, in my view. And we certainly shouldn't be inviting outsiders to paw through our affairs."

Well, there was no doubting that the old man read his Bible, Kane thought. Or that he was being stubborn to the point of obstructionism.

"Bible or no Bible," Kane said, "if you withhold information that's germane, that's going to make people suspicious, isn't it? It might make them wonder if you have something to hide."

Wright laughed.

"Do you really think you're going to get along in this community by threatening its leader your first day here?" he asked. "And with the wagging tongues of idle speculation?"

"I'm under the impression you're not the leader of this community anymore," Kane said mildly. "Your son is."

The old man stood up. He wasn't much taller standing than sitting, Kane noticed. He leaned toward Kane. Anger snapped in his eyes.

"My son couldn't lead a children's parade," he said. "I am the ultimate authority here. You'll do well to remember that."

Kane stood.

"What I'll remember is that you refused to assist in the investigation of your granddaughter's disappearance," he said quietly.

Wright's shoulders sagged and he settled back in his chair.

"You're right, Mr. Kane," he said wearily. "Pride has always been my weakness. Come, sit down again, and I'll do my best to help you. I may disagree with the decision to hire you, but I won't obstruct your investigation. Besides, the sooner you finish, the sooner Rejoice can get back to doing God's work."

Kane sat, but the conversation that ensued wasn't much help. The old man said he didn't know his granddaughter all that well—"the generation gap, you know," he said—and didn't have any idea where she might be.

"She doesn't come to you for spiritual counseling?" Kane asked. "I thought you were the leader of this community."

The old man didn't like the gibe, but he kept his temper in check.

"No," he said, "not everyone is required to confide in me. Or even, as your presence here proves, to heed my counsel."

"So who does she confide in?" Kane asked.

The old man seemed to think about that.

"I have no idea," he said. "I'm under the impression that Faith keeps to herself for the most part."

"Did that bother you? Not being close to your grand-daughter?"

"Are we here to inquire into my emotional state?" the old man snapped.

Kane didn't say anything.

"I can't see how my preferences about the girl have any bearing," Wright said in a milder tone. "Raising her was her parents' responsibility. Of course, after his wife died my son made a mess of that, too."

"*Was* her parents' responsibility? Do you think Faith is dead?"

"No, no," Wright said. "I have no reason to think that. I just meant that Faith is old enough to know her own mind. Besides, apparently teenagers no longer require instruction, even here in Rejoice."

"That bother you?"

"Many things bother me, Mr. Kane. Rejoice is not what it was, and has yet to become what I hope it will be. The world is too much with us, and the other elders don't seem to be bothered by that. We are in danger of becoming a strictly secular community."

"Would that be so bad? Is religion so important to Rejoice?"

"Mr. Kane, please. Religion—faith, anyway—is the sole reason Rejoice continues to exist. Without it, we would just be another hardscrabble town, and why would anyone stay?"

"And the religion that is required here is the one you preach?" Kane asked.

The old man laughed.

"There is only one true religion," he said, patting his Bible, "and that is the one found in this book. Every word in it is God's word, and they are all literally true. I study it and try to interpret it, but more than that I try to be sure that Rejoice operates according to its precepts."

Doors were opening and closing in the building. People

were tramping out of the cafeteria and down the hall from lunch.

"What did you think of the decision to let your grand-daughter attend the regional high school?" Kane asked.

"I opposed it, of course," Wright said. "Our children receive a fine education here. Many of our graduates go on to the best Christian universities. There was no academic reason for her to change, no matter what she said."

"So why do you think she changed schools?"

The old man sat for a moment, looking down at his Bible, as if he expected to find the answer to Kane's question on one of its pages.

"I think she was curious about the secular world," the old man said.

"So she was going to something, rather than away from something?"

Wright's eyes came up from the page and locked with the detective's.

"I'm not sure I understand your question," he said.

Kane paused to marshal his thoughts. He'd been thinking about this a lot since Laurie had told him she wanted a divorce, but he'd never said anything out loud.

"When someone leaves," he said, "there can be one of two reasons. First, they can be going to something: a better job, a better relationship. Second, they can be going away from something: a lousy job, a bad marriage, a problem, a threat. Which do you think Faith was doing?"

The old man picked up his pen and made some notes on his pad.

"I'll have to see what the Bible says about that theory. It's an interesting exercise in logic," he said, "but couldn't a person have both kinds of reasons? Or different reasons entirely. Like enticement by Satan?"

Kane looked at the old man again, seeing something more than he'd seen before. Be careful not to think of Moses Wright as just a Bible-thumping cartoon character, he thought.

"I suppose they can," he said. "And there's always the possibility that they don't leave of their own free will."

"Does anyone do anything of their own free will, Mr. Kane?" Wright said. "Aren't we are all just tools of the Lord's will?"

"If I'm a tool of the Lord, he's got to be scraping the bottom of his toolbox," Kane said. He raised a hand to forestall the old man. "Yes, I know. Blasphemy. But back to my question. Why do you think Faith changed schools?"

The old man shrugged.

"I'm afraid I have no idea," he said. "I always supposed it was because she was drawn to the world in some way. I know of nothing in Rejoice she would be fleeing."

"Do you really think this place is that perfect?" Kane asked.

Wright laughed.

"I don't think Rejoice is at all perfect," he said. "I'm sure that for younger people in particular it might seem small and boring, despite our efforts to keep our children engaged and occupied. But I don't think it is actively hostile in any way. I suppose boredom may have been a goad to Faith, as it has been on occasion to others. But I doubt that was what caused her to change schools. Or to leave, for that matter."

"If, as I said, she left of her own free will," Kane said. "But there's no use guessing when the future might provide facts. Where were you the day Faith disappeared? Last Friday?"

The old man's eyes narrowed, but he answered civilly enough.

"I really can't say," he said. "As I get older, the days seem to blend together. But I expect I was where I usually am, here in this office reading the word of God and offering advice when asked."

"You don't recall seeing her? Speaking with her?" Kane asked.

Moses Wright shook his head.

"Did anything seem to be bothering her lately?" Kane asked.

"As I told you, we weren't close. And Faith is a very private young woman. If there was something troubling her, she was perfectly capable of keeping it from me."

"So you have nothing useful to tell me about her disappearance?"

"I'm afraid not. She wouldn't have come to me, and if she had, I wouldn't help her leave. I'd counsel her to stay, and open her heart to the Lord. Just as I counsel you to open your heart to the Lord."

"But not to stay, eh? I thank you for your advice, Elder Moses Wright, but the Lord and I are going to have to work things out on our own."

He took the pictures out of the manila envelope and laid them in front of the old man.

"Tell me what you know about these people," he said.

Moses Wright looked at the first photo.

"This man is in league with the devil," he said with surprising heat. "He has been a plague on this area since he arrived."

"When was that?" Kane asked.

The old man thought for a moment.

"It was some years after we came here," he said. "Five or six, I think."

He was quiet again, then said, "Yes, he arrived within a few years of us, bringing with him all we sought to escape. Only the intervention of the Lord saved us. 'Though I walk in trouble, thou wilt revive me.' I believe he has made way for his offspring now. The boy—I suppose he is a man now—would be as evil as his father, but he doesn't have the character."

"Character?" Kane said. "That's an odd word to use in this context."

The old man looked at him, the ghost of a smile chasing across his lips.

"Real evil, like real goodness, requires real character, Mr. Kane," he said. "Satan could not be the demon he is without character enough to prevent him from begging God for forgiveness. Pride and stubbornness are as much a part of character as kindness and loyalty. It is all a matter of how God allows them to mix in us."

He slid the photo across the desk.

"The modern world wants to see character as a pure

good," he said, "but like everything given by God, it is a two-edged sword."

The old man looked down at the second photograph.

"That's me," he said, "taken some time ago. Why would you have this photograph?"

Kane said nothing. The old man looked at him, waiting. When he realized the detective was not going to reply, he gave a little shrug, slid the picture across to Kane, and looked at the third photograph. He gave a start and leaned closer to it. He held that pose for so long Kane thought he might have fallen asleep. Or had a heart attack.

"Elder Wright?" Kane said at last. "Are you all right?"

The old man raised his head and stared at Kane. His face was pale and something not quite sane danced in his eyes.

"How dare you?" he said, his voice low but forceful. "How dare you show me this woman's picture? Get out."

Kane reached across the desk and tried to slide the picture over to himself. The old man resisted. Kane pried the picture loose and retrieved it, using plenty of muscle.

"I'm sorry if I've made you angry," he said, "but if I'm to find your granddaughter, I have to follow all leads."

He smoothed the wrinkles out of the photograph and put it, along with the others, back into the envelope. The Lord might armor his children in righteousness, Kane thought, but the old man's armor had a hell of a chink in it.

Wright had his hands on the desk, and they were working like he was trying to strangle someone.

"What would you know about righteous anger?" he asked. "What would you know about being made a laughingstock among people who respected you, among your followers?"

His voice was louder now, like he was preaching a sermon, and spittle flew from his lips as he spoke.

"What would you know about the damage she did to the Lord's work here?" he said, his voice rising and falling in a preacher's cadence, and at a preacher's volume. "Let me tell you about this woman. She was Lot's wife."

The old man's eyes were unfocused, staring into a place Kane could not see. Even as he watched the man rant, Kane couldn't help admiring his performance. With that look and that voice, he could have gone far, the detective thought.

"Jesus said: 'Remember Lot's wife.' Like Lot and his family, we were a small band fleeing the evils of the world. 'And it came to pass, when they had brought them forth abroad, that he said, Escape for thy life; look not behind thee. . . . But his wife looked back from behind him, and she became a pillar of salt.'

"That woman came with us where God directed, but she looked back at the sin and wickedness of the world and fell back into the pit."

The old man smote the desk with his fist. People in the hallway paused to look toward the noise but, with the restraint of people in small communities, passed on without inquiring into its cause.

"You mean she died?" Kane asked.

The old man's eyes refocused on Kane.

"Died?" he said in a normal tone. "What makes you think she died?"

"Well, being turned into a pillar of salt can't be good for you. Or falling into a pit."

"She died to us, as all those who abandon God's word die, even in life," the old man said. Then, more softly, "Margaret left here, a long time ago, and no one has heard a word from her since. She left her lawful husband and her small child and returned to the evil, doomed cities of the plains."

"You have no idea where she went?"

"None. But why are you interested? All this happened long before Faith was born."

"So it did. What happened after Margaret Anderson left?"

The old man sank back down into his chair.

"Nothing happened," he said, "nothing but a lot of loose talk. I hear some of it again now, renewed by Faith's departure. Nasty whispers: 'Those Wrights can't seem to hold on to their women. Do you suppose there's something wrong with them?'"

"Is there?" Kane asked.

The old man waved an angry hand at him and picked up his Bible again.

"This interview is finished," he said.

Kane stood there looking at the old man's strong, veined hands clutching the book that hid his face.

"We'll leave this here for now," Kane said, "but I'd encourage you to reflect on the fact that your granddaughter is missing, and that your obligation is to help find her. Not to protect your pride. You were quoting Isaiah to the elders just the other day. You should think about that yourself."

"I don't need the counsel of an unbeliever," the old man rapped from behind his Bible. "Begone. Speak to me no more."

Kane left the room. He felt happy.

I wonder what it is about upsetting that old man that makes me happy, he thought. That's got to be a sin of some sort. But then, is it better to be a happy sinner than an unhappy Angel?

Let no man despise thy youth; but be thou an example of the believers, in word, in conversation, in charity, in spirit, in faith, in purity.

1 Timothy 4:12

KANE LOOKED INTO THE CAFETERIA. THE LUNCH CROWD had thinned out, but one table was still lined with teenagers carrying on like teenagers. He walked over to them.

"Do you mind if I sit?" he asked what seemed to be their leader, a strong-jawed, dark-haired youth.

"Please do," the young man said, getting to his feet. "Make room," he said, and the other teens shifted down. "I'm Matthew Pinchon. You must be the man who is looking for Faith." That brought a titter from some of his cohorts.

Kane shook the young man's hand. They both sat.

"I am looking for Faith Wright," Kane said. "I suppose you all know her?"

There were nods around the table.

"Do any of you know where she is?" Kane asked.

Head shakes. Silence. Then, "Faith is in the world," said a thin, dark-haired girl of fifteen or sixteen.

"Pardon?" Kane said.

"Oh, that's just Rebecca," the young man said. "She decided about a year ago to become all soulful and mysterious."

"I did not, Matthew Pinchon," the girl said. "You know very well that Faith transferred to the regional high school because she was fed up with Rejoice, tired of the same old people and the same old things."

"Who doesn't get tired of the same old people and things sometimes?" the young man said. "But none of us runs away. I don't think Faith did, either."

"That's because you've always liked her," the girl said. The statement—it sounded like an accusation to Kane—brought color to the young man's cheeks.

"This is hardly proper behavior, Rebecca Lewis," he snapped, "especially in front of an outsider."

"You're not an elder yet, Matthew Pinchon," the girl said, "so you can just stop trying to act like one."

"She's right," said another girl, this one with short, brown hair and about the young man's age. "And if Faith wasn't going to go out in the world, why was she hanging around Johnny Starship all the time?"

"She was hanging around with Johnny Starship?" Kane asked.

The sound of his voice reminded the teenagers that there was a stranger present, an adult at that.

"We shouldn't be gossiping like this," the young man said, looking around the table, and they all clammed up. Both girls began spooning up soup, and the young man took a bite of a sandwich. The other teens, most of whom looked to be a little younger, watched the older ones, their gazes sliding every so often over to Kane, then sliding away again. I suppose they don't have much practice dealing with outsiders, Kane thought, and they're learning from this.

Silence reigned for a few minutes as the teens finished their lunches. When the young man swallowed the last of his sandwich, Kane asked, "What's the name of the woman who runs the food service?"

"What?" the young man asked, confused. "The food service? Why do you want to know that?"

"Is everyone in Rejoice this paranoid?" Kane said.

The girl called Rebecca laughed.

"Some here are," she said, "but Matthew isn't being

paranoid, really. The woman who runs the food service is his mother."

"Stepmother," the young man snapped.

Damn, Kane thought. Married.

"Okay," he said. "I certainly didn't mean any offense to your stepmother. I talked a little bit with her earlier and just needed her name for my notes."

"Her name is Ruth Hunt," the young man said.

"Thanks," he said. He took his notebook out of his pocket and wrote the name in it.

"Do married women keep their own names here in Rejoice?" he asked.

"Only this one," the young man said in a tone that made it clear he did not approve.

Kane let the topic die.

"Are you really a detective?" the brown-haired girl asked after a few moments. "Have you really apprehended criminals?"

"Yes, I am, and yes, I have," Kane said, grinning at the girl, "although I don't think I ever heard what we did referred to so elegantly inside the police station."

"The world must truly be an evil place," the girl said, "to require detectives and prisons and such."

There was an embarrassed silence, which told Kane that even the children in Rejoice had heard he'd been in prison.

Rebecca broke the silence.

"You've been listening to Foaming Moses too much, Judith," she said.

"Rebecca!" Matthew Pinchon said loudly.

It was Kane's turn to laugh.

"I take it Foaming Moses is Elder Wright," he said.

Rebecca blushed.

"I really shouldn't speak so disrespectfully," she said, "but all us kids call him that. Some of the adults, too."

"Then not everyone is religious here?" Kane asked.

"Some of us are more religious than others," the young man said, shooting a look at Rebecca. "Those of us who have accepted Jesus Christ as our personal savior have no doubts about Elder Wright's interpretation of God's will."

"But others do?" Kane asked. "Did Faith share those doubts?"

Judith opened her mouth, but closed it without saying anything.

"Look," Kane said, "Faith might not have left of her own free will. She might be in trouble. You aren't helping her by keeping quiet."

The teens looked at one another. The looks passed a message among them, but Kane couldn't tell what it was. If he'd been a teenager from outside Rejoice, dealing with such a tight-knit group would have been a problem. And Kane was long past being a teenager.

"We've talked about this quite a bit among ourselves, as you might imagine," Matthew Pinchon said. "None of us can explain the situation. If Faith was planning to leave on her own, no one knew about it. If she was in some sort of trouble, no one knew about it."

"People often know more than they know they know," Kane said with a smile. The teens smiled back. "But I've never had much luck finding out what they know by talking to them in groups. Do your schedules allow you to speak with me individually?"

The teens looked at one another again.

"Mine does," Rebecca said.

"So does mine," said Judith.

"I guess mine does, too," Matthew said. "We would have to be fast, though, because our basketball teams are leaving later this afternoon for games in Anchorage, and we're all on them."

So Kane commandeered a small room off the community hall and talked to the teens one at a time, beginning with Pinchon.

"There was a time when Faith and I were much closer," the young man said when he was seated next to Kane on a padded folding chair. He had his legs thrust out in front of him, crossed at the ankles and his hands folded across his belt. "I had hopes that we would be closer still. We were born only ten months apart, and for as long as I can remember everyone, all of the adults, treated us like we were a couple. I guess I started to believe it, too."

He grinned and shook his head.

"Why not?" he said. "Faith was wonderful to look at, she had a sweet disposition, and she was godly without being a pain about it."

"So what's not to like?" Kane said.

"Yeah, that's it," the young man said, "what's not to like? But then her mother got sick. And she changed. And we just kind of drifted apart."

"How did she change?" Kane asked.

The young man stared at his folded hand for a minute.

"I don't know," he said. "She was just different. We were still friends, but we weren't so close. And then, when she decided to go to the regional high school and started hanging out with that Johnny Starship, well, I just quit thinking about her very much."

"Hanging out with him," Kane said. "You mean they are involved? Like girlfriend and boyfriend?"

The young man looked at his hands again.

"I'm not sure," he said, giving Kane an embarrassed smile. "The truth is, I don't know much about relationships outside of Rejoice."

"I don't know much about relationships inside Rejoice," Kane said. "Tell me about them."

The young man looked at his hands, then at the wall, then at Kane again.

"It's okay," the detective said, "what you say to me won't go outside these walls, unless there's a crime involved."

The young man laughed.

"I don't mean to be mysterious," he said, "but it's hard to know what to think about things myself, let alone what I should say to an outsider."

He straightened up in his chair and leaned forward, his elbows on his knees.

"The accepted practice is this," the young man said. "Until you're sixteen, there's no dating and everything is done in groups. After that, if the adults think you are mature enough, you can walk out with someone. But what you can actually do with that person is carefully circumscribed and closely watched. After a year or so of that, if you are still interested in each other, the two of you can become engaged and take instruction that leads to marriage."

"Whew," Kane said, "that sounds pretty strict."

"I suppose it does," the young man said with a smile, "but this is a Christian community, so things like godly behavior and chastity are important here. Besides, like any community, Rejoice has an interest in people knowing one another well enough, and what marriage requires well enough, to make an informed decision."

"And young people accept this and do what they're told?"

The young man laughed.

"Not all of them, but it's not really like a set of rules. It's more like what I think they call cultural norms. Most people do things in this way because that's the way they're done. Some people don't, but enough do that it's the accepted way. Besides, it's not always two young people involved."

"Pardon me?"

The young man gave Kane a funny look.

"I would have thought that would be obvious. Rejoice is a small place, and the number of marriageable people here at any one time isn't that large. So it's not always two sixteen-year-olds walking out. In fact, it is normal to have some disparity in ages, and not at all unusual to have a considerable difference."

"So you could have sixteen-year-old girls and . . ." Kane said.

"Forty-year-old men," the young man said. "Just so. Or forty-year-old women and sixteen-year-old men. There was just such a disparity in the ages of my parents—that is, my father and my real mother."

"So your mother . . ." Kane said.

"Is in her sixties," the young man said, "but she doesn't live here anymore."

"Is divorce common here?" Kane asked.

The young man looked at his shoes for a moment.

"I'm not sure I want to talk about that much," he said. "Technically, there is no divorce in Rejoice. But let's just say that when two people don't want to live together anymore, they find a way."

Kane decided to let that go.

"Did Faith have any older suitors?"

"I wouldn't know, unless they'd started walking out. But I can think of several unmarried men in Rejoice, and I can't imagine that none of them is interested in Faith. Judith might know. She and Faith were best friends once, and I think they still talked."

"Okay," Kane said. "Thanks."

Matthew Pinchon stood up and turned to go.

"Just one more question," Kane said. "You seem like an intelligent young man. Don't you find all these rules and customs a little confining?"

"They are meant to be confining," the young man said. "We are trying to confine ourselves to Christian behavior. Those of us who don't want to do so are free to leave. Those who stay accept the confines of living here."

"What if they don't?"

"Excuse me?"

"What if they don't accept the rules, but continue to live here anyway?"

The young man gave Kane the same funny look.

"Why would anyone do that?"

"Wasn't that, in a way, what Faith was doing?"

"Not really," the young man said, doubt in his voice. "Maybe. I don't know. But given who she is, the elders would be reluctant to act against her."

"You mean, because she is the daughter and granddaughter of the leaders of Rejoice?"

"That, and Faith really is an extraordinary person. If she is truly gone, that's a real loss to the community."

"If the elders had acted against her, what would they have done?"

"I'm not really sure. Counseled her, I suppose. If that didn't work, they might have posted her name on the Wall of Shame in the community hall here. We set a lot of store by public censure. And if that didn't work, they would have banished her."

"Have people been banished?"

The young man gave Kane a look he couldn't read.

"I'm not really the person to ask about that, and I have to go prepare for my trip. So if there is nothing further?"

Kane waved a hand, and the young man left, to be replaced by Rebecca.

"What did you do to Matthew Pinchon?" she asked, sitting across from Kane.

"What makes you think I did anything to him?" Kane asked.

"He didn't offer me any advice or instructions when he came out," the girl said with a laugh.

"Does he usually?" Kane said.

Rebecca gave Kane a shrewd look.

"If you think Matthew was somehow involved in Faith's disappearance, you're wrong," she said. "He still loves her, it's true, and he'd never harm her."

"How do you know that?" the detective asked.

The girl smiled.

"I have been studying Matthew Pinchon since I was twelve years old," she said. "I want to know everything I can about the man I'm going to marry."

It was Kane's turn to smile.

"Does he know about the impending nuptials?"

"Not yet, but when the time is right, he will."

Rebecca sounded thirty rather than fifteen when she said that, speaking with a certainty and maturity that impressed the detective.

"Are all the women in Rejoice so sure of their futures at such a young age?"

"You mean, was Faith this certain?" the girl said. She stopped to consider. "I don't know. When you grow up in a place this small, in a culture that treats you like a woman much sooner than the larger world would, you begin considering your future much sooner than you might otherwise. I think I want to stay here, and if I stay I might end up married to someone twice my age, and I'm not sure I'd like that. So I've settled on Matthew."

"And Faith?"

"Faith doesn't seem to have settled on anything. Everyone used to talk about Faith and Matthew like their marriage was a foregone conclusion. But then, well, Faith just wasn't there anymore."

"What do you mean by that?"

Rebecca gazed over Kane's shoulder for a moment, then refocused on the detective.

"I don't know just how to describe it," she said. "I mean, she looked the same and did all the same things, but it was like she'd shut down all of her emotions. She was more like a Faith robot than the flesh-and-blood Faith."

The girl was silent for a moment.

"Of course," she said with a shake of her head, "her mom was dying, or maybe had just died, so that's probably what did it. Faith and her mother were close, much closer than she was with her father."

"What can you tell me about their relationship, Faith's and her father's, I mean."

"Faith loves her dad, I think, but Elder Thomas Wright is a tortured soul. I think he's trapped by being the son of the founder and, if that weren't the case, would have left Rejoice long ago."

Kane looked at the girl. The silence stretched out. Rebecca blushed.

"Like I said, when every unattached male is a potential partner, if you've got any brains you pay attention."

"Okay," Kane said. "And what about Faith's relationship with her grandfather?"

"Faith avoided her grandfather, but why should she be different from any of the rest of us? Except Matthew, I mean."

Kane grinned at that.

"You seem to be close to blasphemy there."

Rebecca grinned back.

"I know, or at least lèse-majesté. But you can live in a small town and believe in a faith without liking everyone else who does."

"What about Matthew? I take it he has a more charitable view of Elder Moses Wright."

"That's true, and it's something I'll have to break him of. But he takes special instruction from Foaming Moses and is always talking about what a great man he is. If Foaming Moses were a woman, I'd be jealous."

Kane made some notes.

"What do you know about Faith's friends and activities at the regional high school?" he asked.

"Not much, I'm afraid. We don't have much to do with the kids outside Rejoice socially. We see them and know their names and say hi and stuff, but we don't spend much time with them. The rumor was that Faith was seeing Johnny Starship. But if she was, she'd have been careful to hide it."

"Why's that?"

"A girl from Rejoice involved with a boy from outside would be bad enough, but with Johnny Starship it would have been much worse. His brother and father are involved in sinful business. And besides, his father and Elder Moses Wright are total enemies."

"Why's that?"

"Well, one's a preacher, and the other's a whoremaster." The girl blushed at the word. "What more reason do they need?"

He finished with Rebecca soon after, and while he waited for Judith to come in, he thought about what he'd been told. He didn't know what to think about a place that seemed to allow forty-year-old men to marry seventeen-year-old girls. These things were routine in other countries, he knew, but not in America.

"Maybe Rejoice isn't really part of America," he said.

"No, it's not," Judith said, taking a seat. "Rejoice is its own place."

"Sorry," Kane said. "I didn't mean to say that out loud.

I seem to be talking to myself more and more as I get older."

The girl reached over and patted Kane's hand.

"It's okay," she said. "Rejoice must be a confusing place for an outsider."

In the normal course of events, Kane would have thought nothing of the girl's gesture. But after talking with the other teens, he wasn't sure how to react to a young woman who was, in this place, of marrying age. Best to put that out of your mind, he thought, taking up his notebook and pen.

"Are all the young people in Rejoice this mature?" he asked.

"Not all," Judith said, "but in a small place all of the adults know you and have expectations for you. The religious nature of Rejoice adds to those expectations. And because there are so few of us and so much to do, you are given responsibility earlier. Most of us respond to all this in the right way."

"I suppose that makes sense, but I'm not used to speaking with young people who think and talk so much like adults."

"Oh, we can talk like kids, at least among ourselves. But a lot of even that conversation is about Rejoice and our roles in it and what that means for our lives."

"Did Faith talk about those things?"

"For a long time she talked about them more than most. Then she stopped."

"About the time her mom died?"

"Just after, I'd say. I noticed because up until then, we'd been best friends. Then she started spending more and more time alone. I asked her about it, and she just said she needed time to think. So we just kind of drifted apart."

"Do you know why Faith changed?"

"I don't," Judith said, "but Faith has pressures the rest of us don't, being the Princess of Rejoice and all."

"What?"

The girl laughed.

"That's what we called it when we were kids. 'The Princess of Rejoice.' Because her grandfather is the founder and her father has taken over from him, everyone expects Faith to marry the next leader. A dynasty, you know."

"Is she headed in that direction? Does she have older suitors here?"

"I'm sure she could have them if she wants, but I don't think she is seeing anyone here. And I don't see how she could be without the entire community finding out."

"Is that experience speaking?" Kane asked.

Judith laughed.

"I won't say that I haven't thought about it, but it just seems so impossible to do anything here without everyone finding out."

"How does Faith feel about being the Princess of Rejoice?" Kane asked.

"She was okay with it when we were younger. It seemed kind of fairy tale–ish to us then. But as we got older I think it bothered her. I'm not at all sure Faith wants to stay in Rejoice, let alone be its princess. And I think she is having doubts about our religion."

"Did she say anything?"

"Not really, but one of the ways she changed was that she just started watching the services, became a spectator, you know. She just sits there and never takes part."

"Do you know anything about her life outside Rejoice?"

"I don't. I hear the rumors, particularly about her and Johnny Starship. And I did see them together once or twice. But I still find it hard to believe Faith would get involved with anyone as immature as Johnny Starship. Although I always wondered about those extracurricular activities that seemed to take up her afternoons."

"How do you mean?"

"Oh, she is never here until right before dinner. And then there's what she said to me on my last birthday."

"What was that?" Kane said.

Judith gave him an embarrassed grin.

"Well, even though we weren't as close, we are still

friends," she said. "We still tell each other things. Or, I suppose, I still tell her things. I was trying to decide whether to start walking out with one of the older boys who'd asked me, and that started me thinking about love and marriage and sex and all that. So I was telling all this to Faith, and she gave me a funny look and said, 'Don't expect too much from sex. You might be disappointed.' "

"What did she mean by that? Do you think she is sexually active?"

The question seemed to throw Judith off stride.

"I have no idea," she said. "This isn't Iran. We don't have the morality police checking on virginity."

Kane sat thinking for a moment.

"Can you tell me what she was wearing last Friday?" he asked.

Judith gave him a smile.

"I'll bet you didn't ask Matthew Pinchon that," she said. Kane opened his mouth to reply, but she said, "That's okay. Men and women are the same in that way here as everywhere. Men see a pretty girl and think about what she'd look like without her clothes. Women look at her and wonder how they'd look in her clothes. Faith was wearing black corduroy pants, a white turtleneck sweater, white wool socks, and black walking shoes. She had a dark-blue down coat, black overboots, and a white knit scarf and hat."

"Whew," Kane said, "that's as good a description as a cop could give."

"We all know one another's clothes very well, Mr. Kane," Judith said. "None of us has that many outfits. Ostentation is not Christian."

"Okay," Kane said, "thanks. You young people have given me a lot to think about."

Judith got up and started for the door, paused, and turned.

"Can you answer a question for me?" she asked.

"I can try," Kane said.

"What's it like, living out in the world?"

"The truth is," Kane said, "I don't really know yet."

10

For I have been a stranger in a strange land.

EXODUS 2:22

KANE SPENT THE REST OF THE DAY IN INTERVIEWS WITH
the adults of Rejoice, checking names off Thomas
Wright's list as he went. He had no trouble finding people,
because they were all in public places, working. Kane
dodged through the clear, crisp, thirty-below air, going
from building to building and cornering them, introducing
himself and asking questions that the workers seemed perfectly willing to answer without any fear of losing time
from their tasks.

Some of the work was necessary to keep a community
the size of Rejoice going: cooking in the cafeteria, med-
icating in the clinic, tending to livestock in the barns, gar-
dening in the greenhouses, teaching in the school, and a
half dozen people handling the paperwork that any modern
American town, no matter how isolated, generates in the
twenty-first-century.

Most of the rest seemed to be involved in making items
to sell during the next tourist season. People knitted and
sewed, threw pots and worked in wood, even ran a small
printing plant, which, that day, was producing color post-

cards of a Devil's Toe ablaze in summer flowers and fo-
liage and bathed in the summer sunshine that lasted nearly
around the clock. There was apparently no end to the gew-
gaws tourists would buy, and Rejoice seemed determined
to supply any imaginable legal want, and to keep the profits thereof. It was, Kane thought, like visiting Santa's
workshop, if Santa made moose-poop swizzle sticks.

Kane talked to the schoolteachers, the town's doctor,
and a sampling of the residents and got, when he added it
all up, nothing useful. Faith put no strain on Rejoice's social fabric, raised no questions troubling to its religious
consensus, and spoke only when spoken to. The town's account reminded Kane of what people said when one of
their neighbors was revealed as a mass murderer: He was
such a quiet, polite young man.

The town was, of course, concerned when Faith went
off to the regional high school, concerned both for Faith,
among all those outsiders, and for what she might bring
back to the community. But Faith didn't start smoking or
wear revealing clothes or go Goth, and she spoke of her ex-
periences outside Rejoice in steady, judicious, slightly superior tones, reassuring the adults that she was a solid
young woman and that their way of life really was superior
to that of those who lived outside.

Faith insisted to one and all that she was attending the
high school because its course offerings would better prepare her for the Ivy League college she planned to attend,
and explained the extracurricular activities that kept her
away from Rejoice in the afternoons as extra polish for her
résumé. Her first year at the school, she'd played Mrs. Gibbs
in the school's production of Thornton Wilder's *Our Town,*
been co-chair of the canned-food drive, and worked as a
copy editor on the student newspaper, *The Devil's Toe Imp.*

As important to the adults of Rejoice were the things
Faith had not done. She had not become a cheerleader, a
position they were confident her personality and beauty
would have won for her, or joined the girl's basketball team,
which would have suited her natural athleticism. With their
skimpy costumes, either of these pursuits, the town agreed,

would have exposed more of Faith to the world than Rejoice would have been completely comfortable with. That, plus the fact that she did not allow herself to be seduced by the secular teenage world of makeup and boys and parties, reconciled the residents of Rejoice to her choice.

After a year, the town was confident in Faith's ability to mix in the outside world without harm to herself or to them. Once that threat was removed, and the novelty of having a Rejoice teenager in the regional school wore off, the town paid less attention to her comings and goings. So what Faith's extracurricular activities were this school year, no one could say exactly.

The only off note in this chorus came from a couple of twenty-something men Kane talked with, cornering them one by one in the cafeteria when they came in from some outdoor labor for a warm-up. They made a point of saying that Faith seemed to spend a lot of time with Johnny Starship—"Can you believe that name? What a wuss," one of them said—who they figured was just biding his time before taking over the family business of doing the devil's work. Careful questioning by Kane revealed that each of the young men had harbored hopes of winning Faith for himself and, although she had disabused them of this notion in the nicest possible way, were still hurt by the rejection. Feeling that there was nothing wrong with himself, each chose to explain it by believing that she was interested in some other male.

The nonsmitten adults had another view. If Faith was spending time with Johnny Starship, it was during the day and in school, where, despite what you sometimes heard about American public schools, they didn't believe anything seriously sinful could be going on. Besides, the contact didn't seem to be hurting her and could only help him. Everyone agreed that Elder Moses Wright couldn't have been happy about his granddaughter spending time with the spawn of his sworn enemy, but it is, they pointed out, a Christian's duty to proclaim the Good News. Doesn't the Bible say: "Sing unto the Lord, bless His name; show forth His salvation from day to day"?

Kane was sitting in his small interview room turning all this over in his mind when Thomas Wright found him.

"I don't mean to interrupt," he said, "but it is time for the evening gathering."

Kane got to his feet, and the two men walked out into the community hall.

"Have you learned anything?" Thomas Wright asked as they moved through the thickening crowd toward the front of the room.

"Only that your daughter was well liked and respected," Kane said, "although what I heard did raise a few questions I'd like to ask you."

"After the meeting," Thomas Wright said. "If you'll stand here."

Kane found himself in the front rank of a crowd facing the front of the room. After a couple of minutes, during which more people straggled in, Thomas Wright stepped out and turned to face the crowd.

"We are at the end of another day of working in the vineyards of the Lord," he said, raising his voice to be heard in the back.

"Praise God," the crowd answered

"Let us hear the Lord's words," Thomas Wright said, and his father, Bible under his arm, stepped out.

"My text today," he said, opening the Bible, "is from the Gospel of Saint Mark, chapter four, verse eleven."

"Speak to us of God's word," the crowd replied.

The old man looked straight at Kane, then dropped his eyes to read: " 'And he said unto them, Unto you it is given to know the kingdom of God: but to them that are without, all things are done in parables.' "

The old man closed his Bible, fastened his gaze on Kane again, and expanded on his theme: the superiority of those who believed over those who didn't, Rejoice over the outside world, and self-reliance over depending on outsiders. Kane locked his gaze with the preacher's and stood there, a slight smile on his lips.

There was no telling how long that might have gone on if the crowd hadn't started fidgeting. Moses Wright, in tune with his audience like any showman, sensed its unease, wrapped up his homily and, with one last look at Kane, stepped back into the crowd.

His son took his place. He looked unhappy.

"Once again, it is good to hear one of the possible interpretations of God's words," he said, bringing a titter from his audience and a scowl from his father. "Now, who has matters to be brought before the meeting?"

What followed was a mishmash of progress reports, complaints, and news, delivered by people in the crowd, some of whom stepped forward in the same manner the Wrights had, others who stood where they were and spoke. The community gave a prayer of thanks that two of its members serving in Iraq remained unharmed and a third was recovering from her wounds in Germany. It said another prayer for the safety and success of the basketball teams on their way to Anchorage. The rest of the proceeding seemed to Kane to be wholly secular: production reports, plumbing problems, plans for the spring and summer. There was some discussion of the wisdom of opening an espresso stand in Devil's Toe, those for it stressing the profits to be made, and those against it voicing the community's aversion to nonbiblical stimulants. No vote was taken.

When everyone had had a chance to speak, Thomas Wright stepped up again and gestured to Kane to join him. Kane walked up and turned to face the crowd. Seeing so many people in one place, all looking at him, made Kane nervous, but he fought to keep an easy smile on his face.

"As you know," Thomas Wright told the crowd, "a member of our community, my daughter, is missing. The Council of Elders has decided that her disappearance merits investigation that is beyond the abilities of anyone here. So we have employed Nik Kane here to look into it. I know he has talked with some of you already, and may want to talk with others. I urge you to cooperate with him, to answer his questions fully and truthfully, and to aid his efforts in any way you can. For now, though, I would simply like you to bid him welcome."

"Welcome, Nik Kane," most of the crowd said. Moses Wright and a few others kept their lips pressed firmly together.

"Let us go now, walking in the light of the Lord, until we meet again in the morning," Thomas Wright said.

The crowd broke up, several members making a point of going to shake Kane's hand.

"Elder Moses Wright seems to have forgotten his duty to strangers," one middle-aged woman said. "The Bible says, 'Thou shalt neither vex a stranger nor oppress him.' "

"And elsewhere," her companion, another middle-aged woman, said, " 'Be not forgetful to entertain strangers: for thereby some have entertained angels unawares.' "

Kane laughed.

"I appreciate the welcome," he said, "although I don't pretend to be an angel."

"Neither do we," one of the women said, "but others still call us that."

Kane was swept along into the dining room, where he ate spaghetti and meatballs at a long table filled with Rejoice residents of all ages and occupations. They asked him so many questions about life in Anchorage that an elder had to intervene, laughing. "Please, give Mr. Kane a chance to eat. We wouldn't want him to go hungry to answer our questions."

Kane found his dinner companions to be an odd mixture of innocence and sophistication, able to talk knowledgeably about national politics and economics, but completely unaware of things like property taxes or the price of a loaf of bread. They got their information, he learned, mostly from the radio, which meant mostly from talk radio and, thus, mostly from the rantings of right-wing white men. So they thought the larger world was much more dangerous and threatening than it was, much more sinful, much more strident and partisan, much less friendly and compassionate. Most of those who had more recent experience of the outside world had come to Rejoice to escape it, their own fears and disappointments reinforcing that view. Kane's suggestions that this might not be a full picture of the outside world were met with skepticism, so he gave that up and used the time to try to learn more about Rejoice.

What he found out was that the community was hardly monolithic. Most of those at his table were unreservedly Christian in their beliefs and fundamentalist in their practice, but some were less so. That the two groups had worked out a satisfactory relationship was clear, and it appeared to Kane that a person could live quite happily in the town by respecting the forms, if not embracing the content, of Christian fundamentalism. Among the strictly religious, there was a wide variety of opinion on both religious form and content. Some sided with Moses Wright's stubborn adherence to a literal interpretation of the Bible, while others upheld the principle that each person was his own interpreter of the Holy Writ.

"How do you manage to live together with so many differences?" Kane asked as he rose at a sign from Thomas Wright.

"Why, where else would we live?" one of the Bible-quoting ladies asked, in a tone that made it clear that she thought no sane person would want to live anywhere but Rejoice.

Kane followed Thomas Wright back to the small room he'd used to interview the teens, and both men sat.

"You said you had some questions?" Wright said.

"A few," Kane said. "Do you know what Faith's extracurricular activities are this year?"

Wright thought for a moment.

"I don't really. I assume she is pursuing the same sort of things she did last year, but I don't know for certain."

Kane made a note.

"Okay, how about her relationship with a boy everyone calls Johnny Starship? What do you know about that?"

"I've heard the rumors that they are involved, uh, romantically, but don't believe them. Faith came to me and told me about the boy long before the gossip started. She said that he was a nice boy, but troubled about what his father and brother did for a living, and that she was trying to help him through that and, perhaps, into a more Christian life.

"I asked her if she was interested in him romantically, and she laughed and said, 'Oh, Papa, I couldn't be. We're the same age in years, but he is so much younger in every other way.'"

"So," Kane said after finishing his note-taking, "he was just a potential convert to her?"

Thomas Wright smiled.

"Every Christian has a duty to spread the Gospel, but we don't try to trick or seduce or dragoon people into our beliefs. At least, most of us don't. I'm certain that Faith's motives were first and foremost to help a fellow human being, and if through that help he came closer to God, so much the better."

"Does that attitude have something to do with why there's no Bible in her room?"

Wright looked confused.

"No Bible? Faith always has her Bible near to hand. It's the one I gave her when she turned seven and was old enough to begin to understand God's word."

"Describe it for me."

"Oh, it's hardback-book-sized, with a padded cover done up in brown leather with gold, stamped lettering. It was actually quite expensive. I expected it to last her a lifetime."

"And your own Bible?" Kane asked. "I didn't find it in your home, and I don't see it here."

Thomas Wright's ears turned red. He squared his shoulders and thrust out his jaw. Kane began calculating his chances of taking Wright down if it came to that.

"You said you wanted to search Faith's room, not my entire home," Wright barked.

"Calm down," Kane said. "You've hired me to do a difficult job, and to do it I need to know as much as I can find out about your daughter and the world she lives in. That definitely includes the house in which she lives."

Wright sat still and silent. Kane could see him try to

will the tension from his body. He took a couple of deep breaths, unballed his fists, and let his shoulders sag.

" 'He that is soon angry dealeth foolishly,' " he said, as if to himself, then sighed. "I apologize for my reaction. I suppose you have a job to do, and as I am the one who asked you to do it, I shouldn't complain if your methods cause me some discomfort. But do you really need to know about the state of my soul?"

"I don't know what I really need to know," Kane said. "I just pick up information wherever I can find it, and hope that, somehow, it arranges itself into a story that I can understand."

"That doesn't sound very scientific," Wright said.

Kane grinned.

"It's not. It's more like hoping for revelation than waiting for the results of an experiment."

Wright smiled back at the detective.

"How can I refuse a man striving for revelation? I don't have a Bible in my home. When my wife died, I put mine away in a drawer in my office. I have not yet figured out how to reconcile her death with faith in God. I understand all the arguments intellectually, but I don't feel confident of them and, until I do, I guess I am estranged from God."

"Doesn't that cause you problems here? Being in charge of a Christian community without sharing the faith?"

"It does," Wright said, smiling again, "but it also causes many people to pray for me. That can't be all bad."

Kane asked Wright a few more questions, then put his notebook away.

"I'm going to do some detecting outside Rejoice tomorrow," he said, "and one of the things I need is your written permission to search Faith's locker at the school. I'll take the trooper along to make it official, but when you're dealing with the public education system, it's better to be prepared for anything."

The two men walked over to the office trailer, where Kane dictated a permission form. Wright typed it into a computer, printed it out, and signed it. Then he reached

into a desk drawer and came out with a key attached to a
piece of wood by a thin chain. He tossed it to the detective.

"We're putting you into a cabin of your own, so you can
play the violin or use cocaine or whatever it is detectives
do these days," he said. "I could show you where it is, but
I'm late for a building committee meeting. We've decided
it's time for a proper church, and you wouldn't believe the
details involved in that. But there's a map in the community hall, so I can show you where it is."

The two men walked back to the community hall and
stood in front of a big, hand-drawn map.

"This is the way we keep track of everyone, and know
which homes are available for new arrivals," Wright said.
He pointed to a large rectangle. "We are here." He pointed
to a smaller one nearby. "That is my home." He pointed to
a rectangle next to a much bigger one labeled "Airport."
"My father lives here."

"He lives far away from everyone else," Kane said.

"His home is on the edge closest to Devil's Toe, right
on the road that leads to the highway," Thomas Wright
said. He smiled. "My father says he lives there because he
is Rejoice's bulwark against the evils of the secular world.
Others say he lives there so he can keep an eye on everyone
else's comings and goings.

"You will be here," he said, pointing to a rectangle on
the other side of the town, not far from the greenhouses. As
he traced the route to it, Ruth Hunt came into the room.

"I wondered who still had the lights on," she said with a
smile. "Are you lost?"

"No," Wright said, "I'm trying to show Mr. Kane how
to get to the cabin he will be using. I'm late for a meeting,
so I can't take him there."

"You're always late for a meeting, Elder Thomas
Wright," the woman said, walking over and standing next
to the detective. She smelled of cooking and clean skin.
"Where is it?"

Wright pointed to the little rectangle that represented
Kane's quarters.

"That's not far from me," the woman said. "I'll be happy to show Mr. Kane the way and see him settled."

"Thank you very much, Ruth," Wright said. "I'll leave you to it." He picked up a marking pen, wrote Kane's name next to the rectangle, and headed off to his meeting.

"Not much chance of privacy here," the detective said, pointing to the names written next to other rectangles on the map.

"If you live here for a couple of weeks, you don't need this map," the woman said, "but it comes in handy for newcomers."

Kane retrieved his coat from his interview room and followed the woman out into the cold.

"Just follow me," she said, getting into a Jeep very like the one Faith had been driving.

Kane unplugged his pickup and followed the Jeep's taillights through the darkness, thinking about one of the last exchanges he'd had with Thomas Wright during their interview.

"Do you remember anything that might have happened to Faith right after her mother died?" he'd asked. "Anything that might have changed the way she acted?"

Wright had shaken his head.

"I don't. Faith never said anything to me, and frankly, those days aren't very clear in my mind. It was like I was living in some sort of fog. You may not know what it's like to lose someone close to you, someone you love, but it's like a blow that dazes you. It took me a long time to recover. If, in fact, I have recovered yet."

I do know what it's like to lose someone close, the detective thought. Laurie's not dead, it's true, but she's gone and she's not coming back. And that's every bit as inexplicable to me as why Thomas Wright's wife died of cancer. And every bit as final. And I don't have a faith to fall back on or a community to support me.

Whoa, he thought. That sounds a lot like whining. Better to think about what's happened to Faith and get on with it.

He pulled in behind the Jeep at a small cabin, got out, and unlocked the door with the key Thomas Wright had given him. Ruth Hunt walked to a box on the back wall, opened it, and thumbed a set of switches. Then she walked back and switched on a lamp, then another.

The cabin was one room: sink and sideboard at the front, wood stove and a couple of chairs in the middle, bed at the back. A long, doorless closet ran along the foot of the bed. There was a window over the sink and another in one of the long walls near the wood stove. Off the living area was a door that Kane figured led to a bathroom. A trickle of water flowed from the sink's faucet.

"We keep heat tape on the pipes all winter, and leave them running so they don't freeze up," Ruth Hunt said. "We heat-tape the sewer pipes, too. It's costly but cheaper than replacing burst pipes all the time."

She went to the stove and opened it.

"Why don't you bring in your things," she said, "while I start a fire and get some heat in the place?"

It took Kane three trips to bring everything in. By that time, a fire was going in the stove and the woman was putting big chunks of spruce on it.

"This should make the place warm enough for you to sleep in," she said, "and I'll leave you to do that."

Kane was suddenly aware that, for the first time since Laurie had thrown him out, he didn't want to be alone.

"Do you have to leave right away?" Kane asked.

The woman smiled.

"The community will be scandalized if I stay long," she said, "but I have a few minutes." She walked to the table and sat down. Kane took a seat across from her.

"Is your investigation going all right?" she asked.

Kane shrugged.

"People are cooperative, for the most part," he said, "but no one has said anything that is likely to lead me directly to Faith."

They were silent for a moment.

"Well, that topic doesn't seem to be taking us anywhere," Ruth said. "Why don't you tell me about why you went to prison? You said you would."

To his amazement, Kane found himself telling her

about the shooting, about the force's inability to turn up a gun, about the newspaper and TV campaign demanding his prosecution, about Jeffords's refusing to intervene and about the district attorney's deciding to prosecute.

"I could see what was going to happen then," Kane said, "so I told my lawyer to string it out as long as he could so that I could prepare for prison."

"Prepare?" Ruth said. "How?"

"Physically, for one thing," Kane said. "I didn't figure that, wherever they sent me, an ex-cop was going to be the most popular inmate in the place. So I went on a diet and spent my afternoons with the department's hand-to-hand combat teacher. I was glad I did, later."

With the delays Kane's lawyer requested, it took nearly a year to get the case to trial. The charge was second-degree murder, but Kane's lawyer did a good job discrediting the so-called eyewitnesses and calling into question the Breathalyzer test results. So the jury came back with manslaughter, and the judge gave him seven years.

"Is that a lot?" Ruth asked.

"The sentencing guidelines call for five years, first offense," Kane said, "but the judge said, 'If the law tells me to add two years for being drunk when you run over somebody with a car, I'm surely going to add them for being drunk when you shoot somebody.'

"And so I spent the past seven years in prison."

Ruth reached over and put a hand on Kane's wrist.

"You poor man, it must have been terrible," she said. "Couldn't you have gotten out earlier?"

"I could have," Kane said, "but I didn't want parole. I wanted to pay the full price all at once."

"How did you come to be cleared of the crime?" she asked.

"First-class detective work," Kane said with a bitter laugh.

The woman said nothing. She just looked at Kane expectantly.

"The other kid there that night, the one they called Train, got shot in a dispute with another young gentleman and ended up in a wheelchair," he said. "The experience seemed to bring him to Jesus. One of the sins he had to repent was lying about what happened that night."

"Enfield, he had him a gun that night," Train Simmons *told a police sergeant named Tater Therriault who'd been on duty when the young man wheeled himself into the station to confess. "That cop who got shot, he was knockin' boots with a young thing name of Sharilee. Was supposed to be my bitch. Well, I couldn't allow that kind of disrespect, could I? When I find this out, I beat her 'til she told me when the cop was gonna be in our neighborhood. Then I called in a phony crime and shot the cop when he showed up."*

Train asked for a glass of water and drank it down.

"Okay," Therriault said. *"Then what?"*

"I never shot nobody before," Train said, *"so I dropped the gun and kind of staggered back. And that dummy Enfield runs out his house and grabs the gun and starts dancing around like some sort of crazy man."*

"Why didn't you take the gun away from him?" Therriault said.

"Man, I was tryin'," Train said, exasperation pushing his voice up an octave, *"but a dummy with a gun be dangerous. And that other cop got there so fast."*

"Then what?"

"He shoots Enfield and falls down. I grab the gun and book. And the rest you know."

Therriault looked at Train for a minute, then said, *"You know you're in big trouble, right? You're going to prison?"*

Train shook his head.

"Man, I'm already in prison," he said, slapping the arm of his wheelchair. *"But long as I'm right with Jesus, that's what counts."*

There was a silence when Kane finished the story. Kane broke it by saying, "After Train confessed, they had to let me out and exonerate me of manslaughter. Even a drunk has a right to self-defense. But it didn't make much difference."

"Why not?" Ruth asked.

Kane gave a rueful laugh.

"By the time Train found Jesus and all the paperwork was finished, there were only three weeks left on my sentence."

Ruth ran her hand along Kane's arm, and he could feel the fist he'd made relax. Her touch was cool and exciting. Kane reached out and put his other hand over hers. They sat looking at one another for several moments. Then Ruth slid her hand out from under Kane's and stood up.

"I've been here far too long already," she said. "I must be going."

Kane got up and walked around the table to stand in front of her. He took both her hands in his.

"If you're sure you have to leave," he said.

Up close, in the flickering light from the stove, Ruth Hunt was so beautiful Kane had a hard time convincing himself she was real. She dropped his hand, reached up, and, with her forefinger, traced the line of his scar.

"Where did you get this terrible mark?" she asked.

Kane wanted to tell her some story, or just tell her to mind her own business. But standing there like that with her, he found himself telling the truth.

"A man tried to stab me in the temple with a sharpened toothbrush handle," he said. "Fortunately for me, he missed my temple. Unfortunately, he didn't miss my whole head." He could feel the jagged plastic ripping down the side of his face as he said the words.

"How terrible," she said. "This was in prison?"

"It was," Kane said.

"What happened to the man?" she asked.

"He's dead," Kane said, feeling the con's neck snap again as the guards tried to pull them apart.

"You really have had a difficult time, haven't you," she said.

Something big and angry crashed through the window near the wood stove, buzzed past Kane's ear, and hit the log wall opposite with an audible thunk. As he threw himself at the woman, Kane heard the sharp crack of a high-powered rifle. His weight knocked the woman to the floor and he landed on top of her. As they lay there, Kane heard two more bullets plow into the log wall, two more cracks, then only the rushed rasps of their breathing.

11

For, lo, the wicked bend their bow, they make ready their arrow upon the string, that they might privily shoot at the upright in heart.

PSALMS 11:2

KANE AND THE WOMAN LAY THERE AS THEIR HEART-
beats lengthened into one minute, two, three. Then Ruth
Hunt began to stir.

"This is nice," she said, "but I'm really too old to be lying on wooden floors."

Kane moved off of her. She started to rise. Kane
grabbed her arm.

"Stay down," he said. He crawled to the broken window
and lifted himself until he could see through it. Nobody
coming. Nobody in sight. Nothing.

"Crawl over there and shut off the light," he said to
Ruth. "Reach up, don't stand up."

The woman did as he directed. With the lights off, Kane
could see white snow and dark trees. Not enough moon to
see any detail, even with the snow cover to reflect its light.
He crawled back to his belongings, rummaged for a pair of
binoculars, and crawled back to the window. The big lenses
gathered a lot of light, so Kane could see better, but not
well. If someone was just inside the trees, Kane couldn't
see him. He could just lie there waiting for a clear shot.

There was a knock at the door. The woman stood up. Kane started to say something, then realized she was out of the line of sight of the window. She swung the door open. A man and woman Kane didn't know were standing there, showing signs of having dressed quickly for the outdoors. The man held a hunting rifle.

"We heard shots and saw the lights go out," the woman said. "We thought we should come and see if something was wrong."

"Somebody shot at us through that window," Kane said, pointing. "Whoever it was might still be out there."

"Not if he knows Rejoice," the man said. "Everyone within earshot will be here soon. We don't leave anyone unprotected." He looked around the room. "Ruth Hunt, I'm surprised to find you here." There was something in the man's voice Kane couldn't quite identify.

"I was showing Mr. Kane to his cabin," Ruth replied. "I didn't really expect his welcome to be so warm."

Kane stood up. No one shot at him. He walked over to where Ruth stood leaning against the wall.

"Are you okay?" he asked in a low voice. "Do you need to sit down?"

She looked at him with eyes that glimmered, then put her hand on his sleeve.

"I'm fine," she said. "I was a little weak in the knees. I don't get shot at every day. But I'm fine now."

The couple at the door was joined by an entire family, parents and what looked to Kane to be seven children, who arrived like a small tornado, spewing questions and exclamations in every direction. Kane could tell that the kids thought it was very cool that someone had shot at him. Within five minutes there were two dozen people in and around the little cabin, most of the adults armed and all of them asking what had happened.

"It's really too cold for everyone to be standing around," Kane said after answering the same questions for the dozenth time. "Anyway, I think the excitement is over for the night. So why don't you all just go home? With my thanks for checking up on me."

The crowd began dispersing.

"I've got some plywood we can put over that window," the first man on the scene said, and went off to get it. His wife found a broom and began sweeping up the broken glass.

"Where is your husband tonight, Ruth?" the woman asked, looking at Kane. "Isn't he in Anchorage with the basketball team?"

"He is," Ruth said, "as you well know, Clarice."

The smile she gave Kane was full of mischief.

"I'd better be going home," she said, "before I'm the talk of Rejoice. Thanks for a wonderful evening."

Kane laughed and laughed some more, hearing an edge of post-danger hysteria in his laugh.

"You bet," he said, "the next time I'm going to get shot at, I'll be sure to invite you along."

Ruth left, and the man soon returned. He and Kane nailed up plywood on the outside, stuffed the opening with insulation, and nailed another sheet of plywood over the inside. Then the man and woman left, taking Kane's thanks with them.

The detective walked out and, using an extension cord, plugged in his pickup. Then he just stood there. He could hear the crunching of feet on the snow, and the soft voices of his neighbors, then the bang of their door closing. Then nothing. He stood, drawing cold air in through his nose, smelling the faint odor of spruce from the nearby forest and the lingering tang of exhaust from Ruth's Jeep.

Above him, a thin sliver of moon showed cold and white. A multitude of stars made pinpricks of dancing, winking light in the blackness of the sky. He could feel the cold move through his clothes and wrap itself around his body. A small thrill ran along his backbone, as it always did when he enjoyed the cold's seductive threat knowing warmth was near.

Kane stood there and thought about who in Rejoice would want him dead and why. He thought about Faith Wright, and wondered if she had a real life and, if so, where it was hidden under her careful covering of pleasantness and conventionality. He thought about God, and if there was one and, if so, where He stood in all of this. He thought about how the excitement of having death brush past him made his blood sing, and about how good Ruth Hunt felt beneath him. Then he began to shiver, so he went into the cabin, closed and locked the door, and got ready for bed.

12

*And from the roof he saw a woman washing herself;
and the woman was very beautiful to look upon.*

2 SAMUEL 11:2

KANE AWOKE WITH A START, THE HAIRS ON THE BACK OF his neck standing upright, his hands groping for a weapon. Then he remembered he didn't have one. If I'm going to do this for any length of time, he thought, I'm going to have to get over my qualms about guns.

That's the thing about living in the world. So many problems to deal with. Life in prison was simpler. He was beginning to understand why so many cons did things that got them jugged again.

His eyes scanned the room, finding only darkness in varying shapes and depths. His ears sought sounds and heard only the soughing of his breath and the hammering of his heart. He lay there breathing deeply and waited for his pulse to slow. When he was calmer, he unzipped his sleeping bag, put his bare feet on the hard, cold floor, walked across the room, switched on the lights, and looked around.

The little cabin looked like a cave that bears had been wrestling in. Before turning in, Kane had moved the bed out of sight of the remaining window, shoving a chair and small table haphazardly out of the way. There was a short curtain on that window, but nothing to keep someone from looking in to find a target. He'd searched the cabin for a better covering and, finding none, had settled for stuffing the cushions from the chairs into the window opening. Then he'd wedged the door shut, unrolled his bag, undressed, and crawled in. He lay there thinking about how he'd get out of the cabin if somebody set fire to it. Just when he decided he was too wound-up to fall asleep, he did.

Satisfied that there was no immediate danger, Kane put on a polypropylene union suit and socks and started a fire in the wood stove. Then he walked into the tiny bathroom and stood eyeing the phone-booth-sized metal shower stall. The electric water heater that stood next to it was warm to the touch, so he decided to risk it. He stripped off his clothing, turned on the water, and, clenching his teeth, walked into the stall. He showered in tepid water, toweled off, and got dressed. Only then did he think to look at his watch. It was five-thirty a.m., far too early to do much of anything in the way of detecting.

There was no stove in the kitchen, and no refrigerator, either. Cooking was done on the wood stove, he decided, and there was probably a trapdoor somewhere in the cabin floor over a hole in permafrost that served as a cooler. They haven't given me the VIP quarters, he thought, and laughed. More likely they figured a guy just out of prison wouldn't be comfortable in anything fancy.

He rummaged in the single cupboard, found a small pot, and filled it with water. He carried it over, set it on top of the wood stove, and waited. When it started to boil, he rinsed his traveling mug with hot water to warm it up, then poured coffee into a one-cup dripper, set it on the mug, and poured water through it. Just one day in Rejoice, he thought, and I'm already breaking the rules.

He carried the cup into the bathroom and balanced it on the edge of the tiny sink. He filled the sink with water and shaved, maneuvering his face so he could see it in the scrap of mirror, alternating razor strokes with sips of coffee.

When he finished, he examined the result. Even without the scar, not much chance of being chosen as Brad Pitt's stand-in.

He went back into the living room and made himself another cup of coffee. The beans were Guatemalan, bought from an Anchorage roaster, and the brew that resulted was, Kane decided, what they served for breakfast in heaven. Good coffee was one of the things he'd really missed in prison, along with, oh, everything else. He was happy to be able to indulge in small pleasures again.

He sat on the bed and read through his notes, took out a legal-sized tablet and pencil, and began sketching. He put Faith Wright in a box in the middle of the page and started a connections matrix. The problem was, everyone was connected to her somehow, and connected to everyone else for that matter.

He flipped the page over and tried doing the same with himself, to see if he could limit the field of people who might have shot at him. But once he put in the names of the Council of Elders and the people he'd interviewed the day before, he saw that he had the same problem: too many possibilities, too little information. Rejoice had had plenty of warning he would be here, so anyone who didn't want him to find Faith could have been behind the attack. Especially since all they had to do to find him was look at the map in the community hall.

Of the people he'd talked with, only those away with the basketball teams could be ruled out. And that wasn't even counting the people at the mine who knew he was here or, for that matter, the "rough element," who no doubt had heard, especially after his performance in the bar. He couldn't even be one hundred percent sure that the attempt was connected to his search for Faith.

Faced with nothing but dead ends, his mind slipped off to other matters. He thought about making himself breakfast, but all he had was oatmeal and a few freeze-dried meals. He could do better than that at the cafeteria. But he knew his real reason for going there was the hope he'd see

Ruth Hunt again. He thought about her for a while, searching for something not to like.

"Well," he said to the empty room, "there is the fact she's married."

Kane knew he shouldn't be thinking about the wife of one of his employers in quite the way he was, but decided he just didn't have the mental discipline to stop. Laurie's decision to leave had left a vacuum inside him that feelings for Ruth were rushing to fill. He'd tried steeling himself against such feelings, but a few moments standing alone with Ruth in the cabin and his willpower had just run out. Well, he thought, I'll just have to have the feelings, do this job, and leave without acting on them. I did seven years, I can do this.

He thought for a while about Laurie without, as usual, getting anywhere. Her departure still seemed as random as a lightning strike. He knew that living with him was no day at the beach, but she'd put up with him for so long, and stuck with him all through his prison term, that he'd thought they'd be together forever.

But she was gone from his life and she wasn't coming back.

He wrenched his thoughts from that channel and began thinking about Rejoice. He supposed its government was something between feudalism and monarchy, with elements of theocracy and the New England town meeting thrown in. Or was that the way to think about it? Maybe it was just its own thing, a community shaped in part by its beliefs, in part by its circumstances. Primitive because its conditions were primitive; fundamentalist because its members' beliefs were fundamentalist. Still there after forty years because of the stubbornness of those beliefs, compounded by misinformation about the outside world and a growing economic stake in the area.

Perhaps fragile despite all of that, Kane thought, without the deeper historical roots of other communities dominated by religious belief. One good shock to Rejoice's belief system, and the members might scatter like ducks that glimpsed the shadow of an eagle. That prospect alone would be enough to make the more devout members want his search to fail. But was their faith strong enough to send someone out into the cold to try to murder him?

Besides, how could anyone know how Rejoice would react to a shock? History showed that belief systems could be tough and durable. Why else were there people clinging to absurd beliefs in creation myths, to outmoded ideas about women, to exclusionary beliefs in their own righteousness? Why else would a couple of hundred people be living out in this difficult country, clinging to the contents of a book of dubious authorship. Was the Bible really God's word? Was there really a God? Why did that question seem important to him?

These and other thoughts occupied Kane for some time, until hunger and frustration drove him off the bed. He got a folding knife out of his duffel and dug the slugs out of the log wall, weighing each in his hand. He dropped them into his shirt pocket, put on his coat, and let himself out, carrying a flashlight in one hand. He walked through ankle-deep snow to the tree line. Once there, he lined himself up with the cabin, switched on the flashlight, and examined the ground. It took him a few minutes to find where the shooter had stood, using a birch branch as a rest. His flashlight beam lit up the plywood covering the window.

He must not have been a very good shot, Kane thought. With the lights on inside the cabin, it would have been hard to miss from here.

Kane followed the footprints through the trees. They soon came to a well-worn path. He turned toward the town and followed it, but other well-worn paths branched off. No way to tell where the shooter had gone.

He walked back through the trees, keeping his flashlight pointed toward the ground. The shooter must have known the area well, to make his way back without using a light. But otherwise Kane hadn't learned much from his expedition.

Back at the cabin, Kane made a last pass through the bathroom, then drove to the community building. At six-thirty a.m., it was coming to life. Kane walked into the cafeteria and was served powdered eggs, sausage of indeterminate origin, and powdered orange juice. Every bit as good as prison food, he thought. The only thing that set the breakfast apart were freshly baked biscuits with honey. The biscuits were delicious.

As Kane was eating, more people arrived, most of them nodding to him as they passed. He'd just about finished when Ruth came out of the back, waved, and walked over. When he motioned for her to sit, she shook her head.

"I don't have time to visit," she said, "but I wanted to say hello."

"I appreciate that," Kane said, "and I do have a question. Is there anyone here who would try to shoot you?"

The woman laughed, confusion in her face.

"You're kidding, right?" she said.

"Not entirely," the detective said. "The odds are very high that those bullets were meant for me, but I can't ignore the possibility, however slight, that you were the target."

The woman cocked her head to the side and smiled.

"You have the most interesting way of looking at things," she said. "I can't imagine that I've irritated anyone enough to try to murder me." She paused. "But I'll think about it some more and give you a definitive answer over dinner, provided you'd be willing to buy me one."

It was Kane's turn to be confused.

"Buy you one?" he said. "I thought everything in Rejoice was free to community members."

"It is," the woman said, "but ever since I came here I've made it a point to have dinner at the Devil's Toe Roadhouse every other Friday. I did that before I married and continued after. It's something of a scandal in the community, I'm happy to say. I've come to think it's my duty to give Rejoice something to gossip about."

Kane laughed. She was starting to make him feel human again. Feeling human, letting his guard down, had been dangerous for so long that it made him nervous.

"I'll bet," he said, following that thought. "Don't some of the people there make you a little nervous?"

"You don't know me very well," she said, "if you think the crowd at the roadhouse would make me nervous."

So they set a time to meet, and the woman went back to her chores.

Thomas Wright came into the cafeteria just as Kane was finishing his breakfast. He saw the detective and walked over.

"You're up early," he said, waving a hand at Kane's empty plate. "I just heard about the shooting at your cabin. Praise God no one was hurt."

"Someone must have gotten up early to deliver that news," Kane said.

"Gossip never sleeps," Wright said with a smile.

"Can you sit for a minute?" Kane asked.

Wright sat.

"What are you going to do about the shooting?" he asked.

"Well, I'm headed out to see the trooper anyway, so I'll report it," Kane said. "Maybe when it's light enough he'll come over and look at the crime scene, although what a bunch of tracks in the snow would tell him I don't know. Anyway, since the shooter missed, I'm far more interested in his reasons than the actual shooting."

"What do you mean?" Wright asked.

"The fact that someone shot at me makes it more likely that the reason for Faith's disappearance is something more sinister than her desire to live in the outside world," Kane said.

The two men sat quietly for a moment.

"I see what you mean." Thomas Wright said. "Shooting at you seems to represent a pretty serious objection to trying to find her."

"Yeah," Kane said, "somebody must think he has a good reason for Faith to stay missing. And I haven't been here long enough for it to be anything but the job I'm doing. I don't suppose there's any point in asking who has hunting rifles in Rejoice." He pulled a slug from his pocket. "Specifically a .30-caliber or 7.62?"

"I'm afraid not," Wright said. "I think every home in

Rejoice has guns for hunting and for self-defense and defense of the community. We don't have a police force, you know, and there's only one trooper for the whole area."

"That's what I thought," Kane said, pocketing the slug. "I'll turn these over to the trooper, but it's probably just going through the motions. I'd better get started."

Kane left Wright sitting at the table and went out to his truck. As he pushed through the doors of the Arctic entryway, he passed Matthew Pinchon, who was headed in.

"I thought you went to Anchorage," he said.

"I felt like I was coming down with something, so I decided to stay," the young man said. "The team didn't really need me. We'll win this game easily."

When Kane was well away from Rejoice, he put a Beatles CD in the player and tracked along until he reached "Here Comes the Sun King."

I may not have the sun, Kane thought, looking at the dark sky, but I have reason to celebrate this morning anyway. Being alive is a good excuse for song.

He drove through the frozen landscape, singing along. The countryside looked as desolate and forbidding as ever, but the music—and the prospect of dinner with Ruth—buoyed his spirits.

Devil's Toe was still locked up tight, but there was a four-wheel-drive cruiser parked in front of the trooper office, where the lights were on. Kane parked next to the cruiser and walked in.

A young man with close-cropped hair looked up from a computer screen. Kane figured him for about twenty-five, big like all the troopers, wearing the full outfit with his Smokey Bear hat lying on the desk.

"Help you?" he asked in a tone of forced friendliness.

Kane walked over and sat in the chair pulled up next to the desk.

"My name's Nik Kane," he said, sticking out his hand. "I've been hired by the Rejoice Council of Elders to find Faith Wright. I'd appreciate any help you could give me."

The trooper had started frowning at the sound of Kane's name.

"You got some ID?" he asked.

Kane took out his wallet, removed his driver's license, and handed it to the trooper.

"You don't have a private investigator's license?" the trooper asked, handing the license back.

"You are new, aren't you?" Kane said. "Alaska doesn't issue them."

The trooper nodded.

"We don't have truck with private eyes out here in the sticks," he said. "Now, why should I tell a civilian anything?"

"It's like this, Trooper"—he looked at the nameplate on the desk—"Slade. I'm here because some law-abiding citizens hired me. I have the blessing of your superiors. I think it would be in your best interests to help me. And of course, I'd be grateful personally."

The trooper gave Kane a hard look.

"I don't think so," he said. "I've given this matter all the time and attention it deserves. I've got a lot of territory to cover and plenty of crime to deal with, and I'm not giving the departure of a girl who's old enough to make her own decisions any more attention."

Kane was surprised by the trooper's attitude. No cop liked having somebody breathing down his neck on a case, but Slade didn't seem to think it was a case. Why would he begrudge Kane a chance to make some money and, maybe, find the girl? Unless he was just a kid trying to prove how hard-ass he could be.

"Okay," he said to the trooper, "but I have a job to do, a job that would be a lot easier with your help."

"Tough titty," the trooper said.

"You're making a mistake," Kane said. "Who knows, I might be able to teach you a thing or two."

The trooper leaned toward Kane.

"I'm not interested in learning to get drunk and gun down unarmed civilians," he said. "All I want from you is to not let the doorknob hit you in the ass on the way out."

Kane stood up.

"Fine," he said. "I don't know why you're being so

stubborn, but I'll be certain to report your lack of coopera-
tion to your superiors."

Slade opened his mouth to reply, but the phone inter-
vened. The trooper grabbed the receiver.

"Slade," he barked, then listened.

"Uh huh," he said, "uh huh, uh huh, uh huh."

With the first "uh huh" he sat straight up in the chair.
With the second, he rose to his feet. By the fourth, he had
his hat on and a key in his hand. He put the receiver down
and walked to an upright safe, opened it, and pulled out a
shotgun.

"I'd love to keep talking," he said, locking the safe, "but
I'm afraid I have to go. Somebody just stole the mine payroll and killed one of the guards."

And they robbed all that came along that way by them. . . .

JUDGES 9:25

THE TROOPER USHERED KANE OUT THE DOOR AND locked it behind them. He unplugged his cruiser, climbed in, locked the shotgun in its rack, started the SUV, and backed it fast onto the highway, straightened, and roared off, lights flashing and siren wailing.

That seems a little excessive on an empty highway, Kane thought as he tried to keep the trooper's lights in sight. But he could remember what it was like to be young and behind the wheel of a police car, adrenaline racing through his veins. Slade seemed to have that going on in spades. Kane looked at the speedometer. He was doing seventy, but the cruiser was pulling away.

Kane was just able to make out the trooper's brake lights, but lost them as the cruiser made a high-speed turn onto the mine road. He backed off the accelerator and followed at a more sedate pace. By the time he reached the crime scene, in a curve about halfway to the mine, the cruiser was slewed across the road, lights still flashing. The trooper was standing next to it, arguing with a couple of men.

Kane pulled to a stop well short of the cruiser.

"I said go back to the mine," the trooper was shouting as Kane opened his door. "You've already compromised the crime scene, so don't make matters any worse."

Kane walked in the cruiser's tire tracks to where the trooper stood. A couple of yards beyond it, one of the mine's Explorers was nosed into the alders at the side of the road. Both front doors were open. Lester Logan was sprawled facedown in a blood-soaked patch of snow near the rear of the Explorer, a shotgun next to his outflung hand.

"You're standing on mine property," one of the men said, in a tone that said he was trying to be reasonable. They were both older than the trooper and didn't seem at all impressed by him. "Besides, that's one of ours laying there."

"I don't care if it's your brother," Slade said. "I want you to walk, carefully and in your own footprints, back to your rig and go back to the mine. If you don't, I'm going to put cuffs on you and send you into Anchorage."

The two men looked at each other.

"Do what he says, Tony," Kane said. "He's law and you're not, now."

"Hello, Nik," said the man who had spoken. "I guess you're right, but it's hard to remember sometime, isn't it? Especially when you know a kid with a badge is only going to fuck things up."

"Now, listen . . ." the trooper began, but the two men turned and walked single file toward another Explorer parked some distance up the road. The man Kane had called Tony moved with a noticeable limp.

"Was there anybody else with this car?" Kane called.

"Charlie Simms," Tony threw back over his shoulder. "He took a hell of a whack, and they've got him in the infirmary."

The two men reached the other Explorer, got in, and backed up the road and out of sight.

"What are you doing here?" the trooper snapped.

"I'm here to help you," Kane said, "and if you've got any sense at all, you'll let me."

"Just stay out of my way," the trooper said, opening the

door to his car. A blast of warm air from the cruiser's heater washed over Kane.

"How do you know those guys?" the trooper asked, taking a small camera from the passenger seat. "They more washed-up ex-cops like you?" He closed the door and started taking pictures.

"I don't know the one guy," Kane said, "but the other one, Tony Figone, used to be on the Anchorage force with me. He was a good cop, until he tore up a knee and medicaled. If you keep at it long enough and you're smart enough, you might hope to be as good a cop."

The trooper grunted and kept shooting.

"Not much of a camera for crime-scene photos," Kane said.

"Digital, gramps," the trooper said, then moved off to shoot from another angle. Kane followed along, as much to keep moving in the cold as anything else. The trooper made a complete circuit, snapping away.

"I can just load these onto my computer and send them to crime-scene interpretation in Anchorage. For all the good that'll do. Those clowns tracked all over, and the road's packed too hard and been traveled too much for tire tracks to tell us anything. If there'd been some fresh snow, we might be able to see something."

The trooper moved closer to the body, watching where he put his feet. The exit wounds in Lester's back were the size of softballs. Slade moved gingerly around the body, taking close-ups. When he was finished, Kane knelt next to the body and put his palm on the back of Lester's neck. It was already cold to the touch.

"Going to be tough getting a time of death," he said.

"More like impossible," the trooper said. "I called for a doctor on the way here, but the closest one's in Rejoice and doesn't have any medical examiner experience. So it's a good thing we've got an eyeball witness."

"Can I roll him over?" Kane said.

"Don't see why not," the trooper said.

Kane did. Rolling Lester over wasn't easy; the body was stiff with cold. But when Kane finally had Lester lying on his back, he and the trooper could see the dead man's chest clearly.

"You ever handled a murder before?" Kane asked.

"No," the trooper said, "but I know the procedures."

Kane could hear the defensiveness in his voice.

"Okay," he said, leaning over to look closely at Lester's chest.

"Two shots, large caliber. Tap, tap." He rolled the body over. "No obvious powder marks around the wounds, so the shooting wasn't point blank, but the entry wounds are close together, which argues for either close range or a very skilled shooter. There's no telling where the bullets went after they passed though Lester. I suppose if we were to examine every tree within range we might find something."

The trooper snorted. Kane rolled the body over once more and looked into Lester's face. His lips were pulled back in a sick caricature of a smile and his eyes stared unseeing at the sky.

Maybe he's looking at God right now, Kane thought. If so, I'll bet he wishes he'd led a better life.

"You should get on the horn and call for a helicopter," he said aloud. "Get the body to a competent ME and criminologists as soon as possible."

"Right," Slade said sarcastically. "We've got the budget to be flying dead people around."

For an instant, rage reddened the edges of Kane's vision. He fought it back, stood up, and looked at the trooper.

"Listen, kid, and listen good," he said. The trooper took a step back. He could hear the anger in Kane's voice, too.

"I don't give a shit if you're happy in your job. I could care less if you like me, or wish I was a thousand miles away. But here are the facts. I know a lot more about this sort of thing than you do. More than that, I make one phone call, and you've got the brass crawling up your ass asking why you didn't take the advice of a veteran police officer. Probably be the end of your short, unhappy career in law enforcement. So get on your telephone and order that chopper. I'm going up to the mine, and I'll send those guys you ran off back down to guard the scene. When they get here, you can come on up and ask Charlie Simms some questions, if he's in any shape to answer."

The trooper opened his mouth to say something. Kane cut him off.

"And if you give me the slightest reason, and I mean the slightest reason, you're going to be sitting in a little office in Anchorage answering questions from internal affairs, or whatever it is your team calls the shoo flies, about why you blew off the Faith Wright investigation."

Kane and Slade looked at each other for a long moment, until the trooper dropped his eyes. The two men walked back to the cruiser and got in. Kane sat in the passenger's seat, soaking up heat and listening to the trooper's cell phone call requesting a helicopter. He was surprised at the way he'd attacked the kid, but something about being involved in an investigation, two investigations now, the return of the old rhythms and procedures, made him feel more confident.

"They're laughing at me," the trooper said, putting his hand over the mouthpiece.

"Give me the phone," Kane said, digging out his wallet and removing the card the trooper brass hat had given him. He broke the connection and punched in the number on the back of the card.

"This is Nik Kane," he said. "We met a couple days ago. I'm out in Devil's Toe now. Somebody hit the mine payroll and killed one of the guards. Maybe you knew him? Lester Logan? Used to be APD? Anyway, the body needs to get back to Anchorage right away for processing, and whoever is answering the phone at trooper headquarters in Anchorage"—he put his hand over the phone and said, "You did call Anchorage, right?" and the trooper nodded—"yeah, in Anchorage, is being a dickhead about sending a chopper." He listened for a minute. "Of course this is going to cause some shit," he said. "We shouldn't be wasting time talking about the obvious." He listened some more. "Okay," he said, and hung up.

"There'll be a chopper in the air within five minutes," he said.

"Who was that?" the trooper asked.

Kane ignored the question.

"I just thought of something else that needs attention," he said, getting out of the cruiser. The trooper did the same. Kane walked around to where he could see the crime scene.

"From the grooves in that berm beside the road, it looks like somebody pulled up alongside and forced them off," he said. "So the perps must have had four-wheel drive."

"Fat lot of good that does," the trooper replied. "There's hardly anybody out here who doesn't."

"Yeah," Kane said, "but maybe this one left some paint behind. Let's look."

The two men walked over and examined the left side of the Explorer.

"Nothing," the trooper said.

The two men stood there for a moment.

"I'm headed up to the mine," Kane said. "Come on up when you're relieved."

He walked back toward his truck.

"Hey," the trooper called, "you're the one who should be staying here."

Kane ignored him, got into his pickup, drove off the road, around the cruiser and the crime scene, then back onto the road and up to the mine. He found the front gate open and nobody in the box. He drove to the trailer where Simms had his office and walked in. He walked past the secretary, who called, "Wait a minute." He ignored her, opened the door to the conference room, and walked in. For the first time since he'd gotten out of prison, he was feeling like he was in his element, in control.

Richardson, the mine manager, was sitting at the table with a couple of other suits and the two men the trooper had run off.

"Take your pal here, Tony, and go back down and se-cure the crime scene," Kane said. "Then send the trooper on up here."

"You taking over, then, Nik?" Tony asked him.

"Just temporarily," he said, "until somebody with more experience shows up."

Tony and his companion got to their feet.

"Wait a minute," Richardson said, "where do you two think you're going? I'm in charge here."

A slow smile spread across Tony's face.

"That's the way you want it, fine," he said, "but if you want the payroll back, your best bet is to let all of us do what we know how to do."

The mine manager looked from Tony to Kane to the other suits. Finally he looked at Kane again.

"You sure you know what you're doing?" he asked.

Kane waved a hand at Tony and his companion.

"Take off," he said, "and don't let anybody touch anything."

"Aw, jeez, Nik," Tony said, "who do you think you're talking to?"

The two men left the room. Kane took a chair.

"Do these two know about the payroll-shipment arrangements," he said, nodding at the other suits, "or should we be talking alone?"

"They know," Richardson said.

"Great," Kane said. "How many others?"

"Just us," the mine manager said, "and, of course, Simms. It's only the people who need to know. Reynolds here is the chief accountant, and Lewes is the head of employee relations."

"Uh huh," Kane said. "I don't suppose that their secretaries might have found out, or anybody else who works in the office?"

"We keep the information to ourselves," the one called Reynolds said. He didn't sound very convincing.

"Never mind," Kane said. "Tell me about the arrangements for this shipment."

The mine manager hesitated, looking at the other two suits.

"Look," Kane said, "you want your best chance at recovering the payroll, talk. Otherwise, don't."

Richardson sighed and started talking.

"We used to deliver the payroll the same way every time. Armored car from a bank in Fairbanks. But a few months ago, Charlie suggested we start changing up. He was getting nervous about being so predictable. 'It's a four-hour trip, and there's lots of places to waylay that armored car,' he said.

"It made sense to change up the arrangements, so we did. We still use the armored car from time to time, but we've flown the money in in a small plane, and had it driven down in an unmarked car. The four of us pick a method the day before the shipment, and that's how it's delivered."

"How was it delivered this time?" Kane asked.

"Airplane," Richardson said. "Simms and Logan met it at the landing strip."

"Wait a minute," Kane said, "I drove by the landing strip coming from Rejoice. I didn't see anybody waiting."

"That's a different strip," Reynolds said. "The Devil's Toe strip is up the highway a ways."

"How much money did they get?" Kane asked.

Reynolds looked at a printout that lay in front of him.

"One hundred thirty-seven thousand, three hundred thirty-four dollars and seventeen cents," he said.

"Not much for an operation this size," Kane said.

"Some of the men have their salaries deposited directly into the bank," Reynolds said.

"And we're down to a skeleton crew right now," the mine manager said. "Gold prices are kind of soft."

"Still," Kane said, "if whoever did this had waited until summer, they could have gotten—what?—twice that? With enough overtime, three times?"

"True," Richardson said, "but a hundred thirty-seven thousand dollars is nothing to sneeze at."

Kane was silent for a moment.

"Any idea who might have done this?" he asked.

The three men looked at one another and all shook their heads.

"I know Simms was worried that somebody inside the mine would be involved," the mine manager said.

"So he must have thought it would be one of you three," Kane said, "since you keep the payroll information so secret."

The three men looked at one another again.

"Look," Richardson said, "the truth is, I don't know who might have known about the shipment. This office isn't all that big, and the walls aren't all that thick."

Kane got to his feet.

"So you've got—what?—seventy, eighty people working here now, and any of them might be involved?" he said. "And some of them have got families who might have heard, and others get drunk at the roadhouse and might tell anybody? What were you people thinking?"

No one said anything.

"Okay," Kane said, looking at the mine manager, "why don't you show me where Charlie Simms is?"

Richardson went into his office and came out wearing a coat. Kane followed him out the door and across to a prefab wooden building.

"Look, it won't do any good to stress the negative," Richardson said as they walked. "It'll only make trouble. For your friend Simms, as well as everyone else."

Kane followed the mine manager into the building, down a short hall, and into what could only be a clinic. Charlie Simms lay on an examining table under a light blanket, an IV dripping something into his arm, and wires running from his body to a couple of machines. A small black man with a trim goatee sat on a chair next to him, making notes on a clipboard.

"This is Divinity Aaron, our medic," the mine manager said to Kane.

"Mr. Aaron," Kane said, "how's the patient?"

"He took a heck of a blow," the medic said. "Seems a little concussed but otherwise okay. His pulse is strong, and so's his blood pressure. I've got fluid running to keep him hydrated."

Simms's eyes fluttered open.

"Who's there?" he whispered.

"It's me," Kane said, "Nik Kane. How you doing, Charlie?"

"Head hurts like hell," Simms whispered.

"Can you tell me what happened?" Kane asked.

Simms closed his eyes. The silence stretched out so long that Kane thought he'd gone to sleep. Then Simms cleared his throat.

"Can I have a drink of water?" he asked.

The medic picked up a plastic cup with a straw in it and held it to Simms's lips. Simms lifted his head a little, groaned, and drank. His head fell back on the pillow.

"I can't remember," Simms said, his voice a little stronger. "I remember meeting the airplane at the Devil's Toe airstrip, getting the money, driving back. But after turning onto the mine road . . . nothing. God, my head hurts."

"Might be better if you let him rest for a while," the medic said.

"Okay," Kane said. "There's a doctor coming over from Rejoice. I'll send him by here to check Charlie out. There's a trooper helicopter headed this way, too, so if he needs to go to town to get checked out, we can send him on that."

"Don't want to go to town," Simms said. "Want to catch whoever did this to me."

"I'm sure you do, Charlie," Kane said. "I'm sure you do." To the medic, he said, "You take a gun off him?"

The medic pulled open a drawer and handed Kane an automatic. It was a Glock 17. Not Kane's favorite weapon, but dependable and relatively cheap. Kane popped out the clip, then worked the slide. A round arced out onto the floor. The clip was full, and the gun didn't smell of gunpowder.

"Hasn't been fired," Kane said, reloading it and replacing it in the drawer. "Lester's shotgun hadn't been, either. So none of our bad guys is leaking blood."

He looked around the room, saw Simms's clothes hanging on a chair, and scooped them up.

"I'll bring you some more clothes, Charlie," he said, "but these are going to the crime lab."

Simms didn't reply. Kane walked out of the clinic, followed by the mine manager.

"Why are you taking his clothes?" Richardson asked. "You don't think he's involved, do you?"

"Standard procedure," Kane said. "The lab might be able to lift something that tells us about the perps."

The trooper pulled up as they reached the mine manager's office. Kane stuffed Simms's clothes into a big evidence bag. His coat was too big to fit, so the mine manager went off to find a garbage bag.

"You can try Simms if you want to," Kane said to Slade, "but he's pretty loopy and says he doesn't remember anything about the crime."

"I suppose he'll keep," the trooper said. "I wonder if they've got any coffee in there."

"I'm sure they do," Kane said, and led the way into the office trailer.

From there they went to search Charlie Simms's quarters, in a nest of prefabs as far from the mill house as they could be and still be inside the fence. Even at that distance, Kane could feel a light shaking in the floor. The quarters were about the size of a decent hotel suite: bedroom, bathroom, living room, and kitchen.

The search didn't take long. There were a few clothes in the closet and dresser, shampoo, shaving gear, cholesterol medicine, and Viagra in the bathroom.

"Viagra?" Slade said. "What's he want with Viagra out here?"

"Good question," Kane said, "although just because he has it with him doesn't mean he's using it."

There was beer in the refrigerator, canned food in the cupboards and dirty dishes in the sink, a paperback western on a table next to one of the armchairs, a row of videotapes beneath the big TV. About what Kane expected to find in a construction camp room.

By five p.m., they were back in the trooper's office. They'd examined the Explorer thoroughly, searched Logan's locker and Simms's office, and come up with zip. They sent Lester Logan's body and Simms's clothes back to Anchorage on the helicopter. The pilot said that a couple of trooper investigators were on their way out from Anchorage by car.

The doctor from Rejoice had said he couldn't tell how serious Charlie Simms's injuries were, and he'd be happier if Simms went to town for evaluation and observation. So Kane had packed him a bag, and they'd loaded Simms on the chopper, too, along with the medic.

"Just make sure he gets to the hospital okay," the mine manager told the medic. "We'll charter you back here in the morning."

The medic had grinned at the prospect of a night in town.

After the now fully loaded helicopter left, Kane and Slade made one more eyeball scan of the area before the light left completely, found nothing new, and reopened the road. In between all that, they'd done a lot of waiting, eaten a lunch the mine's kitchen had knocked together for them, and drunk a lot of the mine's coffee.

"Any ideas about this?" Slade asked. He had his hat off, his collar open, and his stocking feet up on his desk. His hair was a mess, and he looked about twelve.

"Lots," Kane said, "but nothing that bears sharing right now. I guess what we do for the time being is wait and hope Simms's memory comes back. And you can keep an eye out for anybody spending more money than he ought to have. Or taking any spur-of-the-moment vacations."

The trooper nodded.

"You think we'll catch whoever did it?" he asked.

"Oh, I'm sure of it," Kane said.

Slade dropped his feet onto the floor and leaned forward.

"What do you know that I don't?" he asked, so earnestly that it made Kane laugh.

"There aren't enough hours in the day for me to answer that question," Kane said. "But as far as this holdup goes, just keep your shirt on. Part of being a good detective is knowing when to press and when to wait."

The trooper settled back in his chair.

"I'm sorry I was so snotty this morning," he said. "It's just that life here is a lot more complicated than it might look, and I'm not sure I'm cut out to handle it, even with-out robberies and murders."

"That's not what we were having difficulties about," Kane said. "Remember? We were arguing about Faith Wright."

The trooper tensed at the mention of her name. Kane stood up.

"I'm leaving now," he said. "Monday, if you're still not too busy with the robbery, I'm going to want you to ac-company me to the high school so I can search the girl's locker."

Slade started to say something, but Kane held up his hand.

"Between now and then," he said, "I want you to think about how you're going to handle this. If you're wrapped around the axle in some way that involves doing your job right, decide how you're going to deal with that. Just don't think that one of your options is to stonewall me or lean on me or somehow get me to go away. Because that's not go-ing to happen."

The trooper looked at Kane steadily for more than a minute.

"What makes you think I've got a problem doing my job?" he asked in a voice that sounded as young as he looked.

Kane laughed.

"I've made a few mistakes, too," he said.

He put on his coat.

"Some of them," he said, turning to go, "the not-so-serious ones, happened early in my career, and older and wiser heads helped me out. I'm offering you the same kind of help I got. You'd be smart to take it."

And he went down, and talked with the woman; and she pleased Samson well.

JUDGES 14:7

KANE WAS EARLY FOR HIS DINNER WITH RUTH HUNT, SO he decided to stop in the bar to hear what Devil's Toe was talking about. From the looks of the place, everyone within a hundred-mile radius had made the same decision. Small-town Friday night, Kane thought. The only thing thicker than the crowd was the cloud of cigarette smoke that filled the room. The only thing thicker than that were the rumors flying around.

Kane felt something like panic crawling up his throat. Too many people, too much noise. He took a deep breath and got a lungful of smoke. Coughing, he forced his way toward the bar.

I've got to get past this, he thought, or I'm not going to be worth a damn at anything but sitting in my apartment staring at the walls.

As he shouldered through the crowd, Kane overheard snippets of conversation. Everybody was talking about one thing.

"I heard there was a half dozen mine guards killed," one man said.

"The payroll was more than a million," said another a little farther along.

"They're sending in some kinda strike force," a woman with a snake tattooed on her left shoulder told a long-haired guy with a ring in his nose. The woman had clearly been spending a lot of time pumping iron, and the long-haired guy was muscles from head to toe.

"I heard," the guy said. "Maybe a SWAT team, too. That kid trooper ain't up to this."

By the time Kane reached the corner of the bar, his nerves were twitching like live wires. I really need a drink, he thought as he caught the bartender's attention.

He wanted to order a beer, just one, but he knew there couldn't be just one for him. He forced himself to say, "Club soda with a twist."

The bartender, a thin, greasy-haired, shifty-looking character who had a scar of his own on his right cheek, gave him a pitying look.

"Sure you don't want a glass of milk?" he asked with a sneer in his voice. "That what the fast crowd in Anchorage is drinking now?"

Kane reached across and laid a hand on the bartender's shoulder, pulling him close.

"Believe me, pal," he said in a low voice, "the last thing you want is for me to start drinking."

The bartender drew back, rubbing his shoulder.

"No need to be acting so tough," he said, moving away.

Actually there's every need, Kane thought. Act soft in a place like this, and they'd pull you down like a pack of wolves. The only difference between this place and prison is that there weren't any guards in gun towers to make them think twice.

The bartender returned and set a glass in front of Kane.

"That'll be three dollars," he said.

"For club soda?" Kane asked.

"It's the freight," the bartender said.

Kane smiled at the punch line to the old Alaska joke, handed him a five-dollar bill, and said, "How do you know I'm from Anchorage?"

The bartender gave him another pitying look.

"This here is Devil's Toe," he said, laying a couple of wrinkled one-dollar bills on the bar in front of Kane. "A half hour after you take a dump everybody knows what color it was."

Kane stood there drinking his club soda and taking in the scene, wishing that his fellow drinkers smoked less and bathed more. He wondered which of them, if any, had been involved in the robbery or knew something about it. Or knew something about Faith Wright's whereabouts. Anyone who did would be unlikely to simply walk up and tell an outsider.

The crowd ignored him until the woman with the snake tattoo forced her way over and stood next to him. Up close, she had a flat face that was cracked and seamed like the face of a glacier, a big nose that had been broken and badly reset, and eyebrows that had grown into one. There was a cluster of rings on one side of that brow.

"You're some kinda cop, ain't ya?" she asked, her voice loud to be heard over the noise of the crowd.

"Some kinda cop," he replied. "That's about right."

"What you know about the robbery?" she asked.

Kane set his empty glass down on the bar.

"Robbery?" he said. "There's been a robbery?"

The woman examined his face.

"You just being funny?" she asked.

"I'm here looking for Faith Wright," he said. "You know anything about that?"

"You mean that little Angel that disappeared?" the woman said. "No, I wouldn't be knowing any of the Angels. I'm sort of on the other team."

"You work here?" Kane asked.

"Me?" the woman said. "Nope, you won't find me making beds or slinging hash."

"How about at night?" Kane said.

The woman gave a hoot of laughter and examined his face again.

"You're kidding, right? Who'd pay money to fuck me?" she said.

She giggled and punched Kane on the shoulder. The blow sent a bolt of pain shooting down his arm.

"You got a pair on you, asking me a question like that," she said, turning to leave. "I told Herman what you said, he'd pinch your head off. See you later, Mr. Some Kinda Cop."

Kane waved the bartender over and handed him a twenty.

"Get those two whatever they're drinking on me," he said, nodding to the tattooed woman and her companion, "and keep the change."

He wriggled his way through the crowd and through the partition into the café.

The café was full. Ruth Hunt was sitting at a corner table, chatting with the waitress named Tracy. The two of them were laughing. Ruth put her hand on Tracy's arm. The waitress responded by reaching down and stroking aside some hair that had fallen over Ruth's face. She looked up and saw Kane watching them.

"Oh, Mr. Kane, right on time," she said. "Meet Tracy, our waitress."

Kane nodded at the waitress as he slid into a chair opposite Ruth.

"Tracy and I have met," he said. "In fact, I was an overnight guest in this establishment."

"I'd better get back to work," Tracy said. "That was a G-and-T for you, Ruth. And what are you having, Mr. Kane?"

"Nik," Kane said. "I'm drinking water."

The waitress went off and Kane looked over at Ruth Hunt. She was wearing a long-sleeved black mock turtleneck sweater, just a touch of makeup, and no jewelry. Her long, black hair had been brushed until it shone. The overall effect was neither provocative nor frumpy.

"How do you do that?" Kane asked.

"Do what?"

"Manage to be so much yourself wherever you are?"

"Is that good or bad?" she said, arching an eyebrow.

"Oh, it's good," Kane said. "Very, very good."

She smiled at him.

"Thank you," she said.

They talked for a while about the mine robbery, Kane giving her the pertinent facts and Ruth recounting the rumors she'd heard. Ruth set her nearly finished drink down and said, "So, when you stayed here did you use all of the amenities?"

Kane could see slyness creep into her smile.

"You mean, did I order up a woman?" Kane said. "No, I didn't, and I'm surprised that someone from a religious community would be interested in such things."

"Sin always interests the religious," Ruth said, laughing. "Sometimes it interests them too much. If you don't believe me, just listen to Moses Wright preach about the sins of the flesh. It's practically pornographic."

"Is that why you're friends with the waitress, who I have reason to believe has firsthand knowledge of those sins?" Kane asked.

"No," Ruth said, "I know Tracy from another life."

The waitress returned to take their orders.

"I'll have another one of these, too," Ruth said, rattling the ice in her glass. The waitress looked at Kane, who shook his head. She went off.

"Why are you drinking water?" Ruth asked.

"It's a long story," Kane said. "The short version is that when I start drinking, I have a hard time stopping. But I'd rather hear about you and our friend, Tracy."

Ruth looked at him for a moment and shrugged.

"Okay," she said. "I met Tracy again right after I came to Rejoice. It was summer, and I made a point of introducing myself around. Small towns are supposed to be friendly, and I thought it would be a good way to establish myself, to start fitting in. But when the residents of Rejoice heard about it, several of them decided to counsel me about staying away from the unbelievers. I decided to counsel them about minding their own business. So I guess you might say that Tracy is part of the reason I sort of got off on the wrong foot in Rejoice."

"And have you gotten back on the right foot?"

Ruth shrugged.

"I'm not sure what foot I'm on there," she said. She raised one hand, palm up. "On the one hand, I have my differences with the more saintly element in Rejoice." She raised the other hand, palm up. "On the other, I've lowered the cost of their food service by eleven percent." She made a rocking motion with her hands. "So I guess I'd say Rejoice has learned to live with me."

Their conversation was interrupted by the arrival of her drink. They chatted for a while about Kane's police days, and he found himself telling her things he had never told anyone but Laurie about the life, about the challenges, the scrapes, the satisfactions, and the camaraderie.

"You make police work sound like fun," Ruth said. Then, after a pause, "I don't imagine prison was as enjoyable."

"I don't talk about prison much," Kane said. "I'm trying to put it behind me, in more ways than one."

"More ways than one?" she asked.

So Kane found himself telling her about his problems with open spaces and crowds and all the uncontained vitality of life outside the prison walls. She nodded and made encouraging noises and, when he'd finished, put a hand on his arm.

"I'm sure there are people who live in Rejoice as a way of dealing with just those problems," she said. "I know life here is much simpler than it was in other places for me. But you seem to be a strong person. I'm sure you can overcome this."

Logically, her words made no sense to Kane. They'd just met; she couldn't have any informed opinion about his capabilities. But what she said made him feel better just the same.

The waitress brought their meals and looked at Ruth Hunt's empty glass.

"I shouldn't," Ruth Hunt said. "I'm already feeling light-headed. But then I'm not driving."

"Not driving?" Kane said. "How did you get here?"

"I skied over."

"In this weather?"

"If you wait for it to warm up before you do anything,

you'll never do anything. Lots of people ski here, all the time. Why, even Moses Wright skis."

Kane tried to imagine the old man on skis and failed.

"I suppose that's all right," Kane said. "Still, skiing in this weather is dangerous. I'll give you a lift home, so if you want that drink, go ahead." At that, Ruth nodded and the waitress went off.

"Let's talk about you for a while," Kane said. "What brought you to Rejoice?"

The woman chewed and swallowed a forkful of vegetables.

"Well, I suppose you could call it lust," she said, laughing.

"Do tell," Kane said.

She did.

She was born and raised in North Pole, just outside Fairbanks, the youngest of the six children of devout Christian parents. Her dad was a civilian employee of the Air Force and her mother a stay-at-home mom.

"We went to the public schools—this was back before home schooling became popular—but religion was really the major force in our lives," she said. "We listened to KJNP—you know, King Jesus North Pole—and went to Bible study twice a week and church on Sundays and Bible camp in the summers. We didn't smoke or drink or date." She stopped to take a drink of her new G-and-T. "We were damned holy, is what we were."

But the older she got, Ruth said, the less appealing all of that was.

"I couldn't help but notice that women held only subservient roles," she said, "and that just didn't look like enough for me."

So when her parents were ready to send her off to a Christian college, she rebelled and joined the Army.

"I wanted combat infantry," she said, "and the Army, in its wisdom, taught me how to run a food service. I ran a mess tent in Saudi during the Gulf War. My biggest problem was keeping sand and scorpions out of the food. That wasn't why I'd joined up, so when my commitment was up, I left."

"I didn't know what I was going to do next. I was still in my twenties and kind of floating. I thought about college, but it didn't really appeal to me. Nobody was much interested in somebody who knew how to run a mess tent, so I was waitressing to pay the bills. That's where I met Tracy. We had some fun. Out-all-night, sleep-all-day kind of fun."

"Doesn't sound like the life for a Christian girl," Kane said.

"It wasn't," Ruth said, "and after a while it got to be not so much fun. Seemed kind of hollow, really. So one Sunday I decided to go back to my old family church. And the man giving a guest lecture about life in an isolated religious community was Gregory Pinchon."

She stopped to eat for a while, shaking her head from time to time, then resumed.

"I'd never seen a more gorgeous man. He was such a babe and he made Rejoice sound so good, kind of like North Pole when I was growing up, that I was just sort of swept away. I moved here. A year later we started walking out, and a year after that we were married."

She ate some more, still shaking her head. Kane finished his steak and set down his knife and fork.

"So you've been married for—what?—seven years?" he said. "How is it going?"

Ruth finished her dinner, taking her time, not speaking. Tracy cleared the dishes away and brought them coffee.

"I haven't told anyone this," she said at last. "I can't imagine why I'm telling you, except that you make me feel comfortable somehow. Plus I've had too much to drink. But the truth is, it's not going well at all. Matthew has never accepted me, and his father and I have less and less to do with each other. Maybe I'm telling you too much, but we don't have physical relations very often."

"What's wrong?"

"I don't know what's wrong. Greg is very immature. His first wife was much older than he. She mothered him and then left him, which must have been confusing, and he just sort of retreated into his work and worship. I thought he'd make room for me, and I think he thought he would, too. But after a while he just quit trying, particularly when my independence became an embarrassment. Plus, we don't really agree on religious matters, which is so much more important in Rejoice than anywhere else."

She was quiet for a moment.

"Listen to me, pouring my heart out. I knew that third G-and-T was a mistake. Anyway, I decided a couple of months ago to leave him, and Rejoice, and I've been living with that decision since, sort of seeing how it feels."

"And?" Kane said.

"And it feels more right all the time. I should have my replacement trained in another month or two, and then I'm gone."

"Where will you go?"

"I don't know, and that's one of the things that keeps me here. That sounds sort of low, but it's true."

"I think inertia is a much underestimated force in human affairs," Kane said. "I suspect it's part of the reason Laurie stuck with me for all those years."

"Laurie?" Ruth said.

So Kane, to his surprise, told her the story of his own marriage and how it was ending. Once he started, he found himself telling her things he'd never told anyone else, about his bad behavior and his hurt and his regrets. The story lasted through coffee, through Kane paying the bill, through warming up his truck, through loading the woman's skis and boots into the back, and through setting out for Rejoice. When he'd finished, they drove along in silence, listening to the heater and their own thoughts.

He drove across the river and along the road, past the airstrip and Moses Wright's house, past the community building, and toward Ruth's house. Just short of it, she said, "I'd like to see the flowers." So Kane drove to the big greenhouse, and they let themselves in.

"It's just so . . . so glorious in here," she said. She took off her coat, dropped it, and walked along the aisles with her arms held out, turning slowly in full circles. "I wish my whole life was as wild and beautiful as this."

She ran back to Kane, threw her arms around his neck,

and kissed him. The first kiss was tentative. The second sizzling. The third molten.

"I knew it," she said, pulling her face away from his. "I knew it would be like this."

They stood looking at each other. Kane felt light-headed and a little dazed.

"I so want to make love right now," she said. "I so want to take you home with me, but Matthew is there. Do you think we could make a bed here somehow?"

Kane took a deep breath and tried to slow the blood racing through his veins.

"That might not be the wisest thing," he said. "I'm sure people saw us driving out here and will notice how long we stay. I can't afford to let something like that get in the way of my investigation and you . . . you just can't afford it, period. Besides, I'm not sure my heart could stand it, anyway."

Ruth smiled and started to move away, but he held her there and kissed her again. The kiss seemed to last an hour. Kane could feel his self-discipline melting like snow in the hot sun, so he pulled away. He wasn't sure what would happen if he lost control, and he didn't want to find out. Besides, he was too old to get involved with a married woman, and old enough to know they'd never get away with it in a place the size of Rejoice.

Boy, he thought, I seem to need a lot of convincing about this.

Ruth stepped back and ran her fingers through her hair, shaking it out.

"I'm sure you're right," she said, "but I had those drinks and I'm just so horny."

She giggled and put a hand to her mouth, then stood breathing for a while.

"I'm sorry," she said. "I know I shouldn't behave this way." They stood quietly for a minute. Then Ruth shook her head again. "I don't know why I'm apologizing. I'm sure there's no reason sex shouldn't be important for Christian women, too."

"I'm sure there's not," Kane said, helping her into her coat.

They got into the pickup and drove along in silence until Kane broke it.

"Why did Matthew stay home from the basketball trip, anyway?" he asked.

"If only he hadn't," she said. She shrugged. "I'm not sure why, unless it was to keep an eye on me. He said he wasn't feeling well, but I didn't see any sign of it."

"What kind of a kid is he?"

"Complicated. Self-assured one minute, full of doubt the next. And, I think, beneath all that, pretty angry."

"Angry?" Kane said. "Why?"

Ruth was silent for a while.

"I suppose because his mother left him. And I think his rejection by Faith hurt him more than he will say. He's talking about joining the military now instead of going to college, and the way he talks about it makes me think he wants to do it because there's a chance he'll get to hurt people."

"Maybe I should talk to him," Kane said, as if to himself, "tell him that hurting people isn't all that much fun." To Ruth, he said, "Do you think he's capable of hurting anyone here? In Rejoice?"

Ruth was silent again.

"I don't know," she said finally. "Maybe. Why, do you suspect he had something to do with Faith's disappearance?"

"I don't really think anything yet," Kane said. He paused. "No, that's not true. I think Faith Wright is or was hiding something, and that her disappearance wasn't voluntary."

"Hiding something? In Rejoice? If she is, she's a much more complex person than I, or anyone else, thought. And why would anyone want her to disappear?"

"I don't know yet, but I'll find out."

"You sound confident."

"I am," Kane said. "There are a lot of things in life I'm not good at, but I'm a damned good detective."

They reached Ruth's home, a prefab a couple of houses

down from his cabin. It was ablaze with lights. He pulled into the driveway and helped her unload her skis. He could see Matthew Pinchon's shadow as the young man watched them through the curtains.

"I'd invite you in," she said, smiling, "but I'm sure Matthew wouldn't like that. Besides, Clarice is no doubt watching us, and I'm afraid the sight of that would make her eyeballs fall out of her head."

"We wouldn't want that," Kane said.

Ruth reached out and gave his arm a squeeze.

"Thanks for a wonderful evening," she said. "And take care of yourself. Whoever shot at you last night is still out there."

"Don't worry," he said, "I'm not about to let myself get killed just when my life has gotten so much more interesting."

Ruth went into the house. Kane got back in his truck and drove the short distance to his cabin. No one shot at him as he plugged in his pickup and let himself into the cabin.

He flipped on the lights. The place had been torn apart. His clothes and camping gear were strewn about the single room, his CDs tossed all over. He stood looking at the mess for a moment. Then he built a fire in the wood stove. He went around picking up his belongings and putting them back into their bags. He found his copy of Eric Clapton's *Unplugged* on the floor of the bathroom in two pieces. That had taken some effort, so destroying it had been a calculated act of spite. Having his stuff handled made Kane mad, but the fact that someone had gone to the trouble told him he was on the right track.

I must be onto something, he thought as he got ready for bed. Now if I could just figure out what.

He was actually happy the cabin had been ransacked, until he came upon his coffee, dumped into the kitchen sink with what looked like his shampoo poured all over it.

"I'll get you for that," he said aloud, thinking of mornings without coffee stretching out into the future. "I'll solve this case and hunt you down, and God help you when I do."

But as he lay there waiting for sleep to come, he found himself thinking not about Faith Wright, but about Ruth Hunt.

15

The whole head is sick, and the whole heart faint.

ISAIAH 1:5

KANE AWOKE EARLY AGAIN. THE ROOM WAS COLD, AND with no chance of coffee, the prospect of climbing out of his sleeping bag appealed to him not at all. He lay there thinking about Ruth Hunt and dozing for a while, then wriggled around until he could reach his Bible and flashlight. He turned on the light, held it in his mouth, and leafed through the Bible. He did this for several minutes before setting the book down and shutting off the flashlight. Then he climbed out of the bag, put on some long underwear and socks, and started a fire in the stove. He whistled as he did so. When the stove started throwing off heat, he went into the bathroom, where he stripped and showered, singing Van Morrison tunes in a voice that would have brought the Irish rocker to his knees in tears. When he was shaved and dressed, he loaded everything into his pickup and looked at his watch. Not quite six a.m. He locked up the cabin and drove to the community building.

The lights in the cafeteria came on as he pulled into the parking lot. A couple of men wearing white uniforms and white paper hats were putting out containers of food.

"Ruth Hunt?" Kane said.

"I'll tell her you're here," one of the men said, heading into the kitchen for another container.

When the men finished loading the line, Kane picked up a tray. He spooned canned peaches into a bowl. He filled a second bowl with oatmeal and sprinkled brown sugar over the top. He filled a cup with hot water, picked up a package of tea, and carried his tray to the nearest table. Then he went back for silverware and a paper napkin. He'd just taken his first bite of oatmeal when Ruth came out and sat across from him.

"You're an early riser," she said.

"You should talk," he said. "You must get up before the chickens."

"Not usually," she said, "but my kitchen manager had to go to town for some emergency dental work. I didn't find out until I got home last night, so it's a good thing we weren't any later."

Kane felt himself starting to blush.

"Good for Rejoice," he said, "but not so good for me."

He ate some oatmeal.

"How do you manage to get up so early and stay up so late?" he asked.

"I take a nap in the afternoon," she said, grinning wickedly. "Just me, all alone in a big old bed."

The two of them sat there looking at each other. I must look like a teenager making moony eyes at his girl, Kane thought.

"I woke up early," he said, grinning back, "so like any good resident of Rejoice, I read my Bible. And I couldn't find a word about tea in it."

Ruth looked at him and nodded.

"I might have known," she said. "I've probably told a hundred people the same story, and nobody ever checked up on me before."

"Once a detective, always a detective," Kane said. "But surely Moses Wright knows the truth."

"The truth is, I told Moses Wright that if he didn't allow

coffee, I was going to serve wine with every meal. Wine is in the Bible. So we compromised on tea."

"Moses Wright made that decision?" Kane asked. "I thought his son was in charge in Rejoice, at least in civil matters."

"He is now. That decision was made several years ago. Moses Wright handed the administration of Rejoice off to Thomas after Thomas's wife died. Everyone thought he was trying to take Thomas's mind off his troubles. Moses said he wanted to spend more time with his Bible. The administration runs much smoother now, but the change wasn't all good. Moses' sermons keep getting longer and longer."

Kane laughed.

"I guess Moses Wright has his followers, though," he said. "The older people certainly seem to be behind him, and I hear your stepson is a student of his."

"Matthew is an intensely religious young man. He studies daily with Moses Wright and can't say enough good things about him."

She shrugged.

"To each his own, I guess."

"I'd love to stay and tuck you in for your nap," Kane said, "but I've got to drive to Anchorage and see to a few things."

"What about your search for Faith?"

"My next step is to talk to her high school teachers and friends and search her locker, but I can't do that on the weekend anyway. I should be back by the time school opens Monday. I don't suppose there's any way you could come with me?"

A long silence ensued. Kane ducked his head and ate. When he was finished, he sipped his tea.

"I was impetuous last night," Ruth said finally. "I don't regret it, but that's not really who I am or how I handle things. So, no, I can't accompany you."

"I didn't think you would, but you can't kill a guy for trying."

"That depends on what he's trying, doesn't it?"

She reached out and covered his hand with hers.

"If you're driving to town, you'll need a lunch. I'll go make you one."

He sat sipping his tea, watching the early arrivals picking up their food and chatting. For a moment he wished he were one of them. As his world became more complicated, the appeal of Rejoice's simplicity increased. He knew he couldn't settle here with Ruth, but maybe somewhere else. Maybe having her in his life would help him shake off prison and make sense of the rest of the world. Maybe that's what all this religion on his mind was about, making life make more sense.

Ruth came back with a brown paper bag and set it in front of him, then sat and leaned close to him.

"I'm sorry if I'm giving you mixed signals," she said, "but I guess it's a reflection of my own confusion."

Kane patted her on the shoulder and got to his feet.

"If you aren't confused about life, you aren't paying attention," he said.

He picked up his tray and carried it to the counter, walking along with Ruth like they belonged together. Then he put on his coat, picked up his brown paper bag, and went out to the truck.

He drove to Thomas Wright's cabin. No lights showed. He walked up and hammered on the door with a gloved fist. After he pounded a second time, he heard the sounds of someone rustling around inside. As he waited for the door to open, he realized that the air temperature had warmed some. Must be cloud cover, he thought.

Thomas Wright opened the door. His hair was uncombed and he was wearing an old flannel robe. His legs, clad in long underwear, stuck out of the robe and ended in big fur slippers.

"Mr. Kane," he said, opening the door so the detective could step in. "What brings you out this early? Have you learned something about Faith?"

The inside of the cabin was cool but not cold. Kane made a show of not being able to see his breath.

"We have electric heat," Thomas Wright said. "Rank has its privileges, I guess."

Kane took off his coat, walked into the living room, and sat down. Wright moved in to join him.

"My cabin was searched while I was out yesterday," Kane said. "There was no sign of forced entry, so I assume the searcher had a key. You weren't there looking for something, were you?"

Wright looked at Kane like he'd grown an extra head.

"Why would I search your things?" he asked. "I'm the one who asked you to work for us."

"Why people do things is often elusive," Kane said, "even to themselves. But I didn't really think it was you. How hard would it be for someone to get a key to that cabin?"

Thomas Wright thought for a minute.

"Not that difficult, I suppose. We lock things mainly as a means of impulse control. People, particularly young people, often have poor impulse control. But if someone really wanted to get in somewhere? The head of physical plant has a set of master keys. So does the chief of the volunteer fire department. And there are a couple of sets in the administrative offices. These keys aren't secret, so anyone with a little bit of guile could get their hands on them."

Kane nodded.

"I figured it would be something like that." He took the keys to the cabin from his pocket. "I'm headed to Anchorage. When I come back, I'll find my own lodgings. No offense, but yours are a little too public for my tastes."

"Is the trip to Anchorage connected to your investigation?" Thomas Wright asked.

"To one of them," Kane said.

Wright raised an eyebrow.

"I really can't say more than that right now," Kane said. He got to his feet.

"I'll be back in a day or two," he said.

Wright walked him to the door.

"I'm sorry that Rejoice has proven so inhospitable," he said to Kane.

"Not your fault," the detective said. "You're not set up

for keeping an investigation private, and there's no reason you should be."

"And your investigation?" Wright said. "Is it going well?"

Kane shook his head.

"So far, it's like a winter day," he said. "Mostly darkness with a few glimmers of light. But I'm hoping for better soon."

"We'll say a prayer for you," Wright said.

"Do that," Kane said. "Can't hurt, might help."

When he was halfway to his truck, he stopped, turned, and retraced his steps.

"Sorry to bother you again," he said after Wright opened his door, "but do you happen to know where Gregory Pinchon's first wife is living these days?"

Wright thought for a moment.

"I don't," he said. "She left some time ago, you know. But I can try to find out."

"If it wouldn't be too much trouble," Kane said, "I'd appreciate it."

"Can you tell me why you want to know that?" Wright asked.

"I'm not really sure," Kane said with a smile. "It may not be important at all. But I'd still like to know."

His drive into Anchorage was fast and uneventful. The roads had been cleared, and although the skies were overcast, no snow fell. As he drove, he sorted his CDs into those that still played and those that were trash. There were quite a few of the latter. He knew he'd have to do some shopping to replace the damaged ones. He could live without a lot of things, but not music. The damaged CDs were pretty old—most music recorded since the early '70s left him cold—so maybe he'd be able to find replacements at a used music store.

He tried to sort out his thoughts about Faith Wright and his feelings about Ruth Hunt with less success. He didn't have enough information about the first, and he had too much about the second. Best to stick to what he knew and take one step at a time.

Kane stopped in Palmer to get a large coffee. The temperature was easily fifty degrees warmer than it had been in Rejoice. He took his time driving into Anchorage, sipping his coffee and thinking about what he had to do next.

He pulled into a downtown parking garage just after noon. He walked to the Fifth Avenue mall and spent an hour going through the stores, buying clothes that were not blue work shirts and jeans. He drove home, unloaded his truck, stripped off his clothes, and took a long shower, making the water as hot as he could stand. Then he got dressed: T-shirt, Levi's, athletic socks, and lightweight hiking boots. He stripped the tags off of his new clothes and took them, along with his dirty ones, downstairs to the laundry room. On his way back up, he stopped at the manager's door to collect his mail. Aside from junk aimed at current occupant, that consisted of a fat, white envelope with an Anchorage Police Department return address. Inside were his retirement forms, all filled out, and a note from Emily Lee telling him that if he would sign them and mail them back, she'd take care of the rest. There was even a stamped return envelope. Jeffords wasn't taking any chances.

He was hungry, so he opened the bag Ruth had given him. It contained a large tuna sandwich, a wizened winter apple, and three big homemade cookies. It also contained a handwritten note that said: "I want things to work out for us." The note was signed with an ornate capital R.

He bit into the sandwich, then walked to the refrigerator to get something to wash it down. He passed up the soda there for a glass of water. I must be watching my weight, he thought. But why? In prison, he'd stayed in shape because he knew that he might have to defend himself at any moment. But now? Now, he guessed, he really hoped that things would work out with Ruth and, if they did, he didn't want to be carrying around any spare tire. He hadn't been naked in front of any woman but Laurie for a long time, and he didn't want the sight to cause anybody to go blind. That didn't stop him from eating the cookies, though. One bite and he didn't stop until they were all gone.

Poor impulse control, he said, thinking about what Thomas Wright had said.

He went back down and transferred his clothes to the dryer. When he'd finished the lunch dishes, he picked up the telephone and dialed a number.

"Elder Thomas Wright, please," he said, then waited. "Tom? It's Nik Kane." Pause. "That's right, I'm in Anchorage. Any luck with the former Mrs. Pinchon?" Pause. "Not really, huh? That's too bad." Pause. "Well, what do you know?" Pause. "She used the name Feather, and folks think her last name was Boyette. Spell that for me, will you?" Pause. "Thanks. Anything else?" Pause. "Most people think she's living in Fairbanks but aren't really sure? Did you ask Pinchon?" Pause. "Yes, I can see how that might be awkward. Okay, thanks. See you."

He put the phone down, thought for a moment, picked it back up and dialed.

"Lieutenant Littlefield, please," he said, then waited some more. "Larry? Nik Kane." He paused, then laughed. "Yeah, it has been a long time. Longer for some than for others, though." Pause. "No, Larry, prison isn't as bad as you hear. It's worse." Pause. "I appreciate that, Larry. Anyway, I need some information. Anything you can get by running a name for me. First name's Feather, like 'feather pillow.' Last name's Boyette: B-O-Y-E-T-T-E." Pause. "Nope, I don't know that she has a record here or anywhere. So this could be a complete wild-goose chase." Pause. "Sure, ask the chief for his okay if you want. I'm on an errand for him." Pause. "Okay, let me give you my cell number." He rattled off the numbers. "I'm running around a lot right now, so you can leave whatever you find out on voice mail if you don't get me." Pause. "Yeah, I know, Larry. I'll be in touch and we can get together. Regards to Carol." Pause. "Oh, I hadn't heard. Regards to Heather, then. Bye."

Kane hung up the phone and sat thinking. Littlefield had followed him up through the ranks, been his partner on the detective squad at the time he'd been sent off to prison, and he'd never heard from the guy once. Now, on the phone, he sounded like someone talking to a bill collector. That attitude told him plenty.

"You can't go home again, pal," he said aloud. He took out a pen, signed the retirement forms everywhere there was an X, and sealed them in the return envelope. He might not know what he would do next, but he wasn't returning to the police department.

Kane tried reading Montaigne but couldn't concentrate. He forced himself to keep at it, but finally found himself reading the same paragraph for a third time. He put the book down and turned on the television. He watched part of a basketball game in which all the players could make spectacular dunks but couldn't hit a free throw. He turned it off, looked at his watch, and went down to get his laundry out of the dryer. Back up in his apartment, he hung what needed hanging and folded what needed folding. Then he looked at his watch. Time to go do something else I don't want to do, he thought. He consulted a telephone book and dialed a number.

"Charlie Simms's room, please," he said. After a wait, he said, "Nobody by that name? Thanks." He looked in the phone book and dialed another number, again asking for Simms's room. A pause. "He's in ICU? What happened?" Another pause. "Yeah, I know the rules about giving out patient information. Thanks."

He put the phone down, put on his coat, picked up the envelope, and went out. He drove to the post office and dropped the envelope in a drive-up box, then drove over to see what was up with Charlie Simms.

Providence Hospital was a big pile of building wings near the university. The place was always under construction, adding new facilities and equipment that fueled the increasing costs of health care. It'd been years since Kane had been in the place, so he had to wander around for a while before he found the intensive care unit.

Sitting outside it was Charlie Simms's wife—what was her name?—June, a short, stout woman with graying hair and glasses. She and Laurie had been friends in a casual

sort of way. Next to her sat a small, trim old guy Kane recognized as a retired cop. His name was Burke, and he'd
been Charlie's partner back in the day. Kane walked over
and sat down next to him.

"Hello, Burkey," he said. "June. How's Charlie?"

"Not good," Burke said. "What are you doing here,
Nik? I thought you'd still be in prison, but then I heard
you're back running errands for Jeffords."

Burke had taken an early out, Kane remembered, after
getting crossways with the chief somehow. Nobody who
got crossways with the chief lasted long. I'm a case in
point, Kane thought.

"Nope," he said, "I'm doing a private job. The force
doesn't want me back. You must have heard."

"Yeah, I guess I did," Burke said. "That's what loyalty
gets you. I told Charlie more than once that carrying Jeffords's water would turn out to be trouble."

"Now, Liam, that's enough," June Simms said. "The
chief was always good to Charlie, whatever your experience might have been."

"That's a good thing to say," Burke said, "in front of
Jeffords's old brownnoser."

June gasped.

"That's enough, Burke," Kane said, dropping a hand onto
Burke's forearm and squeezing. "Why don't you take a walk
now, and come back when you feel like not being a jackass."

Burke pulled his arm loose, got to his feet, and walked
away.

"I don't know why Charlie puts up with that man," June
said. "He's so full of hate."

"They're old partners, June," Kane said, "and loyalty
was always important to Charlie."

The two of them sat for a while in silence, which Kane
finally broke.

"Can you tell me what happened, June?" he said.
"When we put Charlie on the helicopter, he seemed to not
be in any danger."

"They don't know exactly what happened, Nik. They
had him in a room here for observation. Standard practice

with head trauma, they said. I was sitting next to his bed and we were talking—Charlie was actually talking about retiring, if you can believe it—when he suddenly stopped making sense. I rang for the nurse and by the time she arrived he was in convulsions."

Her voice had been filling with tears as she spoke, and when she got to this point she broke down. Kane took a handkerchief out of his pocket and handed it to her and waited for her to regain her composure.

"They took him right into surgery," she said, "and he was on the table for four hours. The surgeon came out and told me, he told me . . ."

She started crying again, then shook her head angrily.

"This is no way for an old cop's wife to be behaving," she said. "Charlie would be embarrassed."

She shook her head again, dried her eyes, blew her nose, took a deep breath, and continued.

"Anyway, the surgeon said he'd been bleeding in his brain and then something burst. He told me what it was, but I don't remember. They've got him heavily sedated now to help him recover. They're not sure what shape his brain is in, and they can't make any tests until they take him off the sedatives. So all I can do is sit here and wait."

"Are you okay?" Kane asked. "Do you need anything done? Do you have family coming?"

June Simms smiled, just a slip of a smile that changed quickly into quivering lips. She took another deep breath.

"I'm as good as I can be under the circumstances. Our daughter is flying up from Arizona to sit with me. She'll be here tomorrow. And Liam Burke has been very nice."

"I'll tell them what happened over at APD," Kane said. "I'm sure they'd want to help."

"Thank you," June said.

They quit talking again, and Kane sat listening to the sounds of the hospital: the bong of bells, muted announcements, the voices of hospital personnel as they passed.

"I should be in there with him," June said. "They said I could sit in there. But I just needed a break from seeing him like that."

Kane didn't say anything. After a few minutes, she began again.

"Our marriage wasn't always smooth, you know. Charlie had an eye for the ladies and liked to take a drink. He was a real handful when we were younger. But things have smoothed out now. He cut back on his drinking—doctor's orders—and I told him that the next time he went out alley-catting would be his last, that I'd leave him. He could tell I meant it, I guess. Besides, how many women can a man who's more than sixty need? I was looking forward to the rest of our lives together. He was going to work this job another couple of years, then retire. We were going to move to Arizona to be near our daughter. Now, I don't know if we'll have any future together at all."

Kane couldn't think of a thing to say to that. He put his hand over hers, and the two of them sat quietly. Finally, he stirred.

"I should go let the police department know," he said. "Are you sure there's nothing more I can do for you?"

June shook her head. Kane got to his feet.

"Wait," she said. "I can't see you for the first time in so long and talk only about my troubles. How is Laurie?"

"She's fine," Kane said.

"And how are the two of you doing back together?" she asked.

"Aw, June," Kane said with a wistful smile, "now we'd just be talking about my troubles."

"I'm sorry to hear that," she said.

Down the hallway, Burke, who had been leaning against a wall, straightened up and started walking toward them.

"June," Kane said, "when Charlie stopped making sense, did he say anything at all that you could understand?"

"Not really," she said. "He said something about pictures, I think, about getting some pictures back. When I asked him what pictures he was talking about, he sat straight up in bed, looked at me, and shouted, 'No!' That's when I hit the call button and started yelling for a nurse."

"Thanks. You can be sure we'll catch whoever did this."

"I appreciate that, Nik, but what good is that going to

do me? If Charlie never comes back, I'm going to have to grow old alone. Catching whoever did this won't change that."

She began to cry again. Burke sat down next to her, put his arm around her shoulders and gave Kane a dirty look. Kane turned and walked away.

The hospital reminded him of prison in some ways. Maybe it was the smell or the metallic taste of the air, or that the rooms were never really warm or cold. Maybe it was the lighting or the garbled intercom announcements. Whatever it is, he thought, I guess all big institutions have things in common. And that proves?

Kane didn't know what that proved. Or much of anything else for that matter. He supposed all it proved was that he'd been a prisoner for a long time and, in some ways, was still a prisoner.

With that, he found an exit sign, followed the arrows, and escaped into the clean, cold evening air.

Ye have compassed this mountain long enough: turn you northward.

DEUTERONOMY 2:3

KANE STOOD AT THE BACK OF THE CHURCH, LISTENING to the old priest recite the opening prayer in a thin, quavering voice. He tried to recall the last time he'd been to Mass. His mother's funeral? Probably. A long time ago, anyway.

The church was a long rectangle with the altar at the front, a choir loft at the back, and rows of pews, divided by a center aisle, in between. The ceiling was high to accommodate the choir loft, and the side walls were pierced at regular intervals by stained-glass windows of abstract pattern. The altar had been turned around since Kane's youth, so that the priest faced the congregation instead of away from it, and had been stripped of its ornate tabernacle and raiment. His mother would have said the altar looked absolutely Lutheran.

These were just some of the changes. The Mass was said all in English now, audience participation was encouraged, and there were even women helping out on the altar. That last change would have sent his father off sputtering after the service in search of the nearest drink. But then, what wouldn't?

Maybe the biggest change was in the congregation. This was the main Sunday-morning Mass, and the church was full, but most of the worshippers were Kane's age or older, not the same multigenerational sprawl Kane remembered. Few young people or families seemed to be attending Mass these days.

He knew the Church was having all sorts of trouble. Not enough people becoming priests or nuns. Sex-abuse problems with men who had been—in some cases, still were—priests. The split between what the laity thought about a whole range of social issues and what the old men in Rome decreed. Kane just hadn't realized how much trouble the Church was in. This morning, in this building, the Roman Catholic Church looked like a dying business.

The priest was moving at a brisk clip. I suppose a church service is like a baseball game these days, Kane thought. If it lasts too long, people get bored and stop coming. But it was a far cry from the incense-filled, two-hour Latin High Masses he'd served in as an altar boy.

After leaving the hospital, Kane had gone home and called the police chaplain and a few of the people who had served with Simms on the force. When he figured he had enough aid and comfort headed June Simms's way, he'd repacked for the trip to Rejoice. But he hadn't felt up to driving right back. More proof that age is creeping up on me, he'd thought. That, and he hadn't wanted to leave the safety of the four walls of his apartment just then. So he'd ordered in pizza and spent the evening reading, falling asleep with Montaigne on his chest and awakening with a start just in time to shower and dress and drive to the cathedral for Mass.

He wasn't really sure why he was there. He felt both restless and tired. He felt like something big was going to happen, but he had no idea what. A big break in the case? A big change in his life? Maybe both? He knew that the only way to find out was to be patient, but he didn't feel patient. What he really wanted to do was to make a run for it, to escape this steaming wreck he called a life for someplace he could make a fresh start.

The thought made Kane smile. He'd be the first man in history to run *away* from Alaska to make a fresh start. He thought about the old gag that was probably still making the rounds in lawyer circles, about getting rich by offering an Alaska Special to newcomers: a bankruptcy, a divorce, and a name change, all for one low price.

He thought about his reluctance to try to interview Charlie Simms and to return to Rejoice. He'd never had that kind of problem as a cop. He'd always gone straight ahead. At the start, as a uniform, he'd felt the rightness of what he was doing, working to make the city he lived in safer. The department had been rawer then, full of big personalities and wild behavior, and, far down on the chain of command, he'd rarely run up against political restrictions. As he'd gotten older and come to understand the limitations of his job better, he'd still gotten satisfaction from solving puzzles and from working in an organization that, despite its many flaws, tried to uphold standards and protect citizens. As the department had gotten more paperwork driven, and he'd bumped into political constraints more frequently, he'd managed to ignore it all by just paying attention to what he did every day, to trying to solve crimes and put bad guys in jail.

Then, one day, he'd been the bad guy in jail. Inside the department and out, the wheels had ground him up. Minority groups had called for his head. The newspaper had joined in. Jeffords had decided to do the politically expedient thing. And the machinery inside the department had rolled relentlessly forward, producing the evidence to convict him.

Being on the wrong side of an investigation had hurt. In an organization like the police department, dominated by male values like stoicism and cynicism, he'd never let himself admit that he loved his job or made himself face the fact that it somehow filled needs that couldn't be touched by anything or anyone else in his life. Once he was no longer a part of it, though, he'd seen that clearly.

In prison, without an anchor for his identity, he could feel his drive and certainty slipping away, replaced by the prisoner's apathy and fear. He began to doubt himself, what he'd done, who he was. And even though he'd been exonerated, was free to go where he pleased and do what he pleased, he was still a prisoner of his fears and doubts.

He wasn't a cop anymore, and never would be again. So what was he? A civilian, like the kid trooper said. A civilian whose time in prison and lack of other job skills severely limited his employment opportunities. About all he was suited to was private work. He wasn't happy about that. The private detectives he'd known as a cop were either sleazy or incompetent, and he had a hard time seeing himself as one of them.

But he needed to do something. If he didn't, all that was left was retirement, sitting in some condo someplace warm, collecting his pension, eating cat food, looking at his silly legs sticking out of a pair of shorts, and counting the minutes until happy hour. He wasn't ready for that. He never wanted to be ready for that.

Maybe he was at Mass to seek help with his weakness, a miracle. God, he thought, I'm a drunk. Cure me. I'm a killer. Save me.

"The Gospel for today is from Matthew, chapter ten, verses twenty-four to twenty-six," the priest said. " 'The disciple is not above his master, nor the servant above his lord. It is enough for the disciple that he be as his master, and the servant as his lord. If they have called the master of the house Beelzebub, how much more shall they call them of his household? Fear them not, therefore: for there is nothing covered, that shall not be revealed; and hid, that shall not be known.' "

Is that a message to me? Kane thought. Was this, finally, God answering a prayer, if only in the scratchy voice of an old priest? Is God telling me to quit being afraid and just do my job? "For there is nothing covered, that shall not be revealed; and hid, that shall not be known." It might not be a miracle, but it was a coincidence.

His life was full of uncertainty now. So be it. He'd just

have to accept that and go forward. The police force, prison, his marriage, they were all in the past. He was, amazingly, a new man at fifty-five, a new man in reluctant search of a new life.

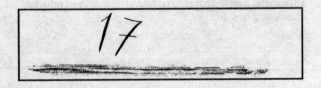

17

It is an honor for a man to cease from strife: but every fool will be meddling.

PROVERBS 20:3

MASS ENDED, AND KANE WALKED OUT INTO THE CLEAR chill of winter. He took out his cell phone, saw he had a message, and called for it. Larry Littlefield's voice told him that there was nothing about anyone named Feather Boyette in any of the criminal databases.

"But one of my computer monkeys found a Feather Collins in the archives of the Fairbanks paper," Littlefield's voice said, "giving money to some charity or cutting a ribbon or something. Maybe she's your girl. How many women named Feather can there be? Either way, remember that I drink the single malt. Here's the Collins woman's address."

Littlefield rattled off an address and the message ended. Well, Kane thought, as he wrote the address in his notebook, that's a long shot.

He walked back to his truck, drove to the grocery store, and emerged with some bags of groceries and a case of beer. He stopped at Café del Mundo for a couple of pounds of ground coffee. He made another stop at Lowe's and bought a set of heavy-duty bolt cutters. He sat in the park-

ing lot, breathing deeply and telling himself: No more excuses and no more hesitations. It's time to go to work. He
started the truck and drove back toward Rejoice.

He stopped at Summit Lake to drink coffee from a thermos. The view was as spectacular as that in any national
park in the Lower 48, and there had been a time when he
could have sat there and looked at it for an hour. Instead, he
found himself thinking about what the priest had said:
"There is nothing covered, that shall not be revealed; and
hid, that shall not be known." He had to keep moving forward now. To lose his momentum was to lose control of his
new life. He gulped his coffee, tossed the dregs out the
window, and drove off.

Slade opened the door of the Devil's Toe trooper office.
Kane handed him the case of beer, then went back for the
bags of groceries. When he returned, Slade led him to the
back and up a flight of stairs to the living quarters. They
walked into a living room, furnished with a couch and a
couple of easy chairs. A pocket kitchen was separated from
the living room by a breakfast bar, and a hallway led to
what Kane assumed were the bedrooms. Two investigators
were sitting in the living room amidst paperwork and the
remains of a meal. Kane knew them both.

"Hello, Harry," he said, "Sam."

"Killer Kane," the one he'd called Harry said.
"Shouldn't you still be in prison?"

"Nice to see you, too," Kane said.

"Knock if off, Harry," Sam said. "He doesn't mean it,
Nik. We're both just unhappy to be told we have to let a
civilian poke around in the case. Nothing personal. Any
civilian would be the same. You'd have felt that way, too,
back in the day."

Kane turned on his heel and walked out, down the stairs
and out the front door. He retrieved his duffel bag and
sleeping bag from the truck, carried them back up the
stairs, and dumped them on the floor.

"Don't anybody get in a hurry to help," he said. "I
wouldn't want you to hurt anything."

He pointed to the case of beer on the countertop.

"It's an assortment of local beers," he said. "They should be cold. Help yourselves."

The investigators looked at one another.

"You going to tell us what you're doing, messing around in our investigation?" Harry asked.

Kane got himself a glass of water and took a seat in one of the chairs at the counter, spinning around to face the room. His smile wasn't friendly.

"I'm not just some civilian, Sam," Kane said, ignoring the other trooper investigator. "And I'm not really here to investigate the mine robbery. The people over in Rejoice have asked me to find one of theirs who's gone missing. Chief Jeffords asked me to help, too, and as I guess you found out before you left Anchorage, I have somebody high up in your chain of command I can call. Plus, I'm consulting with Charlie Simms on mine security. Is that enough for you yet?"

Harry started to reply, but Sam held up a hand.

"We just don't want you tracking up our investigation," he said.

"Fine by me," Kane said. "I'll need to borrow Jeremy here in the morning for a little while to help me with my investigation, and I certainly don't want to get in your way. Just for curiosity's sake, though, what is your next step?"

The two men looked at each other again. It was all Kane could do to not burst out laughing. He dug into the case and pulled out some beer bottles.

"Like that, is it?" he said, handing one to each of the troopers. "Well, let's drink to the fact that most criminals are stupid, and whoever took the payroll will probably fuck up and catch themselves."

The investigators looked at Kane, and suddenly all three of them were laughing.

"You might be a clown, but you got that right," Harry said. "Cheers."

They drank, Kane sipping his water, and told stupid criminal stories for a while.

"You remember that bank robber," Sam said, "the one

who wrote the holdup note on the back of one of his own deposit slips? Had his name and address right on it?"

"Yeah," Kane said, "and how about that guy who killed his wife and tried to burn her up in the fireplace and when he was caught in the act claimed she'd died and fell into the fire on her own and he was just feeding her in because it wouldn't be dignified to let her be seen in a coffin all burned like that?"

After they'd laughed and drunk some of the tension away, Kane unpacked his groceries and made himself a sandwich. The others kept drinking, Harry polishing off two bottles to everyone else's one.

"I tried to talk to Charlie Simms when I was in Anchorage," Kane said, around a mouthful of turkey, ham, and Havarti, "but he'd had emergency brain surgery and was in no shape to be talking. According to his wife, it's touch-and-go if he ever talks again."

"It figures," Sam said. "There's not enough evidence in this case to stick in your eye."

"Got any results back from the lab tests on Charlie's clothes yet?" Kane asked.

"Are you kidding?" Harry said. "With the budget the crime lab's got, the techs are working nine to five, Monday to Friday, and that's it. We won't get any results for a couple of days at the earliest. Medical examiner's office is the same way, so we won't get anything from the body 'til then, either. Doesn't make any difference to any of them that both victims used to be cops."

That set off a round of bitching about the hard life of the law enforcement officer, followed by fresh beers for everyone but Kane.

"Nothing from searching their rooms?" he asked.

"You know the answer to that," Harry said in a sour tone. "You been all through their stuff. All we found is that Simms lived like a monk and Logan lived like a slob. You didn't happen to remove anything we might be interested in, did you?"

"Like what?" Kane said. "The minutes of their last robbery-planning meeting?"

Harry tried to struggle out of his chair. It occurred to Kane that everyone in the room except him had had too much to drink.

"You always were a superior son of a bitch," Harry said, "but I guess you got what was coming to you."

"Harry," Sam said.

"Don't Harry me," Harry said. He looked at Kane. "You know what it was like to wear a uniform after you shot that kid? Do you? All the jokes about drunk cops and the sass from teenagers? 'What you gonna do, off-i-cer, shoot me?' We got new shooting protocols and mandatory alcohol counseling and stricter firearms-discharge reviews. And all because you couldn't hold your liquor, you no-good son bitch. I should kick your ass for that."

Harry was swaying a little now. Kane slid off his stool, walked around the breakfast bar, put his hand on Harry's shoulder and eased him back down in his chair.

"Nobody's fighting tonight, Harry," he said. "It's time for sleep."

He turned to Slade.

"I suppose you've only got enough beds for the three of you," he said.

"There's the couch," Slade said.

"Just give me the keys to the holding cell," Kane said. "I'll sleep down there. It won't be the first night I've spent in a cell. Will it, Harry?"

The trooper investigator waved his hand sloppily but said nothing.

"Guy's a drunk himself," Kane said quietly. "Probably scared to death he'll do something that'll cost him his pension. Or worse."

Slade handed him some keys. Kane picked up his duffel and sleeping bag and walked downstairs. He opened the cell door, spread his sleeping bag on the bunk, and went to brush his teeth in the bathroom off the office. He set his travel alarm for seven a.m. and lay down. He tried to think about Faith Wright and what he needed to know, what he knew, and what he suspected about the mine robbery. But he couldn't. Instead, he thought about what

Harry had said. It might not have been a crime to shoot that kid, but it had been a sin. And he'd done his penance, hadn't he? His penance, and then some. He followed these thoughts into the darkness. When the alarm dragged him into wakefulness, it seemed like he'd been asleep only a matter of moments.

*For nothing is secret, that shall not be made manifest; neither any
thing hid, that shall not be known and come abroad.*

LUKE 8:17

MISS EVELYN WISP, THE PRINCIPAL OF DEVIL'S TOE RE-
gional High School, did not look happy. She gave Kane
and Slade the sort of look Kane's fifth-grade teacher used
to give him after some particularly boneheaded escapade.
In fact, Miss Wisp—she insisted on the "Miss"—looked a
lot like that teacher, whose name Kane could not for the life
of him bring to mind. All the boys had simply called her
Sister Mary Pointer, because a long, heavy wooden pointer
had been her preferred tool for correcting misbehavior.

Of course, Kane thought, that nun would be five hundred years old by now. And he doubted she would have
broken her vow of celibacy, even if she'd been able to find
a man desperate enough to help her do it. Could be a
grandniece, though, Kane thought. It was all he could do
not to ask her, but he and Slade were having enough trouble with Miss Wisp without adding fuel to the fire.

The plain fact was that Miss Wisp did not want them
searching Faith Wright's locker.

"Why, the hubbub will distract the students for a week
at least, and us with the exit exam coming up," she said.

"We could come back after school," Slade said.

"Yes, I suppose you could," Miss Wisp said, as if he'd just said the most obvious thing in the world. "But the students would find out anyway. And so would the school board. I wouldn't want to have to explain this to the school board."

Kane leaned forward in his chair.

"I'll be happy to explain this to the school board," he said, fighting to keep his tone reasonable. "A girl is missing, and we have her father's written permission to search her locker for clues to her whereabouts. Any more delay only adds to her jeopardy. How do you think the school board will like it if it turns out that she could have been helped, but the delay in searching her locker prevented that?"

"You don't know that Faith is in any trouble," Miss Wisp snapped.

"And you don't know that she's not," Kane said reasonably.

The principal sat glaring at Kane, her jaw working as she sorted through her options. She's certainly got that look down, Kane thought. They must be related.

"I'm afraid I'll have to call the school district's attorney and confer," Miss Wisp said. "I'm not even certain we know the locker's combination."

"That's enough," Slade said. "I want Faith Wright's locker number and I want it now. If anything other than that number comes out of your mouth, I'm locking you up for obstructing an official investigation, and you can talk to the school district's attorney through the bars."

What's gotten into him? Kane thought. Aloud, he said, "I don't think there will be any need for that, Jeremy. I'm certain that Miss Wisp only wants what's best for her students."

He poured a little more verbal oil on Miss Wisp's wounded feelings, and after looking in a file, she gave them the locker number.

"But I was serious about the combination," she said. "I'll have to see if anyone knows it."

Kane knew she was bluffing and decided to call her on it.

"That won't be necessary," he said. Leaving Slade in the office, he walked out through the accumulating students.

It felt good to do something, to move forward, to let the role of the detective settle over him and armor him against his fears and doubts. This was a job he knew how to do, and he could feel his confidence, confidence that he could and would do this job, growing within him.

He went to his truck, took the bolt cutters he'd bought in Anchorage out of the back, and walked into the school.

Devil's Toe Regional High School was a rectangle of one-story boxes with peaked roofs around a central courtyard. The front box was divided by a two-story entrance module with a cathedral ceiling that housed the library, administrative offices, faculty lounge, and cafeteria. In the middle of the rear box was a two-story block that Kane assumed was the gymnasium. The school housed about 250 students, Miss Wisp had told them, eighteen teachers, and an administrative staff of six. They really needed more teachers and staff, she said, but the legislature was being tight-fisted.

The first bell rang as Kane reentered the building. Some of the students began drifting toward classrooms. Others gave Kane and his bolt cutters the fish eye. They're probably worried that it's their lockers I'm after, he thought. He walked back into the principal's office, where Slade and Miss Wisp sat regarding each other like boxers waiting for the bell.

"These will get us into the locker," Kane said to Slade, holding out the bolt cutters.

"But the lock?" Miss Wisp said. "Who will pay for the lock?"

Kane extracted a twenty-dollar bill from his wallet and laid it on her desk.

"This should cover the cost of the lock," he said.

Miss Wisp looked at him with pursed lips.

Sister Mary Perpetua, Kane thought. That was her name. At least, her nun name.

"We don't have any way to take in cash from strangers,"

Miss Wisp said. "Besides, I've just remembered. We have a list of locker combinations somewhere."

"Too late," Kane said. He wondered if he was being high-handed because she looked so much like the nun. To Slade, he said, "Let's go."

"I'm going with you," Miss Wisp said.

"Fine," Slade said, "just don't get in our way."

Miss Wisp led them down one hallway, then halfway down the next. Students were still putting things into lockers and taking things out. Miss Wisp stopped in front of a closed locker.

"This is it," she said, "number one-seventeen."

"What's going on?" asked a young man dressed, as were half the students in the school, in dirty jeans and a flannel shirt. He had a knit cap with a Carhartt label on his head.

"Nothing that need concern you, John," Miss Wisp said. "Go to your classroom."

"It does concern me, Miss Wisp," the young man said. "Faith is a friend of mine."

"You Johnny Starship?" Kane said. The boy looked surprised and nodded warily. "Maybe you'd better stick around. We've got some questions for you."

"Mister—what did you say your name was?—you can't just question underage students," Miss Wisp said. "It's against the law."

Slade gave the principal a disgusted look and opened his mouth to speak. Kane cut him off.

"I'm sure this young man wants to help us find his friend," he said, smiling. "And I'm sure that the school board would want you to let him help us. But if you'd rather wait until he can get a lawyer here from from Fairbanks or Anchorage, I'm certain the girl's father and everyone else will understand that you are just looking out for the boy. They might question why you put his rights before her safety, but you can explain that, can't you?"

Miss Wisp's glare would have melted concrete, but he had her and they both knew it.

"Go ahead," she said in a voice that dripped icicles.

"Give me the bolt cutters," Slade said.

Kane handed him the tool.

"You stay right where you are, pal," Slade said to Johnny Starship.

The locker was secured by a cheap combination lock run through holes in its handle. Slade gripped the locking bar with the jaws of the bolt cutter and strained. The lock broke.

"Good bolt cutters," he said, handing them back to Kane. Then he swiveled the locking bar to one side, pulled it through the holes, and snapped open the locker.

The second bell rang.

"Students should go to their classrooms," Miss Wisp said, but none of the students who had formed a semicircle around the locker budged. Kane saw a couple of teachers in the crowd as well.

"Move along," he said, raising his voice. "This has nothing to do with you."

The teachers started herding the students away.

"Have a look," Slade said to Kane.

The locker was as neat as everything else that belonged to Faith Wright. The walls were undecorated gray metal. No clothing hung in it. Textbooks stood in a line on the top shelf. On the floor sat a pale-blue plastic step stool supporting a dark-blue plastic crate. The crate contained binders of various colors, arranged spine up. A pair of sensible-looking shoes sat beneath the stool, to be exchanged for boots, Kane figured, and worn inside the building.

"Clean enough to do brain surgery in here," Kane said. "You take the books, and I'll take the binders."

He picked up the crate and turned to Johnny Starship.

"Go ahead to your first class," he said. "It'll take us a while to go through these. Come and see us when it's over. We'll be . . ." He looked at Miss Wisp. "Where will we be?"

Miss Wisp pursed her lips so hard that they disappeared. She said nothing.

"Surely you have an empty room we can borrow for a couple of hours," Kane said, keeping his tone light and reasonable. Miss Wisp looked like a cartoon figure of anger. All that was missing was steam coming out of her ears.

"Miss Wisp," Slade said, his tone neither light nor reasonable.

"I suppose you can use the counselor's office," she snapped. "The counselor only visits once a week. This way."

"Come and see us in the counselor's office," Kane told Johnny Starship, then followed Miss Wisp's rigid figure down the hallway.

Miss Wisp opened a room with a key, turned on the lights, and walked in. The room was small and windowless, as homey as Faith Wright's locker. Kane and Slade put their loads on the metal desk.

"Thank you, Miss Wisp," Kane said. "We'll find you if we need anything else."

Kane's words set the principal vibrating with indignation.

"This is my school," she said. "Faith is one of my students. I have an obligation to be here while you search her belongings."

"You have an obligation to cooperate with the police," Slade said, none too kindly, "and an obligation not to obstruct an investigation. Good-bye."

Miss Wisp looked from one man to the other, spun on her heel, and marched out of the room.

"There goes someone to make telephone calls to get us in trouble," Kane said with a smile.

Slade laughed.

"Let her," he said. "It won't be the first time I've gotten into trouble with a principal."

The men pulled chairs up on the opposite sides of the desk. Slade slid the first book off his pile and began leafing through it. Kane did the same with the first binder. It was red, and its spine was labeled "Civics." It contained nothing but notes and other papers relating to the class. The notes were in a clear handwriting, feminine but unadorned by the curlicues Kane associated with teenage girls. Each of the test papers in the binder bore an "A" written in blue ink, and several pages appeared to be notes for what seemed to be an ambitious term paper on the separation of church and state.

The next binder, a green one labeled "Trigonometry," was just as well organized, clear, and comprehensive. Kane, who didn't remember a single bit of his high school math, couldn't make heads or tails of it. The blue one labeled "Spanish IV" was just as bad. The marks in both were all A's.

"This is one formidable young lady," he said.

Slade set the last of the textbooks on the pile.

"There's nothing in these," he said. "There's writing in some of them, but it's all different and none of it looks like the handwriting in the notebooks. Probably used books."

Kane took binders labeled "English" and "Chemistry" off the pile and slid them over to the trooper.

"Check these out," he said, then opened one labeled "PE." There wasn't much in that but some handouts on exercises and a couple of physical evaluations that said Faith Wright was in good shape indeed. Kane turned to the last binder, "Extra C." He leafed through fliers for dances and student-body elections and copies of the school newspaper.

"The only thing I see in here," Slade said, sliding the English binder onto the pile, "is notes on a lot of feminist literature: Simone de Beauvoir, Nancy Hardesty, Catherine MacKinnon. Plus a bunch of stuff about feminism and sexuality. That's a little unusual for a Christian girl, isn't it?"

"Maybe," Kane said, "but a young woman who wants to go to the Ivy League probably needs to know that stuff. How do you know those are feminist writers?"

Slade laughed.

"I took a course on feminism in college," he said.

"Know thine enemy?" Kane asked.

"I suppose," Slade said, "but I don't remember a thing about that class. Except that it put me next to a lot of women anxious to demonstrate their sexual independence."

Kane turned a page announcing tryouts for the school's production of *The Taming of the Shrew* and stopped.

"I've got something," he said, sliding the binder over to Slade. "Tell me what you make of this."

What Kane had found were a pair of statements from an Anchorage bank addressed to Dorothy Allison at a Devil's Toe post office box that showed weekly deposits of a thousand dollars or more.

"Looks to me like Dorothy was making pretty good money doing something," Slade said.

The two men sat looking at each other.

"Suppose it's an alias?" Kane said.

"Could be," Slade said. "Why else would she have these statements?"

They were silent again for a few minutes.

"So if it is an alias," Kane said, "how could Faith Wright have been earning one thousand dollars a week?"

Slade looked uncomfortable and said nothing.

"Hard to think of many legal ways," Kane said. "But the illegal ways are completely out of character, at least the way I read her character. Maybe Johnny Starship can shed some light on this." He paused. "I think the conversation might go better if I talked with him myself."

Slade looked at Kane for a moment, then nodded.

"Okay," he said, "I'm sure the investigators could use my help questioning the workers up at the mine."

"You might stop at the post office first," Kane said, "and see who rented that post office box."

Slade didn't look happy about the suggestion. But he nodded, got to his feet, put on his coat, and left.

Kane finished leafing though the binder while he waited, finding nothing else the least out of the ordinary. When he finished, he leaned back in his chair and stared at the ceiling, trying to blank his mind and let this new piece of information settle into the mosaic he was composing of Faith Wright. The ringing of the school bell didn't stop his reflection, but a knock at the door did.

"Come in," he called, and Johnny Starship stepped into the room.

"Please sit down," Kane said, motioning to the chair Slade had vacated. "Thanks for coming."

The young man sat on the edge of the chair, looking like he might take off at any moment.

"I'm not sure my dad would want me to talk to you," he said.

"Okay," Kane said, "but all I'm trying to do is find out what happened to Faith Wright. I'm told you are friends. Don't you want to help find her?"

"Maybe she doesn't want to be found."

"Do you know that? Do you know that she left of her own free will?"

The young man shook his head.

"I don't. The last time I saw her she said she'd see me later, just like always."

"When was that?" Kane asked.

The young man looked over Kane's shoulder at the wall.

"I guess it was Friday before last, here at school," he said.

That's his first lie, Kane thought.

"Were you good friends?" he asked.

The young man shrugged.

"We talked about stuff. She was nice to me. Lots of kids won't have anything to do with me because of my family."

"What kind of stuff did you talk about?"

"Oh, life and stuff. About the problems of life and what to do about them."

"Did you hang out together after school?" Kane asked. "Are you into the same extracurricular activities?"

Johnny Starship's eyes flitted to the wall again.

"I don't do many extracurricular activities. Nobody wants me in their clubs and stuff. And I don't know what Faith does after school."

"So you wouldn't know how she was making money? Lots of money?" Kane asked.

The boy stood up.

"I've gotta go," he said. "I don't want to be late for class."

"Johnny," Kane said, "whatever you know, whatever Faith was doing, she needs your help now. The way you can help her is to talk to me."

"No," the young man said. "No. I can't. I won't."

He turned and hurried out through the door.

Kane sighed, shook his head, and got to his feet. He carried the books and binders out to his truck. Both bells rang as he was doing so. He went into the administrative offices, walked past a student at the counter, and opened the door to Miss Wisp's office. The principal stopped talking to a pleasant-looking woman in her forties to glare at him.

"A closed door is usually a sign that someone doesn't want to be disturbed," she snapped.

"No kidding?" Kane said. "I'm just here to report that we're done for now. Thank you for your help."

He nodded to the other woman and smiled.

"I'm Nik Kane," he said. "Faith Wright's father has hired me to find her. And who might you be?"

"I might be anyone," the woman said, "but who I am is Audrey Lee. I'm Faith Wright's faculty adviser. I'm helping her with her college applications. The girl has a lot of potential. Do you think you will find her?"

"You might be able to help me do that," Kane said. "Do you know which after-school activities Faith is involved in this year?"

"Mrs. Lee," Miss Wisp said, "you know we aren't supposed to talk about the students."

The other woman ignored her.

"Faith wasn't involved in any extracurriculars this semester," she said. "She told me she had an after-school job."

Kane asked a couple of more questions without getting anything, thanked the woman, nodded to Miss Wisp, and walked out to his pickup. Faith Wright is proving to be a very interesting young woman, he thought. But not in a good way.

19

She is gone up upon every high mountain and under every green tree, and there hath played the harlot.

JEREMIAH 3:6

"DID SHE KNOW WHAT THE JOB WAS?" SLADE ASKED.

The two of them were sitting in Kane's truck. Around them, the business of the Pitchfork mine went on as though nothing had happened. The two trooper investigators were set up in Charlie Simms's office, questioning mine workers about the robbery. They still had a lot of people to talk to.

"She didn't," Kane said. "What did you find out at the post office?"

A look of worry passed over Slade's face.

"Those federal bureaucrats are even more secretive than Miss Wisp," he said, "but I finally got them to tell me that the box is rented by our friend Little John."

"Interesting," Kane said.

"Think we should go see him?" Slade asked.

"Absolutely," Kane said, "but since we're here, there's a couple of things I want to do first."

"What's that?" Slade asked.

"Well, first, I want to look over Simms's room again," Kane said.

Slade raised an eyebrow.

"I just want to check on something he said," Kane said.

Simms's room was unchanged, right down to the dirty dishes still in the sink.

"We've got to search the whole place again," Kane said. "I'll start in the bathroom."

"What are we looking for?" Slade asked.

"Pictures," Kane said.

The two of them moved through the apartment carefully, searching the furniture, sounding the walls and taking down curtain rods and closet poles to make sure nothing was rolled up and hidden inside. They found nothing. Kane sat on the couch in the living room and let his eyes wander around. They stopped at the row of videotapes beneath the television.

"You know," he said, getting up from the couch, "there's nothing that says pictures have to be still pictures."

He crouched, pulled a tape from its box and looked at the handwritten label. He repeated that procedure until all dozen tapes were stacked on the floor in front of the television.

"I guess they've got cable here," Kane said. "Charlie seems to have been taping *The Sopranos*."

"What?" Slade said. "No porn?"

"Not on the labels," Kane said. He looked at Slade.

"I suppose we're going to have to watch all of these," the trooper said.

"We are," Kane said. "You've got a VCR back at your quarters, don't you?"

The trooper nodded.

"Then I guess we'll just look at these tapes later," he said.

They carried the tapes out to Kane's truck and put them in the passenger seat. Tony Figone and his sidekick pulled up.

"That's good timing," Kane said. "The other thing I wanted to do was talk to Figone."

"Got a call we're being interrogated," Figone said to Kane. "That you guys?"

"No," Kane said, "a couple of trooper investigators. They're in Charlie's office. But I do have a few questions."

"Come on in," Figone said. "We'll tell the troopers we're here and then we'll talk."

"I'll tell them," Slade said, knocking on the door to Simms's office. Tony led the way to the conference room. Slade followed a moment later.

"They want one of you now," he said.

"Why don't you go first?" Figone said to his companion. After the man left, Figone said to the trooper, "No offense, but this will go a lot easier if it's just me and Kane."

Slade shrugged and left.

"Got a problem with the kid?" Kane asked.

"Not really," Figone said. "But you know how it is in a small town. You hear things."

"What kind of things?"

"Oh, just that the kid might be a little badge heavy. And maybe a little too friendly with the ladies."

Kane laughed.

"That'd describe just about every young cop I ever knew. Including me."

Figone grinned.

"Me, too, I guess. Now what was it you wanted to know?"

"I want to know about Charlie," Kane said. "How he's seemed lately. If he's done anything unusual. You know the drill."

"You think he was involved in the robbery?"

Kane didn't say anything.

"Me, too," Figone said. "The SUV, right? No damage."

Kane nodded.

"He wouldn't have been that easy to run off the road. You'd need something big to overpower that Explorer, and you'd have to hit it pretty hard. Hard enough to leave marks."

"That's what I thought the first thing I saw it," Figone said. "Have the troopers figured that out yet?"

Kane shrugged.

"Don't know. They're putting up with me because they know I've got political backing, but that doesn't mean they're telling me what they're thinking."

Figone grinned.

"Yeah, we always used to hate guys like you when we were on their side of it, didn't we? Anyway, Charlie. Nothing too unusual. Not out carousing at night. Not chasing secretaries around the desk. Three, four months ago he did start getting a little hepped on the subject of theft, particularly payroll theft. Even started working a split shift. Said it was so he could keep an eye on the night crew. Not that there's much of a night crew working right now."

"Got any idea what he was doing in his time off?"

"Not really. He was going off the mine site, but I don't know where exactly."

"Anything else?"

Figone looked off into space for a minute.

"Just one thing. He was due for R-and-R last month and didn't take it. Said he didn't want to leave during a period of heightened danger."

He shook his head.

"Jesus, Nik, I hope he wasn't involved in this. I'd hate for it to be him."

"Me, too, Tony," Kane said, getting to his feet, "but it's got to be somebody."

He put his hand on Figone's shoulder.

"There's no reason for you to volunteer any of this to the troopers," he said.

"I understand, but if they ask me, I'm not lying to them. I need this job."

"That's fine. I wouldn't expect you to lie. I'd just like to keep a step ahead of them if I can."

"Are you a step ahead now?" Figone asked.

"Shit, Tony, who knows?" Kane said.

He left Figone sitting in the conference room and walked into the waiting area. Richardson, the mine manager, waved him over into his office.

"Just thought you should know, we're offering a reward for the recovery of the money," he said. "Ten thousand. Since you're not in law enforcement anymore, you'd be eligible."

Kane nodded and walked toward the door. Gossip and

tips brought out by the reward should keep the troopers busy. Slade was sitting in a chair in the waiting area.

"Get anything from Figone?" he asked.

Kane stopped and looked down at the trooper.

"Not really," he said. "Simms started acting differently a few months ago, but not really in a way that tells me anything. I've got a lot of pieces, but none that seem to go together."

"So now what?" the trooper asked.

"I don't know," Kane said. He put on his coat, ran a hand through his hair, then covered it with a knit cap. "We need to talk to a couple of guys named John, but we don't really have a lever to pry anything out of them yet. So we'd better wait. I think I'll head over to Rejoice to check in and have lunch. I'll drop these tapes off at your place first if you've got an extra key. What about you?"

The trooper shrugged.

"I really ought to be out on patrol sometime today," he said, "but I also need to stick around in case these guys need anything. So I'll probably do that. Just don't go talking to the Johns without me."

He took a bunch of keys off his belt, separated one, and handed it to Kane.

"That'll let you in."

"Okay," Kane said. "See you later."

Kane drove to the trooper office, unloaded the tapes, and drove to Rejoice. Along the way he moved pieces of information around in his head without forming a clear picture. Whatever Faith Wright had been doing with her afternoons, the Johns had been involved. But he couldn't see one of them as the person who'd shot at him. They both seemed too confused and dispirited. I suppose it could have been Big John, he thought, but would he be creeping around Rejoice? Probably not. So it was likely someone in Rejoice was involved as well.

And as for the robbery? He couldn't see Charlie Simms involved in the robbery, but he couldn't see how it had happened without Charlie's help. And if he was going to steal the payroll, why would Charlie be warning everyone of the danger? He'd told Kane that Big John had been a particular danger. That made a clean sweep of the Johns. Did that mean that Faith's disappearance and the robbery were related somehow? Everywhere he looked was fog.

Except on the road. The sun suddenly broke through the clouds and, as low as it was, shone directly into Kane's eyes. He pulled over and put on his sunglasses. I wish the same thing would happen in this case, he thought, and drove on. He pulled into the Rejoice community center just before noon and went inside.

He'd almost finished his cheeseburger when Ruth Hunt came out of the kitchen and sat across from him. She looked drawn and tired, although even like that she looked good to Kane.

"I'm happy to see you," she said.

"I'm happy to see you, too," he said. "I think this case is picking up speed, so I don't know how much time I'll have for the pleasure of your company for a while."

She looked at him and smiled.

"Something's changed, hasn't it?" she asked.

"What do you mean?" Kane said.

"You seem different," she said. "More alive somehow."

"Must be the coffee I get to drink when I'm not here," he said.

"That must be it," she said, "the coffee."

After a silence, she said, "Do you think you will find Faith soon?"

"I don't know, but I think I know some places to look. What's going on with you?"

"I'm not really sure," she said, reaching out to put her hand over his. "Things with Gregory seem to have reached a critical mass. He came home from Anchorage with the basketball teams late yesterday, and we talked for most of the night. Neither one of us is happy with our marriage, and neither one of us wants to do what the other thinks it would take to make things work."

They were silent for several minutes.

"There's an old joke about the definition of mixed feelings," Kane said at last. "They're what you have when you find out your mother-in-law has driven off a cliff in your new Cadillac. I have mixed feelings about your news. I've been left myself, so I know something about how Gregory feels. But mostly I'm happy and hopeful that this means you and I will be spending more time together."

"I hope so, too," she said. "Maybe when you finish your case and I wrap up my obligations here, we can go someplace together."

She looked around the room, withdrew her hand, and stood up.

"I have to get back to work," she said, "and we don't want to start any gossip. The community's reaction will be bad enough when people learn I'm leaving."

"I've got to get going, too," Kane said. "I'm sleeping over at the trooper office if you need to find me."

She waved and went back into the kitchen. Kane finished his lunch and started for the door. As he passed the community meeting room, he saw Moses Wright sitting in his office. Matthew Pinchon was sitting in the chair opposite him and seemed to be crying. Wright looked up from the boy's face and glared at Kane, who kept walking.

As he drove back to Devil's Toe, he pondered his options. None of the ones involving law enforcement officers looked promising. Too damn many rights and warnings. Without them, though, he was limited to scooping Johnny Starship up at school, taking him somewhere, and scaring the shit out of him to make him talk. Or he could grab the boy's father somehow and sweat him. But either of those approaches were far too close to breaking the law. I didn't get into this to become a thug, he thought.

So instead he drove to the trooper office and carried the tapes upstairs. He shed his outdoor gear and made a pot of coffee. When he had a cup, he sat down to look at tape. He'd planned to fast-forward through the tapes, looking for he didn't really know what. But he quickly realized that watching the tapes whiz by made him feel jumpy. So he rewound the tape, put the tapes in chronological order, and began watching at regular speed.

Slade came in as he was taking the fifth tape out of the player.

"What are you doing here?" Kane asked.

Slade looked at him quizzically.

"It's after five o'clock," he said, "where else should I be?"

"No kidding?" Kane said. "I guess I got caught up in what I'm watching."

"Learn anything?" the trooper asked, tossing his coat on a chair and taking a bottle of water out of the refrigerator.

"Yeah," Kane said, "this Tony Soprano is one sick puppy."

Slade laughed.

"So I've heard," he said.

"Where are Sam and Harry?" Kane asked.

"They're damn tired of having mine workers tell them nothing," Slade said, "so they decided to get a few beers and then dinner at the roadhouse. You want to join them?"

Kane shook his head.

"I don't think so," he said. "I really need to know if there's anything on these tapes."

He put tape number six in the player.

"And if there's not?" Slade asked, sitting down beside him.

"If there's not, we're going to have to lean on Little John pretty hard about that post office box and hope he cracks," Kane said, "although we still don't have anything he can't explain his way out of."

He hit the Play button.

"Besides," he said, "I need to see what Tony Soprano is going to do next."

Two tapes later, Slade got up from the couch.

"That's a good show," he said, "but I've got to have something to eat. Think I'll go see if my fellow troopers have progressed to food yet."

Kane pulled the tape from the player and inserted another one.

"Okay, go ahead," he said. "I've only got a couple more tapes to go. Think I'll finish."

Slade walked into the bathroom and closed the door. Kane hit the Play button.

A poorly lit and somewhat blurry image came up on the screen. A young woman with long black hair that had beads woven into the ends walked into the picture. She was wearing a black ribbon around her neck, a black garter belt, long black stockings, black high-heeled shoes, and nothing else.

"Charlie, you devil," Kane said, smiling, "this isn't *The Sopranos*."

The woman was followed by a naked man, an older guy with his gut sucked in and a considerable erection. Kane's smile faded from his lips. The man was Charlie Simms. The woman knelt on the carpet. The man walked up and stood in front of her. Her head began to bob. As she continued, her hands on his flanks worked him around so that his face would be clear to the camera.

"Aw, hell, Charlie," Kane said aloud.

The woman got up and lay on the bed. The man lay down on top of her. He began moving. There was no sound on the tape, but he could see the woman's mouth moving, encouraging the man in his efforts. As he watched Charlie Simms's ass rise and fall with increasing speed, Kane felt sad and a little dirty.

The activity on the screen stopped abruptly. The man lay there for a few moments, then rolled off the woman. She got up and walked out of the camera's view, returning in a matter of moments with a towel. She handed it to the man and, turning slightly, winked at the camera.

The scene jumped to another encounter, then another. Always Charlie and the young woman. She wore different wigs, different outfits, and they engaged in slightly different acts, but it was the same pair and the same result and the same, sassy wink at the camera. At the end of the sixth encounter, the screen went blank. Kane sat there, his brain spinning and a pain growing in his stomach.

"Jesus Christ," Slade said. "I guess we know what Simms was doing with that Viagra."

Kane looked up. The trooper was standing beside the

couch, his Smokey Bear hat crumpled in his hand. Kane hadn't heard him come out of the bathroom or noticed him while the tape was rolling.

"Yeah, we do," Kane said. "Better than that, or maybe worse, we know what Faith Wright was doing during her afternoons. Look."

He rewound the tape, ran it forward until the woman winked at the camera, and paused it. At the corner of her winking eye, the two men could just make out a small scar, the kind a dog's claw might make.

20

*For in much wisdom is much grief: and he that
increaseth knowledge increaseth sorrow.*

ECCLESIASTES 1:18

KANE THUMBED THE REMOTE CONTROL TO REWIND
the tape. Slade walked over and set his hat on the breakfast bar, took two bottles of beer from the refrigerator,
opened them, and walked back into the living room. He
offered a bottle to Kane, who shook his head. Now was
no time to start drinking. Slade sat down in one of the
armchairs. The whir of the tape rewinding stopped, leaving only silence. The silence continued as Slade drank his
beer slowly, pausing between swallows to stare into
space.

Finally, Kane broke the silence.

"Shit," he said. "Shitshitshitshitshit. And fuck." He
sighed. "What could Charlie have been thinking of? That
girl was young enough to be his granddaughter. What
could he have been thinking?"

Slade said nothing.

"And what about Faith?" Kane continued. "What would
make a Christian girl, one living in a religious community,
for Christ's sake, take to whoring? It can't have been the
money."

That's the trouble with detecting, Kane thought. A lot of what you uncovered you didn't want to know, and most of the time answers just led to more questions.

"Well," he said, "we're going to have to find out where that tape was made, where Faith was working. Although it's pretty much got to be the roadhouse, doesn't it?"

"I know where the tape was made," Slade said in a small voice.

Kane went on as if he hadn't heard the other man.

"God damn it, this news will kill her father. Who is going to tell him? I don't want to do it. Maybe we're better off just dropping the whole thing."

"I said," Slade said, "I know where the tape was made."

Kane stopped talking and looked at Slade. The younger man had pain, and what might have been fear, in his eyes. As Kane opened his mouth to speak, he heard Harry and Sam coming up the stairs. He jumped to his feet, ejected the tape, and put it on top of the pile. The trooper investigators came into the room.

"A wasted day," Sam said, tossing his coat on the floor. "You guys get anywhere on the girl?"

"Not really," Kane said. He looked at his watch. "It's early, but I think I'll turn in anyway. Get an early start."

Harry held up the tape of Charlie Simms and the girl.

"What you guys watching?" he asked.

"*The Sopranos,*" Kane said. "Charlie Simms taped them, and I'd never seen the show."

"What did you think, huh?" Harry said. "That Tony Soprano's as fucked up as a real bad guy, isn't he?" He put the tape back on the stack. "I've been watching that show since it started. You should get cable."

Kane put the tapes back into their boxes and picked them up.

"I'll return these tomorrow," he said. "I guess they're still Charlie's property."

Harry and Sam looked at each other, then at Kane.

"The mine manager got a call just before we left," Sam said. "Simms didn't make it."

"Aw," Kane said, "that's too bad. Did he say anything before he died?"

"Never came out of the coma," Harry said.

Kane took the tapes and walked downstairs to the cell. He put the tape of Charlie, and the three he hadn't watched yet, into his duffel. He set the others on the edge of Slade's desk. Then he took a Clif bar from his bag and sat on the bed. He tried to think of nothing while he forced himself to eat. Each bite was like a mouthful of sand; it took a whole bottle of water to wash the bar down. His mind kept jumping to the images of Faith Wright and Charlie Simms, screwing their futures away. His life, in Charlie's case. Maybe hers, in Faith's.

Kane could feel depression clawing at him, and he set his jaw against it. He concentrated on trying to figure out what he'd just seen and heard.

He could understand Charlie being there, he supposed. Few old men would pass up a chance to get next to a young woman, especially a man like Charlie, who'd always followed his dick wherever it led him, even though that was mostly into trouble. Charlie had to know the risks to his job, his marriage, and his reputation, but the chance to get a good-looking young woman into the sack would drive everything else from his mind.

Out in the office, the fax machine started up.

Charlie is easy to figure, Kane thought, because he's not all that different from me. But Faith's motives are much harder for me to fathom. I've never been a teenage girl.

Kane was not naive. If he'd run across a teenage hooker on the streets of Anchorage, he wouldn't have thought twice. The culture spat out rootless children in an unending stream—runaways, throwaways, druggies, adrenaline junkies—and some of them washed up in cities, even cities the size of Anchorage.

But he hadn't expected this here, even though he knew that the trailers and cabins and slapped-together homes at the ends of the dirt roads of Alaska housed plenty of the cruelty and depravity that were epidemic in the world. Somehow, he'd been seduced by the idea of Faith Wright as the dutiful Christian girl, not entirely religious perhaps, but with the moral compass that a religious, small-town upbringing had given her. What was it the psalm said? He picked up his Bible and leafed through it until he found the passage he wanted: "God is in the midst of her; she shall not be moved: God shall help her, and that right early."

Despite a life spent looking all too often into the abyss of human behavior, Kane had retained a belief in the saving grace of religion. Even though he couldn't make himself take what theologians called the leap of faith, he admired those who had and stood safely on the other side. It wasn't the aggressive and hostile religiosity of Moses Wright that he yearned for, or the superstition-ridden faith of his parents, but the quiet and constant right behavior he had projected onto Faith Wright. He wanted it so much for himself that he had imagined it in her.

Well, the videotape was the end of that. Probably the end of Charlie Simms's reputation, too. And he wondered what it would do to Slade, who seemed to know more about it than he should have.

Footsteps came down the stairs, and Slade walked into the office. He picked up the fax, read it, and carried it into the jail cell. Kane straightened up and made room on the bed. Slade handed him the fax and sat, leaning his arms on his knees and folding his hands.

"Looks like Harry was wrong about how long the lab tests would take," he said. "The fax says no gunshot residue on Simms's clothing, so whatever he did he didn't shoot Lester Logan."

"Thank God for that," Kane said. "Where are Sam and Harry?"

"Upstairs watching *Fear Factor*," Slade said. "So they're good for a while. I've got some things I need to tell you, but we have to keep them between us."

Kane shook his head.

"I can try to keep you out of it," he said, "but we both

know if you're involved in a serious crime, it's got to come out."

Slade was silent for a few moments.

"Yeah, I can see that," he said, "but if there's any way you can help me, I'd appreciate it."

Kane sat and waited.

"I'd only been out here a couple of months," Slade said. "I'd had the academy and the on-the-job training, but this was my first solo assignment. I guess I wasn't really ready for it. They tell you all about procedures and precautions, but they never tell you what it's like to be the only cop for hundreds of miles, to never really be off duty."

Slade was quiet again, then shook his head.

"Listen to me, making excuses like some perp," he said. "It was a Friday night and I was tired of my own cooking, so I went over to the roadhouse for dinner. I guess I wanted to look over the action, too, maybe get some of it. The waitress seemed friendly, and we got to talking. I ended up waiting for her in the bar. Maybe me being there put a damper on things, because the bar emptied out about eleven. The waitress showed up a few minutes later with another woman. We had a couple of drinks, and one thing led to another. I suggested we go back to my place, but the waitress said she had a key to one of the rooms. I thought, what the hell. The three of us spent a couple of very pleasant hours in that room, and that was that."

Slade was silent again.

"Only, that wasn't that," Kane said to prime the pump.

Slade shook his head.

"No, it wasn't. A couple of days later, this old guy with a beard and earring comes in here with a videotape under his arm. Says his name is John Wesley Harding and he wants to welcome me to the community. Says the videotape is a gift. 'It's only a copy,' he says, 'but I thought you'd want to see it. In fact, I think you should watch it right now.'

"By now, I've already got an idea what's coming. So I bring the tape upstairs here and put it into the VCR, and there we are, the three of us, doing what comes naturally.

"The old guy has followed me upstairs, so I don't have to go far to get my hands around his neck. 'What are you showing this to me for?' I ask him. 'There's no law against consenting adults doing what they want.'

"The old guy kind of cackles and says, 'Consenting adults? That Tracy there, she's a working girl. And the other one? She's married. You don't want your bosses to see this, especially when you think about the story that can be told around this tape.'

"So I let go of the old bastard and start thinking, and the more thinking I do, the worse it gets. 'What do you want from me?' I ask.

"'Nothing,' he says, 'except for you to remember that I'm providing a necessary service over at the roadhouse and it would be a shame to disrupt it.'"

Slade unfolded his hands and held them up, looking at them like he'd never seen them before.

"Of course, that wasn't all," Kane said.

"No, it wasn't," Slade said. "I figured the odds were good it wouldn't be. So I didn't intervene in the whorehouse part of the operation, but I kept a close eye on it."

"Close enough that you knew Faith had joined it?" Kane asked.

The trooper nodded and dropped his hands.

"Yeah," he said, "so I pulled her over one day on the highway and we had a little talk. She made it clear to me that she was older than sixteen, which is the age of consent in this state, and that she was a volunteer. Needed the money for college, she said. Told me there were no drugs involved or anything else. She just laid it all out, as calm and cool as could be.

"I couldn't see any reason to intervene, especially with the original of that tape in the background."

"What did you do with your copy?" Kane asked.

Slade gave him a startled look.

"Destroyed it, of course," he said. "Why would I leave something like that lying around?"

Slade stopped again. Kane just waited. He'd tell the rest of it on his own.

"Then the girl disappeared," the trooper said. "I heard her father and the others were looking for her, and her dad came to see me. After he left, I went looking for Big John. I found him in the roadhouse office with Little John and braced him about her.

" 'She was just fine when she left work Friday evening,' he told me. 'Maybe she just decided to take off and make a movie.' Then he laughed and gave me a look. I got the point. I went through the motions of looking for her, but with no evidence of foul play I was happy to soft-pedal the whole thing."

Slade stopped then and took a couple of deep breaths.

"If anything happened to her because I dragged my feet," he said.

Kane stood up, walked over, and kicked the trooper's desk. Then he started pacing.

"You should have locked the old bastard up right after he showed you the tape, then gotten on the telephone," he said, trying to sound more confident than he felt. "Your bosses were young once, so if they thought you had any real cop in you they'd have helped you survive this. No matter what we tell the public, we're not a band of God's angels, and we all know it."

He paced some more.

"Here's what's going to happen. You and I are going to question the boy and his brother and fill in the blanks about Faith as best we can. Then we're going after Big John. When we find his stash of tapes, a couple of them are going to disappear. There's no need Charlie Simms's widow should have to see the one, and you'll be rid of the other. With any luck, your bosses will never know."

"What about the women?"

"I'll find them and have a word, and the next time you are deciding whether to do something stupid, you'll remember that I know all about this."

He walked over and put his hand on Slade's shoulder.

"There are several ways this won't work out that well," he said, "but we'll take it one step at a time and hope. Now get upstairs and try to get some sleep. We've got a busy day ahead of us."

21

But thou didst trust in thine own beauty, and playest the harlot because of thine renown, and pouredst out thy fornications on everyone that passed by.

EZEKIEL 16:15

KANE SAT IN HIS PICKUP OUTSIDE THE REGIONAL HIGH school, watching students arrive. They came in beat-up pickups and dented Suburbans and minivans that had seen better days, their lights stabbing Kane in the eyes as they bounced past. Most of the vehicles rattled off again after depositing a kid or two. The kids walked into the building with that draggy, oh-God-it's-Monday step. I wouldn't be a teacher for all the money in the world, Kane thought.

He had the defroster on high to keep the windshield clear. The warm air washed across his face, but left his feet freezing. He could have waited inside, if he'd had the nerve to go up against Miss Wisp again.

Slade had argued hard to be with him, but Kane hadn't budged.

"If you're there, he's got rights and lawyers and all that," he said.

"If I'm not and he resists, it's kidnapping," Slade countered.

"Yeah, and his word against mine," Kane said.

Slade gave in and went off to check on a burglary report

up the highway. Sam and Harry returned to the mine for
more questioning.

"They're going to be pissed when they find out we've
been holding out on them," Slade had said.

"Better pissed than jammed up in a situation where they
have to phony up a report or turn in a fellow cop," Kane
had replied, and again Slade had followed his lead.

A new Honda with tinted windows pulled up and the
driver got out. It was Johnny Starship.

Kane put his coffee cup into a holder, levered his door
open, and slid out into the cold. He walked toward the
young man, who was just straightening up from spread-
ing an old quilt over the Honda's hood to keep the heat
in.

"Hello there, Johnny," he called. "I've got some questions for you."

For a moment, it looked like the young man was going
to rabbit, but there was really no place for him to run. Kane
reached him and put a gloved hand on the his arm. When
Johnny tried to pull away, he jerked the young man toward
him and put his other hand on his neck. Ignoring his "What
the fuck" and "You're hurting me," he marched him to the
pickup, opened the driver's door, shoved him in and over,
and climbed back behind the wheel.

"Don't even think about running away," Kane said,
turning toward the young man. "I'll catch you and cuff you
if I have to."

"I'm not telling you nothing," Johnny Starship said.
"And if you try to make me, I'll sue you for everything
you've got."

Kane reached over, grabbed Johnny by the shoulders,
and shook him.

"This isn't some movie," he said. "This is serious. You're
going to tell me everything you know about Faith Wright."

"I'm not," the young man said, "and I'm reporting you
for assault."

Kane shook his head.

"And you about to graduate from high school," he said,
scorn in his voice. "You figure the troopers are going to do

anything based on the word of a kid whose father is the local whoremaster? Guess again."

"What do you mean?" the young man said, doubt in his voice.

"What I mean is this. I know your father is running whores over at the roadhouse. The troopers know that, too. I also know that Faith was working for him in the afternoons, taking on all comers for a hundred dollars an hour or whatever."

"Shut up!" Johnny cried. He squeezed his eyes closed, put his gloved hands over his ears, and rocked from side to side. "Shut up, shut up, shut up."

Kane waited until the fit subsided, then reached over and pulled Johnny Starship's hands off his ears.

"That isn't going to make anything go away," he said. "You can't hide from the things you do or the things other people do. Believe me. I know. So it's time to act your age now. Tell me, how did Faith get started whoring?"

The young man grimaced at the word and shook his head.

"I don't want to talk about this. You can't make me. I won't."

Kane put an arm on his shoulder.

"I can make you, and you will," he said. "What, are you trying to protect your family?"

The young man's eyes snapped up and locked on Kane's. There was murder in them.

"Family," he said, "I don't care anything about family. My mother took off, my father is a mean, evil son of a bitch, and my half brother doesn't have the balls to stand up to him. I'm just waiting until I'm eighteen, and then I'm going so far away nobody will ever be able to find me."

"Then why don't you want to talk? Is it Faith?"

"I don't want to think about Faith, either. I thought she was good. I thought she was my friend. But she just used me to get to my father."

He shook all over like a dog trying to shed water.

"Just leave me alone," he said. "Just leave me alone."

"I'm sorry, Johnny," Kane said softly, "I can't do that.

But if you tell me what you know, and you weren't part of whatever has happened to Faith, I'll let you go."

"What do you mean, what's happened to Faith? Has something happened to her?"

"I don't know for certain, but I was a policeman for a lot of years, and most of the girls who were doing what Faith is doing and disappeared didn't leave voluntarily."

The young man hung his head and sat there silently for a few minutes.

"I've got to find her," Kane said, "and you can help me. If you have any feelings for her at all, you'll talk."

"She's okay," he said. "I know she's okay. Faith can take care of herself."

"It's not time for that now, Johnny," Kane said. "It's not time to be a little kid and think that if you wish for something hard enough it will come true. It's time to be a grown-up now. You know that."

The young man was silent again, and when he began to speak his words came out in a monotone.

"Faith came to our school last year. Nobody knew what to make of her, an Angel coming to school with all the stoners and nerds and jocks. A few of the guys put the moves on her. Who could blame them? She's a total babe. Because of who my dad is, I steered clear of her, but she was hard not to notice. After the first couple of months, the excitement died down and she fit right in.

"Then, second semester, we started hanging out and talking and stuff. She seemed to be totally real and not all I'm-queen-of-the-world, the way pretty girls usually are. We talked about our families and what we were going to do when we got out of this hole."

"She's planning on leaving Rejoice?" Kane asked.

"She's *so* planning to leave," Johnny said. "There is something there she is totally pissed at. She talked about going away to some good college and living in what she called 'the world.' She would do good at it, too. She's smart. Me, I'm not. I'm going to the Army or someplace, anyplace out of here.

"Anyway, we got to be friends, sort of. I was kind of scheming on her, but she said she wasn't down with boy-girl stuff. I was bummed, but I really liked her, so we just kept hanging out.

"Then, when we came back for our senior year, I was complaining about my dad and, like, out of the blue she said she wanted to meet him. I was like, what for? But she kept after me, so I took her around to the roadhouse, to the office there. My dad wasn't there but my brother was, and she shook his hand and said she had something private she wanted to talk to him about. So he tells me to go get something in the café there and I wait around and like half an hour later she comes out all smiles.

"I'm thinking this is pretty weird. I ask her what they were talking about, but she blows me off."

The young man stopped and shook his head.

"Then, a couple of days later, my brother tells me that he wants to see Faith. I ask him what for, and he says she's going to work for him. Doing what? I say. Waitress-ing, he says.

"I'm like, yeah, right, waitressing. I know what that means. So I ask Faith what's going on. 'I'm going to work for your father as a sex worker,' she says, like it's just any old job. 'I need the money and I want to see what it's like.'"

Johnny Starship was silent for a minute or two, then resumed.

"I couldn't believe it. She was beautiful and smart. She didn't have to be some skanky whore."

He was silent again. Then the monotone.

"When I turned sixteen, my father had one of the women at the roadhouse show me the ropes. He said it would make a man out of me. It was okay at first. The woman kind of liked me, said I was cute, so we kept seeing each other for a while. Only in the roadhouse, in bed. I thought it was great, the sex, but this woman, she had such a negative view of life, of other people, on account of what she did, it totally bummed me out. One day she just up and left, and I actually felt relieved.

"I said to Faith, 'What are you doing? Having sex for

money could ruin your life, your outlook on life.' And she gave me the saddest smile and said, 'I'm already ruined.' But I didn't give up. I told her she could get some disease, something bad. But she said she would take precautions. That's what she said, 'precautions.'

"I said I'd tell her father, and she just laughed.

"Then she said, 'I need you to drive me from school to the roadhouse and back.' She had it all worked out. She'd leave her Jeep at school, and I'd drive her in the Honda—she'd be laying in the back so people wouldn't see her. She'd go in through the door in the warm storage shed, turn her tricks or whatever, and then I'd take her back to school.

"I was, like, totally not. No way. But she told me she was going to do it anyway, and she needed me to take her there and back. I said I wouldn't do it. 'I need you to keep me safe,' she said."

The young man looked at Kane and gave him a bitter smile.

"What could I do?" he asked. "I didn't want her doing that, whoring, but I didn't want her to get hurt by some sicko, either. So I stole a gun from my father, who has them all over our cabin, and kept it in the glove compartment, and I drove Faith back and forth to her goddamn job. And it hurt a little worse every day."

Kane patted the young man on the shoulder. As inadequate as that gesture was, it was all he could think of to do. He took a deep breath and willed himself to ask the questions he knew he had to ask.

"Did she work the day she disappeared?" he asked.

Johnny nodded.

"And you took her there and back?"

The young man nodded again.

"Then why was her Jeep still at the high school?"

"I don't know," Johnny said. "I watched her get into the Jeep and made sure it started, just like I always did. It seemed to be running fine when I drove off."

"There wasn't anybody in the Jeep, maybe lying in wait for her?"

"I don't think so. I didn't see anybody, and she waved to me as I drove off."

Kane was silent for a moment,

"I have to ask you this, Johnny," Kane said, speaking softly. "Did you do something to Faith? Did you hurt her? Do you want to tell me about it?"

The young man leaned away from Kane and swore. Then he began to cry.

"I didn't do anything to her," he said, tears spilling down his face and his voice harsh in his throat. "I loved her. I was part of this nasty, crazy thing she was doing, but I'd never hurt her for it. I hoped that if I was around and was dependable she'd get over whatever it was and we could be together."

Kane watched him cry for a few minutes, then said, "Did she ever tell you what she meant, that she was already ruined?"

Johnny just shook his head and kept crying. His tears turned to sobs, which turned to quiet, deep breathing.

"Okay, Johnny, I guess you'd better go," Kane said. "The smart thing would be to go to school and stay there. I'm going to see your brother next, then your father, and things might happen."

"I hope you kill them both," the young man snarled. He scrubbed his face with his sleeve, opened the door of the pickup, and got out. "They're bastards," he said. "I really hope you kill them both." Then he slammed the door.

Kane watched the young man walk up the steps of the high school. When the door closed behind Johnny Starship, he put the truck in gear and drove to the roadhouse.

22

Surely the churning of butter bringeth forth butter, and the wringing of the nose bringeth forth blood: so the forcing of wrath bringeth forth strife.

PROVERBS 30:33

KANE WALKED UP TO THE COUNTER AT THE ROADHOUSE and hit Little John in the face with an overhand right. Little John staggered backward and went down. The lowlife he'd been talking to started to say something. Kane looked him in the eye.

"Beat it, asshole," he snarled.

The lowlife left, walking fast with his feet splayed out like a duck in a big hurry. Kane moved around the counter, grabbed Little John by the front of his shirt, heaved him to his feet, and dropped him into the chair that sat beside a telephone stand. He watched as the man regained his senses. The side of his face was red and swollen.

That punch is going to leave a bruise, Kane thought. Good.

"Both hands on that table," he said.

Little John didn't budge.

"Now," Kane said, "before I decide your face would look better with matching bruises."

Little John raised his hands and laid them on the table. He opened his eyes and looked at Kane.

"The money's in a cash box under the counter," he said.

Kane gave him a wolfish grin. Without taking his eyes off the man, he felt around under the counter until he found the cash box. He laid it on the top of the counter, opened it, and threw it at the far wall. It struck with a crash. Coins flew everywhere. Bills jumped into the air, then floated toward the floor.

"Now that we've established that this isn't a robbery," Kane said, "let's get down to business. I want you to tell me everything you know about Faith Wright."

Little John took his hands off the table and put them on the arms of his chair. Kane leaned toward him. Moving very slowly, Little John pushed himself erect in the chair and put his hands back on the table.

"I don't know anything about Faith Wright," he said.

Kane's grin got even bigger.

"I think you should know that I'm dying for an excuse to beat the crap out of you," he said. "And when you lie, it just gives me one."

Little John let his shoulders slump.

"Go ahead, pound on me, I don't care," he said.

In two steps, Kane was by the man's side. He wrapped his free hand in the man's hair and jerked. Little John cursed.

"I hope I have your attention now," Kane said, "because you need to know just how the land lies. I've got videotape of Faith with a john in one of your rooms. I've got your brother's story about how she came to work for you. You're nailed for pimping. The only question is what else you go in for."

Little John tried to shake Kane's hand off his head but failed.

"You leave my brother out of this," he said. "He didn't have nothing to do with it."

Kane gave the man's hair another jerk and was rewarded with another curse.

"Oh, but he did," Kane said, "In fact, it's possible he

was the last person in these parts to see Faith Wright. If anything's happened to her, he could be in for some trouble. Big trouble."

"I said leave him out of this," Little John said, trying to sound tough.

"What do you care?" Kane asked.

Little John seemed surprised by the question.

"What do you mean, what do I care?" he said. "He's my brother."

Kane let go of his hair and stepped back.

"That's just biology," he said. "Otherwise, the boy hates you. In fact, he was telling me that he hoped I'd kill you."

Little John was almost on his feet when Kane grabbed his collar and pushed. He slumped back into the chair.

"He didn't say that," he said.

"Oh, but he did," Kane said. "He also said you didn't have the balls to stand up to your father."

Little John looked at his feet for a while.

"Families," he said at last. "What a fucking joke. Nothing but trouble. I'm so sick of this place, and my old man, and having my kid brother look down on me, and the shit I have to do. If I had any brains, I'd roll right out of here and never look back."

Kane leaned against the counter and waited. Minutes passed.

"If I tell you," Little John said finally, "you got to promise not to make any trouble for Johnny. Or me."

Kane shook his head.

"I'm not the troopers," he said. "They want to knock this crib over, or grab you up for something else, there's nothing I can do about it. And if something bad's happened to Faith, and you or your brother were involved, I'll burn you. Otherwise, I could give a rip what you do."

Little John was silent for another long stretch.

"Okay," he said finally, "I'll tell you what I know about the girl. Johnny brought her around, said she wanted to meet my dad. But he never deals directly with anybody if he can help it. So I talked to her. She told me she wanted to spend a few months as a sex worker here—that's what she called it, sex worker—to make money for college. I asked her, what, was she wearing a wire? She just smiled and said no and that she'd prove it and took all of her clothes off, right here in front of me. Then she just stood there, naked, like it was nothing. I told her, all right, all right, put your clothes back on. I mean, anybody could have walked in.

"I was tempted. She was a looker and, frankly, I could've used some new blood around here. The others were looking pretty wore out. Still are. So I told her I'd think about it. Then I went to talk to my old man, to tell him one of the Angel girls wanted to spend some time working on her back."

Little John shook his head again.

"He did what he always does whenever I have an idea," he said. "He said it was stupid. That if we started using Angel girls, we'd be shut down for sure. So I figured, what the fuck, and started to leave. When I got to the door—we were talking in the cabin. He don't come around here much. Doesn't like the risk, even though he takes most of the money, the old bastard—he asked me the girl's name. And when I told him, he got this big grin on his face. 'Faith Wright?' he said. 'Moses Wright's granddaughter?'

" 'Yeah,' I said, 'the old man's granddaughter. So what?'

" 'Well, that makes all the difference,' he said. 'Put her to work. She's fresh, so save her for the good clients. And work her in the video room. I wants lots and lots of tape of her at work.' Then he laughed like he'd just heard the best joke in the world.

"Now, I know Moses is always preaching against us over there in Rejoice, so I figure my old man wanted something to get even with. So I did what he said. I didn't want to, but I did.

"And everything went fine. The girl was mainly servicing the high rollers from up at the mine, so it's not like she was getting knocked around or anything. She was making money and seemed satisfied with the arrangement. We were making money, good money, off her. And my old man got his dirty tapes to cackle over. And then, boom, she just disappeared. And that's all I know."

Kane stood looking at Little John for a while.

"So, you put a seventeen-year-old virgin to whoring, and everything was just hunky-dory?" he said. The look on his face must have been something, because Little John put his hands in front of him like he knew he was going to be hit.

"Hey, look, it was a business arrangement," he said from behind his hands. "It's not like we went out and grabbed her, held her against her will. She came to us. She was of age. And she wasn't no virgin."

Kane could feel himself grinning again. The grin felt so wide he thought his face might split. He wanted Little John to keep talking, needed him to keep talking, because he was sure that this was the way to find Faith. But he also wanted to shut him up, to grind his face into the floor, to punish him for what he'd done, to wash away with Little John's blood the things he'd heard. He could feel the anger boiling up from his stomach to the base of his throat, threatening to make him throw up. He took a deep breath.

"Wasn't a virgin, eh?" he said. "And you'd know that how?"

Little John dropped his hands. Kane watched the bad news pass across his face in waves. First that he'd said too much. Then that he'd have to say more. Then that what he said might very well get him hurt or worse.

"Okay, okay, okay," Little John said. "I gave her a try-out. Who wouldn't? I had to know that she knew what she was doing."

Kane just looked at him.

"Okay, okay, and she was prime, too," he said. "She didn't know a lot about the stuff the girls do, the faking and everything, but she knew where the noses went. She wasn't no virgin."

Kane took in air through his nose and pushed it out through his lips. Once. Twice. Three times.

"She tell you where she got her experience?" he asked.

"Crap, no," Little John said. "I didn't need to know nothing like that. I felt bad enough about turning her out as it was. If it hadn'ta been for that fucking old man of mine, I never would have done it."

The whining note in the man's voice pushed Kane over the edge. He went for Little John, lifting him out of the chair like he was made of feathers and bulldozing him up against the wall. Kane's breath was coming in hot gasps, and red was gathering at the corners of his vision. Everything that was wrong in his life was in that anger. His right hand was around Little John's throat and he was squeezing, squeezing.

"Hey," a woman's voice said, "hey, what's going on?"

Kane looked over his shoulder. Tracy, the waitress from the café, was standing in the doorway with some bills in her hand. She took a step back when she saw his face.

"I just needed some change," she said. "I'll come back later."

She turned, jumped through the doorway, and pulled the door shut behind her.

Kane laughed. He let go of Little John's throat and laughed some more.

"She just saved your miserable life," he said.

He lowered Little John to the floor, spun him around, pulled a pair of Slade's cuffs off his belt and handcuffed the man's hands behind him.

"What's going on?" Little John said.

"I'm taking you somewhere you can't make any phone calls, like to warn your father," Kane said.

"You can't do this," Little John said. "You ain't no cop."

Kane pushed Little John across the room to the outside door, his captive trying to dig his heels into the ratty carpet. Then he spun him around.

"You're right," he said. "I'm no cop. So I'm going to leave it up to you. There's two ways this can go. You can come along and spend a few hours in a nice, warm cell over at the trooper office. Or I can beat you so badly you don't wake up for a while. Your call."

Without a word, Little John turned around and let Kane take him out the door and into the pickup. As they pulled away from the roadhouse, Kane said, "Tell me something. You really think all this shit you do is somebody else's fault? I mean, you're what, thirty? Thirty-five? Isn't that a little old to be blaming everything on your father?"

"Wait'll you meet my father," Little John said.

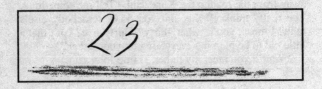

23

So David prevailed over the Philistine with a sling and with a stone, and smote the Philistine, and slew him.

1 SAMUEL 17:50

KANE TOOK THE HANDCUFFS OFF LITTLE JOHN AND locked him in the cell.

"But you promised to leave me alone if I told you about the girl," Little John said as Kane closed the cell door.

"Looks like I lied," Kane said, taking a seat in front of Slade's computer. Ignoring a steady stream of questions, complaints, and demands, he pecked away at the keyboard. When he'd finished, he printed out his page and went upstairs to make coffee. He was back at Slade's desk working on his second cup when the trooper came in.

"Burglary my ass," he said to Kane. "There wasn't anything worth stealing in that dump. Guy probably trashed the place when he was drunk and forgot he'd done it."

He took off his coat and hung it on a hook.

"What's this?" he asked, motioning with his head to Little John.

"That's a citizen's arrest," Kane said. "Turns out he is running a house of prostitution."

"No," Slade said. "Who knew? Are you breaking the law, Little John?"

"Fuck you guys," Little John said. "What are you, comedians?"

Kane handed Slade the piece of paper he'd typed.

"We just want to keep this guy away from telephones while we go see his old man," he said. "This affidavit should be enough to hold him."

Slade read the page and shook his head.

"I don't know," he said.

"Look," Kane said, "the old man is the toughest of this crew and he knows the most. We don't want him running, and we don't want him warned, not with all the guns he's supposed to have. What do we care if some judge says this wasn't legal in six months?"

Slade looked at Kane, then at Little John.

"He does look good in there," the trooper said. "You ask him anything about the mine payroll robbery?"

"Nope," Kane said. "Figured I'd leave that to the authorities."

Slade pondered for a moment.

"If he was involved in the robbery, it's a felony murder rap, two counts now," he said, "so we can't question him while he's locked up on this." He shook the paper. "It might be enough to keep him inside for twenty-four, but anything he says about the robbery won't stand up in court." He paused. "Christ, I hate all these rules and lawyers and shit."

"Welcome to the wonderful world of police work," Kane said. "Do you know where the old man's cabin is?"

"Yeah, it's out a dirt road north of town," the trooper said. "Harding Drive, the old bastard calls it."

"Fine, let's go see him now," Kane said. "If anybody was involved in the robbery, it was the old man. This one doesn't have the sand to do anything by himself. We'll brace his father and see what happens." He thought for a moment. "We'll take my rig. You'll hide in the back. I'll try to talk my way in. If I do, you can sneak out and cover my play. If I don't, no harm done. We'll come back, turn this one loose, and start grilling him. Unless . . ."

He got up and walked over to the cell.

"Listen up," he said. "We're going to see your old man

now. We're going to find out what he knows about Faith, and about that payroll robbery at the mine. If you've got anything you want to tell us about those things before he gets to talk, now's the time."

Little John laughed.

"You're wasting your time," he said. "You won't get anything out of my father."

"Okay," Kane said. "That's not your best move, but if that's the way you want to play it."

Slade rode most of the way sitting next to Kane in the pickup's cab.

"He tell you anything about videotapes?" the trooper asked.

"Yeah," Kane said. "He said his old man has them. Claimed he doesn't know where they're kept."

Following Slade's directions, Kane turned off the highway onto a narrow road that led through the trees. The road had been plowed, and polished in spots to glare ice. Kane drove slowly. After they passed two or three side roads, the trooper told him to stop.

"Time for me to get in the back," he said. "The road you want is the next left. It takes off just where this one starts to climb to the right."

He got out of the truck and, carrying his shotgun, got into the back.

The road to Big John's cabin was even narrower and hadn't been plowed. Kane followed old tire tracks along it.

The cabin was a big log A-frame. The front door faced uphill, toward a large clearing filled with snow. A new four-wheel-drive pickup was parked under some spruce trees off to one side. On the other was a tall woodpile. Smoke curled from the cabin's chimney. It was full daylight, or as full as daylight got, and Kane could see that the A-frame's windows were covered with wooden shutters.

"Doesn't look all that welcoming," he said to himself as he pulled up. He parked the pickup so that Slade could slip out the back without being seen from the door, got out, climbed the steps, walked into the Arctic entryway, and knocked.

No answer.

He pounded this time, his gloved fist making the door rock as he struck it.

"Knock that off," a voice called from inside. "Get off my porch and get off my property, or you'll wish you had."

"John Wesley Harding," Kane called. "I'm here to talk to you about Faith Wright."

"Go away," the voice called.

"That's not going to happen," Kane called back. "I'm staying until you talk to me."

No answer. Kane pounded on the door some more, keeping up a steady battering until the door slid open and a gun barrel poked out.

"You got more guts than brains," a voice said. "Who are you?"

Kane put his hands out to the sides to show that they were empty. Behind the gun barrel he could make out what might have been white hair and a white beard surrounding a lined face.

"My name's Nik Kane," he said. "Faith Wright's father hired me to find her."

"What makes you think I know anything about this Faith whatever-her-name-is?" the voice asked.

"I've talked to your sons," Kane said. "I know she was turning tricks at the roadhouse for you. I don't care about your whorehouse, but I need the answers to some questions about Faith."

The voice was quiet for a moment, then said, "You're a complication. I don't need no complications right now. I could shoot you, but the ground's too froze for burying." The voice laughed. "Come on in."

The gun barrel disappeared and the door swung open with a creak.

"Just keep your hands where I can see 'em, and walk on in here," the voice said.

Kane did as the voice instructed. The interior of the cabin was dark and he couldn't make out much.

"Push that door shut and lock it," the voice said from the shadows.

Kane turned and pushed the door shut, then fiddled with the lock. A hand shoved him out of the way.

"Just get over there," the voice said. Kane moved away, then turned. He heard the lock click into place and saw the old man straighten. The gun in his hand was an Army-issue .45. From where Kane was standing it looked like you could drive a Mini Cooper down the barrel.

"Rightee-ho," the old man said. "Now, take your coat off, careful like, and let it fall to the floor."

Kane did, then followed the gun barrel's instruction to turn slowly in a circle. That seemed to satisfy the old man.

"Well, you ain't got a gun, at least not one easy to get at," he said. "Walk over there to that chair and sit."

Kane's chair seemed to have been made from willow poles, the cushions made of caribou hide and stuffed with God knew what. He sank into them like he wouldn't stop until he hit China.

The old man snapped on a lamp, and Kane got his first good look at the place. It was all done up in rustic, the walls covered in wood paneling, a big wood stove blazing in the fireplace. There was even an honest-to-God grizzly rug in front of the fireplace.

Big John seemed to go with the room. He was of average height and build, with broad shoulders and a big head framed in a lot of white hair that didn't look to have been washed recently. His face was deeply lined and his mouth turned down at the corners in a permanent frown. He was wearing Carhartt pants held up by suspenders and a flannel shirt rolled at the sleeves to expose long underwear. He had some sort of moccasins on his feet.

If Kane hadn't known better, he'd have thought the man was some harmless, worn-out old prospector. But the glint in his eye and the .45 trained on Kane said different.

The old man took a similar chair across from him.

"Rightee-ho," he said, "ask your questions."

"Do you know where Faith Wright is?" Kane said.

"No, I don't. I truly don't. But you know, these hookers aren't too stable."

"Uh huh. Why did you change your mind and put her to work?"

Big John smiled.

"Oh, that. I like to help enterprising young women."

"So it didn't have anything to do with the fact she's Moses Wright's granddaughter?"

The old man's smile grew.

"I didn't say that. Sure, I like the fact the old fraud's granddaughter was doing the dirty for money. After all the wrong he's done me all these years."

Kane looked at the old man.

"You tell him what she was up to?"

Big John's smile disappeared, replaced by a poker face.

"Now, why would I want to do that?"

They sat looking at one another for a few moments.

"You know, you and Moses Wright look a lot alike," Kane said. "You related?"

"Nope," the old man said. "People are always asking me about that. Must be that we're both so godly."

He laughed at that.

"You got any more questions?"

"Yeah, I do," Kane said. "Who are you so afraid of?"

"What makes you think I'm afraid?"

"You're hunkered down here with your cabin buttoned up tight and a gun in your hand. Seems like fear to me."

The old man shook his head.

"Just being cautious. You never know what you'll run into out here in rural Alaska. Now, I think it's time you was going."

"I'm not done," the detective said. "You think one of your sons had anything to do with Faith's disappearance?"

Big John laughed at that.

"Not likely. My oldest boy don't have the backbone, and his brother was in love with the little whore. She probably took off somewhere like they do. Or one of her clients wouldn't take no for an answer. Or maybe them Angels found out what she was up to and is punishing her some way. Ain't nobody more ruthless than a righteous man with a Bible in his hand."

"You mean, like Moses Wright? Why would he hurt her? She's his granddaughter."

"I ain't saying it was the old fraud," Big John said, "or any other one of 'em. I'm just saying all the sin in these parts ain't sitting here in this room. Now, if you're finished . . ."

Kane nodded and started to get up.

"Wait a second," the old man said. "Ain't you going to ask me about the robbery?"

"What robbery?" Kane said.

Big John just smiled.

"You mean the mine payroll?" Kane asked. "I'm not investigating that."

"That's not what I heard," the old man said. "I heard you was one of the first on the scene and was kind of running things."

Kane nodded.

"That's right as far as it goes," he said. "But if you know all that, you should know that a couple of trooper investigators showed up and took over. Told me to butt out."

Big John shook his head.

"Nope, I never heard that part. But if you're saying it, it must be true. You cop types never lie, right?"

"You're a fine one to talk. I've been lied to more times than I can count, and by better liars than you. I figure you haven't said two true words since I came in here."

The old man gave him a sarcastic smile.

"Then I don't see any more reason we should be talking," he said. "Do you?"

"Guess not," Kane said.

He put his palms on the chair's arms and levered himself to his feet. The gun barrel wavered as Big John started to do the same. Kane dove at him. The .45 went off, the bullet going God knew where. Kane got his hands on the old man's wrists and rolled off the chair, bringing the old man with him. When they stopped rolling, Kane was sitting on Big John's chest, pinning his arms to the floor. The old man threw his head to the right and tried to bite the hand that held the gun down. Kane let go of Big John's empty hand and clipped him on the jaw.

"Knock it off," he growled, "or the next punch puts you out. Let go of the gun."

The look the old man gave Kane was feral and full of hate. But he gradually relaxed his grip on the .45. Kane took the gun, rose, stuck it in his belt, and offered Big John a hand. As the old man reached his feet, he lunged at Kane and tried to knee him. Kane turned his leg and took the knee on his thigh, then pivoted back, using his momentum to put some zip into the slap he landed on the side of Big John's head.

The old man staggered back a couple of steps and fell back into the chair. Kane was right on top of him when he pulled a small-caliber automatic from under the chair cushion. The detective swiped the gun away and landed a short, sharp punch to the old man's jaw. Big John's body went slack, but Kane wasn't taking any chances. He dragged the old man to the middle of the floor, away from any convenient hidey-holes.

A shotgun blast blew the front door open and Slade came through like he was storming Omaha Beach. Kane stuck his hands straight up in the air.

"Just be calm," he said. "It's all over."

The light went out of Slade's eyes, and he lowered the shotgun's barrel.

"I heard the shot," he said after he'd collected himself. "I was all the way around at the back of the house. I thought maybe something had happened."

Then he smiled.

"Heard gunfire," he said. "Probable cause."

"You're learning," Kane said. "Now why don't you keep an eye on this fellow while I conduct an unofficial, unrecorded search of this place? And be careful. The old boy is dangerous as a wolverine."

Kane started at the top, in the A-frame's loft, where he found nothing but an impressive number of firearms, boxes of ammo, and some thoroughly illegal explosive devices.

"Looks like Big John here is prepared to fight World War Three," he said to Slade as he came down the steep stairway. He walked to the back of the cabin. As he walked past the old man, he stepped carefully on one of his fingers. The old man jerked his hand away and cursed.

"Ah, awake, are we?" Kane said. "How nice. Perhaps you could direct me to your videotape collection. And, of course, the money from the payroll robbery."

The old man cursed Kane, steadily and inventively.

"You can't search my place," he said when he'd finished. "You got no warrant."

"Guess again, old-timer," Kane said. "I'm not a cop. I don't need a warrant. And by shooting at me, you gave Trooper Slade here probable cause to enter your house. And once he's in, well, there's no telling what he might see right out in plain sight. Now, if you'd prefer to answer a few questions, we wouldn't have to go through this song and dance."

Big John told Kane to do something both obscene and improbable.

Kane went through the ground floor of the house quickly. He found a pile of dirty magazines in the old man's bedroom, and in a drawer some notes in block letters. "Justice is coming," one said. "Prepare to die," said the other. The other two bedrooms, which Kane assumed belonged to Big John's sons, yielded nothing of interest.

When he was finished, Kane got a broom from the kitchen and started tapping the floor and interior walls. When he'd finished every place else, he went back to the living room, where Big John sat on the floor with his arms on his knees and Slade leaned against a wall with his issue sidearm trained on the old man.

"That's quite a collection of reading material in your bedroom," Kane said. "And you such an old man. Shame."

Big John responded with a snarl.

Kane turned to Slade.

"At least I found out why the old guy is holed up here," he said, handing him the notes.

Turning to Big John, he said, "Who's been threatening you?"

The old man glowered at him and said nothing.

"Must have been somebody pretty scary to make you hide out like this," Kane said.

"Ain't nobody scares me," Big John said.

Kane gave the old man a considering look.

"I guess that's why you decided to go for the mine payroll now," he said. "You wanted one last score before you cleared out, and you couldn't wait because you were afraid whoever was after you might get you. Who is it?"

The old man sat there mute.

"Okay," Kane said to Slade, "I'm going to finish checking this room, then we'll take him in for assault and sweat him."

The broom made a hollow sound where a couple of the walls came together. Kane set the broom down and walked back to look at the kitchen, then came into the living room with a smile on his face.

"You know," he said to the old man, "that's pretty good. I suppose that if someone noticed that the kitchen stopped a couple of feet short of square, they'd just think it was the pipe wall. But I'm thinking something different."

He began pressing on the paneling of the hollow-sounding wall. After several attempts, a section of the paneling popped loose and swung open. Kane groped around until he found the pull chain for an overhead light.

He walked in and looked around. The room was the size of a good-sized closet and was lined with wooden shelves. The shelves held all sorts of things, including videotapes and a couple of plastic freezer bags containing money. On the floor of the room sat a half dozen bank bags.

"I expect that's the mine payroll," he said.

He turned to find Slade looking in at him.

"Aw, hell," Kane said. Pulling Big John's .45 from his belt, he stepped to the door and looked out. Big John was sitting on the floor next to an end table with a big revolver in his hand.

"Drop it, old man," he said.

Big John fired, the big handgun sounding like a cannon. The bullet bit splinters out of the doorframe next to Kane's head. Kane pointed the .45 and fired at the old man's shoulder. The gun roared and a red spot appeared on Big John's upper arm. He grunted and flinched. His second bullet crashed into the wall about halfway between Kane and the trooper. As Kane aimed again, Slade began firing, the shots coming as fast as he could pull the trigger. His bullets drove the old man across the room and flat onto his back. His weapon clicked and clicked again as he pulled the trigger after his magazine was empty.

"Get a grip!" Kane barked. He walked over to the old man, looked, and turned away without even taking his pulse. Slade's bullets had made a pulp of the old man's chest.

"That's great," Kane said. "Just fucking great. You couldn't keep an eye on one old man and then you had to shoot him to pieces. Christ almighty. I still had plenty of questions to ask him."

"It was a firefight," Slade said. "They teach you in a firefight to keep shooting until the other guy can't."

"It was only a firefight because you took your eyes off your prisoner," Kane said.

He wanted to hit somebody, but there was really nobody to hit. The old man was a corpse, and the trooper had just made a young man's mistake.

He took several deep breaths.

"Okay, here's what we're going to do," he said. "You take my truck and go to the mine and get the investigators. I'll deal with the videotapes and see if there's anything here that will help tell me where Faith Wright has gone. Stick to the truth. We came out here to question Big John about Faith. I went in while you waited. You heard a shot and busted in. We were questioning Big John when I found this room. He got his hands on a gun and we shot it out. Tell them we found the mine payroll, and that we are as surprised as they are. That way we don't have to explain looking for any tapes."

Slade started to say something, but Kane waved it away.

"I don't want to hear it," he said. "Just go. You killed my best lead to Faith Wright because you underestimated an old man and took your eye off the ball. So I don't want to talk to you right now."

The trooper nodded and left the room. A minute later, Kane heard his truck start, back around, and drive off. He set the .45 down and walked to one of the windows, opening the shutters to look out at the monochromatic landscape. He took deep breaths and felt his pulse slow.

I really like this stuff, he thought with something like surprise. Even getting shot at. Maybe especially getting shot at. I like the matching wits and following clues and figuring things out. Maybe being a private eye wouldn't be so bad after all.

Then, after taking one more look at Big John's mortal remains, he put his gun away and got to work.

24

For they proceed from evil to evil, and they know not me, saith the Lord.

JEREMIAH 9:3

ON THE DRIVE TO FAIRBANKS, KANE TRIED TO FORGET
the events of the previous two days.

There was a lot to forget. He'd had time before the
troopers showed up to fast-forward through Big John's tape
collection, finding the original tapes of Simms and Slade
and selecting another that featured Richardson, the mine
manager. He'd watched Slade's all the way through at regular speed, then one part of it several times. Then he'd sat,
staring into nothing for several minutes.

"God damn it," he'd said at last. "God damn it, God
damn it, God damn it."

He'd stowed the tapes he was keeping in the inside
pockets of his parka and returned the rest to the shelves.
He couldn't do anything about the tapes that were left.
There were too many to hide. Besides, when the troopers
questioned Little John, he'd tell them about the tapes. It
would look pretty suspicious if they'd all just vanished.

So lots of tapes remained of Faith at work. Kane knew
someone would copy a tape or two, and they'd make the
rounds at cop stag parties and poker games for years to

come. The cop world would know Faith as an eager whore, and nothing more.

He knew, too, that word of what Faith had been doing would leak out, which meant he was obligated to tell her father before he heard it on the small-town telegraph. That had been an encounter Kane never wanted to repeat. The blood had drained out of Thomas Wright's face, leaving him pale as the sheets of paper on his desk, his eyes closed, rocking back and forth, saying, "I don't believe it," over and over again. Kane had finally gone in search of help, and when he'd brought the two middle-aged ladies who had been at his table at dinner back to Wright's office, one of them had shot him a baffled look and spat, "What have you done?" He'd made a run for it, and that was the last he'd seen of Wright.

Word of Thomas Wright's pain got out, of course. Many Rejoice residents refused to speak to him after that. When he tried to ask Moses Wright some questions, the old man held up a cross and yelled at him to leave, like he was driving out a demon. Kane's appeal for information at that evening's gathering was greeted by mutters or stony silence. The few who did talk had no idea what might have caused Faith to think she'd been ruined.

Everything else was a collection of negatives. The troopers' search of Big John's cabin had found no clue to Faith's whereabouts. They'd held on to Little John for a while, under the theory that his father couldn't have pulled the robbery solo. But without any evidence tying him to the crime, all he had to do was keep quiet, and he did, about Faith as well as the robbery. So they'd let him go. They might charge him with running a house of prostitution, not much of a charge all things considered. The trooper investigators were pissed off about the outcome.

"If you assholes had brought us in on this when you should have, the old man would still be alive, and we'd have been able to make a case," Sam had shouted at Kane and Slade.

"Wanted that reward too bad, huh, Kane?" Harry had sneered, and Kane was too depressed to snarl at him.

Even Slade was mad at Kane. The trooper wanted the original videotape of himself and the two women, but Kane wouldn't give it up. When Slade demanded to know why, Kane lied and said that he still wasn't sure what Slade's role had been in all this, and he wasn't about to hand over his leverage until he was. After he'd said that, he'd thought he was going to have to fight the big trooper.

After two days of nothing but hostility, Kane was anxious to get some space between himself and the residents of Rejoice and Devil's Toe, so anxious that he pulled out at four a.m., even though the errand that took him north and west was a long shot. He hoped, too, that the drive would help erase the images from the videotape that kept running through his mind like they were on a loop.

He played nothing but the blues on the four-hour drive through the darkness, the music matching his mood and the cold, pitiless land he drove through. The highway took him past Eielson Air Force Base, through North Pole, then into downtown Fairbanks, a small cluster of buildings on both banks of the Chena River.

Kane stopped there, at the post office, where he put all of the videotapes but one in a box and mailed them to himself in Anchorage. Then he walked a few blocks to a mean-looking bar on Second Avenue. Good thing the bars open early here, he thought, and ordered a shot and a beer.

He sat looking at them for a while, debating the wisdom of drinking them. There was no wisdom in doing that, he knew, but it wasn't wisdom he was after. So he downed the shot and chased it with beer.

His impulse was to stay and drink until he couldn't remember Faith or Laurie, until he couldn't remember Charlie Simms or Lester Logan or Big John lying dead, until he couldn't remember his time in prison and the lack of grace in the world, until he couldn't remember anything, especially Ruth Hunt. All that made several more drinks irresistible, but later, he decided. He had work to do. Work was all he had now, so it had better be enough. He forced himself back out into his truck and drove up toward the university with the alcohol rolling around in his empty stomach like liquid fire.

The university sat on a hill above the Chena, west of town. Following the directions he'd gotten off Slade's computer, Kane took the road that ran across the base of the hill, then past a golf course. About two miles past the campus, he took a left onto a road through the trees, then another left. He rolled up a short hill to a big house that sat in a clearing overlooking a creek valley. His knock was answered by a young man with a cereal bowl in his hand. He wore a pair of blue-and-white-striped boxer shorts and nothing else.

"Yeah?" the young man said.

"I'm looking for Feather Boyette," Kane said.

"Got no Feather Boyette," the young man said. "Got a Feather Collins. She owns the place."

"I'd like to talk to her, then," Kane said.

"Step in, mister," the young man said, "it's goddamn cold with the door open."

Kane stepped in. He found himself in a big, open room with a kitchen along the back and a set of stairs leading up to a railing-lined walkway that gave access to several doors.

"Hey, Feather," the young man called as he walked back toward the kitchen, "old dude wants to see you."

The door farthest along the walkway opened, and a woman in a bright red Chinese dressing gown with wide sleeves stepped out. Her hair was jet black and her face smooth, but she moved older than she looked.

"Can I help you?" she asked.

Another young man, this one blond and naked, stepped out onto the walkway behind her and ran his hands into her robe through the sleeves.

"We aren't finished yet," he said, his hands moving beneath the fabric.

The woman writhed against him, then pulled away.

"Not now, baby," she said. "We have company."

"I'm looking for a woman named Feather who used to live in Rejoice," Kane said.

"What do you want with her?" the woman asked. The young man made another grab but she slapped his hands away. "I said not now," she said. The young man grunted and retreated through the door, closing it behind him. "The young are so single-minded," she said.

"I just need some information," Kane said. "History, really."

"You could have picked a better time to talk about the old days," the woman said, "but what's done is done. Help yourself to a cup of coffee in the kitchen and I'll be down soon."

The dark-haired young man was sitting at the kitchen island spooning cereal into his mouth.

"Nice place you've got here," Kane said, pouring coffee into a mug.

The young man nodded and swallowed.

"It's Feather's really," he said. "We just room here. We're college students."

Kane took a drink of coffee. It was very good.

"The rent high?" he asked.

The young man laughed.

"Rent," he said. "Right. There's three of us live here. We each pay the rent once a week. Franklin's paying his right now." He put his cereal bowl into the sink. "Guys been lining up to rent rooms here for years," he said, making little quotation marks around "rent rooms" with his fingers. "Well, gotta go. Classes."

Left alone, Kane picked up his coffee and made a tour of the downstairs. The living room featured comfortable-looking couches. The dining room table was solid cherry and could seat a dozen. Original artwork dotted the walls, and every window had a view.

The dark-haired young man came down the stairs dressed, took a coat out of the closet next to the front door, and left. He was followed not long after by another young man. Kane was just starting his third cup of coffee when the blond one came flying down the stairs, dressing as he went.

"Damn, late again," he said, grinning, as he ran past.

By the time the woman came down the stairs, Kane had about memorized the ground floor of the house. It was all very tastefully and expensively done, right down to the leather-bound books that filled the walls of what appeared to be a den.

"I'm sorry for the wait," the woman said, extending a hand.

Kane took it. The bones were delicate and the back of the hand was lined with veins. Feather Collins looked every bit her sixty-some years around the edges, where spas and cosmetic surgery couldn't hide the effects of aging. But otherwise she looked damn good.

"You're staring, Mr. . . . ." she said.

"Kane," Kane said. "Nik Kane. I'm sorry. It's just that I expected someone older."

The woman smiled.

"Oh, I'm old enough," she said, "but I'll take that as a compliment. Would you care to sit down?"

They sat across from one another in the living room. The woman tucked her legs up underneath her.

"A lifetime of yoga has its rewards," she said. "Now, what can I do for you?"

"It's about a young woman named Faith Wright," he said. "She's missing."

"Faith Wright," the woman said. "Thomas Wright's daughter?"

"Yes," Kane said.

"I'm afraid I can't help you," she said. "Faith was quite young when I left Rejoice, and I haven't seen her since."

Kane nodded.

"I didn't expect you could tell me much about the girl," he said. "But I was hoping you could fill me in on some history of Rejoice, about the Wrights and Faith's grandmother, who also disappeared. Margaret Anderson?"

"Peggy Anderson. We all called her Peggy, all of us except Moses," the woman said. "That takes me back. Do you think the two disappearances are related?"

"I don't really know," Kane said, giving the woman what he hoped was a charming smile. "The truth is, I've run out of real leads to follow, and I'm here grasping at straws."

"Couldn't anyone in Rejoice tell you about her?"

"Not really. Most of the original group that settled Rejoice has died off or moved away. Except for Moses Wright, you may be the last of the people who founded Rejoice who is still in Alaska, not counting a few people who were children then."

"Like my ex-husband, you mean? How is Gregory?"

"He's doing well, the last time I saw him. As is your son."

Something in the tone of Kane's voice made the woman straighten in her seat.

"Do you think it odd, Mr. Kane, that I have severed contact with my son?" she asked.

"A little," Kane said, "but it's really none of my business."

The woman sat staring at Kane for a long time.

"If you're going to hear the whole story of my goddamn life," she said, "you'll need something stronger than just coffee."

She got up, took Kane's mug, and walked to the kitchen. She dumped the contents into the sink, got another mug, poured coffee into the mugs, then added something from a bottle. She got a can of whipped cream out of the refrigerator and sprayed some into each mug. She walked back into the living room, set Kane's in front of him, and took her seat.

"Now, then, we can begin," she said, cradling her mug. She took a sip, licked the whipped cream off her upper lip, and started talking.

"I was coming on fifteen when Mikey Hogan took me out behind the bottling plant in south Boston to show me something. He was about ten years older, and my mother, God rest her soul, didn't want me having anything to do with him. Mikey and his half brother, Francis, who was a few years younger than him, were nothing but trouble, she said."

The woman raised her cup in a mock salute.

"You got that right, mom.

"But I liked it from the first, so I hung around with Mikey when I could sneak away. He was a guy around the neighborhood, running errands for bookies and such, and devilish handsome. We were hot and heavy for a few years. Then I graduated high school and went off to college, and he lost interest. We still knew each other and spent time together during the summers, but we quit having what the parish priest called carnal knowledge of each other.

"I didn't mind, though. There were plenty of guys at college. I graduated and moved back to the old neighborhood and got a job. Then the sixties hit and Mikey had plenty of dope. He still liked young girls and would bring them around to my place. Young boys, too, which is why I let him in. Before I knew it, there was a bunch of us crashing there. Then Mikey started talking about going far away, to Alaska. To get back to the earth, like people were talking then. We pooled our money and bought a bus, and Francis, who was always good with engines, got the thing running. We painted it all up and stocked it and everything, and it just sat there in the lot behind my apartment until one day Mikey said, 'We're going.' And we went."

She stopped talking for a while, then continued.

"You know, I look at these young people now and think, what were we doing then? Mikey and I were old enough to know better, but we didn't give a damn. The rest of them, the oldest was maybe seventeen. Where were their parents?

"The whole thing was weird. Like Francis not coming along. There'd been some sort of robbery out at the airport there, and Francis had been grabbed up by the cops, Mikey said.

"None of us paid much attention then. Like I said, Mikey had plenty of dope and always seemed to have money when we needed it, and we floated across America making love, not war.

"When we got to San Francisco, some people left and some people joined up. By the time we headed north, we were a convoy, the bus and several cars. Mikey started calling himself Moses, because he was leading us to the promised land, and sleeping with the sweetest young thing on the bus, pretty Peggy Anderson."

The woman was quiet again for a while.

"He liked them young, but who doesn't? Anyway, that first winter was rough, living in the bus in the cold. Fortunately, we had more girls than boys, so we attracted a couple of young locals who knew what they were doing. We made it through the winter and everything looked good. That summer we got a few cabins built and some gardens planted and caught some fish and used Mikey's money for the rest. Only everybody called him Moses by then, Moses Wright, and when I kidded him about it in private he gave me such a look that I called him Moses from then on, too.

"About the only attention we attracted, besides the local boys, was from the trooper who was stationed out there—a big, young, good-looking guy. He was always dropping in. At first I thought he was suspicious, but he didn't do anything and we gradually came to accept him. We kept the dope out of sight, but otherwise he was just another visitor.

"Then, that fall, Peggy was pregnant. I was surprised. When I was seeing him, Mikey was never careful about birth control and neither was I, but nothing happened. I'd gotten pregnant once, in college, so I figured maybe it was Mikey who was shooting blanks. But then Peggy got knocked up, so I guessed it had all just been luck.

"The baby, Thomas, was born in June. We had a big celebration, I remember, with a bonfire and fireworks, and Mikey looked proud enough to bust. But he and Peggy started having trouble not long after. We were still living close together then, and I could hear them yelling at each other at night. That winter Peggy disappeared, and not long after Mikey began toting a Bible around. I thought he was just goofing, but he was deadly serious. About the Bible, about being Moses, about the whole religion thing. He even quit chasing the young girls for a while, although everybody was paired up by then, so he didn't have much choice."

The woman drained her cup and got to her feet.

"You want more?" she asked.

Kane shook his head. The first one hadn't been a good idea all by itself.

"I'm having more," she said, "and if you want to hear what I've got to say, so are you."

Kane handed her his mug. He didn't want to hear more, not really. He felt worse now than he had when he'd knocked on the door, and the Irish coffee wasn't helping. But he took the fresh mug from her and drank as she resumed talking.

"The trooper looked hard for Peggy," the woman said. "He questioned us all, especially Mikey, but didn't get anywhere. The next summer, another young girl moved in, and Mikey took up with her, and then another after that, but they didn't stick. Maybe he just wanted help with the baby. Anyway, a few years went by. Mikey was really Moses by now, and most everybody else in Rejoice was getting religious, too.

"Then, one day right around summer solstice, Francis showed up. Everything was cool for a week or so, then he and Mikey had a big row and Francis left Rejoice. He didn't go far, though. Some of the less religious element of Rejoice had moved over into the woods around Devil's Toe because they didn't like all the new rules Mikey was making. Francis moved over there, too, and somehow got the money to buy the roadhouse there."

"He was calling himself John Wesley Harding by then?" Kane asked.

"Yes," the woman said with a smile, "he was. Mikey warned me against having anything to do with him. Not that he needed to. I never liked Francis that much. He was mean and not very smart."

"Why were you sticking around?" Kane asked, interested despite himself. "You were educated, and used to a better life. Why didn't you leave?"

"Inertia, at first," the woman said, "and a steady supply of young drifters. And then I noticed little Gregory Pinchon. He couldn't have been more than eight then, but God, he was a beautiful child. I waited, and when he was sixteen and legal, I took him into my bed. It was quite a scandal. I was in my mid-forties and all the tongues were wagging. But I made sure he got me pregnant right away, and then nobody could stop us getting married. It was about the time Matthew was born that the community decided we needed some rules about young people and sex and came up with all that 'walking out' garbage."

"What happened?" Kane asked. "Why did you leave?"

The woman took their mugs into the kitchen, then brought them back. When Kane tasted his, it was straight whiskey.

"Young men are great for some things," she said, slurring some of her words, "but Gregory didn't wear well on me. He was beautiful, but repressed sexually, probably by all that religious nonsense. And outside of bed we didn't have anything to build a marriage on. Besides that, I was a rotten mother."

Kane could hear a slur in his own voice when he spoke.

"Was that all?" he asked. "The whole reason you left?"

"No," she said. "There was Mikey, too. He was stirring people up against me. By then, I didn't know if that was because he believed I was too sinful or because I was about the only person left in Rejoice who knew him from the old days.

"So I took the hint and left. Came here. Divorced Gregory. Met a man, a nice fellow, man named Collins, who had a lot of money. All that time I'd spent studying the Kama Sutra came in handy then. He married me. Five years ago, he dropped dead. I've been taking in boarders ever since."

Very carefully, Kane set his mug down.

"That's quite a story," he said. "Did you ever have any idea what happened to Margaret Anderson Wright?"

"Nope," the woman said. She shook her head from side to side for what seemed to Kane like a long while. "I thought it was strange she'd run off and leave her baby, but none of us was too stable. I think the trooper thought something bad had happened, but like I said, nothing ever came of it."

They sat looking at one another for a moment.

"That's some scar you've got," the woman said. "What happened?"

"I had a difference of opinion with a sharp object," Kane said. Or that's what he tried to say. It came out sounding like something in Russian.

"You must be a rough customer," the woman said, giving a theatrical shiver.

Kane got carefully to his feet and started to put on his coat. He got his arm into the wrong hole and had to start over. When he looked, the woman was smiling at his antics.

"You don't have to leave," she said. "You could lie down with me awhile. I've got a big, soft bed upstairs."

"I appreciate the offer," he said, "but I'm pretty sure that I'd just embarrass myself, particularly compared to your boarders."

He held out his hand and shook hers, then made his way to the door as carefully as if he were walking on a tightrope high above the ground.

"I hope you don't mind if I don't get up to show you out," the woman called after him, "but my feet seem to be numb."

Kane managed to get the door open. He stepped through and pulled it shut behind him. Then he stood for the longest time, leaning against the door and breathing in the cold, fresh air.

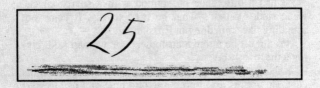

25

And be not drunk with wine, wherein is excess; but be filled with the Spirit.

EPHESIANS 5:18

KANE NEEDED ALL OF HIS CONCENTRATION TO HEAD HIS truck back toward Fairbanks.

"Eleven o'clock in the morning and drunk as a lord," he said as he tried not to weave all over the road. "Great."

He pulled into the big parking lot at a place called Sophie's Station, wrestled his duffel out of the back, and forced himself to walk a mostly straight line into the lobby. The desk clerk cocked an eyebrow at him, but payment in cash in advance seemed to mollify her. Kane made it to his room, transferred the contents of the duffel into a couple of plastic laundry bags, added the clothes he was wearing, put on the hotel's bathrobe and called for a bellman. When the bellman showed up, Kane handed him the bags and a twenty-dollar bill.

"If you get these back to me clean by six, there's another twenty in it for you," Kane said, or tried to say. The bellman seemed to understand him, took the money and the bags, and left.

Kane walked into the bathroom, shoved a finger down his throat, and spewed coffee and raw whiskey. When he was finished, he rinsed his mouth out with cold water, groped his way to the bed, and collapsed.

Pounding on his door woke him from a dream full of malevolent shadows with beaks and tentacles and naked dark-haired temptresses and blond heroines wearing black ribbons around their throats and not much else. He exchanged another bill for his clean laundry, then sat on the bed for a while and listened to the pounding in his head.

"Irish coffee for brunch just isn't a good idea," he said aloud. He rose from the bed, got into the shower and stood under water as hot as he could stand it for as long as he could stand it. He tried to think about nothing, but his mind kept wandering back to images of angels, of Charlie Simms rising and falling on top of Faith Wright, of Laurie smiling at the top of the stairs, of Slade with the two women.

Somewhere in this mess is the answer, he thought. But the answer to what? To what happened to Faith? To why Laurie sent him away? To why religion keeps calling to a man who doesn't believe? To something, anything, that would make his life make sense?

"Well," he said aloud, "there's only one cure for self-pity."

He turned off the shower, toweled off, and dressed. He put some money in his pocket and tucked the rest into his duffel, then went downstairs to the restaurant. He ate soup, salad, and steak at a table by the window, looking out at the vast darkness pierced by a few pinpricks of light. When he finished, he went into the bar and ordered a glass of Silver Gulch pilsner. The first sip spread through his body like the glow from a first kiss.

He awoke the next morning spread-eagled on his bed, fully clothed. His tongue, as someone had once written, felt like the entire Russian army had marched across it in their stocking feet. He heaved himself up and stumbled to the bathroom, where he drank water until he sloshed. He stripped off his clothes and stood under the shower again.

At least I'll be goddamn clean on the outside, he thought.

He had no sequential memory of where he'd been or what he'd done the night before. He remembered riding in cabs and shoving bills down the cleavages of waitresses. He remembered arguing with a big woman dressed all in black about whether Bob Dylan was a better poet than Dylan Thomas. He couldn't remember which side he'd been on. He remembered telling a couple of barflies how his wife had left him to become a hooker and how they'd clucked their tongues and suggested he buy everybody another round.

He got out of the shower and went through the motions of getting ready to face the world. He brushed his teeth and shaved and combed his hair, ate aspirin, put on clean clothes, packed his duffel, went down a flight of stairs, checked out, started his truck, and drove to the library. He spent fifteen minutes checking on something, then got back into his truck and pointed it back down the highway.

He felt, all things considered, like something that had fallen out of a tall cow's ass.

Not bad, he thought. Two literary allusions for one hangover. Wasn't he an educated s.o.b.

His head pounded, and it felt like there was an archery contest going on in his bowels. But his mind had that perfect clarity that often comes after a bender. And he no longer felt sorry for himself.

"Today," he said aloud, "I feel like the avenging angel. I'm the angel of death. And I've got a hangover. That's got to be bad for somebody."

He slid a Rolling Stones CD into the player, cranked up the volume, and stepped on the gas.

26

Thou hast laid me in the lowest pit, in darkness, in the deeps.

PSALMS 88:6

DORA JORDAN ANSWERED NIK KANE'S KNOCK, WEARING
designer sweats and big pink bunny slippers. She had her
long, dark hair pulled back from her face in a ponytail and
wore no makeup. She had a trace of flour on her chin and a
wary look in her eye.

"Can I help you?" she asked.

The Jordans lived in a small frame house in a row of
small frame houses built in the 1980s by the Bureau of In-
dian Affairs. Kane had pried the location out of a surly
Slade and driven there through the gathering darkness of
the winter afternoon.

She's really very pretty, Kane thought as Dora Jordan
swept a stray lock of hair out of her eyes with a hand covered by an oven mitt.

"I'm Nik Kane," he said, "the fellow who bought your
grandfather soup the other day."

The woman was silent for a beat longer than Kane expected, then nodded.

"I remember," she said. "What do you want?"

"No beating around the bush," Kane said, giving her

his best smile. "I was hoping to speak with Abraham for a moment."

She stood there looking at him for what seemed to Kane like a long time. Then she nodded.

"Sure," she said. "Leave your boots and coat in the entryway." She spun on her heel and left him standing there.

Kane removed his outdoor clothes and stepped into the house. He was standing in what he took to be the living room. The room was warm and softly lit. Abraham Jordan sat in a big La-Z-Boy watching television. Kane walked over and sat in a chair near him. The TV showed footage of explosions and bodies from Iraq.

"That damn war," the old man said. "I don't like my boy being at that damn war."

Dora came in carrying a plate of cookies. The old man took one, then Kane.

"He gets confused about what year it is sometimes," she said. "He thinks the war in Iraq is Vietnam."

"Him and all the Democrats in the country," Kane said, winning a brief smile from the woman.

He bit into the cookie. It was hot and moist and loaded with chocolate chips.

"These are wonderful," he said.

"They're his favorites," she said. "Would you like some coffee to wash it down?"

She brought coffee and sat on the sofa. The television set was pitching some new wonder drug for erectile dysfunction. Abraham Jordan was asleep, breathing noisily through parted lips.

"He does that sometimes, just drops off," his granddaughter said. "More often as time goes on."

"I can't blame him," Kane said. "It's warm and homey in here, a perfect place to nap."

In fact, he was having trouble keeping his own eyes open. Too old to go carousing and then just carry on like nothing happened, he thought.

The woman looked at him, smiled, and stood up.

"Trade me places," she said. "You can stretch out on the couch and nap yourself."

"I couldn't," Kane said. But he got to his feet and walked past the woman. She smelled like soap and cookies. He sat down on the couch.

"I know you saved my grandfather some unpleasantness," Dora Jordan said. "Please, accept our hospitality."

Kane was too worn out to resist. He put his feet up, his head on a pillow, and was asleep in an instant.

He dreamed he was arriving at Wildwood Prison in Kenai again, with a fresh scar and a lot of worries. He'd been in the system less than a year and this was his third facility; transferred from Spring Creek, the maximum-security prison, when the warden got word the White Brotherhood was going to kill him, then attacked in the mess hall at Palmer Correctional by a drug dealer named Kelso he'd sent up three times. Three strikes and Kelso was out, and he'd tried to take Kane out with a sharpened toothbrush, maybe on his own, maybe on commission from the Brotherhood. Being a con who used to be a cop was no cakewalk. After he'd healed up, and the prison authorities decided they couldn't tack on any more time because he'd killed Kelso in self-defense, they'd sent him to Wildwood.

The first con he'd seen in the yard had been Amos Titus, a Native guy he'd grown up with.

"Holy shit!" Titus had said. "Nik Kane! They got the whole West High senior class of 'sixty-seven in here now."

"That can't be right, Amos," he'd replied. "There were more than five hundred of us."

Titus had grinned and nodded.

"That's right," he said, "I guess they just got the cool ones."

They'd talked for a while, catching up. Titus had followed Kane's case in the papers, and his time inside on the grapevine.

"You done something to piss the white guys off plenty," Titus said. "And the blacks don't like you much, either. But this here's a Native prison. So why don't we go talk to the elders, see what they think."

The elders were a half dozen guys sitting in the best place for sun. Titus had introduced Kane.

"What you in for?" one of them had asked.

"I killed somebody," Kane said. Then, after a pause, *"I was drunk."*

There were nods when he said this. Alaska Natives knew all about the damage alcohol did.

"You arrested me once," another elder said.

Oh, shit, Kane thought.

"But you weren't an asshole about it," he continued after a moment. *"I was drunk."*

There were more nods, and that was it. From then on Kane was safe, as safe as you could get in prison. He never really knew why he'd been accepted. He'd just been grateful and secure, and that security washed through his dream, just as it had through the rest of his time in prison.

When he awoke, the house was full of cooking odors. Abraham Jordan was watching *Survivor* on television.

"You white people don't know nothing," he said, giggling as the contestants did something particularly stupid.

Dora Jordan came into the room.

"You're awake," she said. "You'll be staying for dinner."

It was a statement, not a question. Kane washed up and joined them at the table. Over stew and fry bread he and Dora talked about the wider world, about her education at the university in Fairbanks and his on the streets of Anchorage. Over bowls of ice cream, she asked, "What was it you wanted with grandfather?"

"I was hoping he . . ." Kane stopped himself and turned to the old man. "I'm sorry, uncle," he said. "I hoped you might show me where you saw the angel."

"Angel?" the old man said.

"It's better you ask him in the morning," Dora said. "His mind is sharper in the mornings." She paused, looking from Kane to the old man and back. "You are welcome to our sofa for the night if you like."

So Kane nestled down in some blankets she brought and fell into a deep and dreamless sleep. When he awoke, Abraham Jordan was sitting in his La-Z-Boy fully dressed, staring at him.

"You sleep all day you'll never see the angel," he said.

Dora Jordan came in from the outside stamping snow off her boots.

"The snow-go is hitched to your truck," she said. "It's full of gas. Watch it, though. It floods easy."

She stopped and looked at him.

"You can drive a snow-go, can't you?" she asked.

Kane smiled at Abraham Jordan.

"I don't know, uncle," he said. "Us white people don't know nothing."

"Don't worry," the old man said, "I'll show you how."

After breakfast, Dora handed him a big brown bag.

"Here's lunch just in case," she said. "You take care of my grandfather."

Kane reached for his wallet.

"I'd like to give you some money for all this," he said.

She shook her head. "But you could bring the snow-go back full," she said.

The old man was dressed in a fur parka, moose-hide leggings, and the beautiful moccasins tied high up on his legs.

He looks better than I do, Kane thought, and he'll probably be warmer, too.

He helped the old man into the pickup, drove to the Pitchfork mine, and stopped at the gate.

"Is Tony Figone running security now?" he asked the guard.

The guard nodded.

"Tell him Nik Kane's here to see him," Kane said.

After a couple of minutes, the guard swung the gate open and waved him through. He left the pickup running and the old man in it and went into the office trailer to see Tony Figone.

"I've got an old man and a snow machine outside," Kane said after they'd shaken hands. "I need to go up into the hills behind here for a while. And I need a map of the old mining sites."

"Mine manager's going to have to approve all that," Figone said. "They guard the maps and all the other mining information like it was nuclear secrets."

Richardson was polite but emphatic.

"Can't allow it," he said. "And it'd cost me my job to give you a map."

"Tony," Kane said to the security chief, "why don't you give us a moment."

Figone left the room, closing the door behind him.

"Now, then, Mr. Richardson, here's the deal," Kane said. "I need to go back in there, and I need a map that shows the locations of the old shafts. I'm sure you've had the whole area surveyed. I'm not interested in the least in where the gold might be or anything else having to do with your operation. And it turns out I have something to trade."

"What's that?" Richardson asked.

Kane took a videotape out of his coat pocket and set it on the mine manager's desk.

"I took that tape out of Big John's collection," Kane said. "Seems he was taping his girls and their clients. This one's got your name on it, and I watched it just to make sure. I hope you don't mind me saying that you're a naughty guy. Or that you don't want your wife to see what you were up to with a teenage girl."

Richardson reached over and tried to grab the tape, but Kane pulled it back out of his reach.

"This is blackmail," Richardson said.

"Absolutely," Kane said cheerfully.

The mine manager thought for a bit.

"I could have Figone take that tape from you," he said at last.

"No, you couldn't," Kane said. "The only way you get this tape is if I get the map."

The mine manager thought some more. Then he got up, walked to a filing cabinet, unlocked it, extracted a map, and spread it out on his desk.

"This shows all the mine sites we know about," he said. "They've all been GPS-located. Have you got a unit?"

Kane shook his head.

"I'll loan you one," the mine manager said. "Wouldn't want you getting lost out there."

He folded up the map and handed it to Kane. Kane handed him the tape.

"If you're thinking about trying anything tricky," the detective said, "you should ask yourself how sure you are that's the only copy."

"There's no need for threats," Richardson said. "I'm certain my best course is to cooperate."

Kane followed Figone's SUV around the face of the mine pit and onto a narrow road that ran up the hill. A crew was working even though it was Sunday. The two vehicles pulled off into a small, cleared turnaround, and Figone helped Kane take the snow machine off its trailer.

"You sure you want to be doing this?" Figone asked. "It's colder than a witch's tit, and you won't have much light."

"It's just a little recreational snow-machining, Tony," Kane said, giving the machine a little gas and thumbing the starter. It fired right up. Kane stowed the lunch and a thermos of coffee under the backseat. He helped the old man onto the seat, slipped a balaclava over his face, wrapped a scarf around his mouth and nose, dropped goggles over his eyes, mounted, and started off, careful to not flood the engine. The old man wrapped his arms around Kane's waist and they were off.

They rode for about twenty minutes, heading due south and mostly uphill before the old man pounded on Kane's shoulder and waved him to the left. Kane made a long, sloping turn. He followed the old man's thumps and waves for another twenty minutes or so. The sky was as bright as it was going to get when the old man signaled him to stop. He pulled up in the lee of a small stand of spruce and shut off the engine. The silence seemed loud after its constant whine. The old man walked a few steps away and fumbled at his zippers. Steam rose from where he wet the snow.

"God damn," he said as he returned to the snow machine. "An old man's bladder is no fun."

Kane handed him a plastic cup full of coffee. He stood, looking around, sipping. Kane looked, too. To him, the landscape looked much the same as it had since they'd left the mine behind them.

"I trapped this country for forty years," the old man

said. "Had me some luck, too. Caught a big lynx in a set right here in these trees. Froze stiff by the time I got here. And a wolf let me shoot him right down in that gully. These are his hairs on his parka hood."

The old man was silent then, as if recovering from what was, for him, such a long speech.

"I like the silence best," he said at last. "In the summer there's birds and animals all over, living their lives, making noise. But in the winter, sometimes the dogs would be asleep and it was so quiet. It was like if you listened hard enough, you could hear the mountains breathing."

The old man slurped coffee.

"I was hoping to get back here before I died. Guess I should thank you for it," he said. "Now, if my son would just come back, I could die happy."

Kane let the silence settle.

"It's been a long time, uncle," he said. "Do you really think he's coming back?"

The old man was silent for so long Kane wondered if he'd heard him.

"A man's gotta have faith," Abraham Jordan said. "If you don't have faith, what do you have?"

The two of them sat there on the snow machine, drinking their coffee and thinking their thoughts. The old man threw the last of his onto the snow and dropped the cup into the compartment under the seat.

"It's just around there that I seen the angel," he said, pointing. "We better get going."

Kane started the snow machine and took them through the gully and around a shoulder of snow-covered hill. There was a frozen, snow-covered creek down below them a ways, and they rode along the side of the hill slowly. Kane had driven snow machines before, but not recently, and he didn't want to tempt fate. They rounded another shoulder of hill, and the old man pounded him on the back. He found a level spot and coasted to a stop.

"This is it right here," the old man called over the rumble of the idling engine. "This is where I seen the angel. He was headed that way." He pointed to the ridge that led down to the creek.

Kane pulled the map from an inside pocket and unfolded it. He checked his GPS unit, then examined the map.

"There's some mine workings right down there," he said, pointing.

"Sure there is," the old man said. "Everybody knows that." Then he gave Kane a big grin.

"It's a lot shorter if you just follow the creek," he said. "You can drive up a dirt road off the highway, unload your snow-go, and be here in ten, fifteen minutes. Don't have to go through the mine at all."

"Why didn't you tell me that, uncle?" Kane said.

The old man grinned again.

"I like to ride the snow-go," he said.

Kane put his things away and took them slowly down the ridgeline, then followed the creek. The old man pounded him on the back and he stopped.

"You got city eyes," the old man said. "There's the trail. There's a drift tunnel up the hill a ways."

Kane untied a couple of pairs of aluminum bear-claw snowshoes from the back of the machine. He and the old man put them on.

"You sure you can make this climb, uncle?" Kane asked.

The old man gave him a pitying look and started off. Kane followed. The snow cover wasn't deep, and they probably didn't need the snowshoes, but the old man kept moving so there wasn't a chance to take them off. A few minutes' slogging brought them to the entrance to the drift tunnel. It was somewhat overgrown by bushes.

"See them broken branches?" the old man said. "Somebody been in there a little while ago."

Kane sat on a fallen tree and took off his snowshoes, then helped the old man remove his. He pulled a flashlight out of an inside pocket and led the way into the drift tunnel, stooping to avoid the low roof. The tunnel led in and down, and the two men followed it for maybe fifty yards, dropping to their hands and knees as the tunnel got smaller. From the marks on the floor, something had been dragged along it.

Finally, the tunnel opened into a sort of gallery in front of the rock face, which still bore the marks of the picks that had gouged it nearly a century before. Kane could rise to his knees and shine the flashlight around. The beam fell on something, and behind him, he could hear the old man suck in his breath. Caught in the beam of the flashlight were a pair of pale hands folded across a big book.

"Maybe that wasn't an angel I seen," the old man said as the flashlight's beam climbed up the body to focus on Faith Wright's dead-white face.

"Maybe it was, uncle," Kane said. "Maybe it was the angel of death."

27

And he said, who made thee a prince and a judge over us?
intendest thou to kill me, as thou killedst the Egyptian?
And Moses feared, and said, Surely this thing is known.

EXODUS 2:14

THE SUNDAY-EVENING SERVICE WAS NEARING ITS END when Kane slid into the back of the community hall. Nobody worked in Rejoice on a Sunday, and there were three religious services, the evening's being the longest and most fervent. Moses Wright stood at the front of the congregation, wrapping up what must have been a powerful preaching. The sweat was rolling off his brow, and most of his congregation were on their knees, arms stretched toward the heavens.

"Jesus calls on us to be vigilant," Moses was saying. "Go out and witness to your faith by the way you live, and be ready to protect it from the evils of the world."

Calls of "Amen" issued from the worshippers. Young Matthew Pinchon stepped forward and turned to face the audience.

"Before we go, let us join our hands," he said, "and pray for Faith Wright, wherever she might be, to come back to the righteous life. And for her family and all of us who know her here in Rejoice, as they seek to understand the ways of God."

He motioned for Thomas Wright to join him at the front of the room. People stood up and took up the hands of their neighbors and bowed their heads.

"I think you might want to wait on that prayer," Kane called. "I have a few things to say."

Heads snapped up. The looks on their faces weren't welcoming. Kane walked through the crowd until he was near the front, facing Pinchon and the two Wrights. All the eyes on him didn't seem to bother him a bit.

"I found Faith today," he said, speaking loudly so everyone in the hall could hear him. "She is dead."

Thomas Wright staggered as if Kane had hit him. He bent over, uttered a low, keening sound, and began to cry. Moses Wright gave Kane a look of pure hatred. Kane didn't like telling Faith's father that way, but he had work to do here, and there was no way to do it that would be easy on Thomas Wright.

"She was lying in an old mining tunnel back up in the hills a few miles from here," he said, his voice rising over the hubbub from the crowd. "Her arms were crossed over this." He raised the brown leather-covered Bible over his head and shook it.

"How did she die?" Matthew Pinchon asked.

"It looked like what we call blunt-force trauma," Kane said. "Somebody hit her or she hit something, and it killed her. But maybe you'd better let me tell this, and then I'll answer questions."

He raised the Bible and shook it again.

"Whoever killed her and hid her body is a religious man," he said, bringing the crowd's attention back to focus on him, "or else wanted us to think he is."

He looked around the room.

"Because of what Faith was doing, there are many suspects," he said. "But the reason Faith died wasn't that she was whoring, at least not directly."

The word brought a gasp from the crowd.

"What's the matter?" Kane asked. "There are whores in the Bible, aren't there? Aren't there, Elder Moses Wright?"

The old man was trying to bore holes in Kane's chest

with his eyes. He looked up and gave the detective a twisted grin.

" 'And behold, there met him a woman with the attire of an harlot, and subtil of heart,' " he said, his voice rising and falling in its preacher's cadence.

"So there would be many suspects," Kane said, "except that Faith left behind an account that tells us who her killer is. Left it behind in this."

He shook the Bible again and pieces of paper flew out and landed at the feet of the three men. Pinchon and Moses Wright bent to pick them up.

"Leave those alone," Kane snapped. The men froze. Kane stepped forward and retrieved the papers. As he picked them up, the people nearest him could see that they were covered in graceful, feminine handwriting. Kane sorted the papers carefully and returned them to the Bible.

The room was hot from all the sweating bodies. Kane had left his coat in the back but was otherwise still dressed for snow-machining. He'd have liked to have taken the time to get out of the snow-machine pants and boots, but he couldn't pause now. Momentum would be important. He took a handkerchief out of a pants pocket and mopped his face.

"Her story is one this whole community should hear," he said, "for it involves one of its leaders. Here is what it says.

"After her mother got sick, Faith needed comforting. She sought the comfort of a man she trusted, but instead of comforting her, he forced himself on her. This went on for some time. Faith didn't know what to do. She was, I imagine, depressed because of her mother and shocked by this man's behavior, and perhaps afraid that no one would believe her.

"But Faith was a strong person, and she fought her way clear of this man. How she got him to stop, it doesn't say. Perhaps she threatened to expose him, I don't know. But she forced him to stop taking advantage of her, and life went on."

Kane stopped and looked around the room. It was completely silent and all eyes were on him. He went on.

"Life doesn't just go on, though, when you are a sexually abused child. Especially when you see your abuser every day. Faith came to be of the opinion that she had been ruined. Whether she blamed herself—many victims do, at least initially—I don't know. I do know that she couldn't seek professional help, and came to think she had been ruined, physically and spiritually. Some of you mentioned that, after her mother's death, she seemed to just be going through the motions of her religion, and that's why.

"That would have been bad enough. But when she was about sixteen, her abuser told her that he wanted to marry her. There were complications to that, but he said he could work them out.

"Faith was sickened and afraid. But as I said, she was strong. So she hatched a plan. She won permission to attend the regional high school and threw herself into after-school activities. That kept her away from her abuser, but there was more to it than that. Once everyone had accepted her schedule, she arranged things so that she could go to work at the roadhouse.

"She wasn't interested in the money, or the sex, really. She was interested in making herself unattractive to her abuser. When she found out her engagements were being taped, so much the better. The tapes would be evidence of her harlotry, evidence that would convince her abuser to look elsewhere."

Kane mopped his face again and looked around the room. Everyone was intent on his story. He turned to face the three men at the front of the room.

"That's what's written on these pages," he said, holding up the Bible. "The rest we have to guess. I suppose what happened was that she confronted her abuser, showed him evidence perhaps, and that he killed her for it. Jealousy, rage, illicit sex. They are often a deadly brew."

He turned slowly, looking at everyone in the room, then faced the three men at the front of the room again.

"What's interesting—ironic, really—is that her killer didn't find her account, hidden in her Bible. A sly child abuser would have searched for evidence. A holy man, or a man pretending to be holy, would have looked in the Bible."

Kane walked forward until he was standing in front of one of the men.

"Why didn't you search this Bible, Moses Wright?" Kane said, poking him in the chest. "Or should I call you Mikey Hogan?" That earned him a look of surprise from the old man. He poked him again. "Didn't you tell me more than once that everything a man needs to know is in the Bible?" Poke. "But you don't really believe that, do you?" Poke. "All this religion is just mumbo jumbo you use to control Rejoice and get what you want." Poke. "Isn't it?" Poke. "Here you have him, folks, your religious leader." Poke. "A murderer and a child abuser and a fraud." Poke. "Too goddamn stupid and evil to look in a Bible."

Moses Wright's anger grew with each poke. His face worked as he fought to control his temper, but the rage grew in his eyes and, at Kane's last words, he exploded.

"I'm not stupid!" he yelled. Spit flew from his mouth and landed on Kane. "There was nothing in that goddamned Bible! I looked!"

The silence that followed his outburst was complete. No one even took a breath. As close as he was, Kane could see the understanding of what he had said come into the old man's face.

"Wait! Wait!" he called. "I can explain."

The crowd wasn't sure what to do. The people of Rejoice had just heard their spiritual leader admit to murder and, to their way of thinking, worse. But they were used to listening to him and, for the most part, obeying him. They shifted on their feet uneasily. Then, one by one, without a word, they turned to go.

"Stop!" Moses Wright yelled. "I am your leader! You will listen to me!"

He leaped back from Kane, pulled an automatic pistol from his pocket, and fired into the ceiling.

Even in a room as big as the community hall, the gun was loud. Everyone stopped moving. Moses Wright waved the gun at his son and Matthew Pinchon, and the two moved away from him.

"You will listen to me," Moses Wright said in a softer voice. Then he straightened himself up and began talking.

"You should have listened to me when I counseled against bringing in an outsider," he said, his voice booming. He waved the gun at Kane. "Without me, Rejoice will just wither and die. And I did nothing wrong! Nothing!

"Maybe I should have waited until Faith was older, but she was willing. Eager. She seduced me with her tears and her need. And she was old enough, as old as her grandmother the first time I lay with her."

Thomas Wright took a step forward.

"You dare to blame my daughter," he growled. He took another step. "She was just a child." He took another step. Moses Wright fired at the floor in front of his feet.

"Stay back, Thomas," he said, "for I will smite you, too."

Matthew Pinchon reached out, grabbed Thomas Wright's arm and pulled him back.

"That's all right, Elder," the young man said. "We will have our time."

"Your time," Moses Wright said with a sneer. "You have no time. Without me, there will be no Rejoice. And I have done nothing wrong. She was old enough, I tell you."

"But she was your granddaughter," a voice called from the crowd.

"Yes," another called, "are you going to tell us that it was not sinful of you because Lot lay with his daughters?"

"No!" Moses Wright thundered. "It was not sinful of me because she was not flesh of my flesh nor blood of my blood."

That brought silence again.

"You are not my son, Thomas," Moses Wright said. "Your mother, whore that she was, lay with another and brought you forth. You are not mine and I will have none of you. 'For their mother hath played the harlot: she that conceived them hath done shamefully.' I had tests done. I am barren."

Thomas Wright gave him a twisted smile.

"Then there is some good news from all this," he said. "I would not be your son for a guarantee of heaven."

Kane put out a hand.

"Give up the gun," he said. "What you did to Faith was still against the law in this state. And there's the fact that you murdered her."

The old man trained the gun on Kane's chest.

"Stay where you are," he said. "I did not murder her. It was an accident. She came to my house that night and told me what she had been doing. Offered to get proof to show me. Described the acts to taunt me. And I lost my temper. Pride and temper are my afflictions. I struck her. She fell and hit her head on the stove and was dead. It was not my will that she died. It was God's."

Kane took a step forward.

"Give me the gun," he said, "and we'll let a jury decide."

Moses Wright laughed.

"Why shouldn't I shoot you, too, then?" he said. "You are the cause of all my troubles with your prying and snooping. And you are an unbeliever. I would be justified in killing you. Just as I would have been justified in killing that evil brother of mine for what he helped Faith do to me, if he hadn't hidden himself from me." Spittle flew from his lips again. "Justified. God be praised."

Kane could see his finger tightening on the trigger when Matthew Pinchon stepped forward.

"And then what, Moses Wright?" he said. "Will you shoot all of us? You were my counselor. I believed in you. I did things for you that were not lawful. I tried to drive this man away with bullets and destroyed his belongings because you told me he was evil. I believed you. I believed in you. And this is your true face? Then you had best shoot me after you shoot him, for I will not let you rest after what you have done."

"Nor will I," said Matthew Pinchon's father, stepping forward.

"Nor I," said another voice.

"Nor I," said a third and a fourth and a fifth. Soon everyone in the room was speaking and walking slowly toward Moses Wright.

The old man looked at the crowd, then at Kane.

"I loved her," he said. "I loved both of them, and they betrayed me. Now so have all my brethren."

He gave Kane a lopsided smile, shoved the barrel of the gun up under his own chin, and pulled the trigger.

And I wrote this same unto you, lest, when I came,
I should have sorrow from them of whom I ought to rejoice.

2 CORINTHIANS 2:3

"YOU TOOK A HELL OF A CHANCE," TOM JEFFORDS SAID
when Kane stopped talking.

The two of them were sitting in a corner of the bar at
the top of the Hilton. Jeffords was wearing civilian clothes
and had had a word with the waiter, so no one was seated
within earshot.

Kane had done several things after Moses Wright blew
his brains out. He'd retrieved Abraham Jordan and his
snow machine from the mine and deposited them, along
with a couple of ten-gallon jerry cans full of gasoline, at
the old man's home. He'd given Slade a statement about
finding Faith and confronting Moses Wright. And he'd had
a painful discussion with Ruth Hunt.

Then he'd driven back to Anchorage. At the top of the
pass, he'd taken the prepaid cell phone out of the envelope
and punched Call. When he heard the connection being
made, he'd said, "It's over. The girl's body has been found.
Her killer is dead. It was Moses Wright." Then he'd thrown
the phone as far as he could into the trees.

Closer to Anchorage, he'd gotten on his own cell phone

and dialed Jeffords to set up this meeting. He'd come straight to it, wearing two-day-old clothes.

"Yes," Jeffords said, "a hell of a chance. Moses Wright might have shot you."

"And put me out of my misery, you mean?" Kane said, smiling. "I suppose he might have, but I was wearing a Kevlar vest. And there really wasn't any other way to play it."

"Why not?" Jeffords said. "You had all the evidence you needed in the girl's handwritten statement."

Kane let some club soda slide down his throat, then resumed smiling.

"True enough," he said, "if there'd been a statement. But all I found between the covers of that Bible was the work of many anonymous writers compiled over about a thousand years, from Genesis to Revelation."

"Then what was on the sheets of paper?"

"Faith's outline for a paper on the separation of church and state. I picked it up at the trooper office when I stopped to tell Slade about the bodies."

"So you were just bluffing?"

"I was, and counting on Moses Wright's pride and temper to do the rest."

The waiter came over and set another drink in front of Jeffords. Kane looked out the window at the darkness, broken only by the lights of the port and homes on the hill behind it. I wonder if I'll ever not want to drink, he thought.

"Then how did you know Moses did it?" Jeffords said. "Why were you sure enough to go up against him like that? If he'd denied it, you'd have been up the creek."

Kane shook his head.

"There might have been forensic evidence," he said. "You never know. But I didn't really need it. There were clues. Dorothy Allison, the name Faith used on her bank account? I found out in the library in Fairbanks that she writes about being abused as a child.

"And there was the fact that Moses was one of the few people in Rejoice who could dump a body unseen, since his house is on the edge of the community. He must have driven as close as he could to the drift tunnel in her Jeep, skied in towing her body on some sort of sled, then skied back out, driven the Jeep to the high school, and skied home from there. A lot of work for an old man, but he was tough as an old boot and he had all night."

"Okay, that's how he could have done it," Jeffords said. "Still, you don't have much proof."

"I didn't really need much proof, at least for myself," Kane said. "You see, Faith wasn't alone in that mine shaft."

"What do you mean?" Jeffords said. Kane thought he heard something in the police chief's voice, but he wasn't sure what it was.

"There was another body laid out in there, too," Kane said. "Mostly skeleton, but with some patches of skin, hanks of hair, and bits of clothing still attached. That mine gallery had been cut into permafrost, and the cold preserved a lot. Enough to convince me that I was looking at the remains of Moses Wright's wife, Margaret Anderson. And there's only one man who could have put both those bodies there, isn't there? Well, two, actually, but I was pretty sure the other one wasn't involved."

"Who is that other suspect?" Jeffords asked. Hesitation, Kane thought. That's what I'm hearing, hesitation.

"Thomas Wright's father," Kane said. "Margaret Anderson's lover. The man who sent me the old pictures and the fifteen thousand dollars cash."

Both men were quiet again. Kane's eyes followed the lights of the traffic along the elevated freeway over Ship Creek.

"But it turned out to be Moses, the most likely candidate," he said, "and that's that."

Jeffords signaled for the waiter to bring him the bill.

"Well, you did pretty well out of this, didn't you, Nik?" he said. "There's what the Angels will pay you, the mine's reward, and the cash you got out of the envelope."

"I am keeping the money," Kane said, "and the reward. I earned them. But I'm not billing the Angels. They've got enough trouble. It's touch-and-go whether Rejoice will survive."

"Do you think it will?" Jeffords asked.

"I don't know," Kane said. "When I left, Thomas Wright was heavily sedated and Gregory Pinchon had taken over, at least temporarily. I'm not sure Wright will ever be up to running the place again, even if the residents would let him. What his father did was a hell of a shock to the community, and many of the residents seem to be re-thinking their commitment to the place. So it's possible Rejoice will scatter to the four winds."

"Maybe it should," Jeffords said.

"Rejoice is more than Moses Wright," Kane said. "And the world still needs faith."

The waiter brought the bill. Jeffords handed him money and waved away the change.

"And what about you, Nik?" Jeffords said. "What are you going to do? More detecting?"

Kane nodded.

"I guess so," he said, "if I can find anyone to hire me. It's all I know how to do, and I need something to keep me on the straight and narrow." He paused for a moment, then said, "And I'm going to try to let the past be the past and figure out some way to live in the present. I think one thing I'll do is try to get used to the wide open spaces, then find some land out of town and build myself a cabin. I find I don't like the city much anymore. And I have plenty of practice being alone."

"And this other woman? Ruth Hunt?" Jeffords asked. "Do you think you'll see her again?"

"I doubt it," Kane said with a sad smile. "I doubt it very much."

The two men rose, donned their coats, and got into the el-evator. They had it all to themselves. As it descended, Kane said softly, "I'm sorry about your granddaughter, Tom."

Jeffords looked at him.

"I don't know what you're talking about, Nik," he said.

"I talked to your pal at the troopers," Kane said. "You got your start with them in 'sixty-six or 'sixty-seven, at the

Tok station, which would have been the closest one to Rejoice in those days. And Thomas Wright looks a lot like you. Has some of the same mannerisms. After I saw him the first time, I thought you two might be related. But that money and cell phone threw me off. After all, you knew I'd tell you what happened. So why would I need the cell phone?

"In fact, it wasn't until I was about to use it again that I realized it was just a red herring. You were trying to throw me off, to keep me from concluding that you are Thomas Wright's father."

Jeffords smiled and patted Kane on the shoulder.

"You always were a bright fellow," he said.

"Why don't you get in touch with Thomas?" Kane said. "A son should know his father."

"My wife would like that, wouldn't she?" Jeffords said. "With my track record, to suddenly produce a grown son? If I had one, that is. Which, of course, I don't. A man in my position couldn't afford the scandal."

The elevator stopped and the two men got off. As they walked through the lobby, Jeffords said, "Come and see me in a few days, Nik. Whenever you feel like it. I have some ideas about how you can find work. And I want to help you, because I know you're effective. And discreet."

Outside, the two men shook hands. Jeffords got into his limousine. Kane walked across the street to the parking lot, started his truck, and drove to his apartment. He collected his mail from the manager, dumped everything on his bed, and unpacked his duffel. Then he opened the box of videotapes the mailman had delivered. He would burn them all, of course. There was no way Slade was ever going to get his hands on his tape.

He looked at the backs of the tapes, selected one, and went into his living room. He put the tape in the VCR and sat on the moldy couch with the remote control in his hand. He thought about his last, painful conversation with Ruth Hunt, then sighed, turned on the TV, started the tape, and fast-forwarded to the spot he wanted to see one last time.

On the screen, the waitress from the Devil's Toe Roadhouse was astride Slade, naked, rising and falling. Another woman stood with her back to the camera, watching. The waitress turned her head and said something to the other woman, then slid off Slade. The other woman threw a leg over him and took the waitress's place. Rising and falling, the woman turned to the camera. The intense concentration and joy on Ruth Hunt's face made it look like she was praying.

Turn the page for a preview of the next
Nik Kane Alaska Mystery
by Mike Doogan

Capitol Offense

Available August 2007
From G. P. Putnam's Sons.

Prologue

BABY SANTOS GOT OFF THE ELEVATOR ON THE FIFTH floor of the Alaska State Capitol. He pushed his cleaning cart to the right, down the hall, around the corner, and through the propped-open door to the House Finance Committee hearing room. At just after 10 p.m., the room, like all of the offices he'd passed, was empty.

Baby had been cleaning offices here for many years. He knew that if it had been May instead of March, the rooms would be brightly lit and full of people. He was glad it wasn't the end of the legislative session yet, because working around all those people talk-talk-talking made his job much harder. And the wastepaper they made. Holy Mother!

He took his CD player from the shoe box that held his music. The CD player was old and heavy and his sons, with their iPod Nanos, made fun of him for using it. But the CD player still worked and he saw no reason to get rid of a perfectly good piece of equipment just because there was a newer one.

Baby put the player into a pouch he'd made from canvas

and clipped it to his belt. Then he put on his earphones, inserted the new One Volce CD into the player and hit Play. If Corazon, his wife, found out he was listening to these young girls he'd never hear the end of it. But he liked the bright, R&B stylings. And the girls. Aiee. Even a man as old as Baby could dream.

He took the thirty-three-gallon plastic garbage can off the cart and started emptying wastebaskets. When he was finished, he took down his vacuum cleaner and ran it over the carpet. He knew some of the other janitors didn't vacuum every night, but this was his floor and he wanted it just so. Besides, they had spent so much time and money remodeling these offices, it would be a shame to let the carpet get dirty.

When Baby finished that room, he worked his way from office to office, around the corner, along the hallway, and past the elevator to the women's restroom. He knocked on the door. When no one answered, he snapped on a pair of disposable rubber gloves, picked up the cleaner and some rags, and leaving his cart in the hall, scrubbed the pedestal toilets and the big square sinks of thick porcelain. When he was finished, he returned all the cleaning materials, hefted his mop and bucket, and scrubbed the floor. Then he moved on to the wing that belonged to the Senate, going in and out of offices with his garbage can and vacuum. One Volce gave way to Rachel Alejandro, then Rachelle Ann Go. These young women could sing and, aiee, did they look good.

Baby liked his job, liked being able to listen to music and move along the floor in an orderly fashion. The older he got, the more he liked everything just so. He even liked being able to work during the day on the weekends, because it gave him time to be with his family on some evenings. His boys were teenagers now and needed watching. Once he had been their hero. Now they clashed all the time. Fathers and sons. It was the way of the world.

Baby reached the men's restroom and looked for his cleaner. It was not in its usual place, with the rags and brushes, but on the bottom of the cart on the opposite side.

Odd. Had he put it there? Baby shrugged. As he got older, he forgot many things.

When he was finished with the restroom, he put a Sugar Pie DeSanto CD into his player. She might not have the shape of the young women, but she had twice the voice. Baby had every CD she'd ever made.

Baby pushed his cart around the corner. The doors of the Senate Finance Committee room were propped open, too. In one of the offices at the far end, Baby saw a light. He switched off his CD player, removed his earphones, left his cart where it was, and walked softly through the committee room. The room was Baby's favorite, a big room that had been a federal courtroom when the building was young, but had been carefully restored and, since Baby had been doing the cleaning, carefully kept up, too.

Baby's sneakers made no noise on the thick carpet. He was glad; he wanted to see why the light was on before revealing himself. Once, years before, he'd blundered into that office and found a man, a senator, on top of a woman half his age, on the office's big leather couch. How embarrassed everyone was. Holy Mother! Baby didn't want that to happen again.

He went through the reception area and peeked into the chairman's office next door. There was a young woman there, but she wasn't underneath anybody. She lay on the floor beside the desk.

She is wearing no clothes, or not many, Baby thought. Where are her clothes? And what is that pool around her head? Water?

Standing over her, holding something in his hand, was a slim, dark-skinned, dark-haired young man. The young man looked up from the woman's body, his face contorted in a horrible grimace.

Baby Santos turned and ran out of the office, around the corner, and down the hall, screaming with all his might.

1

*Politics are as exciting as war and almost as dangerous.
In war you can only be killed once, but in politics many times.*

—WINSTON CHURCHILL

TOM JEFFORDS LEVELED THE GLOCK .45 AND PULLED the trigger. The automatic tried to kick upward, but Jeffords was a big man and held it level with ease as he fired again. When he'd run through thirteen rounds, he ejected the clip and laid it and the automatic on the counter in front of him. He removed his big hearing protectors and motioned to Nik Kane to do the same. The last shot still echoed in the big room, empty except for the two of them. Jeffords pushed a button on a pole next to his shooting station and a motor began to whirr.

While he waited for his target to arrive, he said, "So, you want to go out on your own."

His tone made it sound as if Kane intended to do something distasteful.

"Yes, I do," Kane said. "I'm bored."

Jeffords nodded and examined the target. It was an outline of a man with a gun. All thirteen holes were within the kill zone. Jeffords might be a desk-bound bureaucrat who was pushing sixty-five, but he could still shoot.

The Glock .45 was the Anchorage Police Department's

standard issue sidearm, but the version lying in front of Jeffords was anything but standard issue. It was chrome plated and had honest-to-god pearl handles with TSJ inlaid in ebony. A grateful salesman had given Jeffords the automatic after the department selected the Glock .45, and it went well with his thousand-dollar-a-copy tailored uniform, his full head of well-barbered white hair, and his Maui tan.

It's easy to mistake Jeffords for a show horse and his automatic for a show gun, Kane thought. But not if you watch him on the firing range.

Jeffords clipped a new target to the line and hit the button again.

"I'd think boredom would be preferable to the life you've been leading for the past several years," he said. "I'd think you'd welcome some peace and quiet."

Ah, Kane thought. The oblique reference. A Jeffords specialty. So much more elegant than using words like drunkenness, killing, and prison.

"And if your life were more . . . exciting . . . you would be forced to carry a firearm," the chief said.

Kane hadn't carried a gun of any sort since the night he'd answered an officer needs assistance call on his way home from a bar and shot and killed a twelve-year-old. Of course, for seven of those eight years he'd been in prison, where they sort of frowned on inmates packing. He'd finally been exonerated when a witness recanted and admitted the dead boy had been aiming a gun at Kane, but he'd tried to steer clear of firearms since he'd gotten out anyway. Jeffords seemed to regard that as a form of weakness.

Jeffords put a fresh clip in the .45.

"A man in your line of work needs to carry a firearm for self-defense," he said, as he waited for his target to reach the proper position, "even if his assignments are boring."

The chief put the hearing protectors back on before Kane could reply. Kane did the same, then watched as Jeffords put another thirteen rounds right where he wanted them.

When Kane had gotten out of prison a little more than a

year before, he had wanted to go back to his old job as a detective lieutenant with the Anchorage Police Department. Jeffords had put the kibosh on that, but had seen to it that Kane was hired by 49th Star Security, a firm in which he was a silent partner. Kane had had an interesting case or two, but mostly he'd been doing corporate background checks, some divorce work, a few pilfering cases, the kind of thing they'd left to the newbies when he'd been with the police department.

When his target returned, Jeffords regarded it for a moment.

If he had any emotions, Kane thought, that look might be satisfaction.

Jeffords took the targets up to the range master's stand, returned with a handful of supplies and began breaking down the automatic.

"Aren't you a little old to be chasing after excitement?" he asked.

Kane laughed.

"I'm, what, seven years younger than you," he said. "Are you too old to be bossing cops and politicians around?"

Jeffords shot Kane a look that said age wasn't his favorite topic of discussion, then shrugged.

"If you are really thinking about going out on your own," he said, "then this is a happy coincidence. I have a job offer for you."

Kane laughed.

"And here I thought you just wanted to see my smiling face," Kane said. "I'm heartbroken."

"Very amusing," the chief said in a tone that made it clear he wasn't amused. "There's a woman in town named Mrs. Richard Foster. She has some work that needs to be done. I'd like you to do it."

Kane had so many questions, he wasn't sure where to start.

"You'd like me to do it?" he said. "You mean, this isn't an order?"

"You aren't with the department anymore, Nik," Jeffords said. "I can't give you orders."

Just like Jeffords, Kane thought. We both know he owns the security firm, but he won't admit it even to me. In an empty room, no less.

"Why am I hearing this from you instead of someone at Forty-ninth Star?" he asked.

"I'm told the firm can't take this job," the chief said.

He's told, Kane thought. That's rich.

"Why not?" he asked.

Jeffords was slow to reply.

"The reasons are . . . complicated," he said at last.

Great, Kane thought. Now we're in the world of Jeffordsisms, answers that don't answer anything. Kane had known the chief for more than thirty years. They'd come up through the ranks of the police department together. Jeffords, who had joined the department sooner and had a much better grasp of politics, was always a couple of rungs above him on the career ladder. Since he'd often worked under Jeffords, Kane had had plenty of reason to study him. He had watched the chief become the man he was, each year growing a little more devious and a little less human.

"You want me to take a job the firm won't take for 'complicated' reasons?" Kane said.

"Can't take," the chief said.

"Why not?" Kane asked.

Jeffords looked around to make sure no one had entered the firing range.

He probably arranged for this place to be empty, Kane thought. He didn't want anyone else to hear this conversation, and he's still not saying anything. I wonder who he thinks might be listening.

"The case involves a politician," Jeffords said. "It would be . . . incongruent . . . for me, or the firm, to be involved with this."

And that's as close to an admission that he owns the firm as I'm likely to get, Kane thought.

"Incongruent," Kane said. "I guess those word-a-day calendars really do pay off."

He was silent for a moment.

"If you're trying to lay low on this, why send me?" he asked. "All your political pals will figure you're involved the minute they see me anyway."

Jeffords' job title was chief of police, but for the past decade or more he'd actually run Anchorage, stage managing the elections of mayors and assembly members who did what they were told. Because so much of the money that made the city go came from the state and federal governments, he had made himself a force in state and federal politics as well.

"I'm not responsible for what people may think," Jeffords said. "But if anyone asks, you can truthfully tell them that I am not involved in this case."

Kane decided to let that go.

"This politician have a name?" he asked.

"His name is Matthew Hope," Jeffords said. "He's a member of the Alaska State Senate."

Kane was silent as he thought about what Jeffords had said. Matthew Hope's name had been all over the news in the past couple of days. He'd been arrested for the murder of a young woman in the state Capitol. The victim had been beautiful and "scantily clad," as the newspapers and the TV news readers put it. She'd also been white, and Hope was an Alaska Native. The story had everything needed to crank up the media—sex, politics, violence, and race. The crime had even been given a tabloidy nickname—The White Rose Murder, for the flower embroidered on the front of the garter belt the victim had been wearing.

Maybe that's why Jeffords is being so careful, Kane thought. A case this hot could burn anybody involved. Or even anybody in the wrong place at the wrong time.

"The White Rose Murder case is a lollapalooza," Kane said. "Is Hope one of yours?"

The chief smiled.

"One of mine?" Jeffords said. "What do you think, Nik,

that I have a stable of politicians who jump when I snap my fingers?"

Actually, that's exactly what Kane thought, but he couldn't see that saying so would get him anything but a lecture on how representative democracy worked. Instead, he asked, "Is he a friend of yours or not?"

Jeffords was silent for a moment.

"I think it's fair to say that Senator Hope and I don't see eye-to-eye on some things," he said.

Jeffords was clearly not going to tell him anything useful about his relationship with Matthew Hope, so Kane changed the subject.

"What do you know about the case?" he asked.

Jeffords looked around the firing range, as if expecting to see a grand jury sitting in it somewhere.

"The newspapers have given it extensive coverage," he said.

So he wants to be able to tell people he never discussed the case with me, Kane thought.

"If you don't like this guy's politics, why get involved?" he asked.

"I'm not getting involved," Jeffords said with a thin smile. "You're getting involved."

Kane opened his mouth, but Jeffords spoke again.

"I really can't tell you any more," he said.

Can't, or won't, Kane thought. Either way, he knew trying to pry information out of the chief was useless.

Kane thought about what Jeffords was offering. He wouldn't put it past the chief to dump him into a sticky situation just to show him that he'd be better off staying with the security firm. But the chief had too much at stake to send Kane blundering into the political world just to teach him a lesson. So this was probably a legitimate job, and it did sound more interesting than what he'd been doing. Of course, watching paint dry sounded more interesting, too. As long as Jeffords didn't want him to do anything he just wouldn't do. He watched as Jeffords' fingers, nimble despite his age, danced just above the counter, reassembling the Glock. Then he began feeding rounds into an empty clip.

"So do you want me to try to get this guy out of the trouble he's in or not?" Kane asked.

Jeffords' thin smile became a grin. I'll be damned, Kane thought. He might still be human after all.

"You know I'd never ask you to do anything but what you thought was right, Nik," the chief said. "We both know that wouldn't do any good. What I'd like you to do is go and talk with Mrs. Foster, and if you find it agreeable, work for her."

He snapped the last round into the clip.

"I believe she's prepared to offer you quite a lot of money," he said. "You do need money, don't you, Nik?"

"Everybody needs money," Kane said.

The truth was that Kane was doing pretty well financially. He was drawing a salary from the security firm and a pension from the police department, and since he wasn't drinking, he didn't have any expensive habits. But wanting to go out on his own was part of an effort to gain greater control of his life. Working, as he saw it, was a matter of trading his time for money and, as he got older, time got to be more and more important. More money would buy him more time to do what he wanted. If he could just figure out what that was.

"I'll have to hand off my part of a surveillance," Kane said. "Then I'll go see this Mrs. Richard Foster and I'll try really hard to take the job."

"Good," Jeffords said. He slapped the clip into the automatic and holstered it. "Wait here."

He went back to the range master's stand, returning with a much plainer automatic, a couple of clips, and a black fabric belt holster. He laid them all on the firing table.

"You should have a little practice," Jeffords said.

Kane looked at the gun for a long moment then shook his head.

"I don't think so," he said.

Jeffords blew air through his lips in exasperation.

"Then at least take the weapon with you," he said. "It's a gift from me."

Kane could see that saying no would start an argument. It was easier just to take the gun.

"Okay," he said, picking up the automatic and accessories from the stand and stowing them in various pockets. "But I don't see why you're so concerned. If this case is political, what's the worst that could happen? A nasty campaign ad?"

Jeffords gave him another real smile.

"You have no idea," he said.

Penguin Group (USA) Online

What will you be reading tomorrow?

Tom Clancy, Patricia Cornwell, W.E.B. Griffin,
Nora Roberts, William Gibson, Robin Cook,
Brian Jacques, Catherine Coulter, Stephen King,
Dean Koontz, Ken Follett, Clive Cussler,
Eric Jerome Dickey, John Sandford,
Terry McMillan, Sue Monk Kidd, Amy Tan,
John Berendt...

You'll find them all at

penguin.com

*Read excerpts and newsletters,
find tour schedules and reading group guides,
and enter contests.*

Subscribe to Penguin Group (USA) newsletters
and get an exclusive inside look
at exciting new titles and the authors you love
long before everyone else does.

PENGUIN GROUP (USA)

us.penguingroup.com